THE
GODS
OF
WAR

By David Donachie

A ROMAN REPUBLIC NOVEL

THE
GODS
OF
WAR

DAVID DONACHIE

McBooks
Press
Essex, Connecticut

McBooks Press

An imprint of Globe Pequot, the trade division of
The Rowman & Littlefield Publishing Group, Inc.
4501 Forbes Blvd., Ste. 200
Lanham, MD 20706
www.rowman.com

Distributed by NATIONAL BOOK NETWORK

British Library Cataloguing in Publication Information available

Library of Congress Cataloging-in-Publication Data available

ISBN 978-1-4930-7599-7 (paperback)

♾™ The paper used in this publication meets the minimum requirements of
American National Standard for Information Sciences—Permanence of Paper
for Printed Library Materials, ANSI/NISO Z39.48-1992.

DAVID DONACHIE was born in Edinburgh in 1944. He has always had an abiding interest in British naval history of the eighteenth and nineteenth centuries, as well as in military history, including ancient Rome, the Middle Ages, and the clandestine services during the Second World War. He has more than fifty published novels to his credit with over a million copies sold. David lives in Deal, the historic English seaport on the border of the English Channel and the North Sea.

To Allison Lyddon,
my son's lovely partner,
who will, one day, if she
can break down his resistance,
be my daughter-in-law.

PROLOGUE

Aquila Terentius left the mountain town of Beneventum the morning after he killed the four Greeks, descending from the high hills of central Italy to the coastal plain and a proper Roman road, which would take him north.

Forced by poverty to walk and hunt his food, he had much time to consider the recent events in his life. The experience of Sicily: arriving as a boy, leaving as a man; his own participation in the recent slave revolt: the dilemma of a Roman fighting against his own kind; the way his old friend and mentor had been sacrificed by the men upon whom he had taken his bloody revenge the previous night. They had betrayed the revolt they led and abandoned their slave army to Roman revenge, the beaten slaves – men, women and children – being herded and returned to the back-breaking work on the farms whence they had come. It was hard to see them as they had so recently been, a powerful army large enough to make Rome shiver.

The quartet of traitorous Greeks, once slaves themselves, had been relaxed in their luxurious hilltop villa, feeling secure under the protection of local guards, with slaves of their own now to fetch and carry. The long ladder he had fashioned to get in and out of the villa had been broken up, the bark strips used to bind the crosspieces to the long central staff had become kindling, the wooden slats he had fashioned from tree branches, firewood to keep him warm for the remainder of the night. No one had seen him enter or leave, and he had killed three of the turncoats quickly and in total silence – the leader first, his tongue cut out, because that had been his weapon of choice to both inspire and then betray. Two of the others had been nonentities, lapdog pets of their chief, but the fourth, called Pentheus, had merited special treatment.

He had been present at the death of Gadoric, the Celtic warrior Aquila had seen as a surrogate father, who died as he would have wished, charging his Roman enemies in a fight he could not win – a way to paradise for one of his religion. It was triple revenge; Pentheus had also murdered Didius Flaccus, the ex-centurion who had brought Aquila to Sicily in the first place and

Phoebe, the girl with whom he had formed an attachment, she being consumed in the flames of Flaccus's farmhouse.

Pentheus had died very slowly, his mouth stuffed with the rich garment he had been wearing when he was dragged from his bed. The boy's knife had worked relentlessly on the body, revelling in what he saw in the pain-filled eyes. Finally, with the man still alive, Aquila had chopped off his hands and feet, doing to Pentheus what he had done to Flaccus. The broken body he had disposed of as he had the others, by taking them out to their high balconies and throwing them into the ravine and the fast-flowing river below. Prior to that, using their bright red blood, he had drawn the image that defined him on each of their walls, the same as the gold talisman he wore round his neck, shaped like an eagle in flight.

At times, as he walked, he wondered if he had a future, but taking that object in his hand, he would be overcome by a strange feeling. He had been told it was his destiny but were the predictions true? There was only one place to go now and perhaps the answer he sought would lie there: the centre of his world; the city of Rome.

It was impossible to pass by the only place he had ever called home, not that there was anything left to see, but this was where had stood his adoptive parents' hut. The familiarity was tempered by a strange sensation that everything seemed smaller than he remembered: the stream in which he had learnt to swim which ran into the Liris River, the trees in the nearby woods, even the distance between the hut and the busy Via Appia half a league away. Only the mountains to the east looked the same, rising in tiers, covered in dense forests, with that strange-shaped extinct volcano, with a cap shaped like a votive cup, the tallest of them all.

Standing on the spot, Aquila could almost hear Fulmina's voice, often berating her husband Clodius. It was she who had prophesied greatness for him, with a faith he had never been able to share; how could he, the child of peasants, do what she foretold? Only on the day she died did he hear the truth; he had been brought here as a newborn child, exposed in the nearby woods to die on the feast day of the Goddess *Lupercalia*.

Clodius, occasionally drunk, always on the sharp end of his wife's tongue, had been sleeping off a drinking bout. Woken by a baby crying for food, he had fetched him back to his wife, knowing it would assuage her anger. On his ankle had been the charm he now wore round his neck, an indication that at least one of his true parents

wanted him to live. Had they sold it they could
have lived in some comfort and Clodius would
have been spared the need for service, and
ultimately death, in the legions; then they did not
speak of the power Fulmina felt, and the dreams
that merely touching the charm had brought on.

A wander round the district brought back
other memories, like the day he had met Gadoric,
a slave disguised as an addle-brained shepherd; of
the dog Minca, huge and fierce to a stranger, as
gentle as a lamb to a friend, long dead now. The
shepherd hut was still there, occupied by another,
sitting at the edge of the field where the Celt had
taught him how to fight with a wooden sword,
how to fire an untipped arrow and most of all
how to use the spear he still carried, which
Gadoric had stolen from the guards of his owner,
the fat senator, Cassius Barbinus.

The land he walked on belonged to Cassius
Barbinus; Sosia, the slave girl, with whom he had
enjoyed a tender childhood romance, had
belonged to Barbinus. Didius Flaccus, the ex-
centurion who had taken him to Sicily, had
worked for Barbinus. Aquila had lived with
Flaccus and his ruffian guards on the fat senator's
Sicilian farms, and so, unwittingly, he had visited
cruelty on the slaves in the name of profit. The
man loomed so large in his life and here he was,

standing in the woods that sheltered the cistern that fed the fountains and baths of the Barbinus villa, close to tears as he contemplated life without all the people who filled his memories.

He was tempted to visit the Dabo farm, where he had gone to live after the death of Fulmina, but that was not a place of fond memories. He had hated Piscius Dabo for the way he had duped jolly but dim-witted Clodius into deputising for him when he was called up for a second stint in the legions, this so he could stay home and get rich. Was the old bugger Dabo still alive anyway, or was his farm now in the hands of his sons, Annius and Rufurius, boys he used to fight all the time?

Old neighbours, recognising him, told him, with no sign of grief, that Piscius was dead: Annius Dabo, the eldest son and a born bully, had the farm, now a ranch, while Rufurius, who had at least tried to be friendly to orphaned Aquila, had got nothing, and was no longer in the vicinity. They also told him there was a legacy waiting for him in Aprilium, a bequest made by a general called Aulus Cornelius Macedonicus, who had died commanding a cohort of the 10th Legion at the Pass of Thralaxas in Illyricum, money for the support of the dependants of his fallen legionaries, Clodius being one of that number.

Having established his identity with the priests at the temple, and because there was nothing for him now in the place in which he had grown up, he made his way back on the Via Appia, and continued to head north.

Marcellus Falerius came back to a house on the Palatine Hill that seemed empty without his father. Ever since he could remember, the spacious atrium had been full of supplicants seeking favours from Rome's most powerful politician, the leader of the *optimates*: now it had a hollow feel. The household slaves, normally so busy attending to those petitioners, were idle, in mourning, staying in their quarters, some no doubt praying to their own gods that they would be freed in their late master's will. It was maddening that he had died at the very pinnacle of his career, having just put down a slave revolt in Sicily, not with fighting legions, as was the norm, but by sheer cunning.

Added to that, instead of lining the roads with crucified rebels, he had got them back to work on the farms from which they escaped, saving their owners, his fellow Roman senators, a fortune, as well as ensuring the city a harvest. Had he returned alive, he would have been hailed a victorious general for his defeat of an enemy, famine, that Rome feared more than any other. Instead he had died in a fountain of blood that seemed to come from every orifice in his body, his weeping son holding a hand that slowly gave up its strength.

The study in which he laboured had the same bare feel, and Marcellus sat in the curile chair wondering what he would do next. His father had been such a commanding presence in his life, as well as the lives of many others, that the lack of his aura was almost tangible. Everyone who counted for anything in Rome would attend the ceremonies to mark his passing, though there would be few who would come because they loved him. Indeed, some so-called mourners would no doubt turn up to ensure that his death was not some hoax to catch them out: Lucius Falerius Nerva had been a scourge to those of high station who fell below what he considered the proper standards of behaviour for the patrician class. He had been feared rather than loved, his only guiding principle being the needs of the Republic he served so selflessly; indeed his whole life had been dedicated to Rome and the preservation of its distant borders. The youngster could hear the echo of his voice now, castigating him.

'Rome first and always, Marcellus! Swear to

me that you will always put Rome before everything.'

'Yes, Father,' he said out loud, hoping that the parental spirit would hear him.

He picked up the piece of papyrus on which he had drawn an image from the walls of that villa in Beneventum, gifted to the four leaders of the Sicilian slave revolt, men Lucius had suborned and bribed to betray their people with the prospect of a life of ease and comfort. They had not lived to enjoy their deceit; someone had taken revenge and killed them all in the most bloodthirsty fashion, and had left on the walls of each room this outline, a drawing of an eagle in flight, only the red on the original had been blood, not ink.

Why had the mere sight of that image so terrified his father? On sight of it he had called for his litter in an obvious panic, and made an effort to get back to Rome, perhaps to seek the intercession of *Jupiter Maximus*. It had been in vain; Lucius Falerius, Rome's senior senator, died like a nobody on the Via Appia, several leagues away from the city he revered, ignored, as was his tear-stained son, by those passing by, the citizens for whom he had laboured so long and so hard.

There was a powerful legacy. Not great wealth; Lucius had put too much time into the care of

Rome and its empire to amass much money, though the boy was comfortably off and had the prospect of a marriage that would bring a massive dowry. The real inheritance was political; as the son of a man so influential – with a list of clients almost too long to recount – he could expect to inherit some of that authority. Not all, he was too young for that, but enough to make his mark in the world. It was now time to find out just how potent that was.

Before they left for that fateful journey to Sicily, Lucius had sealed many of his most secret scrolls in chests, to be placed in the cellar. In these wooden containers lay all Marcellus needed to take his place in the world. He took a lamp down the worn stone steps rather than fetch the trunks up to his father's study. That stopped him: he had to remind himself that the study was his now; he was the head of the household. There had been an awkward moment at the Forum, where he had gone to announce his loss, when Appius Claudius, the richest man in Rome, had reminded him of his obligations towards his daughter.

That, more than anything, served to bring home to Marcellus that he was now the master of his own destiny. It also underlined his potential; Appius Claudius still saw the betrothal as desirable. Did he, given that his preferences lay elsewhere? Ever since he had donned his manly gown he had been in thrall to Valeria Trebonia, but the entire Trebonii family was out of Rome, so he had not yet put that to the test. Once he had suggested to his father that he should marry Valeria, only to have the notion ridiculed. To a Falerii, who could trace their family name back to before the Tarquin Kings, the Trebonii were parvenus, too recently elevated, not fit to merit the connection.

That was something to consider later; time now to examine his inheritance. A whole glass of sand later, he sat, surrounded by scrolls, wondering how he had lived with his father all these years without really knowing him. Every scroll made him cringe; they contained personal details, none of them flattering, of all the people Lucius had called friends and clients. Details of financial and sexual scandals: wives who had indulged in adulterous relations, naming the men involved, often more than one; senators and knights who had blatantly stolen from the public purse, hoarded scarce commodities or indulged in impeachable rapacity as they governed the provinces of the empire.

One contained a poem, and scratched in the corner were the names Sibyl and Aulus, which must refer to an oracle and Aulus Cornelius, his father's childhood friend, while the remainder had lots of scribbled notes. The reading of it made no sense.

One shall tame a mighty foe,
The other strike to save Rome's fame.
Neither will achieve their aim.
Look aloft if you dare, though what you fear cannot fly,
Both will face it before you die.

There were a surprising number of scrolls relating to the Cornelii family, which Marcellus opened reluctantly. He could not believe that, locked away, they contained praise of his father's lifelong friend. Aulus Cornelius had been, to him, the very embodiment of Roman virtue, a successful general not once but twice; a soldier's soldier revered by the men he led; tall, handsome, with a noble brow, the very embodiment of the Roman *imperium*. Bound to his father by a youthful blood oath, Aulus and Lucius had been like two peas in a pod until something happened to ruin their mutual attachment. Marcellus now learnt how and when that deep companionship had become fractured.

It could not be just that Aulus had failed to attend Marcellus's birth – certainly a deep breach of his obligations – but enough to threaten a lifelong friendship? Reading on, the reason for that absence shocked him. Campaigning in Spain, fighting a rebel leader called Brennos, Aulus's second wife, twenty years his junior, had been taken prisoner by the Celt-Iberians. It took two seasons of hard fighting to get her back, and when discovered, she was found to be with child. Aulus had failed to attend his birth because he was attending that of his wife's bastard, a fact unearthed by a Nubian spy, a slave that Lucius had placed in his old friend's house.

There were good grounds to believe the child had been exposed, a perfectly natural thing to do, though there were patrician husbands who would have killed their own wife rather than risk the disgrace. More interesting was the information the slave had supplied, which indicated that the Lady Claudia was tormented by the location of that exposure, that she had in fact searched as though expecting to find the child alive, strange behaviour when any sensible person would do whatever they could to put such a damning event behind them.

Marcellus hardly knew the Lady Claudia Cornelia and at first he wondered how her disgrace fitted into these chests, these records of misdemeanour. Then it dawned on him; it would have been a weapon to hold over Aulus, and even though Claudia was only Quintus Cornelius's stepmother, it would also serve as a means to embarrass the oldest son of the Cornelii house, a man Lucius was grooming to a position of power, designated to hold that together till Marcellus could come into his own. Any deviation from that obligation would see the scroll on public display, which would ruin the family name in a world where nothing was held to be more important.

His father had said he would not be pleased by what he found and, as usual, Lucius had been right, but what to do? He could call people in to see him, one by one, and give them the scrolls pertaining to them, but they would then know they had been read. It would only be a matter of time before the city was full of gossip, damaging his father's reputation and, by association, his own. The best thing to do would be to burn the lot, a notion he considered long and hard, knowing haste was a mistake. Clearly some of the crimes listed in these scrolls deserved punishment. If he could not burn them all, which should he keep?

Carefully, Marcellus put the scrolls back. The last bundle in his hand related to the recently returned Governor of Illyricum, Vegetius Flaminus, with a list of the evidence that Aulus

Cornelius, heading a senatorial commission, had mustered against him in the recent rebellion. There was also a true account of the campaign: the number of dead, not all enemy combatants, which negated the Flamian triumph; his venal rapacity as governor; and finally a report from a retired centurion called Didius Flaccus, which told how Vegetius, knowing they were isolated, had deliberately left Aulus and the men he led to die at the Pass of Thralaxas. There was enough here not only to impeach the man, but to see him stripped and thrown off the Tarpeian Rock.

He dropped in the last bundle and relocked the wooden chest, before making his way back to the study to find his father's steward waiting with the latest despatches from the frontiers, asking what he should do with them now that Lucius was dead. This correspondence was not for his young eyes; in reality consular communications, they had come to his father because he was powerful enough to make or break the people who wrote them. Despite that, Marcellus went through them, only half taking in the news that there was more trouble on the border shared with the empire of Parthia.

There was something from each province and potential trouble spot, and Marcellus knew that in the scroll racks that lined the study walls lay years of correspondence relating to every matter of import to the empire. Fratricidal strife in Africa, the bribes necessary to keep at bay various tribes north of Cisalpine Gaul and a positive report from Illyricum, so recently the seat of revolt. He stopped when he came to a despatch from the senior consul, Servius Caepio, in Spain. Having read it, Marcellus decided he disliked the contents. Like the chest in the cellar, it contained written proof that his father would not only condone but actively encourage murder. Never mind that it was a barbarian called Brennos who was marked for assassination. Rome, to his mind, should fight such people, not try to engage renegade Celts to murder them.

There had been scrolls relating to this Brennos in the chests below, old reports from Aulus Cornelius, the man who had fought him first, as well as from Aulus's youngest son Titus, made many years later. They described a man of tall stature and golden hair, a Druid shaman from the misty lands of the north, simple of dress but with a commanding personality. There was only one thing that really marked him out, a device he wore at his neck, gold, shaped like an eagle in flight. For a moment Marcellus's mind went to that image which had so terrified his father, had been, to him, some kind of harbinger of doom.

The notion of a connection was too fanciful; the owner of that gewgaw was in Spain, his father had been near Neapolis. *A powerful shaman* they said about Brennos; no one had power over that distance.

He told the slave to send the scrolls on to the Forum and, alone again, he considered going to the family altar to say prayers for the soul of his father, which reminded him he must order a death mask to place with those of all his other ancestors. But he felt lonely; he wanted comfort, so before going to pray, Marcellus went to visit the chamber of the best gift he had ever had from his father, the slave girl Sosia, who looked so like Valeria Trebonia they could be twins.

And unlike Valeria, Sosia was his property, to do with whatever he wished.

CHAPTER ONE

The return to Rome of Cholon Pyliades served as a sharp reminder to Claudia Cornelia of the limitations placed on her by her situation as the widow of a patrician noble. A freed Greek, the former body slave to her late husband, Aulus Cornelius Macedonicus, he could travel as freely as he wished; she could not. Claudia had missed his company while he had been in Neapolis and Sicily, so she did her best to welcome him warmly, suppressing any feelings of resentment. Not that such a thing precluded the odd barbed comment, especially when she heard of his intention to attend the funeral rites of Lucius Falerius Nerva.

'I never thought that you, of all people, would attend such an event.'

The Greek smiled, knowing there was no real malice in the words. 'I think your late husband must have understood Lucius Falerius better than you or I. After all, he held him in high esteem, despite the fact that they disagreed on so many things. Perhaps the bonds of childhood friendship were stronger than we knew.'

Claudia replied with mock gravity, her dislike of Lucius being well known. 'You're right, Cholon, Aulus would have attended the old goat's funeral, in spite of the way the swine treated him. He forgave too easily.'

'Then I am absolved?'

Claudia had not quite finished baiting him. 'There was a time you would have gone just to ensure the old vulture was dead.'

'True, but I met him in Neapolis only to discover he was an interesting man, and the irony is that when I got to know him, I found his ideas were more Greek than Roman.'

Cholon did not say that Lucius had used him as an intermediary; it had been he who had taken the Roman terms to the leaders of the slave revolt and persuaded them to accept them. Right now, he was amused by the shocked reaction of his host.

'Lucius Falerius saw himself as the complete Roman. He would not be pleased to hear you say that!'

'Not the words, perhaps, but I think the sentiment would please him. He was far from as

stiff-necked as he appeared and I did discover
that he was remarkably free from the cant you
normally suffer from Roman senators. I think
Lucius understood his world and knew what he
wanted to preserve. Perhaps he was illiberal with
the means he needed to employ to gain his ends,
but he was clever. Certainly what he did in Sicily
was positively Alexandrian in its subtlety. Not
Roman at all!'

'What would a Roman have done?' asked
Claudia.

'Put the entire island to the sword or lined the
roads with crucifixions, then strutted like a
peacock, full of virtue because of his actions.'

'I doubt my late husband would have done
that.'

The Greek suddenly looked grave, partly
because she had referred to the nature of his late
master, but more for the wistful look on
Claudia's face. To Cholon, there had never been
anyone like Aulus Cornelius, the conqueror of
Macedonia, the man who had humbled the heirs
of Alexander the Great, yet never lost that
quality of modesty which defined him. It had not
been for his military prowess that his Greek
slave had loved him, but for his very nature.
Sitting here with Claudia, he was reminded of
how she had hurt him, and how he had

withstood that for year after year with a stoicism that made him even more of a paragon. He knew the reason and had to compose himself then; too much deliberation on the life and death of his late master was inclined to induce copious tears.

'No, Lady, he would have freed them all, and then dared the Senate to override him.'

They sat silently for a while, each with their own recollections of a man who had stood alone, not aloof, but one who refused to support any faction, yet was there when the call came if Rome needed him. It was Cholon who finally spoke. 'I am about to commit a shocking breach of manners.'

'You?'

He ignored the irony, given he was always accusing Romans of being barbarians.

'It is not often polite to allude to a friend's private situation, to the lack of pleasure, the emptiness in their lives.'

Claudia wanted to say that he alone had the power to change that, he who had helped her husband, but she had promised never to ask again the only question that mattered to her, the one that haunted her dreams – where had Cholon and Aulus exposed her newborn son that night of the Feast of *Lupercalia* – so she bit her tongue.

'I wonder that you do not take another

husband.' Her eyes shot up in surprise as he continued. 'There, I've said it. I have wondered for some time and now it is finally out in the open.'

'I'm shocked.'

'Please forgive me, Lady.'

Claudia laughed again. 'What is there to forgive? I am happy to know that you care so much for my welfare.'

'Truly?'

She smiled at the Greek, in a way that made her utterly believable. 'Truly.'

'It's just that you spend too much time alone and, if I may say so, too much time in Rome. There are some wonderful places on the coast around Neapolis…'

His voice trailed off; he had said something to wipe the smile off her face, yet whatever it was had not made her sad or angry. No, whatever it was had rendered her thoughtful.

He could not comprehend the sheer size of Rome, nor the quantity of people, rich and poor, who thronged its busy thoroughfares. Here he was, in the capital of the empire, ready to admit that the place scared him more than the idea of facing a herd of elephants armed with a catapult, not that he had ever seen one, let alone a herd.

They were rude, these city folk, treating Aquila's polite enquiries with either a shrug or ill-disguised contempt, eager to be about their business and with no time to give directions to someone who, by his accent, was a country bumpkin and, by his appearance, no true Roman anyway. So Aquila saw more of the city than he should, saw that Rome was full of temples, some to gods he had never heard of, while the sheer wealth of the place was as astounding as its size. Numerous carts fought for the right of way with those walking, everyone pushed aside for the occasional litter, as the rough servants of some wealthy individual demanded passage.

The marketplace was bursting with produce of every kind while behind the stalls, and in the streets that led off the square, little shops abounded. They sold goods of silver and gold, leather and wood, made statues of men whose brows all seemed noble. Aquila, with his height, his distinctive red-gold hair, now down to his shoulders, plus his battered sweat-stained armour, stood out from the jostling crowd. Many a suspicious glance was thrown in his direction, looks which tended to linger on that valuable charm he wore round his neck, with eye contact being broken as soon as he turned to face these curious people. They were wary of a man who had a spear, used by the look of it, wore a sword at his side, and carried a bow, with a quiver full of arrows slung across his back.

He found the bakery eventually, only because, once he realised that he was being ignored, his enquiries ceased to be polite. The people of the city seemed more helpful if you towered over them with a threatening look, and eased your sword in your belt if they showed signs of trying to hurry by. He was directed to the street, but it was the smell that took him to the premises he sought, a whiff of fresh baking that somehow managed to overbear the odour of filth and packed humanity. The shop, with a small crowd outside, was a dark cavern at the bottom of a towering tenement in a street called the Via Tiburtina.

Aquila looked up at the narrow band of light between the two buildings on either side of the street, which seemed to be leaning towards each other the higher they went. Drying clothes hung from every balcony, women screeched at each other across the divide, their voices raised so they could be heard above the din from below, while naked children played in the doorways of walls covered in drawings and messages, some rude, others complaints. Beggars, blind or with missing limbs, sat against those walls, their knees raised to avoid the open sewer that ran down the middle of the roadway.

He called over the heads of those waiting to be served. 'Is this the bakery of Demetrius Terentius?'

There were two women behind a table, one of middle years, bent, with a face ravaged by pain, the other much younger, both coated in flour, with hair stuck to their faces by perspiration. The bent woman, who seemed to be toothless, ignored him; it was the younger one who answered. The older woman spoke sharply and the young girl went back to serving her customers.

'I wish to speak with Demetrius.'

'Round the back, if you can stand the heat.'

Aquila was not welcome, and not because the owner was working. He was done for the day, busy replacing all the sweat he had lost by consuming copious quantities of well-watered wine, none of which was offered to his surprise guest. Demetrius was his adoptive parents' eldest son, long gone from the place when he had been found, no more than a name and an occupation, yet someone to connect him to his past.

'You can't stay here!'

Demetrius was gross, looking as though he

consumed more bread than he sold, with his great belly hanging out over a thick leather belt and the fat, round face, still bright red from his ovens, was scowling. Aquila could hardly blame him for his reserve. After all, he had only heard of this young man, now standing before him, from the odd passer-by who had come in from the countryside around Aprilium. He had never seen him, nor had his wife. They knew he had been found in the woods, which was a pretty tenuous way to claim kinship.

'I don't remember asking,' the young man replied, 'but I'm a stranger in Rome. If you can help me to find lodgings, I can pay.'

'What with?'

'I have money.'

His fat, adopted stepbrother sat forward, resting one podgy hand, and half his stomach, on a huge thigh. 'How much money?'

'Enough,' replied Aquila coldly.

Demetrius let his eyes fall very obviously to the golden eagle, which seemed to reassure him. 'If you can pay, I'll put you up and get your name on the voting roll, provided you're content to share with Fabius.'

'Who's Fabius?'

Demetrius laughed, without humour, but with enough effort to make his gut wobble. 'Why, I suppose he's like your nephew, though I dare say he's older than you. How did you get on with my father?'

Aquila hesitated. He did not want to tell fat Demetrius that he had loved Clodius, as any small boy would love someone he thought was his Papa, so he kept all emotion out of his voice. 'I got on very well with Clodius, from what I can remember. He left home in my fourth summer.'

Demetrius heaved himself to his feet, his fat, red face wreathed in a grim smile. 'Then you'll get on with Fabius. He's the laziest, drunken bastard it's ever been my misfortune to meet. Siring him has given me no pleasure at all.'

Fabius was a shock, so like his grandfather that it was uncanny; as he and his new roommate talked, Aquila had to keep reminding himself that this was not Clodius and it was far from just a physical likeness. His laugh was the same and the way he scowled, when his mother scolded him for coming home smelling of drink, was the spitting image of the way Clodius had looked when Fulmina chastised him for the same offence. He was hearty, amusing company, and when he had enough drink liked nothing better, he said, than to sit with his feet in the Tiber and sing.

'Your grandfather used to go the woods. That's why he found me.'

'Would I have liked him?'

'I did. I loved him, but he went off to the legions when I was small.'

The story of how Clodius had deputised for Piscius Dabo was not long in the telling and no one knew if Fabius's grandfather had signed up because Dabo got him drunk, or he just wanted to get away from being a landless day labourer. It was supposed to be for a year or two, but it had gone on for ten and ended in Clodius's death at Thralaxas.

'Bit of a bugger being exposed,' said Fabius. 'Mind, they left you with that thing round your neck, so one of the parents wanted you back.'

'I'd trade it to know who they are.'

'You're mad. Who cares about parents?'

'Easy to say when you've got them.'

'You can keep mine, and you watch out, that fat old sod of mine will milk you for every penny you've got.' Fabius followed up his words with a deep swig from his tankard, while Aquila wondered if his 'nephew' was being cheeky, given that he had been sitting in this tavern happily spending Aquila's money for several hours. 'And don't leave that charm round your neck lying about, or the miserable old bugger will pinch it.'

'Your father speaks highly of you too,' said Aquila.

That produced a deep growl, and he said for the hundredth time, 'Imagine you being my uncle.'

It was hard; Fabius was ten years older than Aquila and looked twenty. The younger man, still well short of twenty summers, had spent all his life in the open air, eaten when he was hungry and drunk little. Fabius liked smoky, dark taverns, day and night. His complexion was puffy, his eyes bleary and, though nothing like his father, he was rapidly running to fat.

'I'll have to find some kind of work.'

'Work!' Fabius spat, then he looked around the dark tavern, full of people who shared his tastes and his appearance. 'That's only for idiots.'

'You don't work?'

'I do the odd day here and there, down at the Tiber warehouses, but there are other ways of making a crust.' Fabius threw back his head and laughed. 'Even for the son of a baker.'

Aquila soon found out how Fabius made a 'crust'. There was no malice in his thieving: it was petty, opportunistic and harmless, relying on a quick eye and even faster reflexes. Walking down a street with his 'nephew' was quite an experience. Fabius's eyes, never resting, looked for something, anything, to filch as if it was some kind of game in which his wits were pitted against the whole world. He would take things that had no use or value to him, just so he could laugh about it later in the tavern, selling the stuff on if he could get the price of a drink.

His 'nephew' had undertaken to show him Rome, marching up and down the seven hills, pointing out all the places of interest: the Capitoline, the Forum and the Temple of Janus. They were on the Palatine Hill, among the large houses of the very rich, when Fabius spotted the red shoes on a first floor windowsill, freshly cleaned and drying in the sun.

'Cup your hands, quick.'

Aquila obeyed without thinking, taking the weight easily as Fabius stretched up and grabbed at the shoes. He knocked one into the room behind, but came down triumphantly with the other.

'There,' he said holding it up. 'A victory for the bare-arsed peasants.'

'One shoe?'

Fabius waved it gaily. 'A senator's shoe, a trophy, Aquila. The bastards usually put these on our necks to grind us down.'

The shout behind them alerted Fabius to

danger and he looked back to see a servant hanging out of the window, the other shoe in his hand, yelling for them to stop.

'Time to extend your tour, "Uncle",' said Fabius with a wink.

He dodged down an alleyway, Aquila following, their feet echoing off the walls as they raced away, emerging into another street running parallel. Fabius dived across that and into a second alley, this one going steeply downhill until they emerged into the marketplace near the Forum. Fabius stopped running and began walking at a normal pace, weaving his way through the stalls, eyes and hands ranging all over the place. By the time they had reached the other side he was able to offer Aquila fruit, vegetables and an iron poker.

'Just the thing for a chilly night, eh, "Uncle"?'

Aquila laughed; it was the middle of summer, the hottest time of year. 'You're probably the only customer he's had all day.'

The eyes shot up in genuine alarm. 'You're right. The poor sod is probably starvin'.' Fabius turned round and retraced his steps. He gave the bewildered stallholder his poker back, plus all the fruit and vegetables he had snatched from the other stalls.

'Eat hearty, brother,' he said fulsomely,

patting the ironmonger on the back. 'Winter will be here soon, and you can rest easy. If I ever need any irons for my fire, you'll be the first man I'll come to, and I'll recommend you to my friends.'

They were walking out of the marketplace, leaving the perplexed trader scratching his head, when Fabius spoke again. 'One thing, "Uncle". If you don't mind me saying so, you should get your hair shorn. It's bad enough you being head and shoulders tall and still growin', but your hair, bein' the colour it is, and the length you wear it, makes you stick out like a sore thumb.'

CHAPTER TWO

Servius Caepio had the good grace to admit that he was no soldier, which earned him nothing but gratitude from those junior officers he had inherited on taking command in Spain. Many a serving consul, fresh from Rome, shared the fault but was blind to it; with only twelve months in office they were impatient to lead their troops into action and, since senior officers, quaestors and legates were that same consul's appointees, it was rare that anyone sought to check their ambitions. This had in the past, inevitably, cost a number of lives – Roman, auxiliaries and native levies – sacrificed to no other purpose than a senatorial reputation. With his small frame and foxy features, Servius was what he looked, a natural intriguer, a man who had climbed to prominence by his slavish adherence to the cause of senatorial pre-eminence, as expounded by Lucius Falerius Nerva.

Warrior or not, his cohorts were forced to fight many a skirmish, since the frontier was never really at peace, though he did everything he could to keep the conflict in a low key. This sensible approach had nothing to do with modesty. Servius Caepio yearned for military success with as much passion as any of his peers; it was what he faced, allied to what he had at his disposal, which induced caution; that and the instructions he had brought with him from Lucius Falerius.

His mentor had been mistaken in his estimation of the main Celt-Iberian leader. Lucius saw Brennos as a pest certainly, but one that could be contained as he had been in the original campaign fought by Aulus Cornelius. Let him skulk in the interior, with his fantasies about the destruction of Rome, with himself at the head of some great Celtic confederacy. It might have happened before, but Lucius Falerius insisted Rome was too strong now for such nonsense, quite apart from the fractious nature of the beast Brennos was trying to assemble. No two Celts ever agreed about anything; millions there might be, but Rome was homogenous, they were splintered.

Yet faced with the actual physical presence of Brennos, he seemed more dangerous than he had been in Lucius's study. Defeated many years before by Aulus Cornelius, he had retired to lick his wounds, but he had come back with a vengeance in his takeover of the tribe of the Duncani and their hill fort of Numantia. His usurpation had been bloody; having married Cara, the favourite daughter of the elderly chief, Brennos, a one-time Druid bound to celibacy, broke that vow. But he also broke by threat, sword and secret murder the resistance of anyone who stood in his way. He had then attacked the neighbouring tribes, taking back from them lands stolen over the years from an elderly chieftain more interested in wine and fornication than the defence of his patrimony.

His next success was to turn a natural fortress blessed by terrain – high bluffs, natural escarpments, a fertile plateau and a constant supply of water – a place in which the added walls had once been allowed to fall into a near-ruin, into the most daunting stronghold in the whole Iberian Peninsula. Numantia provided security in a troubled land, so the itinerant had flocked to the place, turning it from a hill fort into a bustling town; it had become not only a place to defend, but a base from which to attack Rome. Year on year Brennos was getting stronger, with more men to do his bidding and fewer neighbours able to stand against his wishes. When the chieftains tried, Brennos suborned their younger warriors, holding out his vision, encouraging them to attack the Roman coastal provinces, his aim to keep the border alight.

His own devious nature allowed Servius to see clearly the temptations the man offered, the most obvious conclusion being that patience, as a policy, might prove unworkable. Brennos was clever, a man who dangled opportunity before greedy Roman eyes, the enticing prospect of a victory large enough to earn the winner a triumph to match any that had gone before. His hill fort, Numantia, might be near-impregnable, but there were others less formidable, and therefore more tempting – Pallentia, halfway to Numantia between the coastal plain and the deep interior, being one such. Brennos let it be known that an attack on that hill fort would draw him to its defence, creating the prospect that, out in the open, he could be defeated by superior Roman discipline. There was an obvious flaw to this dream of glory; it might be Brennos who won, which would leave the whole of Spain at his mercy. What could he achieve then?

Not prepared to risk defeat, possible death, and at the very least certain disgrace, Servius Caepio had come round to Lucius's view that, other methods failing, Brennos should be assassinated, preferably by someone who could not command the succession. This would lead to the break-up of the confederation of tribes Brennos already dominated, and that in turn would get them back to warring with each other rather than Rome, bringing peace to the border. Let them fight for their mountains and valleys as much as they liked.

One of the assets vital to a good intriguer is the ability to listen, because only by doing this can he find his opponent's weakness. Servius listened to the centurions who had been stationed in Spain for years, just as he did to those Celts who sought protection and peace with Rome. The governor was patient with these client chieftains, garnering nuggets of information from the midst of their endemic Celtic boasting, but most of all he courted the Greeks, who, being in trade, of necessity needed to take a long view. The two who sat with him now had plenty to relate.

As a race, the Romans had a sharp and immediate sense of their own history; to them, Hannibal, the Carthaginian general who had annihilated two Roman armies and ravaged the whole of Italy, was no distant memory, he was yesterday. The sack of Rome by the Celtic tribes, under another Brennos, over two hundred years before Hannibal's invasion, seemed like last week. The Greeks' protectors knew this, and took some delight in ensuring that the threat Brennos represented seemed real.

Servius Caepio heard, behind their doom-laden words, the hint of the greed he sought. He needed the knowledge of these men who passed regularly back and forth between Emphorae and Numantia, men who could provide a picture of life in the fortress; who could detail the habits and hopes of those with some prominence, warriors perhaps, who at present stood in the shadow of Brennos. But they would not speak for nothing, while he was reluctant to offer an outright bribe, because for gold they might tell him what he wanted to hear. He needed to tempt them to speak, and if possible to do so without paying them so much as a copper ass.

'No Roman could go near Numantia and hope to keep his head,' he said, 'yet we desire an end to this constant upheaval so I must find a way of approaching Brennos. If I can open up a dialogue, who knows what may flow from it.'

'Peace,' replied one of the Greeks, sententiously, 'and from the blessings of that flows prosperity.'

Servius looked him straight in the eye. 'Those

who achieved such a thing could command their own reward.'

'As you say, Excellency, not a Roman, yet neither, I fear, could the task be entrusted to a Celt.'

'Brennos is suspicious of his own race,' said the second Greek trader. 'A man with such power must be suspicious of everybody.'

'Naturally.'

At this acknowledgement the two traders brightened; Brennos had treated them well and they had good reason to feel they would be welcome in Numantia again, and said so. Without a blush they put themselves forward as envoys, not forgetting to add that they lacked the funds to make such a journey, in pursuit of such a mission, on their own.

'No envoy of mine could travel in a fashion that demeans the Republic,' said Servius expansively, his heart warming at the glow of avarice this produced. 'Yet I wonder if it's money well spent. Everything you've told me makes me doubt he would welcome my overtures.' The result of this douche of cold water and reality nearly produced a laugh, so dramatically did the two faces fall; he had allowed them to glimpse considerable wealth then smartly withdrawn it. 'What troubles me is this: that through no fault of anyone, words will be used that will kill off any hope of dialogue before it can be started.'

'Truly it requires skill, Excellency.'

'It also requires knowledge. Perhaps there are others in Numantia, people whom you could approach initially, who hold the key to his thinking. People close to Brennos who could perhaps persuade him to listen.'

They talked eagerly, unaware that in seeking to impress this Roman consul they had missed his true purpose. Servius knew well that, in any situation where power exists, there would always be someone who wished to usurp it and the first act of such people is to talk to others, hinting at those small areas where they disagree with their leader. By the time he dismissed them he had the names of at least ten warriors, some members of Brennos's own bodyguard, others cousins to his wife, who fitted that category. One of them might be prepared to betray him for the chance to enhance his own prospects of ruling the Duncani.

Not inclined to entrust all his eggs to one basket, Servius read avidly, absorbing the mass of intelligence already gathered, going all the way back to Aulus's old despatches and the more recent reports of Titus Cornelius. He knew more of Brennos than any living Roman, so the man, from being a mere name, began to take on a proper shape. Running like a thread though marble was his obsession with the destruction of the Roman Empire, no doubt to be replaced with a Celtic one with him at the head, and physically he seemed to have the stature for such an ambition.

Brennos had, it seemed, aged well these last seventeen years. He stood head and shoulders above most of his fellow Celts, his hair, worn long, was now silver, with the odd hint of gold at the very tips. For all his power and prestige he dressed simply; the outward trappings of his elevated status meant nothing to him, though no report failed to mention his one piece of decoration, a gold talisman he wore at his neck, shaped like an eagle in flight. Many addressed him as if he were a king and there was much to underscore that assumption, not least the size of his family. Too powerful to be constrained by convention, he had taken several concubines, while still acknowledging Cara as his wife. Given his own potency, and that of his women, his immediate family had increased, till he numbered twenty-six in his own household. To an outside observer he could scarcely ask for more, but it appeared that anyone who got remotely close to Brennos soon found him to be a deeply frustrated man. The grip of his obsession had grown, not diminished, with both time and success, till the very name 'Rome' was, apparently, enough to throw him into a towering rage.

So, a powerful thane who troubled his neighbours; who stood at the head of a large and diverse family group? Growing more powerful by the year, who might become uncontrollable; a threat to the Republic every bit as dangerous as his ideas suggested. Servius had at present neither the strength nor the inclination to attack him, and since he had clear instructions as to the proper course to follow, nothing would tempt him to send to Rome, pointing out the dangers and demanding extra legions. When news arrived of the death of Lucius Falerius it changed nothing; an attempt must be made to neutralise this barbarian enemy.

The information he had extracted from the Greek traders provided one strong possibility, a Celt called Luekon who had hinted at a jealousy of Brennos by some of those around him and an ambition to match. Distantly related to Cara, Luekon was a man who could move freely inside the orbit dominated by Brennos, but he would first require his services to act as a messenger, because there was a second possibility. Luekon's first task would be to make contact with Masugori, the chieftain nearest Brennos. He led the Bregones and had great promise, having signed a proper treaty with Aulus Cornelius Macedonicus and held to it all these years, neither siding with Brennos nor taking arms against Rome. Yet he had to be vulnerable to the constantly increasing power of his neighbour; did Masugori realise that the time must come when failure to stand against Brennos could mean annihilation for him? Perhaps he could be persuaded to act out of pure self-interest.

What Servius did not know was that Brennos had called a tribal gathering, something he did often in order to overawe his fellow chieftains. None of the chiefs would stay away for fear of offending him, and that led Luekon to Numantia with the hope that the circumstances necessary for what he had to encourage were most propitious.

'Hannibal could never have invaded Italy without the Celts! In this I speak the truth, on the soul of the great God *Dagda*.'

Masugori nodded as if he were hearing the words for the first time, instead of the hundredth, but he knew better than to interrupt. Viathros, paramount chief of the Lusitani, the numerous tribe of the western shore, was too drunk to hear, let alone respond – not that he needed to be sober, for he had himself been subjected to this speech a dozen times. Brennos, who had also been drinking copiously, slammed the table with his hand, causing the platters and goblets to jump in the air as he addressed the men assembled, chieftains all. As usual, the subject was how to beat the Romans.

'Carthaginians they called themselves. Do you know how many of the men in his army were actually from Africa?'

One word must have penetrated Viathros's stupor. 'The elephants were from Africa.'

If it was intended as a joke, he should have known better; Brennos had never had much of a sense of humour, and unbridled authority had done nothing to improve it.

'That's about all. His cavalry were all Celts and so were most of his infantry. He would never have got near the Alps if the tribes on the shores of the Middle Sea had opposed him, nor would he have got through the mountains without the Boii to guide him.'

Masugori decided on a bit of mischief, being well aware of the weak spots in Brennos's personality. 'The Volcae Tectoganes sided with the Romans, did they not?'

The resounding shout, as the Duncani chieftain responded, could be heard at the outer walls, and so could half the rant that followed. It was the same old litany, of Latin duplicity, with their tactics of divide and conquer which would reduce the Celts to slavery if they allowed it to keep happening.

The chieftain of the Bregones looked away, lest Brennos see evidence of duplicity in his eyes. The man had trained as a Druid and might still have the power to see into men's minds. Luekon, the messenger from the governor of the province of Hispania Citerior, Servius Caepio, had hinted that matters would be eased for the Bregones by the death of Brennos. Masugori was not blind to the danger, yet he had survived by remaining aloof. Perhaps the time would come when he would have to take sides, but not yet. So, tempting as it was, he had sent Caepio's messenger packing after the most perfunctory show of hospitality. That made little difference; if Brennos ever heard of the purpose of Luekon's mission, he would see betrayal in the mere act of receiving him.

Right now he had little to fear, Brennos being too busy diminishing the reputation of Hannibal. Seventeen years the Carthaginian had stayed in Italy. He had beaten the Romans at Lake Trasimene and Cannae, then wandered the peninsula instead of assaulting the city, only to see his brother Hasdrabul, who had come to his aid, crushed at Metaurus. The Celts who helped him died in their thousands for his failure to take decisive action, or found themselves evacuated to North Africa, only to perish in an unfamiliar land at the battle of Zama. And, of course, the implication was clear. Masugori knew what was coming; at this point Brennos would always clasp that damned eagle on his neck, as though he was making a prophecy. History proved it; only a Celtic leader, with greater numbers behind him, could do better than Hannibal and actually succeed in destroying Rome.

The expected words did not emerge, for at that moment Galina entered and a mere look from her was sufficient to stem his flow. Masugori watched her move, quickly lifting his eyes from the allure of her swaying hips to observe the look of amused tolerance that filled her eyes, and he wondered, not for the first time, if such a woman might temper his neighbour's ambitions, and absolve him of the need to either succumb to Brennos, or go to war with him.

Brennos found it harder to deal with Galina than his other women and it was not just because of her youth or beauty, though she had both those attributes in abundance. Her colouring was unusual, for it suggested that she had a different strain of blood in her veins: with her olive skin, dark eyes and black hair, she reminded Brennos of the Lady Claudia, the Roman woman he had captured after his first battle against Aulus, the first person to make him break his vow of celibacy. Cara, plump, matronly and fecund, had turned a blind eye, not to mention a regal back, on all his other concubines, but she hated this latest acquisition with a passion, never losing an opportunity to spit at her, calling Galina a changeling, a Roman-born bastard and a sorceress.

There was an assurance about the girl that intrigued Brennos; she was unlike the others, for neither his prosperity, nor his evident authority, had any effect on her. She talked to him as an equal, and on those occasions he had tried to check the girl, to remind her of the position he held, Galina had simply announced her departure, and walked out on him. Power and wealth corrupts nothing more than a man's relationship with women; he is never sure whether a display of affection is prompted by love, fear or greed. Brennos would not have recognised the problem, having been convinced, all his life, that he required nothing from anyone, but he was, even if reluctant to admit it, human.

Without losing face in any way, he always contrived to entice young Galina back to his bed.

'If you mention Rome once more, I shall leave.' He laughed, as much because of what she had said as the fact that she dared to say it, but the physical position contributed too. Her head was resting on his naked stomach, and this statement was addressed to his erection, which got a hearty tug, and a small bite, as a warning to desist. 'It's bad enough without visitors prattling on about them.'

'Luekon has lived amongst them. He knows the Romans and their ways. What he tells me of their plans helps me to deal with them.'

She was across him in a flash, straddling his body, the eagerness that he loved quite evident in her eyes. 'I know Roman ways. I might even have Roman blood and I want you to do to me, at least ten times, what they always do to their female captures.'

Luekon heard the hearty shout as Brennos responded to Galina's delightful vulgarity. So did two of the chieftain's nephews.

'We are safe. That whore will keep him occupied for the whole night,' said Minoveros, the eldest. As the son of Cara's brother, he had command of the chieftain's bodyguard.

'They say Brennos can see through walls,' said

Luekon, a cautious man, with a healthy fear of sorcery.

The younger nephew, Ambon, spoke, a hint of jealousy evident in his voice. Luekon knew that this young man had an eye on Galina, whom he wanted to take over when his uncle was dead.

'Right now he can't see further than the end of his prick.'

These were the two most prominent names given to Servius Caepio by the Greek traders. Luekon had come to see them, to persuade them to murder, on the promise of a reward large enough to tempt the gods. The Celtic laws of hospitality allowed him the freedom, and the time, to wean them from their primary allegiance, and it had proved simpler than Servius Caepio could have hoped. Related to Brennos's wife, the two could bring Cara into the conspiracy, along with all her relatives, and all because of the voluptuous creature who had just made Brennos laugh.

'Nothing must happen while I am here.'

'Why?' asked Minoveros.

'No good would come of your actions. I have come from Roman territory, and if Rome's hand were seen in this you would be pariahs amongst the other tribes.'

'They hate Brennos as much as we do. I say we do it before their very eyes.'

Luekon snorted derisively; to attempt to kill Brennos at a tribal gathering was madness. 'They respect him as a man who keeps the peace in our own lands. He might talk down to them but he's not taken a single blade of grass that he cannot rightfully claim belongs to the Duncani, yet he has the power to subdue them all, except the Lusitani. How do you think they will feel if they see that power in the hands of others, men they cannot trust, because they've taken Roman gold to kill their leader?'

'It is not a thought that troubles us,' Ambon replied.

'Neither should it trouble Rome,' added Minoveros. 'Tell them we will put one of Brennos's sons in power, and rule through him.'

'Do you think that will fool the Bregones, or the Lusitani, a child as a chieftain? They'll say nothing while they're guests. They may even smile and bless your act, but those chieftains, with all their warriors, will be outside your walls within a month.' The two younger men exchanged thoughtful glances. 'And what if you lose? Not even Numantia can stand against the combined might of all the tribes.'

If his argument lacked a degree of logic, he had at least made these two boneheads worried. Tribes fighting each other, instead of raiding the frontier, would suit Rome very well, and he was of the opinion that it would happen as soon as Brennos was gone, but this tribal gathering, arranged before he arrived, had caught him out. Some of those visiting chiefs would recognise him and might even guess what he was about. As long as he was away from Numantia before the assassins acted, it would not matter. Luekon knew that conspiracies were never as easy as they sounded, that they had a habit of going wrong, and rebounding on those who had instigated them.

Masugori was one of those who knew Luekon; the man had come here from his own encampment, having delivered Servius Caepio's blandishments, but they avoided any hint of recognition, so that Brennos would be unaware that they had met. Caution made them wait until he was fully occupied, greeting another arriving chieftain, before they spoke. Masugori cornered Luekon, in an effort to establish what he was doing in Numantia.

'I could ask you the same question, Masugori.'

'I am here by invitation.'

Luekon clicked his fingers. 'Don't you mean by command?'

The Bregones chieftain, who was a good head shorter than the other man, edged his sword out of its scabbard. 'Have a care what you say. Remember that, in Numantia, you are no guest of mine.'

'I'm not beholden to you. Rome offered you a chance to act yet you refused. The task falls to others.'

Masugori laughed, and pushed his sword back. 'Here? You're mad. Brennos has eyes in the back of his head. If I were you, I'd get out of this while you still have skin on your bones.'

'Whoever would have guessed that I'd take advice from you? I am in the act of leaving this very day.'

They had made sure Brennos was fully occupied, but neither of them thought to check on Galina, who witnessed this exchange. She had also been present when Masugori first arrived and had seen them introduced like strangers, and that made her curious. How was it that these two, who apparently did not know each other, were now engaged in earnest conversation? As always, when she saw anything that might affect her future, she told Brennos.

Just as Luekon was going out of the main gate, he was caught and hauled back to the open space before the wooden temple that stood at the very centre of Numantia.

'That is hardly the way a guest repays a host,' said Brennos. 'To leave without saying farewell.'

'Leaving?'

It was a foolish statement, because the guards had brought both of the horses with them, and the packs on the back of the second animal showed quite clearly what he had intended.

'Masugori!' The Bregones chieftain jumped slightly as Brennos called his name, but he faced the man, determined to keep his dignity. 'You know this man?'

'Yes.'

'How?'

'He came to me from the Romans, to sow the seeds of distrust between us.'

Brennos's voice was low and compelling. 'And you let him live?'

'He was my guest.'

The Duncani chieftain nodded. To a Celt, that required no further explanation. The person of a guest was inviolate. 'Yet you did not choose to tell me that this viper was here.'

Masugori knew he was in danger, knew Brennos was capricious and cruel. He had power of his own, as did his tribe, but it was not enough to stand against this man. 'It is because of me that he's leaving, Brennos. I suspect he came here to do mischief. I told him that he was wasting his time.'

Brennos had picked up the shuffling in the crowd, part fear, part a prelude to action, for anyone with even half a brain would know that their leader would not leave matters there. If Luekon had anything to tell, then Brennos would extract it. He came very close to the Bregones chieftain, towering over him, his blue eyes boring into the other man's soul.

'You seem very sure, Masugori.'

'Less sure now than I was, Brennos.'

Brennos leant forward and pulled out Masugori's sword. 'The wearing of weapons, in my lands, is a privilege only afforded to friends or guards.'

He spun round, his eyes raking the crowd, before walking over to Luekon, who seemed to shrink as he approached. Unable to look him in the eye, he stared instead at the gold eagle round his neck, as Brennos removed his weapon. The charm seemed to mock him, its spreading wings alluding to a freedom he knew he had lost.

'Look at me,' said Brennos softly. The other man shook his head, but Brennos put one sword under his chin and pushed, so that Luekon had no choice. The blue eyes were like ice and the voice droned on, as Brennos spoke to his victim. 'You are a spy, a traitor to your race, Luekon, and you will tell me why you came. A man like you does not travel so far, unless he has come to see someone...'

On and on went the voice, as Luekon felt the power slip from his limbs. Minoveros and Ambon had moved to the front of the crowd, their hands edging towards their swords. They assumed that Brennos could not see them, but they underestimated his powers; he could feel them.

'The names, Luekon?'

'Mino...'

The two nephews, about to be exposed, jumped forward as Brennos pushed Luekon's own blade hard into the man's unresisting gut, then he hacked down Ambon's weapon with Masugori's sword, so hard that the young man dropped it. Minoveros raised his to strike, just as a spear flashed past his intended victim and took him in the chest. Brennos did not look to see who had saved his life, for he had Ambon at his mercy, the point of his sword at the bodyguard's throat. Luekon, still in a catatonic state, stood swaying, as if unaware of the gaping wound in his stomach. Brennos turned back to him, holding his eyes, again talking softly to reimpose his spell. When he asked a question, his victim replied without hesitation and the whole story spilt out, into a crowded arena in which the smallest gasp could be heard. Finally Brennos turned and fixed Cara with a stare.

'Lies, Husband, all lies,' she cried.

Coldly, he ordered her to fetch his children and go into the temple, then gave the same instructions to all his concubines, except Galina, who was childless. When they had obeyed, Brennos took a *falcata* off one of his remaining guards. It was a huge weapon, a thick curved blade, with one razor-sharp edge designed to remove a head or a limb at a single stroke. He entered the temple himself and shut the great wooden door. The screaming started almost immediately, but there were no cries of pain. Within a little time the sounds died away, to be replaced by an eerie silence, then the door opened and Brennos emerged, covered in blood from head to foot.

He looked around the silent crowd. 'They sought to replace me with a child of mine. There are now no children of mine, nor mothers to breed them.'

He walked over to Galina and stood before her. 'Who threw the spear?'

She indicated Masugori, who stood rock still, shocked to the marrow at the barbarity of what Brennos had done, and fully expecting to suffer the same fate as his family. Brennos walked over to look at the conspirators. Ambon was untouched, Luekon badly wounded and Minoveros nearly dead from the spear in his chest. Three swift strokes with the mighty *falcata* removed their heads, sending great founts of blood up from their trunks. He picked up Luekon's head by the long black hair.

'This one should be sent to Rome.'

CHAPTER THREE

Calpurnia, Demetrius's daughter, was a delight; slim and graceful, she was the same age as Aquila. He had seen her that first day in the shop, covered in flour and sweat, which certainly did not do her justice, though the smile never changed. Washed, with her black hair properly combed, Calpurnia was a different girl. She had a happy disposition, which seemed to be at war with an interior sadness, and there was tension in the house, evident by the way conversations between her and her mother were abruptly terminated when their new 'relative' appeared. She treated her father with some reserve, and generally tried to be elsewhere when he was around.

Alone among the Terentius family, she welcomed Aquila without avarice, doing all she could to see to his comfort and seeking nothing in return, washed and repaired his clothes and even polished his battered leather armour with beeswax, restoring it to something that looked reasonably respectable. The charm intrigued her, but Aquila never found it easy to speculate about his birth, and the frown that greeted her first question was enough to ensure her future silence on that subject.

But she did seek him out, making a point of being around when he was at home. Typical of a youth his age, Aquila was unaware of how much she admired him; unaware he was so different, taller, with even the golden tone of his skin so unlike all the other young men she knew. Alone at night, she prayed that Aquila had come to rescue her, and the more she conjured up his image in her mind, the more fanciful her thoughts became. To Calpurnia he was like the son of a god, placed on earth to right the wrongs of mankind, and they were alone in the house the day she told him. That made him laugh and he was able to point out that such a notion was not just a Roman myth but existed in both the Greek and Celtic religions as well. That intrigued her even more, so he was forced to describe how he knew such things.

There was, of necessity, a care in his descriptions: of Gadoric, who had taught him about the beliefs of the Celtic religion; that the gods lived in the trees and in the earth; the same man who had taught him to hunt only to eat, never to merely display prowess. The Celt's most abiding religious conviction was that a warrior dying in battle went to sit with the gods in a special place, where the tales of their heroic deeds became the stuff of legend. Gadoric had certainly achieved that; though he did not describe it to Calpurnia, as he talked, he had the image of his friend's death in his mind, of him charging a line of Roman cavalry with no hope of survival, yelling the war cries he had learnt as a child.

When talking of the Greeks he was even more circumspect. Sicily, and his activities there under the tutelage of Didius Flaccus, could not be mentioned, but he had heard from many members of the slave army of the deities they worshipped, very like Roman gods but with different names, as well as the pantheon of heroes whose deeds were told and retold to inspire the timorous, the fearful, and most of all those brave enough to wish to emulate them. But there was another side to Greek belief; no man should seek too much, certainly no mere mortal should challenge the supremacy of the gods, which led to the sin of hubris, a transgression that would see a man humbled, or even destroyed.

And there were heroines too, for, if *Zeus* was

male, there were enough female and powerful goddesses to make a woman feel equal to a man. Calpurnia was much taken with these Greek tales and made Aquila tell them over and over again. For a girl who rarely travelled outside her own close-by Roman streets, and would only rarely visit a temple, the stories he had learnt from the rebellious slaves brought an embarrassing light of hero-worship into her huge brown eyes, until, eventually, with much gentle chiding that it was a suitable adornment for a girl, he was persuaded to let her wear his charm. With great care Calpurnia put it on, shivering slightly as the metal touched her smooth olive skin.

'I feel impious,' she said, and immediately removed it. 'It has a meaning, this eagle? I felt it when it touched my skin.' The girl could see that she was making him uncomfortable and changed the subject. 'You were never formally adopted, were you, Aquila?'

'No.'

She gave him a dazzling smile. 'Then we're not truly related, are we?'

'That pleases you?'

'Oh yes. The relatives our Roman gods have given me do not inspire me to love the breed.'

'I worry about Fabius. He'll get into real trouble one day.'

She laughed. 'Fabius will take one step sideways, then some innocent fellow, a bystander, will find he's accused of something he knows nothing about.'

They sat in silence and she rubbed the golden eagle between her fingers. 'I sense a darkness in you, Aquila, secrets that you will not tell anyone.'

That made him more guarded. 'I cannot think what they are.'

'You have an aura about you.'

He smiled. 'Only when the sun is at my back.'

His levity did not please her. 'Perhaps because we're not family, I can't be trusted.'

'I trust you more than anyone else in the house, Calpurnia, you know that.'

Her head dropped and she spoke softly. 'That doesn't rate me very highly.'

Aquila moved closer, lifting her chin. 'It was meant to.'

Her upturned face lit up again, with that dazzling smile and she pushed the chain over his head. 'I am too nosy for my own good.'

'Nonsense. You say the charm means something. Why should it "mean" anything? It was wrapped round my foot when Clodius, your grandfather, found me. All it means is that one of my true parents wanted me to live, though not enough, it seems, to want to find me.'

Calpurnia sensed the bitterness in that last outburst and touched the charm again. 'It's very valuable.'

For the first time, Aquila voiced something that had only ever been a thought. 'Perhaps it would have been better if Fulmina hadn't kept it for me. Not that she handed it to me as you see it. She made a leather amulet to hide it, making me promise not to reveal it until I felt no man could harm me.'

'How would you know when that would be?'

Aquila was thinking about the day he had unpicked Fulmina's stitching; the day, on the way to Sicily, he had taken a spear to a beetle-browed bully called Toger, one of the band of ruffians Didius Flaccus had recruited to help him make money on the farms he was going to run for Cassius Barbinus. He had not confronted Toger for what the man had tried to do to him in his night-time cot, but because the ex-gladiator had killed the thing Aquila loved most: Minca, the dog he had inherited from Gadoric. A trained fighter, Toger had scoffed at the notion of a mere boy threatening him. He died with Aquila's spear in his throat, pumping blood into the hard, packed earth at his feet.

'I knew,' he replied, but he did not reveal what he was thinking. 'I could have left it in there and maybe people would stop asking me about it.'

'It is better to wear it.'

Calpurnia said this with total conviction, and then she blushed at her own forcefulness.

'Is it really? Your grandmother had dreams, which she told me about just before she died.'

'What kind of dreams?'

He was even reluctant to answer a question like that, but having said that he trusted her he could hardly stop now, though in relating the notion he tried to make them sound like some kind of joke.

'She saw me on a horse, being cheered by the crowds, as if I was celebrating a triumph. The Feast of *Saturnalia* probably, with me as the city fool. There was an old soothsayer she used to consult as well, a smelly old thing called Drisia. She kept yelling at me to come to Rome. I didn't believe either of them.'

Aquila gave a small humourless laugh, though Calpurnia did not seem to be in the mood for too much jollity. He explained Fulmina's dreams more fully, watching as the girl turned the charm in her fingers. All the time he spoke, her expression deepened, becoming sad.

'Then you will leave here,' she said, when he had finished.

'What?'

'Can I ask you for a favour? That I be allowed to wear it once more.'

Aquila reached for the chain, but Calpurnia held up her hand. 'No, not now.'

'Why are you sad, Calpurnia?'

There was a faint trace of a sob in the voice, even though she was trying to be funny. But he could not see her eyes because she was bent over. 'Don't ever let Fabius get his hands on it.'

'I was just doin' a favour for a friend,' said Fabius.

Aquila sat up in his cot, wide awake enough to see by the tallow guttering in the lantern that his 'nephew's' smock was covered in blood. The story tumbled out; he had told Aquila about some of the tougher criminal gangs in Rome before, and the toughest of the lot was led by a man called Commodus.

'It was Donatus's stuff in the first place, except the bastards took it off him. He knew it was in Commodus's warehouse down by the docks and he set out to pinch it back again. I said I would keep a lookout for him.'

'Surely they would have guessed who'd done it?'

'They'd never think that Donatus had the nerve and he already had a buyer, so the stuff would have been shifted before dawn.' It had not gone to plan, for the warehouse was better guarded than Donatus had supposed. 'I had to leave him in a doorway a hundred paces from the warehouse. He had taken a knife in the guts. I got him away from the dockside, but I couldn't carry him any more.'

Aquila looked at the blood on Fabius's smock; he did not have to ask if Donatus was badly hurt. 'He may be dead by now.'

'What if he isn't,' Fabius protested, jerking his 'uncle'. 'I can't just desert him.'

Aquila shook his head slowly, but he was on his feet and dressing as he did so. 'I should leave you to your fate.'

'If they find him and get him to talk, he'll tell them about me. My life won't be worth much then.'

That was a final plea, a tug at Aquila's feelings; Fabius would go back for him anyway. 'Get hold of something to bandage him with.'

'Why the sword?' asked Fabius, as Aquila strapped it on.

'Perhaps if you or your friend had learnt to use one of these, you wouldn't be in so much trouble.'

He had added his knife and his spear by the time they emerged into the street, coming out through the bakery. The ovens were fired up, full of loaves of bread, the great table covered in dough and flour.

'Where's Demetrius?' asked Aquila, pausing.

He had always been asleep when the morning bread was made. Fabius gave him a funny look, and indicated that they should hurry. They found Donatus, still alive, but in considerable pain, in the doorway where Fabius had left him. Aquila examined him swiftly, but the darkness made any proper assessment impossible.

'We can't do anything here. We must get him to a place with some light.'

'We'd better not take him back to his house. His wife is worse than Commodus.'

'The bakery,' said Aquila, strapping his spear to his back.

Donatus gasped with pain as they lifted him, but he did not scream. Fabius picked the route, staying to the alleyways, and they stumbled a lot, for Donatus was no lightweight and his legs were forever giving way beneath him. Demetrius was still absent in the bakery, though by the look of the loaves cooling on the racks he had been and gone. Aquila put his weapons aside and they laid Donatus on one of the tables and started to cut away his smock.

'Fabius Terentius! Well I never,' said the voice from the doorway.

Aquila guessed this to be Commodus, just by the look of fear on Fabius's face. He was a real hard horse, with a broken nose and scarred cheeks, carrying a sword in one hand and a heavy club in the other. The two men behind him, likewise armed with clubs, looked just as evil, with the kind of low foreheads that reminded him of the fellow called Toger, the first man Aquila had killed.

'We wondered who'd been with him.'

'You followed us?'

'Who's this?' said the visitor.

'Who's asking?' said Aquila, edging closer to his spear.

'It's Commodus's brother, Scappius,' said Fabius quickly. 'This is a friend from the country. I asked him to come and help carry Donatus. He had nothing to do with breaking into the warehouse.'

The man looked Aquila up and down, puzzled by his height, the sword and the colour of his long hair. Then his eyes lit on the charm, opening greedily as he realised it was gold.

'Is that so?'

The spear was up, which caused Scappius to take a pace back. Demetrius walked in, his face red and sweating, as though he had not moved an inch from the front of his oven. He looked and sounded guilty, instead of surprised. 'What's goin' on?'

'Nothing, Demetrius,' Aquila replied, in a voice devoid of emotion. 'These men were just leaving.'

Scappius looked at the spear, then into the stranger's bright blue eyes and he realised that being the brother of one of the most frightening men in Rome meant nothing, since there was no fear in them. He knew that he would die if they started anything right away, so he smiled, sure in the knowledge that time was on his side. There was no threat as he walked slowly toward the nearest table, where he picked up a thick round loaf and sniffed at it appreciatively, then smiled at Aquila and Fabius.

'We'll see you both another time.' Then he looked at Donatus, flat on the other table. 'Don't expect I'll see him though.' Both Aquila and Fabius looked at the same time. Fabius, less experienced, was unsure, but Aquila knew. Donatus was dead. Scappius grinned and turned to leave. 'You should have left him where he was.'

'What have you done,' snapped Demetrius, breaking the silence that followed the trio's departure.

'I ain't done anything,' said Fabius angrily, and

in a very liberal interpretation of the truth.

'Don't give me that, you good-for-nothing bugger. People like Scappius don't go calling for no reason.' Demetrius prodded the dead man on his table. 'And who is this?'

Aquila explained, trying to minimise Fabius's role and maximise his courage in going to the rescue of his stricken friend, but it was having no effect on the father, whose face grew darker at every word.

'I want you out of this house,' he said, pointing at Fabius as soon as Aquila had finished.

'What?!'

'You heard. What do you think Commodus and his gang are going to do. Forget you? And if you stay here, they'll take it out on me, too. I haven't spent all these years building a business to see it burnt out on your behalf.' He stepped forward, poking his son in the chest. 'You're no good, d'ye hear?'

Fabius put a hand on his father's ample belly and pushed him back. 'If I'm no good, I get it from you. Don't you walk in here getting pious with me, especially after what you've been doing.'

'Shut up!' snapped Demetrius, throwing a worried glance at Aquila.

'Why should I?' asked Fabius, with a sneer.

'You don't think it's a secret do you? Go on, Aquila, ask him what he's been up to.' Fabius looked like a man who had gained the advantage, while Demetrius held up his fat hands, imploring his son to be silent. Aquila just looked from one to the other, confused. 'Ask him why a daughter of Calpurnia's age and looks isn't married.'

Demetrius turned his frightened eyes towards Aquila. 'I need her to help my wife in the shop.'

'And at night, Papa. What do you need her for then?'

Aquila dropped the spear, so that the point was close to Demetrius's huge belly. The man started to tremble and Fabius drove home the final nail.

'You've ruined her life, you fat slob. He won't give her a dowry and without that she can't get a decent husband. Not that too many would want her after what you've done.'

'Get out!' Demetrius cried, but the words had no force.

She sobbed in his arms as he held her gently, letting her spill out her grief. The sun had come up and in the bakery below they could hear the noise of the first customers. The pressure from her arms, wrapped round him, seemed to increase with each revelation. It had been going on since she was a child, originally something playful, just touching, but it had grown stronger as her mother's health had deteriorated, and, like every child in the world, she was her father's property.

'Shall I take you away from here?' he asked.

She looked up at him then, through tear-stained eyes, but she managed a smile and her hand ran over the eagle at his neck. 'You have a destiny, Aquila, remember.'

'All I have are dreams and prophecies. I've seen people blinded by those and die because of it. To me it is of no consequence.'

'But it is. Fulmina knew. I think I do, too. Perhaps I've inherited her gift. You're not meant for a life in the back streets of Rome.'

'From what I've heard of this Commodus, I'm not destined to live at all.'

She gripped his arms and shook him. 'Then get out of Rome.'

Aquila smiled, thinking that if Calpurnia did have second sight, it ran totally counter to the advice he had been given by Drisia. 'Where to? Besides I've barely been here two months.'

Calpurnia looked at him closely, her wet eyes narrowing slightly. 'You've already made up your mind to leave, haven't you?'

He tapped her on the nose, which produced that smile he liked so much. 'You're too clever.'

She kissed him suddenly, taking him by

surprise, then with her hands round his neck and her eyes full of pleading, she spoke. 'Once, Aquila. Just once.'

He knew what she meant and shook his head.

'It would make me happy. I will ask for no more, I promise.'

He shifted uncomfortably, to try and hide the fact that though his mind considered it a bad idea his body did not.

'I cannot have more, I know that. I have told you how I've suffered. Perhaps, now that it's out in the open, my father will give me a dowry and I'll find a husband, but once, Aquila, just once, it would be nice to hold someone I love inside me.'

Her kisses took away what little resistance he had, leaving her with no need to exert much strength when she pulled her conquest down onto the bed.

'Go to Commodus.'

'What do I say?' asked Demetrius. He was plainly afraid of Aquila, his great fleshy jowl shaking even as he listened.

'You will tell him that Fabius and I have left your house.'

The small eyes brightened as Fabius interrupted. 'Where are we going?'

'When you registered me with our tribe, so

that I could vote, which class did you put me in?'

'The fourth class, like Fabius, not that he deserves it. On his own he would never qualify to vote.'

'Good!' said Aquila, who was not interested in anything but Demetrius's initial statement. He turned to Fabius. 'You and I are off to join the legions, "Nephew".'

Fabius shuddered. 'Never.'

'Thanks to the foresight of your father, we will be required to apply as *hastarii*, taking our own equipment.'

'You go,' replied Fabius with a dismissive sniff. 'I'll stay here.'

'You'll be dead in a week. Commodus will see to that.'

Fabius went pale, but Demetrius spoke. 'You still haven't told me what I am supposed to say to that robber and thief.'

'You're to tell him to leave you and your family alone.'

'He's not going to listen to me.'

'He will, because you will say that in the next week, I will deliver him a message, one that will remove whatever desire he has for revenge on you, Fabius, or me. If, in seven days, he's not satisfied, and prepared to say so publicly, then he can do what he wishes. That is, as long as he's prepared for the consequences.'

Demetrius scowled. 'You seem pretty sure of yourself.'

'You have two choices, Demetrius. Either wait here for Commodus, with his brother, to visit you, or go to him and deliver my message.' The older man nodded, aware that there was no choice. 'The other thing you'll have to do is dig under your floorboards and get out some of that hidden money.'

The fat man was too frightened to ask how Aquila knew about that. 'Why?'

'To pay for our equipment, Demetrius. You wouldn't want anyone from your family turning up for service in the legions improperly dressed.'

Demetrius puffed up angrily, as if he was about to explode in protest, but he saw the look in Aquila's eye and the words died in his swollen throat. The young man walked over to him, towering over the fat baker.

'Lay another hand on Calpurnia and I'll castrate you personally. I'll make you eat you own balls, d'you understand?'

The fat face held a look of absolute terror and his hands had, involuntarily, gone to cover the top of his portly thighs.

* * *

'I want you to have the choice, Calpurnia.' She moved her naked body closer to him, thrusting with her pelvis. The eagle slipped round her neck, brushing over her breast.

'Again Aquila, please?'

He laughed. 'Just once, you said, and that was two days ago.'

The vibrations of her words tingled on his neck. 'That was before I knew it could be so nice. And I don't want your money.'

He pulled himself away, pushing up on his elbows. 'If Demetrius gives you a dowry, he can make it conditional on you marrying someone of his choice. If I give it to you, then you can decide for yourself.'

She lay silently, her head in the crook of his arm, and Aquila sensed she was crying. 'Perhaps the gods will be kind.'

'You deserve their kindness. Use the money to find somewhere else to live. Get out of here. When I'm not around, how can I be sure that Demetrius will keep his hands to himself?'

The wheel fell off Commodus's cart the first day, tipping him into the street. He was still aching from the bruises the following morning when he woke to find the stone-cold body of Donatus in his bed. That day, as he walked through the streets, on his way to tell Demetrius that he was a dead man, a whole pile of wooden scaffolding cascaded down. Commodus was as aware as anyone that the shout, coming from nowhere, had saved his life, giving him just enough time to duck into a doorway. He screamed and cursed at his men, especially his brother, for their inability to protect him, but he stayed away from the bakery. What finally convinced him were the three arrows that arrived the following day. They came through his open warehouse window, one near his right arm and another near his left, with the third thudding into the desk right in front of him. He went personally to see Demetrius, swore on all the gods that he would not take revenge, and even paid for his bread.

'I'm enjoying this,' said Fabius as they watched Commodus making his way home, surrounded by bodyguards, his eyes darting around the buildings.

'I think it may be over,' Aquila replied.

The vengeful look was quite gone from Commodus's face, to be replaced with one of fear, as the gang leader's head swept from side to side, to seek out his invisible attackers. Demetrius, who reluctantly handed over the funds they needed to buy their equipment, confirmed that Calpurnia had taken lodgings with Donatus's widow and that was their last port of call. She was brave; no tears or tearing of garments, and she even kissed Fabius on his podgy cheek.

'I look forward to the day when you celebrate your triumph, Aquila.'

He wanted to argue, to tell her he was a mere mortal and point out that legionaries were not awarded triumphs, but the look in her eyes precluded that, so he bent and kissed her softly.

'Take care, Calpurnia.' Then he spun round to face Fabius, slapping him on his spreading stomach. 'Come along, "Nephew". Time to get some of that weight off you.'

His 'nephew' insisted on one last sweep through the rich houses on the Palatine Hill, certain that the gods would not let him go off to war empty-handed, and he was right. They caught a vintner delivering ampoules of wine to the Cornelii villa, a man foolish enough to leave his cart unattended while he lifted the clay containers into the rear of the house. Not that his eye was off his possessions for more than two seconds, but that was enough for Fabius. He was spotted, of course, which led to a commotion, as well as a hue and cry.

* * *

'Remarry?' asked Quintus Cornelius, ignoring the noise of shouting that suddenly erupted from just outside the kitchens.

Claudia thought that his eyebrows were arched in a rather theatrical way. Quintus was like that, always behaving as if there was part of his personality outside his body observing his actions. They had been at loggerheads ever since the day she had married his father, not least because he esteemed his own dead mother, but also as she had been younger than her prospective stepson at the time of the nuptials. Quintus could never accept that Claudia had loved his father, as well as admiring the most famous general in the Roman world, and, after his conquest of Macedonia, one of the richest men in Rome. The twenty-year age gap had not made any difference to their relationship either; that had changed after she had been taken prisoner by the Celt-Iberians.

It was Quintus who had found her, and he was one of the few people who knew her secret. Not that he would say anything; the Cornelii name and his political ambitions meant too much to him. She did not doubt that her intention to remarry had surprised him. On top of that, he had the air of a man who was anticipating the pleasure he could gain from a negative response.

Time to disabuse him of that notion!

'I am aware that I don't really require your permission.'

'Oh, I think you do, Claudia. I am the head of the Cornelii household.'

'Which your father saw fit to place me outside.'

Quintus bristled. 'As long as you reside under this roof…'

Claudia cut him off sharply. 'I can move today if you wish it, Stepson, and buy a house of my own.'

'I will not let you do this, Claudia!'

'Yes, you will,' she said softly.

The eyebrows shot up again; he was unused to that tone of voice from his stepmother. 'I don't think so.'

'Not even if you were to have a hand in my choice of husband?'

There was nowhere left for his face to go, being shocked and surprised already, so it seemed as if her words had failed to register. But she knew her stepson too well for that; he was not stupid, despite his manifest faults. He would have covered all the possibilities relating to his personal advantage in a split second. After all, he was, since the death of Lucius Falerius Nerva, the titular leader of the *optimates*, the faction that

Lucius had led, but he lacked the authority of his predecessor. His hold on power was shaky and his position, to his mind, was perilously assailable.

'I am aware of my responsibilities to the family, just as you are.'

Quintus treated that remark with a mocking smile. 'Then it is a sudden and somewhat overdue conversion, Lady.'

Claudia let the insult pass; her goal was far too important for that. 'You may draw up a list of candidates, Quintus, men who stand to gain by an alliance with the Cornelii. I will not let you choose, but I shall certainly take a husband from the names you provide.'

'I find this hard to believe.'

'Why? I want to remarry, preferably without a public fuss.'

'Which I could most certainly cause,' said Quintus coldly.

'So let it be a person who will give you something in return, like more vocal support in the Senate.'

They stood, eyes locked, for what seemed an age, while Quintus ran through the pros and cons in his mind. Finally, he nodded abruptly. 'I agree, but on one condition.'

Claudia's heart was pounding fiercely; she was

afraid he had guessed her motives and would make her swear an oath that would block them off. 'Which is?'

'That you make a will, returning, on your death, all the money my father left to you to the Cornelii family coffers.'

Claudia felt, and heard, the breath she had built up escape from her body. 'I agree!'

CHAPTER FOUR

———•———

Marcellus had two problems to consider, which had nothing to do with the chests full of documents in the cellar; first, he had to decide what to do about his forthcoming nuptials, and secondly, he had received his summons to join the legions as soon as he got home, though the death of his father excused him from immediate compliance in both cases. As Lucius's sole heir he had to oversee everything; Titus Cornelius, his mentor in Sicily, now quaestor, and more experienced in these matters, helped him to make the arrangements. The death of someone as potent as Lucius Falerius was the occasion for one of the greatest sights in the Roman Republic, a patrician funeral, and Marcellus had to request the attendance of famous men, people of enough personal standing to grace such an occasion and act as family mourners.

They readily agreed, though Titus declined the

premier post. He advised Marcellus that he would be wiser to ask his elder brother Quintus, certain to be elected as the next junior consul, to undertake that prestigious role. The catafalque was arranged, borne aloft by the most imposing slaves from the Falerii farms. Marcellus followed on foot, while behind him came Quintus in his purple-edged toga, driving his own chariot, wearing the death mask of Lucius's most famous ancestors, Maximus Falerius, a great administrator and Roman soldier, who had helped to conquer the Celts of the Po valley.

He was followed by ex-consuls, generals, praetors, governors and men of standing, all wearing a different family death mask, all driving chariots adorned with their own rewards for service to the state. This was a sad occasion yet, more than that, a deeply religious one, in which the cult of the family was celebrated to its greatest extent. The cupboards in the chapel were bare, for each important guest, by agreeing to attend, had taken the role of a Falerii. The family genius of his house, on that day, reigned supreme in Rome.

They made their way from the house, down the Palatine Hill and through the silent, crowded, marketplace. When they reached the rostrum before the Forum, the representatives of all

Lucius's ancestors exchanged their chariots for thrones. The crowd that had followed the procession now gathered before the rostrum to hear the funeral address, delivered by the Falerii heir. Marcellus spoke of things lost in the mists of time, of deeds performed by the giants of legend who were connected with his house. Each ancestor of note was revered, his exploits and offices catalogued. The crowd stood silent; even Lucius's enemies would not have dared to utter a word at the great man's funeral. They carried the body, now followed by the procession on foot, to the Campus Martius, in the middle of which the pyre was prepared, the timber seasoned by the wind and sun so that it would burn with a high flame, carrying the spirit of Lucius towards the heavens, where those gods he claimed in his family tree would surely care for him. Marcellus held the torch in his hand, facing the crowd, and spoke the valediction.

'There are those who saw my father as a stern man, unbending and strict. He was as hard on me as he was on himself. I was not spared, and Rome can thank *Jove* himself that my father was not either. He never put himself above the needs of the Republic he served, seeing that, in our system of government, Rome had achieved mastery in a dangerous world. He had one abiding care, that this city and its citizens should never fall under the yoke of some foreign power, or succumb to the ambitions of a man who would seek to reign supreme. He worked to ensure the Senate should remain as a place of debate, the great initiator of legislation and no man therein should be anything other than the first among equals.

'No well-born Roman, in my father's eyes, had any right to avoid service to the state. It was a duty and it should be counted a pleasure. I, Marcellus Falerius, reaffirm a vow I made to my father, that in all things my primary concern will be for the safety of Rome and the laws that serve her citizens so well. No man, while I live, shall aspire to, or reach, a higher status than that of a citizen of the Roman Republic. As long as I have strength to raise my sword arm, no other power shall impose upon our world.'

Marcellus's peroration in the Campus Martius, to many an ear, was seriously flawed, not nearly flowery enough – lacking in rhetoric. They had felt the same when he spoke from the rostrum, but it would have been a hard-hearted wretch, looking on so handsome and noble a youth at the moment he put the torch to his father's funeral pyre, who did not shed a tear. Men who had cursed Lucius Falerius Nerva all their lives, wept copiously, either moved by the ceremony or suddenly conscious of their own mortality.

The message waiting for him when he returned to the house caused Marcellus to curse heartily. The Trebonii were back, and sorry they had missed an opportunity to pay their respects at the funeral. He wanted to see Valeria badly, but he had asked Quintus Cornelius to call on him to discuss his father's last wishes. Desire was one thing, but he could hardly insult a man who was soon to be consul by being out when he arrived, yet neither could he let the opportunity pass. He sent a slave to cover the road to the Forum, with instructions to give him plenty of warning, then ran to the Trebonii house. The time it took to complete the polite exchanges with her parents was extremely galling, but unavoidable.

Flustered, Marcellus did not pick up the look of anticipation in their eyes, for his attraction to their daughter was no secret in the house. Now that his father was gone, perhaps Marcellus would exercise his rights, as a free spirit, to change his mind and marry their daughter. They also mistook his impatience, being unaware of his impending visitor, and put it down to barely controlled desire. When they finally left the two youngsters, bidding her brother and Marcellus's friend, Gaius, to remain for the sake of propriety, Valeria's parents were happy. They could feel reasonably sure that their wish was about to come true; that a Falerii would consent to an alliance with the Trebonii, something that would raise the prestige of their family enormously.

'I shall stay as far away as possible,' said Gaius, wickedly. 'I've just had a huge meal. If I have to listen to you two exchanging sweet nothings, I fear I'll be sick.'

Marcellus was too occupied to hear the sarcasm. His eyes were glued to Valeria, who had dressed for the occasion, with her auburn hair carefully plaited above her beautiful face. Her eyes were green, large and steady and the upturned nose added something to that slightly mocking smile which always entranced him. He could recall the first day when he had seen her as a budding woman rather than a teasing pest of a girl, smelt her, seen the shape of her body through her dress, and lost the will to fall out with her.

'If we sit over here,' she said, pointing to a bench by the garden wall, 'Gaius will be unable to see us.'

Marcellus had no idea he was holding his breath, but he was, and it escaped in a rush. The sound made her grin impishly. 'You sound as though you don't need me to...'

He didn't let her finish. 'I do need you, Valeria.'

She was piqued at the interruption, since she had been about to say something designed to shock him. Having so many brothers, and being a curious individual, the shape and nature of men's bodies was no mystery, and with Marcellus, so upright and priggish, it would have been wonderful to say something really vulgar.

'Valeria, I don't have much time,' he gasped, taking her hand.

Her green eyes opened wide at that. 'What do you mean?'

Marcellus saw her face close up, becoming angry, as he explained, which made him gabble the words in a way that made them sound worse than they truly were. And secretly he cursed her. Clearly Valeria was unconscious of the honour he was bestowing on her by being here in the first place. He was winding himself up to protest when she surprised him by suddenly smiling again.

'Never mind. Your slave has not come yet. So let us sit down for a moment.'

He allowed himself to be led to the bench, with only one over-the-shoulder glance at the door, and sat down. She slid close to him, so that he could feel her thigh pressing against his leg, launching into an anecdote about her stay in the country, which Marcellus barely heard, he was so taken with her proximity, and the way her every movement communicated itself through the thin tissue of their clothes.

Valeria was disappointed; she had graphically described the dimensions of the horse's genitalia twice, using her hands to do so, as well as making a crude allusion to its mounting of a mare. Perhaps Marcellus was not so much of a prude after all, the thought making her bolder, more vulgar; whatever happened, she must keep him here, make him miss his appointment with Quintus Cornelius. So, in the act of describing her shock, at the sight of a bull put to a cow, Valeria allowed her hand to brush over Marcellus's lap.

Feeling the very tip of his erection, the girl allowed her hand to linger tantalisingly close. She also felt a surge of power, since Marcellus was plainly close to bursting, and so enamoured by her proximity that he had barely heard a single word she had said. She pulled her hand away and folded them both in her lap, in a maidenly way, but she ran her tongue along her lower lip, before she spoke.

'What would you like to do now, Marcellus?'

The slave, who dashed in and called to his master, spoilt the whole effect of this delicious teasing. 'The lictors are coming, Master.'

She suppressed a laugh, tempted as she was to shout at him, 'Damn you, cretin, so too is your master.' But Marcellus was on his feet, trying to arrange his toga so that it covered the very obvious bulge in his groin.

'I must go.'

'How can you leave me like this?'

Compared to the way he felt, Valeria looked like coolness itself, so the plea had a staged quality. 'I have no choice, I told you.'

She grabbed his hand to stop him. 'Tell me you love me, Marcellus.'

'I do, Valeria, but I must go now.'

'Stay, please.'

'I cannot, you know that.'

'How can you say you love me, then desert me for some old goat?'

'I can call round later.'

The green eyes flashed for the first time since he had arrived, demonstrating that look of haughty disdain that he so dreaded and her voice, delivering that single whiplash word, was enough to attract the attention of Gaius, who had been studiously avoiding the scene.

'No!'

'Valeria,' he pleaded.

'If you go now, Marcellus, don't come back. Ever!'

'Master,' called the slave, with increased urgency.

Marcellus had to drag his eyes away from her, which, since Valeria clung to him, was nearly as difficult as letting go of her hand. Eventually, he had to pull hard to free himself. He rushed out of the door, hard on the heels of his slave.

'Well, Sister, have you destroyed Father's hopes of a Falerian alliance?' Valeria pretended she had no idea what he meant. Gaius, who knew her better than anyone, did a very fair imitation of her voice. 'If you go now, Marcellus, don't come back. Ever!'

'He'll be back, Brother, and I hope that Father enjoys having him as a son-in-law. I certainly don't think I'm going to get much pleasure out of him as a husband.'

Gaius yawned. 'I think I'll go to the brothel. It would be nice to have some decent female company.'

He was delighted when Valeria stuck her tongue out at him, just as she used to when she was a little girl.

'You must see, Marcellus, that I cannot accede to what you ask.' Quintus thrust the scroll back at the young man, as if merely holding a request to give some small rights to Sicilian slaves might contaminate him. 'It would be political suicide at a time like this.'

Marcellus took the papyrus, turning it round to point at his father's seal at the bottom. 'You must, Quintus Cornelius. It was attested to by my father. If anything it is a valedictory request to the Senate.'

Quintus wanted to get up and leave. To his mind this youth had that same expression of arrogant disdain habitually worn by his late father. It was hard to take in someone with the gravitas of age and long service to the state, intolerable in one so young, and it would have been nice to throw it back in his face, telling him that the man they had just buried was a slug, who had become so warped by power that he had even spied on those he called his friends, to tell him that he had caught the Nubian slave Thoas in the act of ransacking his study. Happening just after an attempt on Lucius's life, one which had nearly succeeded in seeing off the old goat, Quintus had taken no chances. He had stabbed Thoas, but it had been too hard, leaving the man no time to tell him all before he expired. But the slave's dying words named his father as the man for whom he was working and, given that knowledge, Marcellus would cease to be so smug.

But being a politician, he put that aside,

effortlessly keeping his emotions under control. 'Please do not think that I am ignorant of that, Marcellus. But your father was, above all things, a realist. He may have made promises regarding the Sicilian slaves, but I doubt he saw them as binding.'

Marcellus, too, fought to control his anger; this man would be nothing like as powerful as he was soon to become without his father, who had taken him under his wing and elevated him to occupy his present eminence. Left to his own devices, Quintus would have been just one senator amongst many and the bargain was simple; Quintus Cornelius would have the support of all the Falerii clients and hold matters in trust till Marcellus could come into his own and take over the leadership of the *optimates* faction. That the man should fail his mentor at the first real hurdle enraged him.

He was less successful than his visitor at masking his feelings and the way he spoke betrayed how he felt. 'You're saying that you lack the will to use the one thing he bestowed on you, his political power?'

Quintus went white, yet somehow he maintained the necessary air of calm; quite remarkable, when his sole desire was to give this upstart youth the toe of his boot. 'I doubt whether your father would have got this through the house. His energy must have been sapped by illness, to even contemplate such a course.'

'If the conditions don't improve for the Sicilian slaves, we'll have another bloody revolt.'

The older man smiled, deciding that he needed to be emollient. He was not yet supreme in the Senate; Lucius had left him strong, but not as formidable as he needed to be. Insulting patricians, even those barely grown up, was a luxury he could not afford.

'I imagine they're rather chastened by what happened. They certainly seem to have gone back to their labours with the minimum of fuss. I should think, by now, with the overseers back in charge, they have had any notion of rebellion beaten out of them.'

Marcellus had to stop himself from saying how important Sicily and the grain grown there was to the security of Rome – Quintus knew as well as he that sustaining the distribution of the corn dole which kept the Roman mob from riot depended on steady supply. Nor was there any point in underlining that his father's tactic, of suborning the slave army leaders by bribery instead of fighting the whole mass, had been based on that one fact; nothing would interfere with the grain convoys more than a protracted conflict and a mass of dead slaves at its conclusion.

'They have gone back to the farms in peace because of the promises my father made on their future rights, and I would point out it is the beatings they suffered which caused them to revolt in the first place. Please remember, Quintus Cornelius, I was there and I saw what I saw. If you doubt me, ask your brother. Titus, you will recall, was there too.'

'I have my own sources to consult, and they tell me matters are settled. The slaves are cowed.'

'I suppose the kind of information you have comes to you from people like Cassius Barbinus, whose sole guiding principle is profit. I am shocked, knowing the man as you do, that you give it credence.'

Quintus cracked finally, the veneer of diplomacy tearing wide open. He was soon to be elected consul, not some nonentity to be lectured by this boy. 'You will not insult Cassius Barbinus in my hearing, Marcellus Falerius, and you will show the proper respect due to my dignity. Lucius is dead and his ghost holds no sway over the Senate. But I, and those who share my views, do.'

He stood up, intending to intimidate the boy by towering over him, but Marcellus forestalled the senator by standing too, and, being much taller, he reversed the situation, so Quintus's admonishing tone lost some of its effect by being delivered upwards.

'You must make your way in the world, Marcellus. I am bound to assist you by the vows I made to your father, but the most compelling oath I swore, in his presence, was to uphold the power and majesty of Rome. Do not thrust scrolls at me which ease the lives of slaves, and demand laws that could fracture the fragile structure that holds the entire state together.'

'I am concerned for my father's honour.'

'And Rome?'

'Rome's honour is at stake here too.'

Quintus laughed at that. 'Honour? Rome has power, Marcellus. We are absolved of the need for honour. Surely your father taught you that.'

Marcellus pulled himself fully upright, as if standing to attention. It was bad enough that his father had died before he could complete his life's work, but to have this, his last act as a senatorial commissioner, set aside, like the work of a freedman clerk, was intolerable.

'To have heard one of the leading magistrates at Rome utter such words makes me ashamed.'

Quintus, who was thinking that for all his height he was a pious little shit, brushed aside the approbation. 'You are young. It is right that you should have high ideals. I held to the same tenets, myself, at your age, but I am now older and wiser, just as your father was. He didn't let honour stop him when he needed to protect the Republic.'

Marcellus made to speak, but Quintus silenced him, pointing to the pile of scrolls held by one of the lictors.

'Look at those, Marcellus. Every one is a plea from the Governor of Hispania Citerior, Servius Caepio, asking for legions to quell a new revolt. I helped to get him appointed. Servius is clever. He managed one thing few of his predecessors achieved by bringing some order to the frontier in Spain. It seems only days ago that he looked set to bring about a more permanent peace, but now, all that is changed. The place is on fire again, if anything, worse than before, which is only one problem amongst many that I must face in my consular year.'

Quintus paused, looking worried, as if the weight of all those responsibilities was a burden too heavy to bear, but he recovered and fixed Marcellus with a hard, unyielding look.

'When your affairs in Rome are settled, you must take up your duties. I have enough honour to remember mine, to recall the vows I made in this very room. You need a military posting by which you can advance your career. You will soon have your orders, appointing you as one of my tribunes. We march for Spain in a matter of days. When you have held your funeral feast, received the contents of your father's will, and put the affairs of the house of Falerii in order, then join us.'

'And the agreement with the Sicilian slaves?'

'Let us be successful in the field, Marcellus.' He pointed to the scroll, still open in the young man's hand, with Lucius's seal at the bottom – the agreement he had made to ameliorate the lot of the slaves in return for their passive surrender. 'Then we can return, so potent that no one would dare block any motion we put to the house, even one as hare-brained as that.'

That last, careless remark betrayed him: Quintus would do nothing. The aspiring consul departed and Marcellus was left with his last words, delivered in that mock-jolly tone, accompanied by the kind of playful punch an adult uses to impress a child.

'We'll go to war and show them what we're made of, eh?'

Quintus was thinking, as he walked down the street, that an impetuous young man like Marcellus could get into some very dangerous situations, but the boy, no doubt, craved success.

As his commanding general, and his patron, he felt he should do all in his power to aid him. If Marcellus succeeded, he would be grateful, and if he died a glorious death, he, Quintus Cornelius, would be spared a future thorn in the flesh.

Marcellus watched him go, aware for the first time of just how naked his father's death had left him. The argument he had just had with Valeria was a blessing, and it was at that moment he decided to go ahead with his marriage to the Claudian girl. He would need her dowry in the future, if he were to have any hope of standing against men like Quintus. She would have to wait a while, till he came back from his first campaign, but he would reassure her father this very day. The second decision he made was just as important; he put aside all thoughts of burning any of the documents in the cellar.

CHAPTER FIVE

'Are you sure this is the right list, Quintus?' asked Claudia, waving the scroll she had just read at him.

'What do you mean?'

'If we were in a stable I would say you'd assembled, for my edification, all the spavined nags and blown stallions in the whole of Italy.'

Actually, for her purpose, the list was perfect. The last thing she wanted was some stalwart husband, full of ardour; she wanted someone meek, malleable and preferably stupid. In her opinion, finding such a creature should be no problem in the Senate. Like her list, it was full of them.

'I have complied with your own wishes, Lady.'

She nearly laughed. He was so serious and stiff, forever striking a pose in his new consular toga, fiddling with the thick purple stripe along the edge, but she fought back the temptation. 'We must invite them to dine then, so that I can look them over.'

'There's no time for that, Claudia. I march for the north within the week and I do think it will be difficult for you to invite anyone to the house with no men around. It would cause a scandal.'

Cunning swine! she thought. *He's got somebody picked out already.* But there was no hint of that thought in her reply, more a feigned anxiety. 'North? I thought you were sailing for Spain, and not for at least a month.'

Quintus threw his head back slightly, as though he were being sculpted for a marble bust. 'There's trouble on all the borders. We march to Massila, effecting a demonstration for the tribes of Cisalpine Gaul, a reminder that they should stay on their own side of the border.'

'Then should I wait till you return, Quintus?' Claudia asked in a meek voice.

'No!' He snapped, reacting too quickly, which he tried to cover with a winning smile; all it did was to make him look like a thief. 'It's up to you, of course, but you did give me the impression that it was a matter of some urgency.'

Claudia put as much sensuality and longing into her reply as she could, causing her stepson to blush. 'Oh, it is, Quintus. You've no idea how I long for a man to take care of me.'

'Yes, well, as you say,' he stuttered, reaching for the reassurance of the edge of his toga.

'Perhaps then we could go through the list and see who you think will be suitable.'

That restored him; indeed he could hardly contain his eagerness. 'There are one or two on there who I think would be eminently so.'

Her silent thoughts were again in total conflict with her smiling face. Putty in your hands, you mean. Well that suits me, pig, for if they'll grovel to you, they'll very likely grovel to me as well.

'I chafe for action.'

Titus smiled at his stepmother, mightily amused by Cholon's words, as well as the languid wave of his arm. 'One campaign in Sicily, without bloodshed, and you've become a warrior.'

'I cannot see myself armed,' Cholon replied, quite missing the irony, 'but being in such danger, surrounded by the threat of imminent war, excited me.'

'I should write a comedy about it, Cholon,' said Claudia. 'After all, no one ever has.'

The Greek sat up suddenly. 'You have hit on a brilliant idea!'

'Interesting, Cholon, hardly brilliant,' said Titus.

Claudia looked at him with mock-seriousness.

'Can you not see your stepmother as brilliant?'

'Radiant, perhaps, Claudia,' replied Titus gallantly.

'Not a play,' said Cholon, still lost in his reverie. 'Something more substantial.' Both his fellow diners looked bemused. 'Plays are ephemeral, not meant to last.'

'I doubt Euripides would agree,' Claudia chided, with a smile.

'He stuck to the eternal verities and, between them, my Greek forefathers quite used them all up. There's little serious left to write about, especially for the theatre, but what of a history?'

Titus gave Claudia a perplexed look before replying. 'A history?'

Cholon was excited, so much so that he passed up the usual sarcastic riposte that would normally have followed from Titus repeating what he had just said. 'Of course, the proper account of a real campaign, like Herodotus and Ptolemy. Who fought and where, the numbers involved, with none of that exaggeration that so plagued the likes of Homer.'

'Are there any Greek writers you admire?' asked Claudia, who was unusual in many ways, not least in that, for a woman of her class, she was well read.

'Of course there are,' replied Cholon, with an

arch expression, but he didn't go on to name them. 'You will go on campaign, Titus, will you not?'

'To do what you suggest would be better realised at the side of a general.'

'Which you will be in three years.'

Titus shrugged. 'That is in the lap of the gods, and, of course, my brother. Quintus wasn't too keen on my being a magistrate at all. I don't know if he'll back me for the consulship.'

'Lucius Falerius's death hasn't helped you,' said Claudia.

The Greek cut in, practically snorting with indignation. 'You can't rely on him, I agree, but you do yourself no favours, Titus. For instance, you could cultivate important people, instead of snubbing them, which, I may say, is your usual way.'

'I promise you, Cholon. If I get a command, you can come with me.'

'Good,' replied the Greek, eagerly, 'but you will forgive me if I take a few precautions, just in case you don't.'

'Then you agree, Lady, to marry Lucius Sextius Paullus?'

His impatience grated on her. Quintus would never have dared to treat another man this way, however dull his wits, but her stepson suffered from the same natural prejudice as most of his gender; he assumed that all women were stupid. In the case of his silly wife, he was right, which made the final condition she intended to extract all the more pleasurable, but first she must seem reluctant, a poor woman who needed to be persuaded.

'Is he not much older than me?'

It was delicious to see how shocked he was. 'You would not wish a husband younger than you, Claudia. That would be most improper.'

She dropped her eyes in submission. 'Of course, how silly of me.'

'Besides, he's a fine figure of a man. What dignity he has. How many men can boast such a noble profile? That mass of silver hair makes him stand out from any crowd and he is rich, Lady, so you'll want for nothing.'

He's also as supine as a cub and as dull and pompous as you, she thought, but she smiled again when she spoke out loud. 'Do you think he'll agree?'

'My dear Claudia, you underrate yourself. You are still a very handsome woman. Sextius will be flattered.'

'You cannot be sure.'

That speared him; she could see the mind

working flat out to counter that objection, but he could hardly tell her that Lucius Sextius Paullus would do exactly what Quintus Cornelius, the newly elected consul, told him to do.

'I must make a confession,' he said smoothly, 'for the very thought you have espoused did worry me. I could not see you risk a rebuff, so, I took the liberty of sounding out Sextius Paullus in advance.'

'You shame me, Quintus!' she cried, her hands going to her mouth.

'Do I?' He was confused. Not having done any such thing, he was wondering what the result would have been if he had. 'It was not my intention.'

'Well, now I have no choice. You have forced my hand.'

'I apologise, most heartily,' Quintus replied swiftly, trying to keep the triumph out of his voice.

Claudia's voice changed completely and her simpering tone went, to be replaced by the true timbre, strong and direct. 'And because you have done this, Quintus, I must extract one more condition from you before we proceed.'

'What?'

She looked him right in the eye, not in the least deflected by his obvious anger. 'I want you to swear, before witnesses, that you will do everything you can to help Titus to the consulship.'

'Titus?'

She couldn't resist being sarcastic. 'You may recall him. He's your brother.'

'I know who he is!' Quintus shouted. 'Did he put you up to this?'

'Would you believe me if I said no?'

'I agree.'

He said it suddenly, which caught her off guard, but the look in his eye was enough to tell Claudia he had no intention of complying. Once the wedding was over, he would renege, no matter to whom he swore an oath and he did not think she had it in her power to force him. Time to disabuse her stepson of that notion.

'That pleases me, Quintus, and I know you will keep your word. After all, you are one of the few people alive who realise the harm that I, provoked beyond endurance, can do to the Cornelii name.' He went white and she could see him beginning to explode. 'I think it would be a good idea to fetch Lucius Sextius Paullus, don't you?'

'There is nothing you can do,' said Cholon, shrugging. 'If Quintus will not move this bill in the house.'

'Cholon is right, Marcellus.'

'You should attend to your guests and put the matter out of your mind.'

Marcellus sighed. If these two said it was hopeless, then it must be so. 'Titus, since your brother is absent, would you do me the honour of sitting at my right hand?'

'The honour is mine,' Titus replied with a slight bow.

He knew as well as his young host just how comprehensively the boy had been insulted. Quintus, who would have crawled to attend upon Lucius when he was alive, had, by pleading pressure of work, declined an invitation to the first dinner Marcellus was hosting as his own man.

Just then, he was distracted from the discussion as Marcellus caught the eye of Valeria's father, who had practically stormed out of the house earlier, and had only been restrained by his friends, who had reminded him of the harm he would do to his house by insulting the host. Marcellus had been a little ingenuous when the man had mentioned marriage with his daughter, disabusing him of the idea, in a voice that sounded stuffed with pride, but was in reality full of pain. Truly, the youngster had reasoned, coming upon your inheritance was not the bed of roses it had, at first, appeared. And he still had to face Valeria!

* * *

'Odd, Marcellus reminds me a little of your father,' said Cholon, as they walked back to their respective homes. 'You do too, of course.'

'He asked me all about him when we first met. Told me that Father was the noblest Roman he'd ever met.'

'The boy was right in that!' said the Greek, proudly.

Titus put a hand on his shoulder. 'I wonder whether nobility is an asset in these times.'

Cholon stopped as they were crossing the Forum Romanum, right outside the Curia Hostilia, home to the Senate, and looked Titus in the eye. 'I think the late Lucius Falerius was right. You're so lucky, you Romans! How many times have you stood on the threshold of disaster, only to find that the very man capable of saving you is at hand, merely waiting for the summons? No other state has had such good fortune.'

'Careful Cholon, or you'll be saying we Romans are doing something right.'

'Much as it pains me to admit it, Titus, I think you are.' He pointed to the building behind. 'There's more corruption and venality in that building than there is anywhere in the world, yet the same system that produces them, produces the likes of Marcellus and you.'

'I agree about Marcellus,' said Titus quickly.

Cholon grinned, his teeth showing white in the light from the torches in the Forum walls.

'Your father couldn't bear a compliment either, but he was there, like you and Marcellus, standing by to take over if the Republic faltered. That is your Roman strength. You have created a system that encourages corruption, that makes men rich beyond the dreams of avarice, yet when it becomes too rotten to sustain, when the fabric tears, it falls into the hands of men of honour, men who would not sully their hands with a bribe.'

Titus tapped him on the chest. 'You are, like all Greeks, an incurable romantic. One day the gods will decide they've had enough of us Romans. One day these honourable men will fail.'

'Then let the gods beware,' said Cholon, who had probably drunk more than was good for him.

'Are we not too close to a temple for such impiety?'

Cholon grinned again. 'What has a Greek got to fear from a Roman temple? After all, you're mere barbarians.'

'Of course I wish you joy,' said Titus, though his face could not help but betray his true feelings regarding someone like Sextius Paullus.

'And me too,' added Cholon.

'You think I've made a poor choice?' asked Claudia. They both gave a negative reply in unison, but in a flustered way. 'Good. Then I would like you to give me away, Titus. I could not bear it if Quintus had the honour.'

The air of congratulation did not last a second after they had left her room.

'The man's a buffoon!'

Cholon looked at Titus, who was confused rather than angry. 'I fear I am to blame. I suggested it in the first place.'

'Sextius Paullus!'

That annoyed Cholon, who knew the bridegroom to be an empty vessel, a handsome spineless nobody with money, and a pederast, to boot. 'What do you take me for, an idiot?'

'I'm beginning to wonder if Claudia has lost her wits.'

The Greek emitted a small but potent moan. 'One evening with Sextius should convince her that she has done just that.'

Titus shrugged. 'It is, of course, her life.'

Cholon looked at the heavens, as if seeking support. 'Let's just hope she doesn't invite us to dine with him too often.'

'Lucky Quintus,' said Titus, mournfully. 'Suddenly a year of hard campaigning in Spain sounds very enticing.'

CHAPTER SIX

The Roman army was a conscript, not a volunteer force, with each man called up slipping into the military class his social standing demanded, but like most things in the Republic, the theory differed widely from the practice. Rome had legions operating on a permanent basis in so many places that recruitment had ceased to be just an annual levy. True, the consuls, on taking office, raised their legions each year, since nothing enhanced a man's career more than a successful war. Where things differed from the old days was that such soldiers were rarely disbanded.

The hoary old legionary doing the recruiting, a fellow named Labenius, festooned with decorations, looked at the two of them with a jaundiced eye. A pair of well set-up young fellows volunteering like this usually meant that they had committed a crime; quite possibly they had murdered someone, and were trying to escape justice. This was not a notion that bothered him; as long as they killed Rome's enemies, he was content, and in an army where officers of his rank were selected, with stiff competition for the posts from other experienced soldiers, the number of recruits he brought in was a matter of great importance. The tribunes would more readily appoint him to a centurion's command if he proved that he could keep his unit up to strength.

The praetor would check their class against the census roll, but they had brought in their own weapons and armour, so he had little doubt that they would qualify as *hastarii*. The legion broke down into four social groups, based on wealth. The Velites who acted as lightly armed skirmishers, the *hastarii* who made the first attack in battle, and the *principes*, old experienced troops, the best in the legion, who would follow up the *hastarii* to press home the assault. The final group were the *triani*, who made up the premier line in a defensive battle, or provided a screen for the others to pass through when retreating from a failed attack.

This was the unit, based primarily on the social standing of the recruits, that had conquered the world, through sound tactics, tough training, coupled with a system of generous rewards and ferocious punishments, both designed to encourage valour and discourage sloppiness. Aquila had to unlearn a great deal, for the way the legionary fought did not often lend itself to individual skill. It was the combined weight and iron discipline of the legions that made them feared by formal armies, just as much as barbarian tribes.

'Drill, drill, drill,' said Fabius, gasping, his face red from the heat and exertion, while sweat ran freely from underneath his helmet. 'I can hardly remember a life without it. My spear has become so much a part of me I tried to piss through it the other day.' Aquila gave his 'nephew' a look of mock-disbelief. 'Easy to make a mistake, "Uncle". I'm a big boy, didn't you know that?'

Aquila, who was breathing heavily, but evenly, had no difficulty in finding the breath to reply. 'Just look at your belly, that should remind you.'

Fabius summoned up enough energy and oxygen to protest. 'What belly?'

'The one you used to trail around with you in Rome, "Nephew". You were a disgrace to the name Terentius, and your prick would have had to be the length of your spear for you to see it.'

Fabius hooted with strained laughter. 'Nobody is that bad! Anyway, as long as you can feel it.'

'Come on you two,' shouted their instructor, 'or I'll give you a bag of rocks to carry.'

Fabius hauled himself to his feet and, picking up his sword and shield, he resumed his attack on the padded wooden post, slashing and cutting, but, typically, still summoning up the breath to talk. 'Where does that man find his rocks? They weigh twice as much as any stone I've ever seen.'

That was a mild punishment; a bag full of stones strapped to your back to remind you that slacking was not allowed, weight that made every task, from marching to spear throwing, that much harder. To protest would be worse than useless; once you joined the legions, the officers owned your life. You could be beaten, flogged, scourged, broken at the wheel or even killed if you stole from your fellows or fell asleep on guard duty. Fabius was fond of telling his 'uncle', with the little breath he could muster, that joining the legions was the worst idea he had ever had. Yet Fabius was getting fitter, for Aquila's remark about his belly was right; it was flat and his face had lost its puffy appearance. He was now lean and tanned, and he could run and jump with the best of them, cast his spear, wield his sword and ram hard enough with the boss on his shield to maim a man.

Being a witty rogue, Fabius was popular, and

though he never actually stole anything, an offence punishable by death, he had the ability, when it came to interpreting the rules, to sail very close to the wind, especially in the matter of acquiring extras like food. Added to that, he had an utter disdain for permanent ownership, happy to share with his fellows, particularly one that seemed a little down. He also maintained, unchanged from his days in the taverns and wine shops of Rome, his ability to drink to excess – no mean feat in a legionary camp where such things were rigidly controlled.

Quintus Cornelius, whose consular legions these were, came frequently to examine his troops. The tribunes assembled their men before the oration platform to witness the appointment of the centurions, men who only held their office on a temporary basis, facing reselection by ballot every year. In practice, unless the tribunes thought they had failed or held them to be too old, those who had held senior positions were usually reappointed. It was a matter of some importance to the men; the last thing they wanted was to be led by some idiot whose only talent lay in pleasing tribunes.

To the rankers, these noble electors were a group of men much easier to hoodwink than the

officers they were set to appoint. Tribunes were
the sons of senators and the wealthier knights;
they varied in age from youths on their first
military posting, to men who had started on the
cursus honorum and held office as aediles. No
man, in theory, could stand for office until two
years had passed since his last appointment, and
the best way to enhance a reputation, and repair
the costs of being a magistrate, was in the army,
on a successful campaign.

Aquila could not keep his eyes off the cavalry,
the wealthiest of the intake. They had to be able
to supply their own horses, as well as their
weapons. The sons of knights, they seemed
overdressed and pampered, and, to his mind,
indifferent horsemen. They had little to do with
the other legionaries, holding themselves aloof
from the foot soldiers, even when those men were
set to guard their animals. The social difference
was maintained in camp somewhat more rigidly
than it was upheld in the city, but, in company
with the auxiliary cavalry – mercenaries drawn
from places like Numidia and Thrace – they
would perform their task when the time came,
undertaking reconnaissance and screening the
legion before a battle.

The men cheered and groaned as the
appointments were made, depending on their

maniple, but all agreed that the tribunes had done a good thing in reappointing old Labenius to the senior centurion's job, the *primus pilus*. He had more decorations than anyone in the army, was as fanatically brave as he was fair-minded, and not above giving an upstart young officer a tongue-lashing if they sought to condescend to him.

The new consul ordered the centurions to put them through their paces, proving that he had a sharp eye by the way he dispensed praise and opprobrium. Soon they would begin the long overland march to the north, picking up the mercenary cavalry plus two auxiliary legions supplied by Rome's allies. The whole would form a column five leagues long, with catapults and siege equipment, while the baggage train, camp followers, merchants and prostitutes, plus all the mules needed as transport would add a tail some thirty leagues long in the army's wake.

A Roman army trained en route; first, in the way it was assembled and marched, secondly, in the way it pitched camp. Those responsible for surveying, tribunes and centurions, would ride ahead, select a site for the camp and mark out the perimeter, then they would raise a red flag on the side nearest to water, and lay out the positions for the roads and the ramparts. Each unit, as it marched onto the site, would take up its appointed task, the consul's tent being pitched on the highest point. A deep trench was then dug, using the earth to form a rampart, thus doubling the height of the defensive perimeter.

Quintus's legions were in no danger as they marched north through Italy, but he desired that they should be thoroughly efficient long before they encountered any opposition. The camps they constructed often resembled those they would throw up near an enemy position, with deeper ditches, higher ramparts, and stakes driven into the top of the rampart to add to the protective wall. While they constructed the first wall, half the army and all the cavalry would deploy, in battle order, to protect the working parties. Once completed, the others would withdraw in sections to finish it off. Only when the camp was complete, the oath sworn, and the guards set for the night, could those not on duty relax. That is, unless one of their officers wanted them to undertake weapons drill.

It did not take long for the experienced legionaries, who undertook the training, to see that Aquila was already adept in the use of weapons. His thrown spear travelled further, and straighter, than the others. When they progressed from slicing at posts to fighting each other, his swordplay was far superior to the accepted norm. All the men in his maniple were visibly impressed except, of course, his 'nephew'.

'Danger!' Fabius exclaimed, stirring the pot vigorously. 'How can I be in any danger? All I have to do is hide behind Aquila. I suggest we all do the same, since he likes fighting so much.'

The other men in his section smiled, and not just at this oft-repeated joke. The smell from the pot was a lot more interesting in Fabius's section than in the others; how he had managed to find the time to filch a chicken baffled them. As soon as the rampart had been raised, he had also dug up some vegetables and picked a selection of herbs from just outside the ramparts.

'Does that mean my back is safe?' asked Aquila.

'My shield will be tight against it, "Uncle", with the boss up your arse. Don't worry, you'll be getting pleasure on two fronts.'

They heard the crunch of feet on the earth and looked up. Labenius, accompanying a tribune called Ampronius on his rounds, tried to lead the officer past them without stopping, but the odour from the pot was too enticing and the tribune stopped, his nostrils twitching. He was young, his face thin, with large eyes and a fine-boned nose, giving him a haughty expression.

'What's in there?' he demanded.

Fabius was on his feet in a flash, prepared to give an honest, if vague answer. 'Our food, sir.'

The others were pulling themselves upright when the tribune responded, his lips pursed and his voice a hiss. 'Don't be insolent, Soldier.'

Fabius had a look of purity on his face, a bland expression devoid of meaning, which is the most insolent expression a man can adopt in the face of a superior's stupidity. The tribune stepped forward and stuck his vine sapling into the pot and a large thigh rose to the surface, unmistakable in its shape.

'Chicken?'

'No, sir!' barked Fabius. He could see the expression of distaste on the tribune's face, see him working up to issuing some form of punishment for this blatant denial of the obvious truth. Fabius could live with that, but the bastard might confiscate his supper.

'It's not a chicken, it's a pigeon. I ain't never seen one like the bugger. It fell out of a tree, your honour, right onto the tip of my spear. Committed suicide, so to speak. Probably couldn't fly because it was so fat.'

The tribune's jaw dropped, seemingly fooled for a second by the utter sincerity of Fabius's reply. The others around the fire had to look away from him, struggling not to laugh and Labenius cut in quickly, his own weather-beaten face showing the strain of containing his mirth.

'Why, that's a good omen, Soldier. We must tell the general about this, sir.'

The mention of Quintus Cornelius halted whatever Ampronius was about to say, but the anger was obvious in the set of his jaw and the look in his eye. Labenius had, with his interruption, adopted a hearty tone, which was as insulting as that used by Fabius.

'Nothing like a good omen at the start of a march to give the men heart.' Labenius added. 'The general can tell them about it in the morning, say the auguries are brilliant. It could mean this army is never going to go hungry.'

Labenius had stymied him and the tribune was furious, the vine sapling twitching in his hand as he fought to control his temper, but he spun on his heel and strode away. Labenius walked up to Fabius, still standing to attention, head back and staring into the night sky.

'If that turns out to be one of the chickens from the priest's coop, I'll fire a flaming arrow up your arse.'

Fabius's head came down sharply. 'I'm not that stupid!'

'Which is why I stepped in, Soldier.' Labenius turned slowly, taking in the entire section in one long look. 'The next time you steal a bird, take one for the officers as well, and make them a present of it.'

'He doesn't look like the type to accept the gift of food,' said Aquila.

'Not here in Italy, he ain't. But when we're in Gaul, lad, or Spain, far away from all those handy, nearby markets, and the sod's been on polenta for a fortnight, he'll kiss your breech for a taste of proper meat.'

'You're welcome anytime, Spurius Labenius,' said Fabius.

The old centurion smiled wolfishly. 'I know that, Soldier. People like me are always welcome.'

They were between Vada Sabatia and the Alpine foothills when Marcellus finally joined the legions and the auxiliary forces, approaching the first area where it could truly be said that the army was in danger. The Boii, a Celtic tribe, still occupied the hills, often raiding far to the south if nothing stood in their way. These were the same men who had helped Hannibal get his elephants, and his army, through the high, snowbound mountain passes. For all his brilliance, the Carthaginian general would have died in that snow if the local tribes had not shown him the way. And they had also reinforced his army, so that when he made contact with Roman legions, they were routed by his generalship, allied to raw Celtic courage. Consequently, they were afforded great respect.

Not that they were impressed by that! Their attitude had altered little in the intervening decades. Quintus had done battle with them as a young tribune. Eager for a fight, he relished the thought that they might descend from their mountain fastness, in numbers, for a proper contest; the general who defeated them and finally brought the Alpine tribes into Rome's orbit would have a great triumph, since they were perceived as a sword aimed at Rome's heart. He elected to proceed slowly, to present them with a chance, because he knew, to the men of the hills and mountains, the legions would present a tempting target. Rome was the ultimate enemy, seeking to destroy their ancient pastoral existence and to bring them into the fold of the despised agrarian empire.

The command tent was full to overflowing when Quintus issued his instructions. Marcellus, as the most junior of the tribunes, stayed well to the rear, able to identify most of the other men in the tent, for he had met them,

at one time or another, at his father's house. It
was evidence of Quintus Cornelius's growing
stature that so many of Lucius's old clients were
eager to go campaigning with his nominated
successor, just as his own diminished standing
was easily deduced by the way they politely
ignored him.

'I hope they do attack us,' said Servilus
Laternus, another young tribune standing beside
him, his face as eager as the words he had used.
'It will blood the men.'

Marcellus looked at him closely. Short, squat,
with an open, honest countenance, he was
tempted to ask Servilus if he had ever seen battle-
blood spilt, as he had in the waters off
Agrigentum in Sicily, knowing it was easy to be
brave beforehand. He had cast a spear for the
first time at a human frame and achieved a kill,
his excitement so great he had failed to see the
danger he was in; if Titus Cornelius had not
swept his feet from under him, he too would have
died. But he decided against disclosure; the other
youth would be bound to ask him where he had
seen action and telling him would be impossible,
since even the most mundane rendition of that
seaborne fight would sound very much like
boasting.

Quintus silenced the murmuring his orders had

produced. 'Any sections of the road that have been damaged, we will repair on the way. I want the baggage trains between the legions from now on, with the cavalry forming a screen on the inland flank.'

His face took on a sad look, matched by the way he dropped his voice. 'In truth, we are unlikely to encounter any heavy forces. We are too strong and I must warn you that we're not truly seeking battle. This is only a show of force. Our destination remains Massila, from where we will take ship to Spain, but this demonstration will be worthless if we are seen to be vulnerable. What we must guard against is small raiding parties after a few trophies.'

Marcellus wanted to ask what would happen if they attacked from the seaward flank. It seemed obvious to him that a small raiding party could do just that, moving across in front of the legion before it arrived, but he was too young, and too inexperienced, to be questioning the instructions of a consul.

'At no time are we to engage in pursuit, gentlemen. Our job is in Spain, not here at the base of the Alps.' That set up another babble of noise, some approving, most the opposite. The junior consul's raised voice silenced them all. 'It is a favoured tactic of the Celts. They send in a small party, which we pursue with our cavalry, then a larger force cuts them off, too far away for the infantry to interfere. I need hardly tell you how handicapped we would be in the future without the cavalry.'

More instructions followed, but there was a rigid pattern to the formation of a legion on the march, so the order in which they, and the allies, would go was already laid down. The horn, which had sounded to rouse them an hour before, sounded again, and as the officers filed out of the tent Marcellus looked at Quintus. Command suited him, for that slightly sly expression was gone; in his decorated armour, with the baton that denoted his consular *imperium* in his hand, he looked every inch the competent general.

'Come on, Marcellus,' said Servilus, taking his arm. Everything had started to disappear: tables, chairs and the regimental symbols at the far end, as the consul's servants prepared to depart. 'Don't hang about in here, or the men will take down the tent with you inside it.'

Over the next few days Marcellus caught up with the requirements of his duties, which had nothing to do with fighting, and everything to do with administering and disciplining those under his command. He led his men on the march, checked the work they had done on the camp defences, supervised the issuing of rations and assigned them to guard duty.

'They've given us the new one,' said Fabius, unfolding the tent. 'Maybe we can have some fun with him.'

'I should take care, Fabius,' replied one of the others. 'He might take it into his head to have a bit of fun with the skin on your back.'

Fabius grinned. 'I'm told he is as noble as they come, this one, with a big house on the Palatine.'

Aquila laughed. 'Then he might have had the honour of being robbed by Fabius Terentius. See if he's only got one red shoe.'

Fabius gave him a wink. 'He might at that, but don't you go hinting at it, just in case.'

'What's his name, again?' asked another man, who was sorting out the poles and ropes.

'Marcellus Falerius.'

Everyone's work rate shot up as Tullius Rogus's voice sliced through the air. If the tribune's tent was not up in double-quick time, then their centurion would have to answer for it and he was not the type to suffer in silence. Aquila had frozen at the mention of the name, one that was burnt into his memory and he shook his head violently. A Falerius had been the man ultimately responsible for Gadoric's death, but he had also been an old man, so surely it could not be the same person.

'Move, Terentius,' snapped Tullius.

Aquila heard the vine sapling swish through the air. The centurion was still several feet away, but he was approaching quickly, and that sound meant that he would use it. Aquila stood to his full height, turned quickly and looked at Tullius, his bright blue eyes blazing with anger. The gold eagle flashed at his neck, somehow adding a frightening dimension to the image he presented and the sapling stopped abruptly, as did the centurion. The look in Aquila's eyes was not insolence, it was something else, something far more dangerous and, given the fellow's height, his broad build and the powerful shoulders, Tullius reasoned that now could be the wrong time to tangle with him. The person before him could not be treated lightly, but the day would come when Aquila Terentius did something serious, an offence punishable by death. Tullius, in his position of authority, could afford to be patient, yet he had to say something, for dignity had to be maintained.

'Get a move on, slug. Or you'll feel this on your back.'

Aquila went back to work, but the centurion knew that his threat had little to do with it and he was right; the soldier, who had taken hold of that charm round his neck, had not heard him.

Aquila drew the first duty, so he was outside the tent while Marcellus had his evening meal. It being a warm night, the flap was thrown back to expose the brightly lit interior. The tent was sumptuously furnished, with every luxury that a young Roman noble felt he needed on campaign, and a great deal of the contents were gold, silver and highly polished wood, while perfumed smoke rose from a brazier to keep the insects at bay. Marcellus had invited several guests and the conversation was, of course, dominated by that which surrounded them: the legions and the prospect of battle. Aquila could smell the food, which he tried to identify as each of the numerous courses appeared, but the odours eluded him. These young men were eating things he had never seen, or smelt, in his life. Being so close he could also hear every word they said through the open flap. Though he had mounted many a guard duty, this was the first time he had really bothered to listen to the conversations that took place around him.

He did now, paying particular attention to the

voice of his tribune, Marcellus, and he could hardly fail to notice that there was a very high degree of arrogance in these young men. They spoke freely and disparagingly, frequently labelling their soldiers as ignorant peasants. It was as though he and the man on the other side of the entrance were not there, somehow made invisible merely by their rank. The tribunes in the tent assumed that they had the right to their commands because of their birth. When they were not discussing the prospect of military glory, they were speculating on their political future, laying wagers as to whom would be the first to hold magisterial office.

He found himself becoming annoyed; for the first time since he had enlisted, he missed being in command himself, as he had been for a while in the Sicilian slave army. Nothing he had seen indicated to Aquila that these men were inherently better at soldiering, yet they constantly alluded to their superior prowess. Had he been in the mood to be fair, Aquila might have acknowledged that Marcellus Falerius did not participate in such boasting, but he was not, and his anger was quite profound by the time he was relieved. The men in the tent had consumed a lot of wine, which made their laughter, plus their attempts at wit, both louder and more galling to the man outside.

Marcellus noticed vaguely that the process had commenced by which the guard would be changed, but he was too taken up with listening to Ampronius to pay any attention. That was, until the soldier being relieved shouted the responses to the guard commander, this done in such a loud voice that conversation within the tent became impossible, so he lifted himself off his divan and went outside to investigate. The legionary, tall, with a hint of red-gold hair under his helmet, stood rigidly to attention, as did his opposite number and the centurion in charge of the changeover.

'Tullius Rogus, I am all in favour of strict discipline, but I'm also entertaining. Please ask the men to keep their voices down.'

He was standing right in front of Aquila, the culprit, and since they were much of a height, their heads were very close. But Aquila was not there, it being no part of a noble tribune's job to even notice a ranker unless, that is, he wanted him flogged. Aquila had a vague recollection, in the light from the flickering torches, of having seen him somewhere before – this while Tullius acknowledged the order and, since the change-over was complete, marched off with the men standing down. He did not address Aquila until they were well away from the line of tents.

'What was that about?' he said angrily. 'All that shouting? I get into enough difficulties without the likes of you inventing new ones.'

Inside Aquila was boiling. He knew the danger he was in, being set to explode with Tullius standing in front of him, but he managed to control the desire to hit the centurion. It was nothing personal; the man just represented authority.

'Never fear, Tullius,' he replied, through clenched teeth. 'You'll always get voted in. These noble bastards will always need someone to run errands for them.'

Tullius flushed. He had once successfully run in an Olympiad in Greece, which made him quite famous amongst a certain section of Roman society. That a number of those were tribunes, and that his distinction as a runner had helped him to his present rank, was no secret. But such elevation had not brought with it confidence; command was very different from mere soldiering. The centurion worried about it himself, afraid that his lack of ability in that area would lead to disaster. In truth, he was not a bad soldier, but he thought he might be and that invoked a fear he sometimes found hard to control.

'If you're looking for a flogging, Aquila Terentius, I can easily oblige.'

The growl in Tullius's voice contrasted sharply with his thoughts. He knew the man he was addressing to be ten times the soldier he was; it was obvious from the way he handled himself and his weapons. Aquila was also a natural leader, popular with the other legionaries, just the kind of man Tullius needed to make him feel more secure in a battle. True, he could punish him, probably, in time, contrive to have him executed, but if he was seen to do it out of spite, he would need to be very careful about going into battle with his remaining troops. He could very easily find himself, one bright day, being pushed forward on to the enemy spears, with a solid wall of shields closing behind him. Being a centurion gave you power, but it was not unlimited and the rankers had their own way of ensuring that their immediate superior could not go too far.

Aquila saved him from making a decision, having realised, as he spoke, that he was taking his ire out on the wrong person. His apology was delivered in the regulation manner, sounding stiff and insincere, but it was enough for Tullius.

'Just watch it!' replied the relieved centurion.

CHAPTER SEVEN

———•———

Claudia leant over her new husband, her hands on his shoulders and her eyes scanning the papers before him. She could smell his body, or more truthfully the faint odour of the perfumed oils he used to cover it. His silver hair, carefully brushed, gleamed by the side of her eyes.

'Does my presence annoy you?' she asked.

'Never, never, never,' he said, quickly and sincerely, his head lifting and turning while one hand patted hers. His nose was in profile – imposing, hooked and patrician. Claudia thought that for all Quintus's subterfuge and downright lying, he had managed to find her the perfect husband. Sextius knew nothing of Quintus's machinations, but he heartily shared Claudia's sentiments. Being handsome and vain, and quite possibly the richest man in the Senate, he had always feared that if he married, it would be because he had been targeted for his considerable wealth.

The idea had never appealed to him; Sextius wanted to be loved for himself, the one person he cared for most in the world. Claudia had been a godsend, rich in her own right, from a famous noble family. He could forgive the touch of Sabine in her bloodline, for she was also a beautiful woman, who fortunately did not make excessive demands on him. The consummation of their union had not been a resounding success, yet Claudia had not chastised him; instead she assured him, while taking all the blame on herself, that she valued his companionship. So Sextius was spared the trial of the marriage bed and he took most of his pleasure elsewhere, discreetly, of course.

'To be utterly and completely truthful with you, Claudia,' he said, as usual, using ten words where two would do, 'I am frankly amazed that you show the slightest degree of interest.'

'It must be the Sabine in me, Husband, that's caused this interest in agriculture.'

Sextius frowned; that reference to her lineage disturbed him, it being something he could forgive only as long as it was not alluded to. 'I must take issue with you. I would describe what you have just said as actually very Roman.'

'I never realised that one man could own so much land, and all of it so close to Rome.' Her finger moved across the map. 'North, south, east and west, it's wonderful.'

'My dear, Claudia, one does not wish to be too far away from the city. Life outside Rome can be exceedingly dreary, unless you go far to the south. Even then, you know…'

It was rare for him not to finish a sentence, but he could not utter the words that would conclude it. Sextius liked the south; the Greek cities were so much more accommodating and pleasant for him than Rome, though things had improved in the north since he had been young. But it was part of his fiction, as the upright Roman, to visit places like Neapolis only very occasionally: too many visits and malicious tongues could wag.

'When you visit the farms, may I accompany you?'

His silver eyebrows twitched. 'Whoever heard of such a thing, Claudia?'

Her voice was low and urgent. 'I know it's unusual, Husband, and people might then make jokes, saying we are inseparable.'

Sextius scarcely paused for breath; for all his lack of intellectual weight, he had a fair degree of guile and the idea clearly appealed to him, as Claudia intended that it should. He, of course, considered himself to be very clever, adept at discerning the deeper motives behind the simple words of others. He also held himself capable of deep subterfuge, an opinion that was totally at odds with the truth.

'So they would, Claudia. Let them do so, I say. By the way, have you ever visited the Greek cities of the south?'

Aquila, once more standing guard outside Marcellus's tent, pulled his spear to his chest in salute as the young tribune approached. The officer could look him up and down without trouble, while Aquila had to try to examine Marcellus while maintaining his stiff sentry pose. They were both taller than most of their contemporaries, but there the similarity ended, with the officer's dark skin and black hair contrasting sharply with his own colouring. Marcellus nodded to him as he came to attention, adding a smile. Natural and unaffected, it failed its purpose, being perceived by the sentry as a deliberate attempt to underscore the gulf between them. Then the tribune stopped and looked him up and down and his eyes took in the gold chain round Aquila's neck and that was when the man being inspected recognised him.

Suddenly, he was back outside the Barbinus villa, close to the woods, on the other side of which he lived with Fulmina, the day the leopards came. Occupied with guarding the senator's sheep, he had seen the cage arrive and had spoken to the man who had brought these beasts to the villa, sleek spotted animals that moved with a grace he admired, their dark eyes never still. This bastard had been present, and even then he had got Aquila's goat with his perfumed perfection: carefully barbered hair, clean oiled body and neat clothes. Had it been this shit or Barbinus who had set the leopards on the sheep? It made no odds – it ended in blood. It was also a time etched in his memory for another reason; the next day, when he had gone looking for Sosia, the Barbinus overseer had taken a savage delight in telling him she was gone.

The charm was hidden beneath his uniform and it was evident that Marcellus Falerius was wondering what the chain held. Aquila's blood boiled again at this close and, to his mind, unfeeling examination. He was still smarting from the thoughts he had had the night before and the flash of real anger he felt now was because he had to wait upon this officer. This man, whose father had issued the orders that had killed Gadoric, could have him flogged at a whim, order him towards a certain death, and there was nothing he could do about it. Fabius, marching alongside him the following day, and listening to his complaints, did not see what he was driving at.

'It's the way of the world, Aquila. There's them that's born rich, and then there's us. Nothing will ever change it.'

'So I stay a legionary all my life, while he will one day command the army.'

Fabius handed him a fig. 'He's been bred to it.'

'We don't even know if he can fight,' snapped his 'uncle', his eyes glaring at the decorated armour on Marcellus's back.

'He'll do me, Aquila.'

Aquila was thinking that riding a horse must be easier than marching on foot. 'You like him, don't you?'

Fabius eased his shield up his back to keep the sun off his neck. ''Course I do. He's polite, always greets the men with a smile, and doesn't go poking his nose in places that don't concern him.'

'That's because he doesn't know they exist and that smile could mean he's a dimwit. He leaves everything to Tullius.'

Marcellus hauled his horse over to the side of the road, dismounted and stood, rubbing the animal's neck, as the men marched by. He could not miss the face that stared at him, nor feel comfortable with the look, a mixture of dislike and contempt almost designed to challenge him to react. He was saved from the need to do so by the soldier marching abreast, who shoved the blue-eyed legionary so hard he had to respond sharply to avoid a collision.

'Eyes front,' said Fabius in whisper. They were past the tribune before he spoke again. 'What are you trying to do, earn a flogging?'

'I'm trying to see what he's made of.'

'He's made of flesh and blood, Aquila, same as you an' me, and we'll find out the quality of that the first time we get into a proper fight.'

Marcellus fell in beside Tullius, pulling his horse along behind him. 'Tell me, Centurion, what do you think of these men?'

The centurion paused a while before replying, having been a soldier long enough to suspect a trick question. His motto was to tell his betters what they wanted to hear, without exaggerating too much and making them suspicious, but something in this young tribune's eye told him that would never do. Still, a little bragging would not harm him, a reminder that, in this group of soldiers, he was one of the few men who had been in a battle.

'Hard to tell, your honour, not many of them have seen combat before. And since they're new to campaigning, I daresay they're still a bit soft.'

Marcellus smiled. 'You don't seem the type to be easy on them.'

'I ain't, sir, but you can never tell what a legion's like in Italy. Life's too easy there.'

'We're not in Italy now, we're in Gaul.'

Tullius looked first at the sea, blue and sparkling, then at the hills, criss-crossed with fields and terraces. 'But it's still gentle country, sir, easy pickings. I'll wait till they have to kill, just to eat, before I trust their mettle.'

That made Marcellus frown, recalling that his father's greatest attribute, as a soldier, was his ability as a quartermaster. 'If we supply them properly, they won't have to.'

Tullius nodded but said nothing. He was not about to tell the tribune that he, too, was a mite soft, nor that he thought him a smug young bastard, who knew little or nothing about life in the army.

The *primus pilus*, Spurius Labenius, was on the rampart, looking north, when Aquila walked up behind him. The older man did not turn round, so Aquila joined him, gazing at the distant, moonlit mountains. He wanted to speak, to ask this wel-decorated soldier about his past and it was not just their differing rank that stopped him. It was almost as if Labenius was lost in some silent prayer, holding himself rigid, his breath forcibly contained. Eventually the shoulders eased and the rush of air through his nostrils indicated that he had relaxed. He spoke, his voice deep and sad.

'Those mountains hold the bones of a lot of legionaries.' He turned and looked at Aquila, his eyes resting on the young man's hair, growing again after the shaving he had endured when he enlisted. 'Not just there, mind. I've been in the legions for over twenty years. Sometimes I think I've buried more men than I've led in battle.'

Aquila was reminded of Didius Flaccus; the man who took him to Sicily had, too, been a centurion, hard and battle-scarred, yet forced to beg for work from Cassius Barbinus when his service was complete. Twenty years of service to Rome had earned Didius Flaccus only enough for a constrained life; no luxuries or a young wife to warm his bed, just more toil. Yet fate had taken him past Dabo's place on his journey south, and having had command of Clodius, it was he who had told Aquila of his adopted father's death at Thralaxas.

For all his rough nature, Flaccus had been good to Aquila, though it was painful now to recall the way he ignored the truth, shutting his eyes to the cruelty visited upon the slaves the older man was working to death. Such blindness had made it a happy time; the spearing of Toger meant the others Flaccus had recruited from the gutters of Rome respected him. He had become a man rather than a boy, and had even had in the girl Phoebe his own Greek concubine. What would have happened to him if, on the day he and Flaccus rode to Messina to meet with Cassius Barbinus, he had not seen Gadoric near-dead on a crucifix? What he had seen was the way Flaccus had died, a victim of the very slaves he had previously tyrannised.

'And still only a centurion?' said Aquila, unsure of who he was referring to, the ex-soldier who had seen him grow to manhood, or this serving one standing next to him. 'Not much for such a dedicated life.'

Labenius, when he replied, seemed resigned rather than angry, which he was entitled to be considering what this youngster had said severely breached the bounds of discipline. 'Was a time I would have flogged any man who addressed me like that.'

Aquila turned and looked at the older man, the moonlight catching the decorations that covered the front of his breastplate, plus the gold torque on his arm. Labenius had won six civic crowns, the second highest honour in the legions, given only to a soldier who saved the life of a Roman citizen in battle and held his ground all day. The light also picked up the gleam of tears in his old eyes.

'Why not now?'

'Who knows, perhaps it's the presence of those mountains and the souls of the departed.'

'Would that make you answer my question about your rank, too?'

Labenius looked him up and down, his eyes taking in the charm at his neck, glinting in the moonlight against the background of his dark red tunic. He wondered if the boy knew how much his trinket had been a subject of discussion amongst the junior officers.

'I've watched you, Aquila Terentius.'

'I'm surprised you know my name.'

'Don't be!' replied Labenius with a touch of asperity. 'I marked you out the day you joined up.'

'Why?'

Labenius looked north again. 'We fought Celts all the time when I was your age, took the whole of the northern plain off them and made the tribes subject to Rome.'

'But not the mountains?'

'There are tribes to the north that see those mountains as their defence. They're different men, taller and stronger, who believe that the way to happiness is to die in battle, so they come south, through the passes, helped by the mountain men, to burn and destroy. I fought against them with the general's father, Aulus Cornelius, before he was consul.'

'Did you win?'

'We took back the mountain passes, but I don't think we won, not against those men from the north. I think when they'd had enough they just went home.'

'And I remind you of them?'

'I don't suppose that I'm the first to remark on it,' replied Labenius, looking at him again. 'And that thing at your throat isn't Roman.' His voice took on a different, more serious tone. 'But it's not just that. Young as you are, you're a fighter. You've got scars that only a man who's soldiered carries, yet you're just old enough to be in the legions. Where did someone like you fight, Aquila? You say you're from round Aprilium. Not with hair like that, you're not. Was it up in the north, among the bones of dead Romans?'

'No.'

His voice grew angry, but it had a hurt tone as well. 'My two sons are buried up there, Aquila Terentius, killed by men who looked just like you.'

'I was wondering why, with all your decorations, you're not in command of an army?'

'I was born poor, lad, that's why. Perhaps my sons, if they'd lived, would have had the luck to rise to a higher class.'

'I'm told that if you win the civic crown, patrician senators stand up in your presence.'

'It costs them nothing to do that, boy.'

'So being brave gains you little. You still have to be voted in?'

'Why are you asking?' growled Labenius.

Aquila had been thinking about this for days, ever since the arrival of Marcellus Falerius. He had recalled seeing the *primus pilus* salute the new tribune with stiff formality. The image, added to the old centurion's question, which he had to answer, finally crystallised his thoughts and made him realise the true source of his distemper.

'I don't want to end up as nothing.'

The word shocked Labenius. 'Nothing!'

'I look at a tribune like Marcellus Falerius, with his father's wealth and his famous name. Why is he where he is, and I am just a legionary? Why will he command armies, while I will require his vote to command cohorts?'

'Are you so sure you'll command men at all?'

The question took him back to Sicily again, to the army he had helped Gadoric to build, to the runaway slaves he had led and the skirmishes he had fought against his own people. 'I have already, Labenius. I won't say where, but it's not in those mountains, and I shall again. You have risen through your courage, yet that is still not enough. I was hoping that you could tell me what else I need?'

'You're an insolent pup, boy, and you don't deserve an answer.'

Aquila pointed to the mountains. 'What would you have said to your sons, Spurius Labenius, if they'd asked you the same question?'

The older man's head dropped and his voice had tears in it again. 'I would have said it's no good just being brave, you have to be lucky too.'

'In what way?' asked Aquila, ignoring the pain he had engendered in the old man's memory.

'Money helps, that and someone powerful who holds you in such high regard he'll adopt you.'

He put his hand on Labenius's shoulder, which was shaking slightly. 'I've been adopted once already. That is sufficient for any man.'

Aquila did not see the rope, but he heard it whistle past his ear and saw the effect as it slid over Labenius's head. The old centurion jerked forward as the noose tightened, his breastplate pressed against the sharp spikes on the low rampart and Aquila had his sword out in a second. He could see the shadowy figures, each with a line hooked round the stakes, hauling themselves up to attack, but he ignored them. The huge shout, used to raise the alarm, seemed to add force to his sword arm as the weapon slashed down, parting the rope that held the centurion's neck. The shout did alert the guards, but that would do these two precious little good. Their enemies, using animal hides to blunt the spikes, were pouring over the ramparts. Aquila hauled Labenius upright and spun him round, then turned himself, just in time to fend off a thrust by one of the Celts. He and the *primus pilus* stood back to back, holding the rampart for what seemed like an age, all on their own.

'It was only luck that we were there,' said Labenius.

His arm was in a sling since, dazed and winded, he had taken a spear in the left shoulder before he had managed to get his sword out. Quintus, who must have been curious about the centurion being alone on the ramparts with a young recruit, knew better than to pose that kind of question. He turned to Aquila, standing unmarked and to attention. He was, like the *primus pilus*, without his breastplate and the gold eagle flashed on the chest of his tunic.

'You should have seen them!' he snapped.

Aquila was not afraid or overawed, even if he had never been in the command tent, nor exchanged anything other than a salute with his general. Normally, in these surroundings, rankers, called upon to report, became tongue-tied but his voice was even as he replied. 'We would have done, if they'd approached while we were standing there. The moon was full up.'

'What are you saying?'

'I'm saying that they took advantage of the clouds, earlier in the night, to get into position. They covered themselves with animal skins and hid in the ditch until it was time to attack.'

'How would they know when it was time?'

'There are ways, General.'

Quintus did not like his insolent tone, that was clear. He looked Aquila up and down, his eyes drawn inexorably to the flashing eagle, with an expression that seemed to demand an explanation as to why this lad, a ranker, was wearing something so valuable. Yet by his action this young man had saved him a number of casualties, since those Celts would have caused havoc amongst his men, sound asleep in their tents. As it was, he had lost several of the lightly armed skirmishers who had been allotted the duty of guarding the walls.

'I owe Aquila my life, General,' said Labenius,

who had seen the look in Quintus's eye. He had known the general since he was a young tribune, so he felt free to talk out of turn. 'And I'm not alone.'

The consul turned to the old centurion, effectively cutting Aquila out of the conversation. 'How many were there?'

'Ask the boy,' replied Labenius calmly. 'He saw more than me.'

Aquila did not volunteer, but waited till Quintus turned back to face him. 'Well?'

'More than ten, less than twenty.'

'That's not very precise.'

'We have ten bodies, General. In my opinion more than twenty men could not have hidden in the time available.'

Quintus exploded. 'In your opinion! What makes you think that's worth anything?'

The reply Aquila gave him went the rounds, with much shaking of heads, and many a question as to how he had missed being broken at the wheel for such effrontery. 'I am just the same as you, Quintus Cornelius. I give you an opinion, as a mere citizen of the Republic.'

Had he turned round, he would have seen the look on his tribune's face, a mixture of shock and anger.

* * *

'No civic crown for you, Uncle,' said Fabius in a mocking tone. 'You're incapable of holding your tongue, that's your trouble. Let this be a lesson. If you're going to save a Roman's life, do it in daylight.'

He had not seen Labenius approaching or he would have kept his mouth shut, but Aquila had, so he manufactured a frown that convinced Fabius he was wounded by his ribbing, which encouraged his 'nephew' to continue.

'Never mind, Aquila. You can take me along the next time. What you need on these occasions is an honest witness. They're all the same.'

'Who?' asked Aquila, maliciously.

Fabius put his hands on his hips and leant forward to emphasise his point. 'Centurions. You saved old Labenius's life and what did you get for your trouble? A wigging from the general, then not so much as a single sestertius from the old goat, and him festooned with gold.'

Labenius's iron-shod boot hit Fabius square on the behind and Aquila dodged to the side, so that his 'nephew' fell flat on his face.

'He was just telling me to mind my tongue,' he said, grinning at the fallen Fabius, whose mouth was open in a silent scream.

Labenius, too, looked down at his victim without sympathy, but his words were clearly intended for Aquila. 'The general wants you.'

That wiped the grin off the youngster's face. 'Why?'

'Don't worry, it's not to flog you, which is what would have happened in my younger days. This lot aren't a patch on their fathers. Don't know the meaning of the word discipline.'

Fabius got slowly to his feet, rubbing his backside painfully. 'I was only joking, Spurius Labenius.'

'Were you?' snapped the centurion, making it plain that he had found it far from funny. 'It so happens, turd, that I've spent half the morning trying to convince our noble general to do his duty.' He turned to Aquila. 'And I've done myself no favours in the process, 'cause the last thing Quintus Cornelius likes is to be told what his papa would have done.'

If Quintus was still angry, he hid it well. Marcellus was present as the tribune who commanded his section of the army, but standing to one side, taking no part in the proceedings.

'Aquila Terentius, I have listened to Spurius Labenius and there is no doubt, by your action, that you have saved the life of a Roman citizen.' He emphasised the last two words, as if to point out that he had not forgotten the way Aquila had used them. 'It is my intention to award you a *hasta pura* at morning parade. Please present yourself, with your tribune, outside my tent at the appointed hour. Dismiss.'

As they came out of the tent, Labenius cursed him. 'A silver-tipped spear? You'd have had a civic crown if you'd kept your mouth shut.'

Aquila was pleased, despite his lack of regard for officers, but he kept his voice low, not wanting those in the tent to hear him. 'Don't worry, Labenius. Civic crowns can't be that hard to come by. After all, you've got six of them.'

'I'd box your ears if you hadn't saved my life.' There was no venom in those words, more a warmth that Aquila had not heard since Clodius left home. The old centurion put up his forearm. 'Give me your arm.'

Aquila did so, putting his hand just below Labenius's elbow. The centurion grasped him in the same way. 'Six men have done this to me. I'm proud to acknowledge you in the same way, even if our general won't. Aquila Terentius, I owe you my life. You have the right to demand anything of me you wish.'

CHAPTER EIGHT

———•———

Cholon rubbed his hands over his sweating brow, while outside, though no rain fell, the rumble of thunder filled the sky. The atmosphere was oppressive enough without the prospect of the impending meeting. He and Titus were expecting a delegation from the *Equites*, a group in constant battle with the Senate over the division of powers. It was really the lack of division that was the problem; the Senate hogged it all, denying the other classes the right to sit in judgement in the courts, and they were just as opposed to sharing the franchise of Roman citizenship with their allies. The peoples of Italy could provide troops to die for the empire, they could help to feed the increasing beast that was Rome, but they had few if any rights, and the man who had fought to keep it that way was the late Lucius Falerius Nerva. Now that he was gone, an opportunity arose, while his successors were weak, to seek redress.

'I fear I am developing a talent for intrigue,' he said.

Titus was aware, as was Cholon, that the Greek was merely the messenger, yet it took a man adept at the messenger's art to play the game; to entice suspicious people to treat with those they thought were their enemies, and he had also provided his apartment for the purpose. Knights calling here would excite no comment; the only person who had had to take precautions to get in unseen was Titus himself, yet those they had arranged to meet arrived, seemingly determined to arouse suspicion. Instead of making a noisy approach, like men calling on an old friend, they crept towards Cholon's apartment silently, whispering encouragement to each other. Even the way they knocked on the door smacked of conspiracy, a soft tap instead of a confident hammering. Cholon opened the door quickly and shepherded them in.

They were three very different men, as though they had set out to find a cross-section of their class. One, Cassius Laternus, was tall and thin; the second, Marcus Filator, was round in face and body, like a human ball. The third was the most important, though the least imposing in appearance. Frontus was small and thin, more like a child than a grown man, but you only had to look into the eyes to see the strength of his character. Chairs were arranged, wine poured and the general enquiries that preceded any meeting flowed, with questions about family friends, wives, children and the state of the finances of the Republic. They all knew each other well; Rome might be a teeming metropolis and sit at the centre of a huge empire, but the people who ran it were small in number, tended to live close to each other and, because of their incomes, shared similar taste in entertainment. There was not a man in the room that Titus had not had a bet with at some time or other, he backing one chariot team, while they backed another. Gambling was one thing, politics another.

'I take it you have discussed my proposals?' asked Titus, formally bringing the meeting around to its true purpose.

The other two looked to Frontus to speak. He, like a dwarf beside Titus, shook his head slowly. 'Nothing is decided.'

Cholon cut in, for he had held the first meetings with these men, trying to encourage them to see reason. 'Yet you saw what Titus Cornelius was driving at.'

'It is hard for men who have nothing to accept that they can only ask for a little.'

That was a somewhat disingenuous statement; all three men were quite powerful, especially in the constituent assembly. They had all schemed at one time to increase that power, only to find themselves up against the prerogatives of the Senate – men who were richer by far, and determined to keep things that way.

'You'll get to sit in the court and judge senatorial behaviour.'

'Without a clear majority?'

'A wedge, Frontus,' replied Cholon.

'Yes, I know. You have used that expression before, but who is the wedge for?' He turned to Titus, the question clear in his expression. 'Some of us feel we are being used.'

'Are you one of them?' asked Titus, sharply.

Frontus was not alarmed, either by his height or his threatening manner. 'I most certainly am.'

'That is just as well,' said Titus. 'If you think I'm doing this for the love of the knights' class, you're wrong.'

Cholon's pained expression spoke volumes, having carefully painted the picture of a noble senator, moved to act only by motives of pure altruism. 'What Titus Cornelius means is…'

Frontus interrupted, his palm raised. 'I know what he means.'

'So what do you stand to gain?' asked Marcus

Filator, his fat head wobbling as he spoke.

'Justice.'

Even Cholon, having heard his friend's previous words, raised his eyebrows at that response. Titus had just used the most abused word in Rome; every charlatan in the Senate would stand on his hind legs and demand 'justice', when what he really meant was that he wished to be left in peace to continue his larceny.

'I want Vegetius Flaminus brought to trial for what happened to my father. He deliberately abandoned him and his men at Thralaxas.'

'Personal justice, or revenge?' asked Laternus.

'Call it revenge if you wish,' replied Titus, ignoring Cholon's shaking head. 'I would also like to see the Senate more accountable to the people, but I have no reason to see why you should believe that. And I have a clear sense of my place in the world. The Cornelii are patricians. I've no desire, for instance, to be numbered amongst the *populares*.'

'Agrarian reform?' asked Filator.

'Not possible and, to my mind, of questionable benefit.'

'So you will not support a law that gives land to the poor?'

'I might, if someone could guarantee to me that those with money wouldn't buy it off them.'

Titus smiled to take the sting out of the words, but his message was blunt for all that. He was telling them to their face that if he was not prepared to indulge in hypocrisy, neither could they. There were plenty of *Equites*, including these three, with the financial resources to stand for the Senate. The censor might take some persuading to admit them to the roll, and insist that they disabuse themselves of some of their more lucrative operations, but if they wanted it badly enough it could be done. If they chose not to it could only be for one reason; they would rather be big fish in the knights' pond than minnows in another. The power struggle was not about money; it was about which personalities held the reins of government.

The three knights exchanged worried glances. It was left to Frontus to speak. 'My own view is that we should accept what you offer.'

'Good!' said Titus.

'I haven't finished. You quite rightly surmised that the time is right, with your brother away and Lucius Falerius newly dead. You are also correct when you say that we can easily produce senators prepared to propose and second these changes.' Frontus paused for a bit, letting these words have their effect. 'What you have failed to appreciate is just how close the vote would be.'

'I was given to understand, by you, that we had arranged a majority,' said Cholon, the newest member of the knights' class.

'What people say and what they do are often at odds. No vote is safe until it is cast.'

Titus looked Frontus in the eye. The little man smiled at him, which did little to take the sting out of his words. 'But if, just before the debate closes, the most noble Titus Cornelius were to speak on behalf of the motion, some in the chamber would have the impression that it has your brother's secret support.'

'You're asking me to commit political suicide,' said Titus angrily. 'Quintus will never forgive me.'

The little man's eyes bored into his, and he had a wicked grin on his face. 'Perhaps you could even add a late amendment, handing the appointment of all the jurors over to the knights, or at the very least giving us a majority. You must decide, Titus Cornelius, how much you want revenge for your father.'

For Quintus and his legions the rest of the march to Massila was uneventful. They boarded their transports, provided by the Greek city state that sat at the mouth of the Rhone, and sailed for the coast of Spain. Marcellus was blissfully happy, for he loved the sea; the clean smell, the fresh wind and the sound of the galley oars digging into the deep blue water. Fabius, when not required to take a turn at the oars, spent his time catching fish, which he would then offer, filleted and raw, to his seasick 'uncle', turning his countenance an even deeper shade of green.

Aquila had been ill from the very moment he had stepped aboard. Romantic allusions to the wine-dark sea brought forth nothing but feeble curses, and this when the weather was clement. He cursed *Neptune* and all his works, then recanted at the insistence of his fellow sufferers, who were afraid that the Water God might whip up a storm by way of revenge. Their fleet ploughed on, never out of sight of land, until they reached Emphorae, just south of the Pyrenees, which stood at the very tip of the first of the Roman provinces on the peninsula, Hispania Citerior, a slice of valuable land that ran all the way down the eastern seaboard.

Quintus, who could not assume his command without his troops, was in a hurry to get them ashore. Messengers were sent to Servius Caepio to tell him that he had now been superseded, and should prepare to hand over control of all his soldiers to the newly arrived commander. Neither could the new arrival afford to be too long away from Rome: yet another reason for haste; if he was going to make any money in Spain, and possibly grab some glory, he had little time to achieve anything, so he avoided a formal handover ceremony and gave orders to be ready to march away from the coast into the interior.

Servius was allowed one short interview, to bring Quintus up to date on the situation, before being bundled unceremoniously onto a ship for the journey home. Quintus then rode hard to catch up with his troops. The legion that had seen action on the frontier was marching the other way by a different route and Quintus did not intend that they should mix. Troops who had been in Spain for any time tended towards low morale; the country was difficult, the natives cunning and fierce, while the war seemed endless. He detached several tribunes, including Marcellus, and gave them the unenviable task of trying to turn these broken legions back into a reasonable fighting force. Having harboured a desire to cut Marcellus down to size, Quintus took great pleasure in telling him that he was being moved to a posting that would be far away from any chance of glory. His voice was positively silky with insincere concern.

'Who else can I trust, for I know you to be as single-minded as your father. And never fear, you will get your chance to fight, Marcellus Falerius, just as soon as you've whipped these men back into shape.'

The young man was not alone in thinking that this was a lie, suspecting that Quintus would drain off any men he trained as reinforcements. He had promised that Marcellus would join him on his first consular command and that promise had been kept, but Quintus was in no hurry to furnish Marcellus with an opportunity to distinguish himself.

Quintus Cornelius was a good general, but like most of his contemporaries a greedy one and there was always the question of time, or the lack of it, to make his military dispositions seem like sound sense. Servius Caepio had told him all the latest information he had about Brennos, leaving the new governor in no doubt of the man's influence on the frontier tribes. He was like a cancer at the heart of Celt-Iberian resistance, which would continue until it was cut out, but he was also far away, and in an impregnable position. The other, closer hill forts, like Pallentia, could be invested, but Quintus did not want a lengthy siege; he wanted gold, silver, slaves and enough dead bodies on the field, all in the space of his consular year, then he could return to Rome to take up the true struggle: to stamp his dominance on the floor of the Senate.

He made an immediate adjustment to the standard tactics; normally the Romans operated in large units, since this was the way their force was structured. The cavalry were used as a protective screen, tying their pace to that of the infantry. Of necessity, this impeded overall mobility, and since the tribes were careful never to be caught in numbers, a battle of any size was rare. The legions marched and counter-marched, their looming presence ensuring that no major incursions took place, their snail-like pace guaranteeing a steady rate of tribal attrition, but they could not subdue their opponents in any meaningful way.

Haste, allied to his ambition, forced Quintus into a radically different method. He marched his men away from the established bases and picked a site that stood at the apex of three valleys, all of which led into the interior. Having built a strong base camp, he split the legions up into four groups, keeping the auxiliary legions, four thousand men, plus the majority of the cavalry, under his personal command. The others formed three triple cohorts. Each legate commanded a striking force of a thousand men with orders to emulate their opponents where possible; to fight, burn, steal and withdraw. Client tribes, those on the frontier who had treaties with Rome, were coerced into revealing what they knew about their fellow Celts, providing the new governor with sound intelligence.

The natives fought back, adept at ambush, forever setting traps to draw in the Roman troops, then attacking in force to try to annihilate them. Quintus Cornelius at the head of his mobile reserve, and with a good system of communications to aid him, would then fall on their rear, killing hundreds and capturing thousands of men. The countryside could then be scoured for the women and children who would be shipped off, like their men, to the slave markets of the empire.

But eventually success meant that the available targets soon diminished. Quintus had to send his cohorts further and further afield. Aquila and Fabius marched and retreated, fought when required, and moaned incessantly like the true legionaries they had now become. And Tullius could at least congratulate himself on being right; Aquila, almost without effort, had assumed a position of authority with his men and he was vocal on their behalf, often saving him from making a decision at all, through offering sage advice on the best way to fight without loss.

And all the time, Quintus received good intelligence about his main opponent, the man whose efforts and subversion kept the war alive.

Brennos could barely contain his disappointment; yet another Roman governor had arrived and declined the opportunity to make an attempt on Numantia. He realised now that he had made his hill fort too strong; it had such a fearsome reputation that no Roman wanted to risk failure by trying to take it. Worse than that, their present tactics were producing results and some of the tribes he had relied on were, out of sheer exhaustion, going over to the Romans, to become clients, who could live in peace, grow fat on their crops and watch their children grow to manhood.

He did not understand the Romans, and there was no one with enough knowledge, allied to a strong personality, to tell him where he was going wrong. To a man with complete power, who made decisions on his own without consulting anyone, the fragmented way that his enemies went about the affairs of state baffled him. He could not comprehend that he was dealing with a hydra-headed monster, with tentacles that prospered by an uncompleted war, and saw no advantage in outright victory. To him, the solution was obvious; all the power of Rome should be used to subdue him. He could not comprehend that the ability to concentrate that power did not exist, there always being voices on the floor of the Forum to counsel caution. The safety of the empire was very rarely their primary motive; jealousy, the opportunity for personal profit, or even the prospect of future glory animated more breasts than good sense.

Being stubborn, Brennos stuck to his aim, with little alteration in the basic concept. Harass the Romans until they saw, without blinkers, that they had to destroy him and Numantia; lure them to a battle which, with all the tribes combining to fight them and far from their bases, they would lose, then use the victory to further his own ends.

One of the most corrupting things about power is that few dare tell the holder of such supremacy the truth. They flatter instead, so when Brennos expounded his plans, again and again, there was no one prepared to tell him he was getting too old, that experience should tell him he was wrong, and that his opponent, Quintus Cornelius, was slowly but surely, by his novel tactics, isolating one tribe after another and pacifying the border area.

He addressed the pertinent problem first, not

by calling a tribal council but by sending for Costeti, the leader of a bellicose yet mobile tribe called the Averici. Though close to the land the Romans controlled, they, because of the broken nature of the terrain and their sturdy ponies, had the choice to raid without too much threat of retribution. But Costeti had another problem: satisfying his younger warriors who longed for a fight, egged on by Brennos appealing to their greed as much as their martial spirit.

Brennos knew he had to stop the haemorrhage of tribes making peace and the best way to achieve that was to show them one thing: that they stood in as much danger from a Rome that claimed friendship as they did from that state's declared enmity. The plan he had evolved had the added bonus that it would, at the same time, inflict a resounding defeat on one of Quintus's columns, which would be laid at his door, proving, once more, where the resolution of the conflict lay.

CHAPTER NINE

———•———

The tribune Ampronius Valerius had taken over command of one-third of the flying column when the titular *legatus* fell ill. His instructions had been clear: to act as a screen and lead the tribes to believe that the whole column was still in the field, while he fell back with the majority of the force to the base camp, where he could ask Quintus to replace him. Ampronius had disobeyed that order, and pushed his troops to the very limit of their supplies. Once there, he had set up a temporary camp, though being only part of a legion it was not a defence that could be manned properly. Such lack of judgement was bad enough, but he had stayed there longer than military prudence dictated.

If the Romans could not defeat the tribal warriors because of their mobility, the need to avoid set-piece engagements also constrained the defenders; it was bad tactics to stay still unless the unit was of sufficient strength to deter attack and the feeling of danger was palpable. Something was brewing and the men could smell it; they felt as though they were being watched, a notion reinforced by the arrival of three mounted men, a paramount Celtic chieftain called Costeti and two of his senior warriors. From the Averici tribe, they spoke of peace, but few took that at face value; many a tribe espoused amity just before springing an ambush.

Ampronius relished the sudden acquisition of power, the fact that he could now make the decisions, and he conversed privately with the three Averici tribesmen for more than two hours, while the rest of his men stood back from the gathering, muttering to themselves and wondering what these three horsemen had to say to their ambitious tribune. Whatever it was obviously delighted him and he was in high spirits when he ordered his men to break camp, seemingly well able to ignore the worried looks they gave him when he kept going west, moving away from the main army base. Soon they were well past the point that Quintus had laid down as the boundary beyond which his flying columns could not operate with any degree of safety, and, as soon as this was realised, the complaints became vocal, as Aquila and Fabius engaged in a mock-argument as to their precise location, to the point where they were ordered forcibly to remain silent.

'Permission to speak, Tullius?' said Aquila.

The centurion, who had been standing at the top of the rise gazing into the fertile valley, turned to look at the younger man. Ampronius Valerius, standing beside him, frowned darkly; it was not fitting for the senior centurion to talk, in his presence, to a mere legionary, especially this Terentius fellow, who thought that the possession of a silver spear entitled him to some form of special consideration. He had spoken before, he and that other reprobate called Fabius. Tullius should have shut him up then, and reminded him to do as he was told, instead of leaving it to him. Ampronius thought the senior centurion was hardly much better, and wondered if he shared the opinions of the rankers. Tullius had obeyed orders on this day's march, but with such a sour expression that the tribune knew he doubted their wisdom.

'Permission denied!' Ampronius snapped.

The centurion, who had nodded, had to shake his head quickly, with Aquila cursing under his breath, having overheard the tribune's orders to march down into the valley. Having sneaked a look while the officers' backs were turned, he had a clear idea of what the orders entailed. There was only one route in and out, through a narrow defile, and the local tribesmen could be waiting there for them, hidden in the rocks that covered the floor of the pass, as well as on the steep sides of the ravine. Tullius, even if he was not much of a soldier, shared his reservations. What the tribune could see was visible to him, but it represented a different picture and within the bounds of good discipline he had tried to persuade Ampronius that merely being this far into the mountains was dangerous enough. They were surrounded by tribes, friendly and hostile, with no real way of knowing which was which, and in some danger of being cut off by trusting the wrong ones.

The Averici had informed Ampronius that the tribe occupying this valley, the Mordasci, who claimed client status with Rome, had fallen under the spell of Brennos and were planning to turn against the conquerors as part of a grand alliance with other tribes from the interior. They also told him it was a rich plum, ripe for picking, with others, more loyal, waiting to take over the land once the Romans had stripped the place bare. So, on this information, and to Tullius's mind ignoring common sense, the tribune had marched his men into what they considered the wilderness.

'Perhaps a small force first, sir, just to test out the enemy?'

Ampronius laughed and spoke loudly; he knew his men were restless and in need of reassurance. 'Enemy? They don't even ride horses. They're nothing but a bunch of farmers.'

Fabius spoke under his breath. 'What does the twat think the Roman army is made up of?'

Aquila shook his head sharply, telling Fabius to shut up, and quieting the murmuring of the others, who had not only overheard the orders but shared their fears. Most of the men Ampronius commanded would obey blindly, too stupid or lazy to examine what they were doing; for those who were a bit sharper, short of killing the tribune, which would make them outlaws, they had no choice but to follow him. Ampronius, no doubt thinking he could lift his men's spirits, waved an arm at the valley floor, which was out of sight to most of them, lined up on the other side of the rise.

'In a minute! You'll see it for yourselves in a minute. These people are rebels, who claim our friendship, but want nothing more than to stab us in the back.'

'We wouldn't want to spoil their fun, would

we?' said Fabius loudly, turning his back on Ampronius so he had no way of seeing who was speaking.

The tribune flushed angrily and gave Tullius a filthy look, but he could do nothing that would not make him look more foolish, so he kept talking. 'My information is correct, you can count on that, and we are looking at a rich prize. They pan the river for precious metals. There's gold down there, and silver, with fat cattle and women waiting to be roasted. All we have to do is go and get it.'

The senior centurion had one more try. 'Might I suggest a runner to return to the general, telling him what you intend?'

'No you may not!' replied Ampronius coldly.

He was well aware that Quintus could forbid him to proceed. Besides, if the consul had the same information, and thought that there was something in this place worth having, he would try to take it for himself. Ampronius would have to share it with him, of course, but by doing this, stretching his orders, he could earn a great deal of money and do wonders for his personal and family prestige.

He issued the necessary commands and the cavalry, fifty strong, moved out first, in pairs. Once they had threaded through the pass, they would fan out, riding hard to seal off the other exits to the valley. Ampronius was not completely stupid, so next he sent in the skirmishers. He had these lightly armed men move into the rocks on either side of the pass, some climbing up the steeper face of the defile to check for an ambush. The other side was less precipitous, and to Aquila represented the greater danger; men charging down that slope could, with sheer momentum, smash through any defensive line.

With Ampronius and Tullius in the lead, Aquila's cohort moved out next, shields up and javelin at the ready. As they came abreast of the rise, the whole panorama opened up before them and from this height, in the distance, they could just see the end of the valley floor. But it was the immediate view that preoccupied the legionaries. Grey rocks, some as tall as a man, lined the actual track: the hill on the right rose at a sharp angle to a line of thick gorse; on the left a small stream ran along the opposite face of the defile, which seemed to act as an overhang, cutting out a great deal of light from their route. As they entered the narrowest part of the ravine, the sound of their boots echoed eerily off the walls, then, at the end, the whole scene opened out to reveal smoke drifting lazily from the roofs of tiny huts, with people working in the fields, and herds of cattle grazing peacefully. It was a perfect pastoral setting.

'They must know we're coming,' said Fabius, marching alongside Aquila and sharing his surprise at this tranquil vista. 'Maybe they're as dozy as Ampronius Valerius hopes.'

'It smells,' replied Aquila, his eyes turning back to search the wall of rock that towered above his head.

The whole mood of the detachment had lifted at the sight, changing from fearful apprehension to something close to pleasure. Even Fabius was infected by it. 'You just don't want to admit you were wrong.'

'When we see the camp of Quintus Cornelius, I'll do more than admit I'm wrong. I'll even go to Ampronius Valerius and apologise.'

'I shouldn't bother. He'd only have you flogged for insolence.'

'For telling him I was mistaken?'

'No. For informing him that you had the gall to think, for even a second, that he wasn't a genius.'

The river, which had been a babbling stream at the top of the hill, became an increasing torrent as the drop increased and the water was forced into the narrow defile. The spray billowed up and covered their faces, a welcome relief from the stifling heat. They came to the neck of the defile and fanned out onto the valley floor. The cavalry had done as ordered, ridden ahead, and in the process had alerted the tribe to their presence, so that a party of men were approaching on foot, bearing gifts of food and wine. The man in the middle, who seemed to be the leader, was richly adorned, with a silver and gold necklace, plus several golden torques about his arms. All the others wore some kind of precious decoration, which caused a great deal of nudging and excitement in the lines of Roman legionaries.

The other units had come through and deployed to the rear of Aquila's cohort and now Ampronius stood out in front, sword still out, as the tribesmen approached. The leader stopped and addressed the Roman in his own tongue. It was not quite the same as that which Gadoric had taught Aquila, but he recognised some of the words. Another tribesman, wearing flowing robes, had come between his leader and Ampronius and he looked as though he was quietly interpreting the speech, which seemed to be one of welcome, into Latin.

The chieftain spoke loudly so that those with him could share the solicitations and Aquila heard the word 'peace'. He also recognised the expression the chieftain used, indicating he was a client of the Roman state. The name of the previous governor, Servius Caepio, was plain, since that was rendered in Latin, but the rest he lost. The baskets of food were laid at Ampronius's feet, the men bearing them bowing to him. All the while he stood, stiff and unbending, interjecting with the odd, softly spoken question, then, when the leader finished, he spun on his heel and walked back to where Tullius stood, close to the line of legionaries.

'This is going to be even easier than I thought. They claim they're still friends of Rome. They don't know that we are aware of their plans.'

'Are we aware, sir?' asked Tullius. 'We only have the word of the Averici and I wouldn't trust them as far I could throw them. Shouldn't we leave them be until we're sure?'

'And leave them to rebel? Have you seen what they are wearing? That chieftain is decorated with enough gold to buy a chariot team.' His voice grew excited. 'And it's local metal. They've even offered to show me how they extract it from the river.'

'But if they're a client tribe...'

Tullius wasn't allowed to finish. 'Why do you always question my orders? If you want to remain in your present rank, you'll do as you're told. They're Celt-Iberians. If they are clients of

Rome, that means they've betrayed their own kind. How long do you think it will be before they do the same to us? If it's not this year, it will be the next.' Tullius was now standing to attention, looking over the tribune's head. 'At my command you will kill them!'

'All of them?'

'Spare that fellow in the flowing robes, since he speaks Latin. He can help to persuade the rest of the tribe to surrender.'

Ampronius could see that Tullius was worried. The killing would not bother him; he had been too long in the legions for that; it was the nature of the intended victims that was causing the centurion problems. If these tribesmen were indeed clients of Rome, they should be immune from attack.

Ampronius was watching him closely and made a sudden decision. 'You suggested that we send a message to Quintus Cornelius, centurion. I have reconsidered your request. I now think it wise to do so and, since you are a famous runner, it is only fitting that you should take it. Inform him that I am in the act of putting down a rebellion of the Mordasci, that I will be heading back to the main camp with substantial livestock and a quantity of prisoners. You may take one maniple.'

The tribune threw out his arm, pointing straight at Aquila. 'Take that one.'

'What's going on?' asked Fabius, alarmed by the look in the tribune's eye.

'Whatever it is, Nephew, we're well out of it. The bastard is sending us away.'

'I'd be better off alone,' said Tullius, aware that eighty marching men presented a better target to potential enemies than a lone runner.

Ampronius was still looking at Aquila and his voice was full of sarcasm. 'How can you say that, when you have an acknowledged hero in the ranks to protect you?'

There was nothing the centurion could do. As Tullius turned to order Aquila's maniple out of the line, he heard Ampronius call to the next senior centurion. The man wanted him, and his doubts, out of the way and Terentius too, along with the men around him whom Ampronius suspected of being infected with Aquila's pessimism. He called his own commands, which had Aquila and his men step forward, turn to the right and double back in regulation fashion, through the spaces between the other formations. As they made their way back into the narrow defile, they could hear Ampronius giving the orders for the troops to close up into the positions they took just before a battle.

'Who are they planning to fight?' asked Fabius, still confused by what had occurred.

Aquila wasn't listening. He was concentrating on the ground beneath their feet.

'Silence!' yelled Tullius, angrily, his voice echoing off the bare rock. He was not a happy man, for he suspected that his career as a centurion had just about come to an end.

The men hiding in the hills watched them go, resisting the temptation to attack. Perhaps, after they had destroyed the Romans in the valley, they could set off in pursuit of this smaller force, but even those they had trapped could wait. Let them do their worst to the Mordasci, let the other tribes see how the invaders rewarded those who sided with them against their own. When the true enemy had pillaged the valley and gathered all the booty in one place, that would be the time to let them know they were cut off.

'It smells like rank cheese.'

'Don't you mean your feet?' said Fabius and Aquila glared at him, hoping that the look would shut him up.

'I have my orders,' said Tullius grimly. 'If Ampronius wants to get himself into trouble, that's his business.'

'He might be in something a bit worse than trouble.' Tullius just shrugged, dipping his hard biscuit into the gourd full of sour wine. 'Come on, Tullius. One of the tribes we've had to fight time and again tells us that the Mordasci are planning to turn against Rome. What does our noble centurion do, laugh in their face? No, he listens to the tales of the wealth the Mordasci have accumulated, licking his lips and thinking of the money he can make.'

Tullius was uncomfortable, stuck out here in the middle of nowhere. He could assert his authority, but he doubted Aquila would acknowledge it, just as he knew that if the men were asked, they would side with their fellow legionary, rather than him.

'How do you know they're not planning to rebel?'

Aquila decided a little exaggeration would do no harm. 'I speak a bit of the language.'

All the doubts that Tullius, and people like him, had about Aquila's height and colouring were in the look that he gave him. 'What?'

'The Mordasci spoke of peace, restated their allegiance to Rome, and offered to feed us. Doesn't sound like people rebelling to me. What did Ampronius say to you, before he ordered us away?'

Most of the men had gathered round now, eager to hear what he had to say. They would never accept a refusal. 'He said he was going to kill them.'

Aquila slammed a fist on to the rock he was sitting on. 'I said it stank. Did you notice anything when we marched out of there?'

'Like what?'

'Like a lot of hoof prints in the track.'

'So what?' said Tullius with a triumphant sneer. 'Our cavalry used it.'

'Before we did, Tullius. The entire detachment marched over that track. Any prints left by our men would have been obliterated. Those horses belonged to someone else, someone who came that way after we did.' Aquila could see the look on Tullius's face. The conflict in his mind was mirrored in his eyes. 'Before you tell me that you're only following orders, let me tell you something. I don't give a fuck about Ampronius Valerius, but there are a lot of good men down there, and I think they've just been marched into a trap.'

CHAPTER TEN

Aquila was in command now. He was, by common consent, the man best fitted to lead, while Tullius was doing what he was good at, running – without arms or armour, a water bag slung over his shoulder, to try and contact Quintus and apprise him of what had happened. Aquila assumed that whoever they were planning to face would follow the maniple to see where they were going, so he marched off after the centurion, looking for a suitable spot to set up an ambush. It was not hard in this mountainous region, even for eighty men: in fact, the more he thought about it, the more he cursed Ampronius. A proper look would have told anyone with an eye to see, an eye not glazed over by greed, that a force their size could only pass this way if someone wanted them to. He cursed himself as well; he should have seen it earlier, even if their tribune had failed to make the observation.

The men had their orders and when he whistled, twenty legionaries in the front ducked off the track, hiding behind boulders. Bringing up the rear, he was in a good position to see if they were visible and he issued the odd command to lower a spear or lay down a shield as he passed, calling for the men to stay still and silent, before ducking behind a boulder himself. Busy looking down the track, he missed seeing Fabius, behind him, do the same. The remainder marched on, with orders to go a thousand paces, then stop, and once they heard the sound of a fight to return quickly.

The soft thud of the hooves grew louder and Aquila concentrated hard, ear pressed to the ground, trying to use the skills he learnt from Gadoric both at home and in Sicily, expertise he had put aside since joining the legions. Four mounted men, not hurrying, but not cautious, matched their pace to the men marching ahead. With luck he would take one of them alive, and just one would be enough. Then he would be able to find out what lay behind them and how many men they might have to fight. He stood up as the first horseman passed him, spearing the second with a well-aimed javelin and his shout alerted his companions, who would handle the other pair easily.

Aquila turned, bending his knees to jump at the first horseman. The man had spun in his saddle, trying to slip off and out of danger, but the javelin took him in the side, adding impetus to the movement, jerking the rider off his mount. Fabius was on him before Aquila could open his mouth, and his shout would have had no effect, given the noise. His nephew was across his victim's chest, both hands pushing his sword, piercing the breastplate and crushing the ribs as it entered his body. The feet kicked wildly and the arms flayed uselessly, but the man was like an insect pinned to a wall. Still with his entire weight on the sword, Fabius turned and grinned at Aquila, an expression which changed to bewilderment when he realised that his 'uncle' was angry.

There was no time for remonstration; they had four horses, animals that could be put to use. Men could be sent off after Tullius, with further information, but first he would have to take a look himself, to find out what it was they faced.

It was easy to mistake Aquila for a local tribesman, stripped of his uniform and wearing an enemy helmet, though he had to crouch over to disguise his height. The whole party made their way back, with Aquila well ahead on the horse, so he was the first to see the smoke in the blue sky, the first to smell the burning. His nose also picked up the smell of horses, a lot of them, the rich odour of fresh manure strong on the faint breeze. They had closed the entrance to the valley as soon as they had seen him leave, taking positions in the hills above the track so that they could catch Ampronius as he left.

Their horses, under a small guard, were now tethered in lines near the river. The Romans would have to come this way, because all the other exits from the valley led them further away from the safety of their base camp and they would come, encumbered by slaves and booty, if the smell of burning was anything to go by.

As Aquila pondered the alternatives, three things stood out as paramount: first, even vastly outnumbered, the Romans would fight better in open country than they could in the narrow defile. Secondly, they would come through that defile unless they were warned of the danger. But it was the third factor that determined the course of action. Ampronius had a force composed mainly of infantry; the Averici normally fought on horseback, so he got out of sight and ran back to join the others.

'Who can ride?'

Several men put their hands up, though the

chance of their being skilful was remote. Roman
farmers never bred horses for anything other than
toil, so they were rarely competent riders, but if
they could stay in the saddle they would move a
lot faster than a man on foot, and for the same
reason, two would stand a better chance than
one. He sent off the first pair with a verbal
despatch, outlining the situation and what he
intended to do, then he had ten men divest
themselves of their arms, and some of their
armour, leaving just enough to identify them as
Romans. They were then ordered to roll
themselves in the dust, Fabius being included
because he begged, and Aquila agreed because his
nephew was good at anything smacking of
subterfuge. The soldiers were roped together by
the neck, apparently hobbled, covered in even
more dust, and told to act like prisoners who had
been severely beaten.

The warriors guarding the horses were already
on their feet as the party came into view, because
Aquila, shouting Celtic oaths he hoped they
could barely hear, had alerted them. Knowing
they would be wondering where the prisoners
came from, he laid into the stumbling line with a
piece of wood, causing them to stagger and fall,
which served to increase their wretched
appearance and, he hoped, to distract the

tribesmen. Fabius, in a piece of overacting that infuriated Aquila, dropped to his knees, hands clasped together, and begged loudly for mercy.

'Get up, damn you. Do you want to ruin everything?'

Fabius dragged himself to his feet, then started beating his chest and wailing. Incomprehensible to the men guarding the horses, it was clear enough to Aquila, as Fabius told him where to stick his silver spear. As they came abreast of the tethered horses, the guards lined up to jeer at these Roman pigs, but that changed abruptly as those porkers leapt at them and it died completely when the hidden knives found their targets.

'Bodies!' snapped Aquila. These were quickly dragged away and flung into the bushes lining the river. 'Fabius, get some of the men dressed up as locals, then get the others out of sight.'

The next two messengers were then sent off, these to inform Quintus that the Romans held the entrance to the pass. Over the next hour, the rest of his men were brought into the horse lines in small groups. He set some to making torches, while those in disguise made bundles of dry brushwood. Aquila, without helmet or shield, was up in the hills to the left of the track, using all the hunting skills at his command to get close to the besiegers without being observed. It was not as hard as he had feared; they sat in groups talking loudly, sure that their lookouts would give them ample warning if Ampronius finished his looting and formed his men up to leave.

He struggled hard, as he listened, to understand the dialect they were speaking. The odd word was clear, but he could make no sense at all of their conversation. Not that he needed to, for the moment they stopped talking and moved into position, he would know it was time for him to go. Aquila was in an exposed and dangerous position, but he was happier than he had been for an age, free to make his own decisions, away from the interference of superiors and right at this moment he relished the solitude – not something often afforded to a soldier in the legions.

The command – hushed but urgent – killed the conversations around him. He heard the clink of metal on rock as the tribesmen moved and the noises ceased. Aquila crept round the rock, behind which he had been sheltering, looking for a spot that would afford him a view into the valley beyond. It was his eagle that saved him, because the man who put the short sword at his throat hesitated just long enough, unsure of his identity. The question, in the guttural local dialect, was easy to comprehend and he answered with a local name, which gained him another second, as the Averici warrior took hold of the eagle, exerting the pressure necessary to pull it off. The sword on Aquila's throat, being in the way, was eased just enough for him to move and his knee made contact at the same time as his hand grabbed the warrior's wrist. The mouth was open, ready to scream but Aquila got one hand on his helmet and jerked it up, using the strap to pull his head back. The other hand was in the Celt's mouth, pushing down on his teeth till Aquila heard the jaw break. His opponent dropped to his knees with Aquila's arm now around his windpipe, cutting off the air. The other still tugged at the helmet as slowly, and as silently as he could, Aquila strangled him.

It was clear up to the next level and one look told him what he wanted to know. He could see the Romans, tiny figures in the distance, but visible by their regular formation. The crowd of future slaves, in the middle of the two detachments, formed an untidy mass, but they moved at the same pace as their captors, heading towards the exit from the valley and the road back to the Roman base camp. The whole fertile plain was dotted with the carcasses of dead cattle; what Ampronius could not take he would kill. The huts had burnt easily, but the embers still sent wispy plumes of smoke up into the air.

He watched them for a few minutes, gauging their pace, and confirmed that the mass of the attacking force was on the other side of the ravine, ready to rush down the slope, before turning and making his way back to where his men were waiting. Ordering those in disguise to get back into uniform, he changed himself, all the while counting, trying to match the pace of the marchers in the valley to the mental image of the landscape he carried in his head.

'Will Ampronius get the message?' asked Fabius.

'He'll get the message all right, but it's what he does next that counts.'

'Like nothing?'

Aquila nodded. 'He's got food, water and a perfect place for a pitched battle, even outnumbered.'

'I think we should get away.'

'Don't worry, Fabius. Most of them are on the other side of the pass. There are only a few of them on this side, because it's too steep to get down amongst our men when the trap's sprung. We'll be safer up there, and if the worst happens, we can always find a way to join Ampronius.'

They lit the torches, then the brushwood

bundles, using their spears to hold them near to the horses. Others dragged more bundles across the track, so that the animals, if they wanted to escape the flames and smoke, had only one way to go. They dragged on their lines, hooves flying to accompany the din of their fear until Aquila shouted the command and the ropes were cut. Those doing the cutting had to move smartly because the animals, once released, took off en masse, heading away from the flames and the yelling legionaries, straight for the rise that led to the route through to the valley.

Aquila had to shout his orders to be heard above the sound of the thundering hooves, as his legionaries ran for the boulders on the left of the track, where there was a route to the top of the sheer-faced cliff, which they immediately started to climb. There was no way he could command them in these rocks; it was every man for himself and, if he had judged the numbers on this side of the defile correctly, and if his men fought well, they would take the high ground. If not, and Ampronius Valerius did nothing, they would, in time, be killed by superior numbers.

The horses raced through, between the narrowing rocks, a solid mass of flesh that nothing could withstand, so that those who had taken up position on the floor of the gorge, and who could not get out of the way, were swept aside or trampled. A huge cloud rose up behind the horses, filling the whole ravine with dust, and the Averici tribesmen, who knew that surprise was gone, were on their feet yelling, as if by calling for their horses they could make them stop.

Ampronius, at the head of his men, had heard the sound of the stampede, magnified as it was by the narrow confines of high rocks. The soldiers and the slaves halted without the need for an order and Roman discipline told as the first of the animals appeared at the mouth of the exit. Commands were automatic as the legionaries formed lines, shields raised, leaving avenues between the units for the horses to charge through. Those the soldiers had captured, dazed by what had happened to them that day, just stood still. Some died under the animals' hooves, but with the increasing space afforded by the valley floor, the momentum had started to go out of the stampede. The horses, now well away from the flames, were beginning to run in circles. Ampronius, who could now see the tribesmen on the rocks above him, turned to the centurion who had taken over from Tullius and issued a single command.

'Kill the remaining prisoners.'

The sound of men, women and children dying reached Aquila as he fought his way up the hill, but it was just background to the noise of men yelling, swords clashing, and the sound of weapons beating on hard wooden shields, all echoing off the rocks that surrounded each individual conflict. Fabius was beside him, cutting and slashing, cursing the gods, Rome and his 'damned uncle'. In the valley, the blood-soaked Romans stood amongst the last of their victims, spearing those who still showed a semblance of life. Ampronius ordered them to fall back behind the mass of bodies and form up as Aquila reached the crest on his side of the ravine. Now that he could see into the valley, he was presented with the sight of Ampronius Valerius in a defensive posture, behind a rampart of dead bodies, content to wait in the open to see if he was attacked.

He had judged right; his men outnumbered those on this side of the defile, who had been posted to hurl rocks down onto the Romans. And it was not just numbers, they were the least tenacious fighters, older warriors, and had been put in a position where they could be of some use. Hand-to-hand fighting, with battle-hardened Roman legionaries, was not what they had expected, so some had tried to surrender, but they died like their comrades who fought; there was no room on this hill to take prisoners.

Out of the seventy men with whom he had started, some sixty made the crest. Aquila lined them up, shields together, to present as imposing a sight as possible, but it was not this show of strength that persuaded the enemy commander to withdraw, it was sheer logic. The same devious minds that had got Ampronius into this trap unlocked it for him. They had lost the element of surprise, their horses, and the initiative. Aquila's men would find a way to join the Romans in the valley if they were attacked and the combined force of infantry would meet them head on at a point where their superior numbers would be useless, especially on foot.

No genius was required to guess that reinforcements would soon, very likely, be on the way, so the whole tribe would have to move out of the sphere of Roman action to avoid retribution, and if they were going to save anything it had best be done quickly. Night was coming, so Aquila formed his men into a tight circle, told them to preserve their food and water, then set the various watches. No one really slept, aware that if the tribesmen were going to attempt anything to redress the balance, it would be here. They could see their comrades camped in the valley, almost smell the meat roasting on spits over the winking fires, and they knew that Ampronius, by not trying to scale the heights opposite, had left them in the lurch, prepared to let them die rather than risk casualties amongst his own soldiers.

Ampronius's men were on a high state of alert and the fires blazed all night, until eventually the inky, star-filled sky was tinged with grey and the light from the fires faded as the sun came up. Aquila's party, who had crouched in the rocks all night, hardly daring to move, could stand at last and stretch their limbs. All looked across the ravine to the rocks on the other side to find they were empty; silently, in darkness, the enemy had departed, leaving them victorious. They would have cheered if they had not been so weary.

Ampronius delayed his march through the ravine until Aquila's messenger informed him it was safe to do so. They left behind nothing but devastation, the sky full of vultures, waiting for these interlopers to depart, so that they could gorge themselves on the mass of corpses. Aquila had his men lined up, parade-ground fashion, their backs to their approaching comrades until Aquila gave the command as they came abreast. His maniple opened their ranks so that Ampronius Valerius could march through at the head of his troops.

The tribune searched in vain for Tullius and when he failed to find him, it did not take him long to realise who had saved him. The look of hate he gave Aquila Terentius was returned in full measure.

Quintus Cornelius looked at the pile of gold and silver ornaments that lay heaped on the floor of his tent. Torques, necklaces, finely decorated breastplates and helmets. The rest of his staff stood around silently, awaiting their general's decision. Ampronius stood to attention before him, while outside Aquila and the others waited, equally mute. The tribune would, at the very least, be sent back to Rome in disgrace: perhaps his fate would be death, which is what he deserved, since he had massacred the Mordasci for nothing other than personal gain.

But their general was reflecting on other things. He was thinking of his father; he had been very young when Aulus had celebrated his triumph, but the image of that occasion was as vivid in his mind as if it had taken place the day before. Nothing meant as much as that, the day when all Rome bowed the knee, the highest pinnacle of military success a soldier could achieve. The valuables before him were as nothing, in quantity, compared to those his father took from the Macedonians, but they gleamed in the same way, and in his imagination he saw them piled high, with captured weapons, in the ceremonial war chariots.

All his life Quintus felt he had lived in the shadow of other men; first his father, then Lucius Falerius as a more powerful politician. When he returned to Rome, as he must, to take up the leadership Lucius had bequeathed him, he would come into an insecure inheritance. He wanted a triumph of his own, so that he could emulate his father and enhance his own position. Nothing would stifle opposition to his leadership more than that; no one would dare challenge his supremacy in the Senate if he had just ridden his chariot down the *Via Triumphalis*, especially one achieved on soil that had witnessed so much failure.

He looked up at Ampronius. 'How many did you kill?'

'Over two thousand, General.'

'And this because the Avereci told you they intended to betray us?'

The tribune looked as though he wanted to be swallowed up, subsumed into the compacted earthen floor of the tent. His fine-boned face was pale, the upper lip glistening with sweat. It had all seemed so simple at the time, so straightforward. Now it had come to this, the point where his life was in danger. He fought to control the fear in his voice and spoke loudly.

'I was convinced I was doing my duty.'

Quintus gave the pile of gold objects a meaningful look. His eyes wandered round the sea of faces before him, all the eyes that had stared at him turning quickly away. He could punish Ampronius, but what would that achieve? Nothing, except that the young man's father, at present a dependable client, would become his enemy for life. But he could not ignore it either; he had to acknowledge it, or punish it. The sound of the mounted party cantering up the *Via Principalis* might just provide him with an answer. Bidding everyone to stay still, he went out to talk to the men he had sent to reconnoitre the Averici camp. No one overheard his exchange with the decurion in command, but the cast of his features as he returned to his tent convinced those watching that Ampronius was about to be condemned.

'Fetch me the map!' he snapped.

Senior officers rushed to obey; the table was cleared and the map laid out for the general's inspection. Quintus paced around, looking down, trying to decide. Few would cheer him if he backed Ampronius, but the good opinion of these men counted for little, since they all owed their appointments to him. It was the impression in Rome that mattered. Finally he stopped pacing, put behind him the idea that enemies would laugh, and issued his orders.

'We must destroy the Averici and they will not wait for us to come. I've just received intelligence that the whole tribe is on the move.' He jabbed his finger at the map. 'All units of the legion to assemble here, at the head of the central valley. I want the cavalry out within the hour. I need to know where the Averici are now, if they stopped and, if not, where they are headed.'

The trumpets and horns calling them to arms surprised Aquila, and they broke camp quickly and were on the march before noon. The cavalry had left hours before, but not without telling everyone who asked them what they were looking for.

'He's going to get away with it,' said Fabius.

'It might be worse than that,' replied Aquila.

'How can it be?'

But Aquila would not be drawn. 'Wait and see!'

Marcellus fretted at the time it took to get his men ready, yet deep down he knew that they were performing well. The order had arrived only an hour before; he was to join the general with all the men he had available, with Quintus wanting to make sure he comprehensively outnumbered his enemy. The young Falerii had worked hard, bringing these weary and cynical soldiers back to the point where they could be considered fit for action. He had never laboured more, nor slept so little. There had been no ringing declarations of the power and majesty of Republic, or the nobility of serving in the legions; he had succeeded through pure personal example, by issuing a simple challenge. Marcellus would not ask these men to do what he would not do himself, so, far from leading the life of luxury available in what was really a garrison duty, he had dug ditches, thrown up ramparts, marched with and without equipment; fought with spear, shield, sword, fists and sheer bodily strength, shouting, encouraging and cajoling, until the first gleam of spirit returned to the disgruntled legion.

As soon as that happened, he sent a despatch to Quintus, which stated that his men needed only combat to weld them back together into a proper fighting unit. Was the consul really too busy to accept the invitation? Perhaps, considering he failed to come to see for himself, nor did he send for these men to join him, replacing those of his own legions who must, by now, be weary of campaigning. The sharp edge began to blunt and Marcellus felt his legionaries, and their morale, slipping through his fingers like fine sand. Hoping Quintus's sudden change of heart had come in time, he put aside the insult that being ignored had implied, and marched off, eager to get into his first real battle.

CHAPTER ELEVEN

———•———

If the Iberian tribe of the Averici had ever had any chance, it evaporated when Quintus received the despatches from Rome; they caught him just as he was breaking camp. It was bad enough finding out that the *Equites* had finally won equality on the juries; Quintus had suspected that, with Lucius gone, the Senate would have to surrender that privilege at some time. It was the fact that his brother had supported it that inflamed his rage. He could protest until his dying day, but no one would believe that Titus had acted without his blessing. Now it was not a case of a triumph to enhance his position, it had become essential that he have one just to save it.

Marcellus joined him when he was still tearing out his hair, so gained no plaudits for the smart appearance and military bearing of his men, nor were the consul's own legions happy to see this addition to their force, since it would only increase the numbers available to split the proceeds of their plunder. Quintus had calmed down somewhat when Marcellus was finally allowed into his presence.

The reception was icy, the mere sight of the young tribune being enough to bring all the general's resentment bubbling to the surface, so he could barely bring himself to be polite. When Quintus had sent for him, he had fully intended that Marcellus Falerius should play a leading role in the coming battle; only a general truly gained prestige from such a thing, but a little could always be allowed to rub off on others, though whatever they gained would always be overshadowed by the commander's role. Not for Marcellus; he was abruptly informed to take station behind his men, and form up as a defensive shield behind the main body.

They caught the whole tribe in the open, a long string of carts, men, women and children on foot, trying to flee the wrath of the Romans. Costeti, their chieftain, who had sent word to Brennos asking for help, had his eyes firmly set on the western horizon. If the Duncani and some of their client tribes came to his assistance, the combined numbers would check the pursuit. They might not be able to defeat the Romans in an open battle, but at least the Averici would get away.

The only dust cloud was in the east, as the legions, for once moving faster than their foes, overhauled their quarry. There was nothing in the west except a clear sky. Emissaries were sent to Quintus offering to pass under the yoke, even to eat the grass of the field, if they could have peace, but they were rejected. Likewise, the offer of the tribal leaders to give themselves up, if the rest could be spared: Quintus wanted a battle.

With no option but to fight, they slew their livestock and burnt their carts, so that they should not fall into the enemy hands, then formed up, in silence, waiting for the Romans to come on, trying to ignore the actions of the skirmishers. Aquila, in the first line, started to advance at the sound of the horns, cursing under his breath that he should be forced to this. Their quarry, finally enraged and goaded into action by the skirmishers, salved his conscience by charging the Roman line, simply because, since the only other option was to die, there was less disgrace in killing now. It soon ceased to be a battlefield, a broad vista with lines of opposing warriors; the fighting narrowed down to the enemy in front and the two men on either side, cutting and slashing.

The horns blew again and the heavier infantry,

the *principes*, with old Labenius at their head, passed through the first line and took up the fight. The Averici, more at home on a horse than fighting on foot, could not stand against the weight of the Roman attack. Their line broke, but there was nowhere to go, for Quintus had sent his cavalry round the flanks to cut them off. They died where they stood, an ever-diminishing circle of tribesmen, none of whom were to be given quarter. Aquila did not see Labenius, as brave as ever, die from the thrust of a spear that took him just as he was calling to his men to make the final charge. Marcellus, well to the rear, watched as others did the fighting, sure now that his men would not be required. It was a measure of how far he had gone in bringing them back to be a proper fighting unit that he was not alone in his disappointment.

They counted the dead on the field at the end, and the total made Quintus a happy man, since they numbered well over five thousand, the total required by a general to claim a triumph. His own casualties were minimal and the spoils, once the possessions of the Averici were gathered in, these being added to those Ampronius had taken from the Mordasci, would please the public treasury, while the heap of weapons would be high enough to gladden a crowd when they were paraded through the streets of Rome. The women and children would fetch less as slaves than the men, but given their quantity, they would help to make Quintus a wealthier man than he was already. The Averici land would be his, to divide amongst his officers, and the mining and panning of silver, now that the Mordasci had been annihilated, fell to the consul as well, a long term source of revenue to the Cornelii coffers.

'Well, Ampronius Valerius, do you have any suggestions as to what we do next?'

The tribune, alone in the tent with his commander, said nothing, for the way Quintus was looking at him boded ill. Ever since the general had given the orders to attack the Averici, he had considered himself absolved of blame for the massacre of the Mordasci; he now guessed that he had been over-sanguine.

'I have you here alone for one reason. I do not wish that others should hear what I'm about to say to you.'

'I understand, Quintus Cornelius.'

Quintus pulled an unhappy face. 'I doubt if you do, Ampronius. You nearly lost two hundred and fifty men and in the process obliterated one of the few tribes in the province whose loyalty was without question.'

'General, I...'

'Silence.' Quintus interrupted without raising his voice, but the effect was the same. 'You deserve to be stripped of your rank and whipped, the kind of public humiliation that would have your family covering their heads in shame.'

Quintus waited to see if the younger man would say anything. It pleased him that the tribune just stood silently to attention. 'However, there are other considerations. I want you to know that, since you forced my hand, I have acted for the good of Rome. You come from a patrician family of good standing, a family whose support I have always enjoyed.'

Ampronius was not a complete fool. He knew that the support would now need to be unquestioned, or Quintus would bring a case against him in the Senate. The charge would be hard to refute, and impossible to survive with the newly staffed juries full of knights, thirsty for a patrician scalp. There was no time limit on this; Quintus could hold the possibility over his head for years, and that too applied to his father as long as he lived. The consul held up a single finger, making a gesture with it to underline each point.

'As a matter of principle, Rome, in the case of barbarians, must be seen to be powerful, before we are seen to be just. Now, what do you propose we should do about this Aquila Terentius?'

The question threw Ampronius, who, when he had thought about it at all, had usually conjured up the image of a swift knife in the back. They had exchanged not a word since the affair at the pass, but the man's looks had been enough to engender true hate in Ampronius's mind.

'We can, by stretching a point, award him a siege crown,' said Quintus.

'What?' Ampronius blurted out the word without thinking.

'Certainly a civic crown,' Quintus continued smoothly, as though Ampronius had not spoken. 'He would have had one of those before, if he'd kept his mouth shut.'

The tribune spoke hurriedly, angry that the consul was thinking of decorating the man at all. 'He didn't raise a siege, General, and what he did accomplish was done with my men, nominally under the command of a centurion. The siege crown is supposed to be for the actions of a man acting alone.'

The consul's voice was icy. 'Don't presume to lecture me about the rules governing the awarding of decorations. I will have to justify your actions to the Senate, including the massacre you carried out in that valley.'

'The good of Rome,' replied Ampronius lamely, attempting to use his commander's words against him.

'Is not something that everyone can be brought to agree about. We must stick with the fiction that the Mordasci were set to rebel, since that alone justifies your actions. All that leaves is the question of a proper reward for the man who saved the day. He must have something, even if he is the most ill-disciplined peasant it's ever been my misfortune to encounter. I assume you agree?'

Given the alternatives, there was no real choice. Quintus smiled. 'Good. You will submit the required report to me, I will accede to your request and the award will be granted.'

Quintus went back to his papers and Ampronius, assuming he was dismissed, saluted and turned to leave. Quintus spoke to his retreating back. 'Another thing. Since Spurius Labenius is dead, we will need to have a vote for the *primus pilus*. Have a word with your fellow tribunes and tell them that I would take it amiss if Terentius failed to receive all their votes. After all, we can hardly give this fellow the highest decoration in the Republic and not promote him. Given that these men are staying here, and there is no more dangerous place in the legion, with a high incidence of death for the holder, I would want him to have it.'

They buried their dead with due ceremony and Aquila, as the replacement, spoke the funeral oration for Spurius Labenius, composing a simple speech, but one with the power to wound. He spoke of an ordinary family of farmers, which included the sons of the *primus pilus*, who had died for the Republic, asking for, and receiving, little reward compared to that bestowed on less worthy men who garnered great wealth and power from the blood of the ordinary Roman. Quintus was angry at the tone of the address, which was clearly aimed at him, but needing to restore senatorial dignity, he decreed that as a signal mark of honour, Labenius's arms and decorations should be taken back to Rome, to be dedicated to *Mars*, the Roman God of war, and remain in his temple, where they would serve as an inspiration to others. After the funeral ceremonies, Quintus mounted the oration platform to thank his men and say farewell.

'There was a time, not so very long ago, when I could take you back to Rome with me. Should the Senate seek to adorn my humble brow...'

There was a loud raspberry blown from the ranks. Aquila, standing in front of his men, suspected it was Fabius, newly elevated into the *princeps* to serve with his 'uncle'. He did not turn round, since to do so would acknowledge that the sound had come from his section of the legion. Quintus was thrown slightly, as much by the sound as the suppressed laughter that followed.

'You will not march behind me, as in the old days, for there is too much to do here in Spain, but you, my own legions, will always be in my thoughts.'

Aquila shouted in a parade-ground voice, 'Silence in the ranks!' It had very much the same effect as Fabius's earlier insult.

'Goodbye,' said Quintus hurriedly. Then his voice took on an angry tone, and he looked directly at Aquila. 'And may the gods bring you what you so richly deserve.'

'Come, Marcellus,' said Quintus, with a warmth that had been singularly lacking of late. 'You have had your first campaign, taken part in a battle and now you can return to Rome and participate in my triumph. Not bad for your first posting.'

'I would rather remain here.'

'What, and serve under someone who doesn't know you?'

'The fighting is here, Quintus Cornelius.'

'Wrong boy, the real fight is in Rome. It's time to go back and light a fire under all those pampered senatorial arses. Speaking of pampered arses, I wonder how the Lady Claudia is getting on with her new husband?'

Sextius travelled in style. He was a man who disliked discomfort, so each property he visited had a suitable villa to accommodate him. Finding the company of bucolic peasants almost intolerable, he was eventually inclined to admit that having Claudia along eased his journey. They always put on a show for him, organised by his bailiffs to demonstrate how happy was the life of his slaves and tenants. This consisted of food roasted on a spit, plain and unspiced in a way that he despised, followed by singing that hurt his ears and dancing so primitive it made him wince, the whole washed down with rough wine that tasted as if it had just come out of the bonfire. To so fastidious a man, it was all a sore trial, a necessary part of his patrician duty.

Claudia, on the other hand, seemed to enjoy it, to the point that her husband wondered just how much of that rough Sabine blood had survived in the Claudian veins these last four hundred years. However, it was pleasing the way she played her part; tending to the sick, mending hurts both physical and spiritual, discussing women trouble in a way he found excruciatingly embarrassing, anointing and washing the squalling babies, ignoring their filth. Sextius, closeted with his bailiff, being bored to terminal distraction with lists of figures, saw such activity as very noble and very proper, without having the least desire himself to indulge in it.

'I wonder if I could not hand all this work over to an agent, my dear. It's so fatiguing, all this traipsing around the countryside.'

Claudia, who even on such a short acquaintance could play Sextius like a well-loved lyre, knew better than to respond with an immediate no. 'If you think best, Husband, perhaps you could set a new trend amongst the better class of citizen.'

'In what way?' demanded Sextius eagerly; he was a man who had always fancied having something named after him, like a law or a road. Even a trend would do.

'Take a lead. Tell all your fellow landowners that you've had enough of farming. After all, it might be a very Roman way to go about things, but it can hardly be said to be work for someone of refined sensibilities.'

Sextius's face, so eager, had collapsed as she spoke; he had spent years protecting his image as the upright Roman; the last thing he wanted was people alluding to his sensibilities. To the simple-minded, there were two ways of living life in Rome; men were either designated as living their life in the sun, soldiering, farming and debating, or they were accused of living their life by the lantern, reading, studying and espousing an interest in philosophical concepts and there was little doubt, in so martial a society, which group excited greater admiration. Sextius had eschewed the army, avoided magistracies and loathed the idea of arguing in the open with a crowd. Given these character traits, he was not left with much more to protect his reputation, so not taking an interest in agriculture, for him, would only lead to him being considered effete.

'How goes your little project?' he asked, abruptly changing the subject.

'If I'd known how many children are exposed I'd never have started on it.'

Her husband leant forward, his face full of concern. 'You mustn't tire yourself out, my dear.'

Claudia sighed, then her face brightened. 'I've just had an idea, Sextius. I shall submit it to you, to see what you think.' Her hand caressed his forearm, this followed by a sigh full of wonder and gratitude. 'You're so much wiser than I. Do you think it matters, the numbers of exposed children?'

Clearly he did not think so, even if he did favour her with an enthusiastic nod. 'That is one of the pillars of the state, Claudia. We Romans always have a clear notion of what is happening in the lands we control.'

'And yet that information is not, as far as I know, available.'

'No?' he replied suspiciously.

'What if I continue my work, record the number, though not the names of exposed children, then you could present the figures to the Senate, neither praising the practice nor condemning it, to shed some light on a murky area of behaviour. Perhaps they would be impressed. They would certainly name the survey after you, if they were.'

Nothing interested Sextius less than babies, especially ones exposed to die on barren hillsides. 'And I would do everything that's required,' Claudia continued, 'but of course, as a mere woman, I would not dare to seek any credit.'

That appealed mightily to her husband; in his mind he could see himself standing in the *Curia Hostilia*, men gasping at his profile and equally amazed at his noble purpose. 'Sextius,' they would say, 'we all thought was a bit of a dilettante, and all the while he's been beavering away at this. Here stands a true Roman.' All that praise and no work to do for it!

'But I thought I'd already said that to you, my dear, or did I just imagine it?'

As he journeyed to the villa, which sat just outside the Servian walls, Cholon was actually afraid, though there was nothing Quintus could do to him. But somehow he had found out about the Greek's role in the affair of the juries, and had thus commanded him to attend upon him to explain; being still in his consular year, it was a summons that could not be refused. He was not afraid of physical violence, but he disliked confrontation, even with people for whom he did not care. There was no doubt that this was a triumphal general's headquarters; soldiers, not lictors, guarded the occupant, and the trophies that would not suffer from the elements were stacked in the courtyard. Cholon deliberately delayed his arrival in the consul's study by an over-elaborate interest in the numerous decorated chariots.

'Am I to be asked to sit down?' he asked, when he was finally commanded to attend, wondering if the trembling in his voice was obvious.

Quintus just waved his assent. His eyes had been on Cholon since he entered the room and they stayed there, as if, by boring into the Greek, he would get the information he wanted without the need to ask a question. Intended to intimidate his visitor, it had the opposite effect; the ploy was so obvious it nearly made him laugh and he felt the tension in his mind evaporate.

'You're getting fat, Quintus,' he said.

'What?'

'Soldiering normally slims a man down. That is, unless he's prone to gluttony.'

'Do you have any loyalty to the Cornelii family, at all?' asked Quintus, his eyes blazing with anger.

'I esteemed your father, I like Claudia and I am friends with Titus.'

'You'd be penniless without us!'

Cholon refused to let his annoyance show; he had learnt, a long time ago, that Quintus found it difficult to deal with a purely rational argument. 'I'm sure you would have given me everything that your father bequeathed, out of the pure goodness of your heart.'

'I would have left you to rot in the gutter.'

'My word, Quintus,' he replied, with affected languor. 'Have a care. Do you realise that you've just told the unvarnished truth?'

The thought occurred to him that Quintus, as he shot out of his chair, was going to hit him. The knot of fear returned, but he remained still, determined to keep the smile on his face. Instead the other man slammed his desk.

'You work against us, and what's worse is that you're using our money to do it.'

'Don't you mean your money, and your interest, Quintus?'

'It amounts to the same thing.'

'Hardly.'

'You persuaded my brother to this foolish act. Damn it, Titus will do anything you tell him.'

'How did you ever manage to command an army?'

That shocked him, especially as he was busy, at this very moment, preparing for his triumph. 'What do you mean by that?'

'Well, for one thing, you've got a very high opinion of my capabilities. And secondly, your brother does what he wants. No man tells him what to do, including, if I may say so, you. If you are such a poor judge of character, I think it is dangerous to entrust you with a military command.'

'I wish we were in Spain now, Cholon,' he hissed. 'I'd feed you to the wolves.'

The Greek stood up abruptly. 'I don't know

why I came! Even with your consular *imperium* I should have refused. Let me give you some advice, Quintus.' The consul opened his mouth to speak, but unusually for him, Cholon actually raised his voice to cut him off. 'Listen! The law has been passed. You'll never get anyone to believe you had no hand in it. If you want to salvage anything for yourself, make a virtue out of necessity. The first time you see Titus in public, embrace him.'

'I'd like to embrace him between two axes.'

'I give you that advice because you're Aulus's son. Personally, you can go to Hades in a papyrus boat, for all I care.'

Marcellus Falerius, still wearing his tribune's uniform, was waiting to see Quintus. He nodded to Cholon as he came out, not alluding at all, even with an eyebrow, to the raised voices he had just heard. Quintus was still fuming when he went in, but the consul smiled, putting the words the Greek had used to the back of his mind.

'I am honoured that you choose to visit me,' he said, as Marcellus sat down.

'I am troubled, Quintus Cornelius.'

The consul's face took on a look of deep concern. 'Troubled?'

'Yes. As you know, the next governor of

Hispania Ulterior is to be Pomponius Vittelius.' Quintus nodded, but said nothing. 'I had approached him about returning to Spain as one of his tribunes.'

'Go on,' said Quintus, as the young man paused.

'I had good grounds to believe he favoured the idea. Indeed he seemed positively enthusiastic, yet this morning when I called on him, his manner had totally changed. I was brusquely informed that such a posting was impossible.'

Quintus opened his hands, in a gesture that said he understood the problem, but was at a loss to know what to do about it.

'Well, I was wondering if you could intercede on my behalf. I believe you have some influence with Pomponius.'

'I have a little, but I doubt that I have enough to change his mind.'

Marcellus's face fell. Quintus actually leant forward and patted the young man's hand and his voice had an unctuous tone that would have made an older man suspicious. 'You do not need any Pomponius to aid you. I am your patron, so I will see you get proper postings and in time I will help you towards all the necessary magistracies.'

'I am aware of that, Quintus Cornelius, but I

would wish to go to a place where there is some fighting.'

'Commendable, Marcellus, very commendable,' Quintus replied, inwardly glad that Pomponius had taken the hint. 'But with your wedding coming up in a few weeks, surely it would be better if you let the matter rest.'

Valeria Trebonia had become a Vispanii while he had been away in Spain; her marriage to Gallus Vispanius had, of course, been arranged by her father, though the girl had, in a manner almost unique to the Trebonii household, been consulted in advance as to her preferences. It hardly seemed to bother her that Gallus, her future husband, was a dissolute rogue, a regular customer of half the brothels in Rome, prone to turning up blooded and drunk on his doorstep, with the contents of his dinner all over his clothes. Gallus was not Marcellus's type at all, but he decided to call nevertheless, his excuse being that he must congratulate Valeria. Advance notice to the Vispanii house was required of his intentions, which he saw to before setting out to visit Quintus, so he was therefore annoyed, on arrival, to be told that Gallus was absent – which was nothing to his surprise when he was invited to enter anyway, and then shown into Valeria's private apartments.

'I called to congratulate both you and Gallus.'

Valeria gave his a conspiratorial grin. 'Are you sure you didn't check I'd be alone first?'

'I most certainly did not,' snapped Marcellus, angry as well as embarrassed.

'No. Perhaps not.' One finger flicked out to stroke the gold embossing on his breastplate. 'And I thought that you'd come in uniform, especially for me.'

'I must leave, it's unbecoming,' he snapped. 'And I would be obliged, in future, if you will cease this behaviour.'

'You're right, Marcellus, after all, I am married now. It would be cruel of me to tease you.'

The emphasis on the word *tease* made him flush slightly. She moved forward till she was standing very close. Her mouth was open a little, just showing the upper row of her white teeth and her eyes ranged over his body, mistaking the care he had taken in preparing himself for this visit as being attributable to her, not Quintus Cornelius. Her voice was slightly husky when she spoke.

'You have been in a battle, Marcellus. My brother told me.'

He wanted to say no, to be honest and admit that he merely watched from the sidelines, but her tone of voice stopped him. He knew she would admire him more if she supposed him valorous.

'A barbarian tribe, caught and annihilated,' she said. 'They say the captured women numbered thousands. Imagine the treatment they must have received from our victorious troops. You must tell me all about it. The noise, the clash of weapons, the sight and smell of blood.'

His hand was halfway to taking her arm when she skipped away, her voice now light and girlish. 'But you must not call on me when Gallus is at the races. What would people say to an unmarried friend calling on another man's wife?'

The meaning was plain enough, but deep down Marcellus felt that this was really just an extension of Valeria's teasing. That after his wedding, if he did call, she would find another way of arousing him, just as she would contrive to avoid a real entanglement.

'She's a sweet little thing, your Claudanilla. Almost like a boy. Perhaps after you've had her, you won't want to cast your net any wider. But if you do, Marcellus…'

Valeria laughed, for she had no intention of committing herself to anything, even her new husband.

* * *

The Falerii house was host to yet another event. Marcellus stood in an unadorned toga on one side of the family altar; his eye kept turning towards Valeria, who stood with her new husband. Gallus was short and rather squat, his face puffy and his eyes seemed watery, as if he had done without sleep. The cymbals sounded and Marcellus turned away from inspecting Gallus to make sure that everything was in place, especially that the two sheepskin-covered stools were ready to receive the bride and groom.

Claudanilla entered wearing a bright orange veil; on her feet she wore saffron-coloured shoes, and they knelt on the stools as the auspices were taken by the priest, a chicken sacrificed and its entrails examined and pronounced propitious. Marcellus poured the libation and the couple ate the holy cake. Claudanilla then anointed the doorposts of the house to seal out evil spirits and presented Marcellus with three coins as a token of her dowry; he in turn gave her the symbols denoting fire and water.

The whole party set out in darkness to walk the streets in a long, winding, torch-lit procession, so that the populace could call good luck to the couple, with the odd ribald comment about how the night was set to end, interspersed with heartfelt wishes that the union be blessed with healthy children. Having descended to the marketplace and then returned back up the hill, the party assembled outside the gates of Marcellus's house. Two Falerii relatives lifted the bride over the threshold to loud cheering, and then everyone entered to partake of the wedding feast. At the appointed time, to many a catcall, Marcellus led his bride away from the chamber full of family and guests. Handmaidens removed Claudanilla's wedding garments, leaving her in a loose shift, alone in a bedchamber with a man she did not know.

Marcellus felt as awkward as the girl. She was, after all, only fourteen years old. He took her hand in silence and led her to the bed. Claudanilla sat down while Marcellus dimmed the oil lamps. Convention debarred him from a sight of her naked, but he could see the outline of her unformed breasts under her shift. He raised the material above her waist, exposing the lower half of her body. In the faint lamplight, Marcellus could see that it was slim, still childlike, with only the faintest hint of pubic hair. He took her quickly, ignoring the scream of pain as he broke her hymen. She cried like a child, though in decency she attempted to hide the fact from her new husband, trying to convince him, by her movements, that her sobs were brought on by pleasure.

The scream produced many a nod at the feast, where those who had waited, the close relatives of the bride and groom, could be satisfied that all the proper forms had been observed. The Claudians had delivered a virgin to the marriage bed, and the Falerii could hear that Marcellus had done his duty by the girl. They toasted the couple and the possible fruits of their union.

In the bedchamber, Claudanilla lay alone. Her lower belly seemed to be on fire and she prayed that Marcellus would leave her be until the pain subsided. Her wish was granted, but not in a way that she would have liked.

In her innocence she did not know that Marcellus had failed to complete their union. He saved that up for Sosia, the silent slave girl who, in the pitch dark of a curtained room, could be anybody Marcellus wanted. Even she, normally so passive, was tempted to cry that night, for by his presence, her master had dashed any hope she had of any relief from her carnal servitude.

CHAPTER TWELVE

Quintus Cornelius, by his actions and the rewards that accrued, unwittingly set the tone for future operations in Spain. Those who watched him parade down the *Via Triumphalis* observed not just the event, but the means by which it had been achieved, while few discerned that the other result of this particular victory was the way their most persistent enemy had been undermined. What had happened to the Mordasci and the Averici might have united the tribes in a way that had hitherto proved impossible, but the role of Brennos in both events could not be hidden and his duplicity caused resentment.

While fearful of engendering an open breach with the Duncani chieftain, many who might have joined him, had he chosen to attack Rome, now demurred. If he would sacrifice one tribe for their amity to Rome, and another for their enmity, he was capable of any treachery. Careful diplomacy might have exploited this, which would have isolated Brennos and left him impotent, but the sight of Quintus Cornelius, painted red and crowned with laurel, acted like a drug on human ambitions, ensuring that the man who replaced him, Pomponius Vittelius Tubero, had no desire to even consider peace.

His first act upon arrival was to summon his officers to a conference; this included Aquila Terentius, as *primus pilus* of the 18th Legion, which Quintus had left behind. His advice, given that they were short of cavalry, was to go on to the defensive along the frontier and let any revolts by the tribes peter out. At the same time, the whole army should train in siege tactics, then invest the nearest major hill fort, Pallentia, and offer the inhabitants a proper peace. If not accepted, it should be subdued, razed to the ground and touted as an example of Roman power. Whatever the result, the loss of that bastion would provide a springboard to the next hill forts, and being less formidable they would likely surrender rather than face a siege. Once enough tribes swore peace, they could forget Brennos, who would be too far off to cause any trouble.

That enraged his new commander, who knew as well as anyone that there was no glory in the idea of a just peace, and no time to finish a siege on such a formidable fortress within his consular year; the fact that Aquila identified both these problems, while everyone else present espoused euphemisms, led to a heated exchange. What transpired in the tent led to a determined attempt to have him removed, an attempt thwarted by the tribunes of his legion, who were well aware of the standing he had amongst the men. Pomponius responded by shipping the reluctant tribunes back to Rome, and replacing them with his own appointees. So Aquila found himself back in the ranks, serving with a maniple of very discontented legionaries, this under a centurion who wondered if he would survive his first battle, so much was he hated, the whole cohort controlled by an young officer who had no experience in warfare at all.

Quintus Cornelius had been a good soldier; Pomponius was not. The advice that Aquila had given him made the senator more determined than ever to achieve a quick result, so with minimum preparation he marched his entire force into the hills. The landscape provided few places where so numerous an army could deploy their full strength. Pomponius, without a comprehensive cavalry screen, found himself attacked daily from a different direction.

Wherever he concentrated his strength, that was the position his enemies avoided. Finding a weakness, a flank denuded of troops for action elsewhere, they would exploit it without mercy, inflicting casualties out of all proportion to the numbers they engaged.

Going forward was bad enough, but once the consul had realised his error and sought to withdraw, matters took a turn for the worse. The morale of the legions suffered from a sense of failure, discipline began to fracture, and the tribesmen, fired up by a sense of achievement, called for others to join them in expelling the Romans from their soil. Pomponius was never actually outnumbered, but the terrain suited the Celt-Iberians. Rather than retiring in good order, the general was obliged to undertake a series of forced marches, just to put a secure distance between him and his enemies, which allowed him to build camps that were safe against attack. The army was only two days away from base when Pomponius, stung by the low opinion of his officers, ordered a rash dawn sortie designed to catch his enemies off balance.

To prove his own bravery, he led the operation personally, for once taking a conspicuous position at the head of his own consular legion, the 20th, but in calling his troops together, he had underestimated his enemy. They could tell the difference between horns blown to rouse an encampment and those same instruments used to commence an attack. Enough of them stood their ground to give the Roman general the impression that his tactic had succeeded, but when they broke in disorder, Pomponius ordered a pursuit that fractured the cohesion of his men. He thought he was pursuing a beaten enemy until the Celt-Iberians counter-attack caught them in extended order, in broken hilly ground. The most disciplined troops formed a line that would hold but two cohorts perished to a man, caught as they were on a rock-strewn hillside.

The message that came back to the camp was clear. Pomponius's quaestor had had the good sense to prepare one legion, holding it ready to cover the withdrawal of his commander, an event which had been contemplated from the outset, should the initial attack falter. This, the 18th, was now ordered to go, under the command of a legate, to the consul's rescue. So Aquila found himself running hard, with Fabius puffing beside him, towards a battle that he believed should not have been fought in the first place. They could not hope for surprise, given the pace and angle of their approach, so the only tactic left was sheer weight of numbers.

The legate made no attempt to sort out the distended formation he now commanded; his aim was to get to Pomponius with the utmost speed, form up the remnants of that legion with his own, and retire. It was a sound idea that foundered in his general's pride, for Pomponius would not countenance withdrawal, calling retreat a mere prelude to defeat. He used the reinforcements to cover his own manoeuvres and initiated a flank march with part of the 20th designed to cut his enemy off from their own tribal lands and squeeze them between the two Roman divisions.

But those same tribesmen held the surrounding hills, the high ground; they could see Pomponius's manoeuvre almost as soon as he set out and, being mounted, they could move at a greater speed than he. So, instead of attacking a weak sector of his opponent's defences, he found himself up against their full strength, with the bulk of the 18th too far away to help, finding his own flanks threatened by a mass of horsemen. Inexorably, the Celts pressed home their attack – for once their actions coordinated in a way that was unusual. The wings of the legion began to crumble in upon the centre.

That was when the *princeps* of Quintus's old legion arrived; the best and most experienced men in Pomponius's army, they sliced through their opponents, an irresistible wall of shields that covered not only their sides but their heads. With a discipline born of many a fight, they held their shape against all comers. Their *primus pilus*, out in front of the line, was one of the first to die and the young tribune appointed by Pomponius lost control and found himself at the rear of the detachment. So, when the *princeps* of that legion broke through to rescue their general, the man at the head of them was none other than their former senior centurion, Aquila Terentius.

'Extend out lines,' he shouted. 'Slot in the 20th's men between two of ours.'

'Who's that giving orders?' yelled Pomponius. He strode towards Aquila, the gold decoration on his armour flashing in the sunlight. In his hand he held the tied bunch of *fasces*, the symbol of his *imperium*. 'I command here.'

'Do you want to die here as well?' shouted Aquila. He waved his arm and his men, who had paused at the consul's shout, moved quickly to obey him.

'You!'

'Yes, General.' Aquila gave him a regulation salute, even though to his mind the man was not one to deserve it. 'If you don't withdraw from this position we'll all die and while I respect that thing in your hand as much as the next man, I'm not about to spill my blood so that you can carry it with pride.'

Pomponius was very close now, his red, sweating face pressed close to that of his insolent subordinate. 'You'll do as I say.'

Aquila took out his sword, handing it pommel first to the general. 'If you're so determined, fall on this, but I'm leading my men out of here, and something tells me your legion will want to follow.'

The confusion on the consul's face was clear, so Aquila dropped his voice. Even though the death of this man would not affect him at all, he knew that if he wanted to survive, the general's dignity must be maintained and he had no time for niceties, since the man's staff officers were approaching in a group.

'You're being as stupid as a mule. We have no choice but to withdraw, so why don't you give the orders? Make it look as though it's your idea.'

'I...'

'Death or disgrace for you and your family?'

That drained the blood from his face. He spun round just as his officers engulfed him. 'Form up with the *princeps* of the 18th. We're going to fight our way back to the main body.'

Pomponius paused then, as though in his

mind he could not envisage what should happen next.

'Then we will retire in good order,' said Aquila.

The general's staff, seeing a ranker address a general, looked at him strangely as Pomponius repeated his words.

There was no way that Pomponius was going back to Rome with only a futile march and unnecessary losses to his credit. He had the good grace not to intervene when the 18th held their election, which brought Aquila Terentius back to his former position as senior centurion, but that legion was not included in his next operation. They were left in Emphorae while the consul, short of time and without a true enemy to fight, marched the rest of his army against the Scordesci, a client tribe that had been at peace with Rome for a decade.

He burnt their camp, slaughtered their warriors, stole their treasure and livestock and enslaved the women and children. He then set off for Rome to petition the Senate for a triumph. He left behind a land in total turmoil, as every tribe on the frontier that had sworn to keep the peace, for their own self-preservation, attacked the nearest Roman outposts. Even the Bregones and Lusitani, if they held back from full-scale participation, sent men from the interior to help. It was no longer tribal uprising the legion had to deal with. It was now outright war.

Marcellus, looking out at the snow-covered landscape, which lay ghostly white under a lowering grey sky, yearned for some decent light. Not just light, but space, for here in the north, in the province of Gallia Cisalpina, houses were built very differently from the way they were in Rome. The windows were small and shuttered, the walls thick, and a huge fireplace dominated each room. The villa had no atrium, a place open to benign elements where a patrician could receive his guests; instead there was an earthen courtyard, either frozen solid at this time of year, or covered in mud if they had a thaw.

Beyond that lay the town of Mediolaudum, the furthest outpost of Roman power in Italy, lying to the south of the towering Alps, which sat like a protective rampart at the head of the Republic. It was a rampart that had been breached of course, and vigilance was necessary. The local Celtic tribes, the Boii and the Helvetii, hated Rome with a passion, but, deep in their mountain fastness, they kept themselves aloof. The odd raid occurred, when cattle were stolen, but there was nothing that would justify a pursuit, and even if he wanted to, Marcellus had no troops with which to achieve anything. The Boii and Helvetii even avoided trouble in the winter, retiring north, east and west for winter pasture, leaving the Romans to bring agricultural order to the foothills.

The weather had been like this for over a week, with only the odd blizzard to break the monotony, depressing his spirits even further than the appointment that had brought him to this part of Italy. Those whom he controlled, the local officials, assured their new provincial praetor that when the sun appeared he would he amazed at the beauty of the landscape. Even snowbound, he would find the heat of the day pleasant, and what could be nicer on a freezing night than proximity to a blazing fire? Good manners, as well as prudence, barred him from telling them that he had been sidelined. Quintus had waxed eloquently about the need for him to hone his magisterial skills, insisted that Marcellus was too young for any office in Rome itself; his mentor also seemed determined to keep him away from any form of war. The excuses he gave for that were as threadbare as those he had used to send him here: the need to protect him from danger, so that the Republic could be sure of his services in the future.

So he found himself, at his first court, adjudicating in disputes so tedious as to make it difficult to remain awake. There were none of the scandals in this part of the world that made advocacy in Rome an exciting occupation; the local lawyers he had met were a bone-headed bunch, more inclined to string out a trial through sheer inability than eloquence, and the cases themselves, as he examined the court records, seemed just as mundane.

Arbitration of land boundaries, chasing those who failed to pay their taxes and endless litigation over inheritances, these were his daily lot, but the really galling thing was his inability to refuse Quintus Cornelius's offer. To do so would release his patron from any obligation to him, an avenue that Quintus would take with alacrity. The Sibyl he had consulted just days before Lucius died had said he would inherit from his father; perhaps one day he would, like Lucius, come to believe in it, but right now, in his present melancholy mood, it was a hard concept to grasp.

He turned away from the small slit of a window as the physician entered the room. The man walked to the fire, holding up his hands to the blazing logs, then rubbed them vigorously before turning to face the praetor. He was smiling from ear to ear, which made the question Marcellus posed seem superfluous.

'Well?' he demanded.

'Definitely with child, Excellency. The gods and the west winds have been good to you.'

Marcellus had to bite his tongue. Did they still believe, in this godforsaken part of the world, that a benign wind was needed to ensure a pregnancy? He wondered what his father's old doctor, Epidaurianus, would have said, faced with such primitive beliefs.

'And my wife's health?'

'Excellent,' the doctor replied, rubbing his hands before the fire again as if to emphasise the point. 'Though the Lady Claudanilla is slight of frame. The actual birth may be a difficult one.'

The conception had been far from difficult. After their wedding night he had managed to quite successfully avoid sexual congress with his young wife. On those occasions when he had shared her bed, he had merely gone through the motions, leaving her as free from pleasure as he was himself. Sosia was still the companion of his dark hours, both physical and metaphoric. Meek and submissive, and entirely lacking in experience, Claudanilla accepted this as the norm, but someone, probably her mother, or perhaps her older friends, had enlightened her as to the true nature of conjugal matters. At the same time, someone in his household had informed the new mistress of the duties performed by the Greek slave girl.

Marcellus flew into a rage when both these things were mentioned, forbidding his wife to allude to them ever again, but she had shown some cunning, as well as determination, in opposing this injunction. Within a matter of days, Marcellus received a visit from her father, who made it plain that the massive dowry he had bestowed on the young man was not provided for decoration. The couple were married in accordance with strict Patrician rules. Appius Claudius expected his son-in-law to behave like a member of his class, instead of some new man, and dismiss the slave girl. Then he should confine himself to favouring his wife with what was her due.

Marcellus was in no position to disagree. In theory, a man owned his wife and could do with her what he liked. This, like most ancient laws, was more form than substance and his father-in-law made it plain that if he failed Claudanilla, then he would not find himself able to keep his complaints about such behaviour within the confines of the family. To any patrician with ambitions, an accusation of that nature was too deadly to ignore. Sosia was removed from his house on the Palatine and sent to the ranch he owned nearest to the city. Marcellus decided on abstinence, partly out of pique, partly out of anger, but then he had left Valeria out of the equation.

All it took to make Claudanilla pregnant was one meeting with Valeria and the most galling thing that happened, when he treated his wife in the same way he had abused Sosia, was the way she took to it, deriving a pleasure from their lovemaking which was completely at odds with what he desired. That had been a matter of weeks ago and on the journey north she had started to be sick. What followed was a sudden emergence of an extremely healthy appetite, a sure sign she was with child. Deep down, her husband suspected that she conceived on that very night, which did nothing to cheer him up.

'Tell me, Doctor, have you ever heard a Sibylline prophecy?'

'I've never dreamt that such a thing was possible for the likes of me, Excellency.'

Marcellus turned to look out the window again. If anything, with failing light, the

landscape was even more grey and forbidding.
'Believe me, they're not all they are cracked up to
be.'

It was harder to be melancholic the day his son
was born. The snow had gone from everywhere
but the very highest peaks and the sun shone on
green, flower-filled meadows. The sky was a blue
of such startling clarity that it hurt the eyes and
little Claudanilla, so slight of frame, delivered
their child with an ease that would have shamed
a brute of a fishwife. Everyone came to the
praetor's house to observe the ritual of sacrifice
and acknowledgement. They noticed that
Marcellus Falerius was no longer like the ice that
bound them in winter; today he was close to a
smile, as he raised the black-haired bundle above
the altar which held the family masks, specially
brought from Rome. He named the child Lucius
in honour of his father and he vowed that like his
father he would raise his child to be a proper
Roman.

The feast that followed was a great event for
those in the vicinity. Most had never seen a
patrician noble; that they had one serving as their
praetor they took to be a sign of great good
fortune. He was, to them, as strange a creature as
the hairy giants said to inhabit the mountains,

and Marcellus, who had all the innate regard for his class that went with his birth, was not stand-offish. They knew him to be stiff-necked and strict in pursuit of his duty, but on the day of the birth they saw the true face of nobility; they saw a man at ease with his station in life, who saw no need to be condescending to those who had emerged from a less exalted bloodline.

To them, the Lady Claudanilla, equally noble, was a delight. Each guest, as was the local custom, had brought gifts of food to the celebration. She obliged them all by tasting their offerings, laughing and preening as she accepted the toasts to her fecundity. They were still talking about it when they discovered how fecund she really was; before the first snows once more reached down from the mountains to coat the valley floor, or tinge the pitched roofs of Mediolaudum, Claudanilla was with child again.

The birth of the first child changed Marcellus. Always assiduous in duties pertaining to his office, he became more so, determined that his area of Gallia Cisaplina would be the best administered in the region. Originally reluctant to explore the furthest reaches of his responsibilities, he now instituted a mobile court, taking justice to the very edge of Roman power. He met and spoke with the Celtic chieftains, restating his predecessor's vow that overzealous rustling would not go unpunished and while he traversed the land they controlled, he studied the terrain, which so benefited the inhabitants that conquest appeared impossible. To those who worked alongside the praetor, it was obvious that his whole attitude to his position had changed. They nodded sagely, casting favourable opinions on the effects of fatherhood.

On the night of the birth, when Marcellus walked under a star-filled sky, he felt, for the first time, that sense of immortality, which is a child's gift to any new parent. It was a defining moment, one at which he felt some understanding for his own father. There and then he cast off the torpor that had affected him since he came north; he was young, he had time, just as he now had responsibility. Quintus Cornelius would not succeed; somehow Marcellus would get back to the centre of things, to take his rightful place in the City of Rome, and to gain and hold a power that he was determined would one day fall to his son.

CHAPTER THIRTEEN

They came year after year, new proconsuls sent
by the Senate to fight what had become known as
'The Fiery War', all with the same aim; Aquila
watched them come and go, despising each one a
little more than the last, because Roman
legionaries would die for the careers of these
avaricious politicians. They arrived mouthing
words of noble purpose and, naturally, the
soldiers hoped this new man would be different
from the last; they were usually disappointed and
their discipline suffered for it.

The legions they brought did nothing to
increase the strength of the army; with conflict
now permanent, these new levies were needed
just to replace the losses. The Roman base camp
on the frontier had been in existence so long it
was now like a small town. Nearly every soldier
had a local 'wife', an attachment that did little to
keep them out of the wine shops and brothels,

which had been set up outside the camp walls. Most cared only for the spoils of war, so that they could sustain their drinking and whoring, as well as satisfy the raucous demands from their local women that they provide for their bastards. They killed without thinking, marched wherever their commander sent them, and ceased to moan about their use as fodder for another's ambition, as long as they received their share of the spoils.

Aquila, alone in the *princeps* of the 18th, avoided permanent attachments, enduring the good-natured ribbing he got from Fabius, who enjoyed a complicated series of liaisons. He consolidated the position of senior centurion in his legion and had become, without trying, someone to be reckoned with, even impressing the local levies of axillaries by learning the language. It was only after he had returned to Rome that Pomponius realised that the tribunes he dismissed for electing Aquila Terentius had all been appointees of Quintus Cornelius; that, and the whispering campaign they mounted against him, cost him his triumph. The message, to avoid interfering in legionary elections, was not lost on his successors. Aquila was always voted in, and by so comprehensive a margin that he held the post no matter who he offended.

He tried to keep his men up to the mark by

personal example, and garnered decorations, as
well as scars, for his personal bravery on every
operation. After the first few years, a succession
of young tribunes, usually clients of the serving
general, arrived from Rome to take command,
replacing more experienced men. Most found,
after an initial attempt to overawe him, that it
was better to work through, as well as learn
from, the formidable *primus pilus*. He took as
much care of them as he did the rankers, well
aware that their birth and background sometimes
caused them to be foolishly brave. Whilst their
attitude to personal danger was something he
admired, it did nothing to alter his feelings for a
system that elevated such novices over soldiers
with long experience.

He was cherished by the men for the care he
took for their safety, while being heaped in an
equal measure of verbal ordure for his
uncompromising methods. His training, in an
army remarkable for that attribute, was
exhausting. He commanded troops who, once
they had been separated from women and the
wine gourd, could run five miles and still fight.
Given their efficiency, they were always in the
thick of the battle, often, as in the case of
Pomponius, engaged in snatching victory from
the jaws of defeat, yet, thanks to his iron

discipline and tactical common sense, the 18th's casualties remained relatively low.

The senior commanders generally loathed him; first for the way he questioned their orders, but more seriously for the annoying habit he had of being right. Time and again he informed them that they were fighting a war which required lightly armed, mobile forces, backed by a powerful cavalry arm, or one with high-built towers and ballistae to destroy and overcome fortifications. And he gave each new senator the same message; there was only one way to actually stop the war, and that was to go beyond the pastoral tribes who inhabited the frontier and attack the hill forts of the interior, starting with Pallentia.

The determined ones, already aware of this, would nod sagely, before they looked at the problem. Certainly, they would lay plans and make arrangements, but, with only a year to make their mark, the idea evaporated as the weeks of preparation slipped into months. Aquila watched the process with a jaundiced eye, until the day came when he and the men under his command were ordered to attack a softer target. No senator wanted to go home with nothing, and that led to a great deal of hard, brutal fighting; it also made a bad situation worse.

With a really lazy general it sufficed to accuse some innocent tribe of revolt, sack their camps, steal their wealth and sell the people into slavery. The idea that the system was corrupt had first occurred to Aquila before he ever set foot in Spain. Little of what he had observed since did anything to change his opinion: that the Republic was a rich man's pasture, from which the mass of citizens were excluded.

The day she found out that her son might have survived, Claudia could not contain herself. All her normal reserves deserted her. Sextius, full of concern, found her weeping, not aware that these were tears of joy, mixed with the fear that this was yet another false trail, but, as ever, he was concerned with appearances. What would his host, Cassius Barbinus, say if he emerged from his bedchamber with his wife red-eyed from crying? Then, remembering the reputation of his fellow-senator, he smirked; the old satyr would probably approve, assuming that Sextius had ill-used Claudia. Doubtless, with such a gossip the story of his marital debauchery would be all over Rome in a flash.

Dinner was a trial; Claudia wanted nothing to do with food, she wanted to go back to see Annius Dabo on his farm, to ask him more about

Piscius, his father, a man whose ashes had long since been scattered in the wind. Not that the son was very forthcoming; he had given her a name, a bit of a description; an age, younger than Annius, that placed this Aquila near the right year. She knew that this boy had left the farm with some soldiers many years before, heading for Sicily, but there was little else; no mention of that golden charm she had wound round his ankle on the night of his birth, the eagle that would positively identify him.

'The name,' she said, not aware that she had spoken out loud.

'Sorry, my dear?' said Sextius, while Cassius Barbinus and the other guests looked at her strangely.

'It's nothing.'

Claudia forced herself to smile, but in her heart she was thinking that Aquila was an unusual name for a child. Yet you might choose that name if something about the infant led you to do so.

Mancinus dragged his eyes away from the gold eagle round the senior centurion's neck. For reasons he could not understand, this object unnerved him; come to that, the owner got under his skin merely for the way he looked at his commanding general.

'I want you to take a small force and reconnoitre this fort. I intend to invest it and I want up-to-date intelligence. And I will move the army to a forward area to be ready, away from the camp and its comforts.'

Mancinus pointed to Pallentia, clearly marked on the map before him. Aquila leant forward, the decorations that adorned his tunic flashing in the light from the lamp. His charm swung free, so he took it in his hand to hold it out of the way. Mancinus, now that he could not see it, felt relieved, but that did little to dent his curiosity. It was very Celtic in appearance, very likely the property of some rich Iberian chieftain. That was what he wanted, a cartload of similar trophies to take back to Rome.

'Even a small force should be a tribune's command,' said Aquila.

The senator was annoyed, and not for the first time. Terentius seemed to be totally unaware of the respect due to a man of his rank. He sought to put him in his place, quite unaware of the pit he was digging for himself.

'None of the men I brought out with me have the necessary experience.'

Aquila looked at him without speaking, but the glare said it all; the wisdom of arriving in Spain, every year, with a whole new batch of tribunes, was the question in his eyes. Mancinus was thinking that those same tribunes were fools; they should never have elected this man as *primus pilus*. He was unaware that he would have faced a mutiny from his soldiers if they had dared appoint anyone else. Aquila Terentius might wear the golden eagle on his neck, but to the rankers of the 18th it was just as much their talisman as his. The legionaries had seen him kiss it just before a fight, watched him go into situations where no man had the right to survive and emerge with barely a scratch; take cohort after cohort through the enemy lines without loss, and damn tribunes, legates, quaestors and generals openly for their stupidity.

He kept them fed and warm where the means allowed, and never left a comrade to die if there was any chance of rescue. And then, to temper his power, there was Fabius, who debunked his 'uncle' at every turn, and acted as a conduit for any man with a grievance. Little flogging occurred in Aquila's legion unless it involved the theft of another man's goods and no one could remember anyone being broken at the wheel. Discipline was tight, and all the more effective for being, in the main, self-imposed. He was a paragon, and all the more unwelcome in the tent of a poltroon because of it.

Mancinus struggled to hold the stare, then coughed and turned away, silently cursing the horns of his personal dilemma. He had come here, like the others, anticipating easy conquests and personal gain, and on the way it had looked simple. Break an alliance with a tribe that had already submitted to Rome, kill their warrior menfolk and enslave the rest; demand a triumph to display your booty and retire to a life of ease, interspersed with a little politics. Quintus Cornelius had done it, as had practically every commander in the ten years since, and the Senate, for all the huffing and puffing of some members, had usually left well alone. The majority howled down the cries of the few with honour that these men should be impeached, and used procedural motions to nullify the machinations of the new juries manned by the knights.

But that was the problem; the war had dragged on too long. The siren voices were growing ·louder, demanding results from a conflict that drained the resources of the state while it enriched the generals. His predecessors had swept things pretty clean, so that all the tribes with anything worth taking now occupied heavily fortified positions and refused to deal with Roman proconsuls. Mancinus had to satisfy the Senate, as well as make his own mark; if there was no other way to achieve his aim, he would have to attack this fortress.

'Might I suggest that I take a pair of the new tribunes along? It will be good for them.'

The consul turned back to look as the other man stood upright. Aquila was a foot taller than him with closely cropped hair, red-gold against his tanned face. He had as many scars as decorations, but it was the eyes that commanded attention. They pinned you like an unlucky fly, demanding that you pay heed to any words he uttered. It was as though Aquila were the general and noble Mancinus a mere ranker.

The senator sniffed loudly. 'How can I ask a tribune to take orders from you?'

'Just ask them if they want to stay alive, General.'

He had already thought of a pair he wanted to take; the pick of a pretty poor bunch, twin brothers, and he had a definite suspicion that one of them was a pederast. But Gnaeus Calvinus kept his hands to himself, and showed proper care for the troops he commanded, never putting his comfort before theirs. His brother Publius also had all the makings of a proper soldier, being physically tough, and he led from the front during training. As a new tribune, he had quietly stopped the habitual ribbing that anyone in his position was subjected to by choosing the toughest man in his unit, taking him to a quiet spot, and beating the living daylights out of him.

'Besides,' Aquila continued, 'the two I have in mind don't seem the type to stand on their dignity.'

'You have in mind!'

The centurion was not the least bit abashed at his general's reaction. 'They seem the most promising. Better they learn now than that they learn too late. If you want to go into battle with even your best men floundering around, wondering what to do, then deny my request.'

'So you're going to be ordered about by a peasant?' asked Gaius Trebonius, as he watched the Calvinus twins preparing to leave.

'I'd like to see you call him that to his face,' replied Gnaeus.

'Fancy him, do we?'

Publius reacted angrily. 'You will oblige me, Gaius, by keeping quiet.'

'It's just as well,' lisped Trebonius. 'I don't think your men, even the roughest and toughest, would be too keen to go off to a quiet place with Gnaeus. I think that they'd rather take you.'

'That's another thing I don't want talked about.'

Trebonius laughed. 'Too late, my friend. What you did to that ranker is common gossip in the camp. Mind, I wouldn't try anything on Aquila Terentius, either of you.'

'Will you shut your mouth!' said Gnaeus quietly, who felt that having endured such a ribbing all his life, he deserved some peace.

Trebonius pouted. 'You better hurry, dears, your peasant will be getting restless.'

The dust of North Africa was no more endearing than the snows of Gallia Cisaplina, though Marcellus was fortunate to occupy a villa that overlooked the sea, so that the breeze took some of the heat out of the noonday sun. This was his fourth provincial posting in ten years, each one interrupted by a very brief sojourn in Rome. He had borne these travels stoically, having realised, after the expiry of his duties in the north, that Quintus was inadvertently doing him a service. Having held posts in Macedonia, Syria and now here in Utica, his knowledge of the problems of governing the Roman domains, which would have been superficial and second-hand had he stayed in the city, was comprehensive and personal. His understanding of the law, endlessly honed in the trivia of far-flung courts, would be unrivalled should he ever find himself pleading a case in Rome.

Each day he rose before dawn, carrying out his own exercises before the sun could make such effort intolerable. First, to warm his muscles, he would wrestle. The bout would begin gently enough, but would soon take on all aspects of a true contest, since Marcellus only employed opponents who had a good chance of beating him. This would be followed by practice with javelin, spear and short sword, the wooden posts he used for these shuddering with the weight of the blows he delivered. Finally, a swim in the sea, followed by a dousing in fresh water, would prepare him for his breakfast.

Then he would meet with his son's tutors, both Greeks and both strict, to check on the progress of their studies, martial and educational. After a brief word with Claudanilla he would mount his chariot, taking the straight road to the provincial city, using that to put his animals through their paces. Locals had grown used to this quaestor who, every morning at the same hour, flew past them, lashing his whip above the heads of his black, foam-flecked horses.

Here in Africa, he had responsibilities that transcended what had gone before. Avidius Probis, the proconsul to whom he served as second in command, was the wrong type of man for government. He hated effort, preferring instead the luxury that this province, which had once been Carthage, provided. Avidius had also taken a Numidian wife, Inoboia, one of the many sisters of the king, Massina.

This had cemented relations with the man who ruled the lands to the south, all the way to the Atlas Mountains, but the other effect was less positive; the governor tended now to favour local interests over that of the Republic and he had hinted that, once his term of office expired, he would probably settle in Utica, since Inoboia disliked the idea of living in Italy – first, because it was not home, and secondly, because of the prejudices which her near-black colouring would inevitably create amongst the notoriously snobbish Roman elite.

Marcellus found himself doing both his own work and that of his nominal superior. Most quaestors, faced with such a situation, would have lobbied to have him replaced. Not he! Marcellus was governor himself in all but name; provided he deferred to Avidius in those matters about which he cared, and treated his royal Numidian wife with the respect due to her rank, he could do very much as he pleased. This responsibility did not end at the Utican border. In the name of the Republic, the quaestor was required to treat both with the King of Numidia, as well as the ruler of Mauritania, people who supplied paid cavalry to the armies of the empire. And the time was rapidly approaching when he could stand for office in Rome itself. He would do it with Quintus's help if it were available, without if necessary. That would, of course, make it harder. So, from time to time, his mind would turn to that chest of documents left to him by his father.

Many of the men named in them had died in the last ten years, but most were still alive, probably still committing the kind of misdemeanours that Lucius had uncovered. If all else failed, he would use that information to assist his election to the aedileship.

Aquila set out with the two tribunes, accompanied by twenty of his fittest men. They left the encampment after dark and headed south, this to avoid the prying eyes of those engaged in watching the activities of the Roman garrison. An hour before dawn they turned inland, climbing up through the hills, their movements guided by strong moonlight. A wooded copse provided shelter as the sun rose and the party ate their cold food by a trickling brook. The smell of pine needles was strong and the copse hummed with insects. They took off the bulk of their uniforms, breastplates, greaves and helmets and threw them into the extra cloaks that Aquila had made them bring along.

'Do we bury them?' asked Publius.

Aquila shook his head. 'No. Very little sunlight gets in here, so fresh-dug earth will be obvious for a long time and anyone spotting them will be bound to dig them up.' He looked up into the trees. 'Tie the bundles tight and hide them high in the trees. Up there, if anyone sees them at all, they'll look like beehives.'

'What if the person who does spot them collects honey?'

'Then they'll get a surprise,' he replied with a smile, 'and since not many of our enemies are given to honey gathering, I doubt we'll be in too much danger. Now, let's look at our route.'

They had been studying the map for two days, so they knew the way, but Aquila was concerned about how they would use the terrain. Patiently, standing at the very edge of the trees, he explained to the youngsters how they would use the hillsides, clumps of trees and bushes and the shadow caused by the position of the sun to minimise the risk of being observed. Gnaeus wondered why he was bothering, since he was there to lead them, then he realised that this strange self-contained man was going out of his way to teach them everything he thought they should know, and what he said could not have been further from the rigid protocols of formal combat with hand or weapon that they had learnt on the Campus Martius.

'You can't move in open country without being observed, and people don't actually have to see you to know you're around. The skyline has to be avoided, for, as a silhouette, you are too obvious, but even down below that is the case. Every bird you startle tells an enemy where you are, just as the silence of the animals will let them know you're coming, minutes before you arrive. But the same applies to them, so keep a sharp lookout for unusual movements. We, ourselves, will move at a steady, gentle pace. I will go ahead to a point where you can see me, then the men will follow in pairs and you can bring up the rear.'

He smiled to take the sting out of his next words. 'By the time you two blunder along in our path, every fly will be used to a human presence.'

'Meaning we won't startle too many birds,' said Publius.

'That's right, and by the time we return I fully intend that you'll take the point, while I'll be bringing up the rear.'

'And if we are seen?' asked Gnaeus.

'Let's hope it's not someone we'll have to fight.' Aquila turned back into the trees, followed by his twin trainees. They saw that the soldiers had dug a shallow hole and filled it with water. They were now busy adding the earth they had dug up. 'Smear your smocks and the metal parts of your weapons with mud. It'll make you harder to see.'

It took a full week to reach Pallentia, by which time the Calvinus twins wondered if they were actually cut out for life in the army. Not that they alone had suffered; filthy and gaunt, there was no way now to tell they were Romans. It was just that their inferiors seemed more able to cope than they, but during that time they grew to understand Aquila Terentius, and to appreciate some of the problems that beset the Roman army in Spain.

They knew there had been casualties in this ongoing war, but neither had realised that they numbered well over one hundred thousand men lost in the last twenty years – more than half of them Roman citizens. Aquila was careful to point out that the men they were with now would probably be soldiers regardless of the dilectus; most, indeed, had slipped through the property qualifications for service and acquired the right to serve as *princeps* because of experience.

It was hard to argue with the centurion's case that neither Rome, nor her allies, could afford losses at the rate they were suffering and expect to field armies sufficient to hold all the frontiers; that the solution lay in the removal of the archaic class- and property-based system of recruitment: if you owned land, you were eligible for service; if you were penniless, you were passed over. This would allow the farmers to tend their land, lessen the Republic's dependence on imported corn, and end the abuse by which rich men bought up derelict farmland for ranching, the land having been let go to the bad because the men needed to tend it were serving as legionaries.

Little did they know that he was expressing the very things that had ruined his adopted parents. Clodius had been a legionary and had served the Republic of which he was a citizen; the reward was ruin, because when he returned from service, the land had gone to rack – Fulmina on her own could not tend it – while he lacked the funds for implements or seed to bring his land back to fruitfulness, and, in truth, it would have broken him to try. The Terentius farm had been sold to

Cassius Barbinus and the already filthy rich senator had turned it into pasture for sheep and cattle. Reduced to a gimcrack hut by a stream, and work as a day labourer, no wonder Clodius had agreed to serve in place of his prosperous neighbour Piscius Dabo, when the latter was suddenly, and unexpectedly, called back to the colours.

'And where will we get our soldiers?' asked Publius.

'When was the last time you looked in the streets of Rome? It's bursting with men. So is every city in Italy.'

'That useless mob. They're a rabble,' said Gnaeus.

'Wrong, Tribune.' He waved his arm around to include the men he had brought along with him. 'They're probably just like us. I mean no disrespect, but any man here, given a chance, could hold your rank. All this talk of needing noble blood to lead men into battle is a lot of patrician shit.'

Aquila grinned, noticing how their loyalties fought with their logic. He stood up, making his way to the crest of the hill they would have to cross to avoid a ten-league detour. 'But we could talk all day and change nothing. The old windbags in the Senate have got it all sewn up.

Personally, I couldn't care if someone lopped off their heads.'

'And what about being governed?'

'Would you use that word to describe what we've got now? Go ask the men in the auxiliary legions what they think. Those togate bastards are happy to spill their blood, but they won't even give them citizenship.'

Publius adopted a bland look. 'You are aware, Aquila Terentius, that our father is a senator?'

''Course I am. Just as, in time, you'll be one too. What worries me is that people like us will still be here in Spain doing drawings of places like Pallentia. Let's move, quickly. We'll do the crest one at a time and through the trees.'

The report they eventually submitted to Mancinus, ostensibly a tribunate one, did little to please him. He had called a full conference of his officers to discuss the prospects, placing Aquila, the true author, well to the rear so as to avoid his negative interventions, but that failed to work, since the Calvinus twins, who had taken Aquila's observations and turned them into the proper, educated Latin form, seemed to share his pessimism. The general was now regretting the obligation to their father that had manoeuvred them onto his complement of officers, let alone the fact that he had allowed them to go on the reconnaissance, but his biggest mistake had been to ask Gnaeus Calvinus to read the report, assuming that he would put a gloss on matters to please his patron.

'So, to conclude, sir, there's insufficient forage and food in the vicinity to supply the whole army. We will be required to build a road and at least three bridges, all of which will have to be held so that supplies can be maintained, if Pallentia can't be taken by direct assault, which in our opinion it cannot.'

'Why not?' demanded Mancinus's quaestor and second-in-command, Gavius Aspicius.

Gnaeus gave him an odd look. Gavius had read the report so he knew as well as anyone that the place would withstand an army if those within the ramparts were numerous and well fed, so the only hope was a siege. Carefully Gnaeus went over the arguments again, returning in due course to the proposed solution. The hill fort had a supply of water that good engineering could divert. It was the one fault in the comprehensive system of defences that Aquila had spotted. The Celts, not themselves as talented in that field as the Romans, had failed to secure it absolutely.

But the method of cutting the supply would

involve the engineers working very close to the earth bastions that jutted out from the main walls. If the Romans gathered to assault that section, the defenders would gather to oppose them. Aquila's idea was an attack elsewhere, not designed to breach the defences but to hold their enemies at that point. This would allow a second group to engage the lightly protected alternative and damn the water supply. Then Mancinus could sit back and wait for the cistern inside the hill fort to dry up. Once that happened, the defenders would have to come out and fight, just to try and restore the supply. If they did, they would face defeat against any enemy who knew exactly where they would strike. Failure to do anything would see them expire from thirst within the walls.

'And how long will all that take?' barked the quaestor, clearly as displeased by the prospect of a siege as his commander.

The voice from the rear made them all spin round to look at Aquila. 'If you can tell how much water they store and predict that we'll have no rain, I'm sure we can provide an answer. With luck it will be weeks. If not, it could take a year.'

Gavius Aspicius turned back to face Mancinus. 'This is nonsense. These are barbarians we're facing. I say that one determined assault, delivered quickly, will breach the defences.' A murmur of agreement came from the senior officers present, all of whom had a vested interest in a quick result. 'If we stop to build a road, to construct bridges, they'll have weeks to get the place ready and, since we can't be sure that the other tribes will not attack, guarding that route will deplete our forces.'

Aspicius stepped forward and swept his arm in an arc over the map. 'But if we force-march the entire army to Pallentia, and press home the attack without resting, we'll catch them unawares.'

The general was nodding, since these were the kind of words he wanted to hear, and so were most of the others, either through a conviction that Aspicius was right, or merely a desire to agree with their patron. The quaestor, ramming home his point, slammed his fist down on the table to emphasise the point. 'That's the lesson we want to teach these tribesmen. That Rome can destroy them whenever we have the will.'

Mancinus stood, chest puffed out, clearly showing his spirits had been raised by those stirring words. 'Gentlemen, it is time to sound the horns, time to march, and time to let our foes know that their years of causing turmoil are at an end. Call the priests and let us look for an auspicious day to begin our campaign.'

Unseen, Aquila marched out of the tent in disgust, knowing that, for no purpose, more men were going to die.

CHAPTER FOURTEEN

'Such a journey would exhaust me, Marcellus,' said Avidius, waving his hand. 'The heat, the dust.'

'Is it wise that your wife should go to Citra without you, sir?' asked Marcellus. 'Will not King Estrobal take such a thing amiss?'

The governor waved aside his quaestor's objection. 'He would be foolish to do so. I will expect both you and my wife to inform him of my intention to retire here in Utica, and since you, Marcellus, will be the one returning to Rome, it is better that you're the one he converses with. It will be your duty to tell him that this continual fighting with Mauritania must cease. We will also want to know whom he designated as his successor, for that is something Rome must approve. You would, in any case, be carrying any messages he wants to send to the Senate, one of which is, I hope, a promise of more Numidian cavalry for Spain.'

'Does your good wife agree with this, sir?'

'A good wife, Marcellus Falerius, does what she's told!'

The younger man flushed slightly. In a small place like Utica, the doings of those in power tended to become common gossip. His own household did not escape scrutiny, so it was well known that he had a running feud with his wife about the way their children were being raised. Claudanilla sought, at every turn, to temper the harsh regime that he had instituted. The Greek pedagogue he had employed complained that if he punished the sons, Lucius and Cassius, then he immediately had to face the wrath of their mother. The tutor engaged to teach them martial arts sought to keep them from so much as a scratch, clearly an impossible goal for youngsters engaged in boxing, wrestling and sword fighting. The boys knew, and took advantage of this, and with the head of the household absent for the whole day it was becoming increasingly difficult to maintain discipline.

'Besides,' Avidius continued, 'the Lady Iniobia can assist you. She knows everyone at Estrabal's court and I'm sure her voice, added to yours, will carry extra weight.'

Both men knew that the governor was engaged in a shocking dereliction of duty, but since

Avidius had decided not to return to Rome, he cared little for what his peers thought. He maintained that the coastal strip of Africa, and great heat tempered by a sea breeze, suited his old bones. Marcellus could have refused, though when he weighed matters in the balance, he knew Avidius would carry any blame for failure, while he, delivering his own report, would garner any credit for a successful mission.

'Then it would be best if we depart within the week.'

'Nonsense, Marcellus,' cried Avidius. 'The Lady Iniobia is the wife of a Roman proconsul. She's also a princess of the Numidian royal house. She cannot travel in anything less than regal splendour.'

That took a month to prepare, during which Marcellus fretted at the continual delay, while any suggestion that he go ahead with a small troop of cavalry was rejected. Finally the caravan was ready, hundreds of camels and porters, dozens of litters, with an escort consisting of almost the entire garrison. There was the princess herself, travelling in a huge double litter borne by relays of a dozen Numidian guards, along with her household, which consisted of maids, cooks, seamstresses and a personal astrologer. The tents necessary to accommodate such an exalted personage followed on a train of carts, along with the servants to raise and lower them, as well as the household slaves who would see to any cares not already covered. The whole assembly depressed Marcellus; rather than being pleased by its grandeur, he was given to thinking how much more appropriate it would be for a plainly clad Roman senator, carrying his rods of gubernatorial office, to call upon a client king unescorted. Nothing could underline the *imperium* of Rome more than that.

As the only two elevated personages in this caravanserai, Marcellus and the Lady Iniobia dined together and, claiming precedence over the quaestor, she declined to use an upright chair, reclining on a couch just like him. She was an attractive woman, much younger than her husband, and in the lamplight, which made her ebony skin shine, it was easy to imagine that he could go beyond the bounds of prudence. That he was at liberty to do so was made plain on their first evening, with Iniobia alluding to the fact that her husband's inertia was not confined to his official duties. This caused no embarrassment, since the governor's wife left him several escape routes, nor was she offended that he used them, showing remarkable sensibility to the constraints of his office.

Instead, without ever once alluding directly to mutual attraction, they became friends. Her conversation was fluent and entertaining, and during the journey Marcellus learnt a great deal about the northern littoral of Africa, of the various peoples, their rulers, their past and the future they looked to. He was forced to see the journey, regardless of his frustration at the slow pace of progress, as a pleasant interlude in his life. On arrival at Citra they parted, she to seek out family and friends, he to the quarters assigned to him as a visiting dignitary, where his first task was to have the naked female slaves sent to bathe him replaced by males. This was nothing to do with prudery – they were striking young women and his for the taking – but let such indulgence get back to Rome and someone might use it to diminish him.

He and the princess came together the next day for a joint audience with King Estrobal, where he discovered that the Lady Iniobia, despite her husband's opinion, had little influence with her father, leaving him to diligently carry out all the tasks set him. This mainly consisted in listening patiently while the king blamed every frontier problem on his rival in Mauritania. Having been present when Avidius received an embassy from that country, and taken note to the opposite view, Marcellus suspected both parties to be at fault.

'You must understand, Majesty, that Rome cannot allow conflict on the frontiers of the empire, regardless of where blame lies. We must intervene to put a stop to it, by force if necessary.'

Clearly King Estrobal, in late middle-age and accustomed to due deference, took exception to being so addressed; that was bad enough, but the fact that Avidius had entrusted the task of chastisement to someone else, an inferior, deeply offended him. On the subject of his successor he was adamant; none of his sons was as yet old enough to indicate their ability, though he was prepared to send his eldest boy, Jugurtha, to Rome with a contingent of cavalry.

It was made plain that this in no way favoured him as a potential successor; perhaps, when his other sons had grown to manhood, he would select another. If Marcellus had been the true governor in his own right, he would have said that such an attitude smacked of useless prevarication; that, failing a decision on the succession by the king, Rome might be called upon to make it for him to ensure peaceful continuity. But he lacked the stature to expound such a view and remained silent, though it was the first thing he said to Avidius on his return to Utica.

'I think he declines to name any one of his children for fear of his own life. As long as they are competing with each other for his favour they will not act to remove him. If, as I suspect, we are going to be involved in the choice, sir, might I suggest that King Estrobal be invited to send his other sons to Rome, as well?'

'On what grounds?'

'If they're going to be clients of Rome, it would be wise for them to see the extent of our power. Then they will be less likely to emulate their father and ignore it.'

'Will he not see them as hostages?' asked the governor.

'I hope so, sir. If his entire bloodline is in our hands, he might stop raiding Mauritania.'

'That seems very harsh to me, Marcellus,' Avidius replied, as usual taking the side of the locals against his own kind. 'Let us leave things be.'

'Will that be the recommendation in your final despatch, sir?'

The old man looked at him, and for once Marcellus could see the sense of purpose there that had, at one time, carried him to the consulship. 'It will.'

'I think the boy Jugurtha is too young for command.'

'He is of royal blood, and will be obeyed. Besides, someone of experience is bound to be sent to keep him in check. You're sure my wife will return to Utica with this cavalry?'

'Those were her words, sir. She intimated that with her presence in Citra, the king would bend all his efforts to fulfilling his promise.'

There was a great degree of dissimulation in that reply. The truth was that his wife was happier amongst her own than she was here in Utica, and, having attended several feasts while in the Numidian capital, and having observed her behaviour with some of the noblemen of that city, he fully suspected that she had taken at least one lover. But she had promised him that she would return in time, well aware how her husband would view her continued absence.

'It would have been better if you'd stayed.'

'The Lady Iniobia was quite insistent. I did not have the strength to change her mind.'

'When do you leave for Rome?' Avidius snapped, changing the subject abruptly, making his subordinate wonder if he suspected the truth.

'As soon as your despatch is ready, Excellency.'

He hoped, desperately, that his superior would show more diligence than hitherto in executing that task. If he were delayed for any time he would miss the annual elections for the aedileship. True to his character, Avidius was excessive in that article, so by the time Marcellus and his family landed at Ostia it was too late, but his disappointment at that fact was outweighed by his reaction to the news, brought back to Rome by the Calvinus twins, of what had happened to the army of Mancinus at Pallentia.

'You could see the disaster looming,' said Gnaeus, 'as soon as the first assault failed.'

'Then why didn't Mancinus withdraw?' asked Marcellus.

It was Publius Calvinus who replied. 'Only the gods know that. He had plenty of advice.'

Gnaeus laughed bitterly. 'Most of it bad.'

Marcellus failed to see the joke and his saturnine face was black with anger. 'Twenty thousand Roman troops taken prisoner. He should have fallen on his sword rather than let that happen, and so should every officer he led.'

Publius was stung; it was as if his friend was rebuking him for his own survival. Yet he had told Marcellus everything about the conferences that had taken place before the attack of Pallentia. Mancinus was as impatient as all his predecessors, wanting the spoils and the triumph so badly that military prudence was abandoned.

'Aquila Terentius is the only one to emerge with any real credit. Without him, the 18th would have suffered the same fate. How he got us out of there I don't know.'

'He didn't get you out, Publius. The legate in command did that.'

'That's all you know. If it'd been left to him, our bones would be spread across Iberia. Thank the gods that Aquila Terentius refused to obey his orders.'

'I didn't think I'd ever live to hear a friend of mine praise a centurion for disobeying a legate. To think we studied under the same tutor, and learnt the same lessons, and this is how you speak. Timeon would turn in his grave.'

'You haven't met the man in question!' said Gnaeus, sharply, wondering how Marcellus, who had hated their Greek tutor as much as he, could now talk as though the man was something other than the tyrant with a vine sapling he had been. Ye gods, his old school friend had once boxed the man's ears and been whipped by his father's servants for it. If Marcellus saw his ire, it had no effect on him.

'I think I've met this fellow, years ago,' said Marcellus. 'He was in my cohort on the march to Spain. Tall, red-gold hair and a cocky manner.'

'He has every right to be cocky.'

They all stood at the sound and turned to see the imposing frame of Titus Cornelius filling the doorway. The black hair was now tinged with grey, but the soldierly bearing had survived, so much so that Marcellus was reminded of the first time he had seen his father. He had stood in a doorway too, reminding their tutor, who was about to whip Marcellus, that one day the boy would be his master. The newly elected junior consul looked as tough and determined as ever so the greetings were swift, for he had known these young men since they were children and nor did he have time for pleasantries. He looked hard at the Calvinus twins.

'The first thing I want to know is how, when a whole army was captured, one legion escaped and you two survived?'

'Perhaps we're better soldiers than Mancinus,' said Publius, who was still smarting from the implied rebuke of Marcellus, and refusing to be cowed either by Titus's reputation, or his consular *imperium*.

'I have a pig that meets that criterion.'

'We're here at Marcellus's request, Titus Cornelius,' said Gnaeus. 'We've already made our official report.'

'If what you tell me is to be of any use, I

need to know how you got away.'

'Then you must ask the senior centurion of the 18th Legion, Titus, for it was entirely his doing.'

'Explain!' snapped Titus.

He realised, by the looks on their faces, that his tone offended the Calvinus boys and that they were not going to be browbeaten. Perhaps, in their time in Spain, they had become proper soldiers after all, so he softened his look and added a polite supplication. 'Please?'

'Would it be in order to start at the beginning?' asked Publius.

'Essential,' said Titus, before addressing Marcellus. 'Perhaps we could have the use of a scribe?'

The young men had been talking for nearly an hour, everything they said attesting to the fact that Mancinus was entirely the author of his own misfortunes. They recounted the facts of the original reconnaissance and the way their recommendations had been ignored, of the assaults launched without proper preparation, which had resulted in terrible casualties; of the day when, in front of all the other officers, Aquila Terentius bluntly informed his general that the other tribes were gathering behind him, telling him that if he did not withdraw they faced disaster.

'He was plainly correct,' said Titus without pleasure. 'None of the other senior officers questioned Mancinus's commands?'

'He's not the type to welcome questions,' replied Gnaeus. 'And Gavius Aspicius was egging him on.'

He and Publius, really too junior to take such a risk, had backed Aquila Terentius, but to say so now would sound like special pleading.

'This *primus pilus* seems to be an exceptional person.'

'Does this help?' asked Marcellus, who was a little bored with hearing about this man. The twins thought him a paragon, while he knew him for what he was, an insubordinate menace. Titus looked at the scribe, then at his host and Marcellus immediately sent him away.

'We must wait to see what happens in the house,' Titus replied. 'What I need now is your opinion of what must be done.'

'That's easy,' said Publius. 'Give Aquila enough legions and he'll bring the war to a conclusion in one season.'

Marcellus cut in. 'Please be serious, Publius.'

'He was being serious,' said Gnaeus.

'This fellow has turned your wits. No one is that good. Besides, he's an illiterate peasant, you told me so yourself. You're not seriously suggesting we give command to someone like him?'

'Being serious...' said Titus, with a quizzical expression.

'Pallentia wasn't worth the effort. They knew that we could take it if we wanted, so long as we were willing to enforce a siege. That's why they let Mancinus pass under the yoke and he only chose it because it was the lesser of two evils. He prayed it would fall easily, then he wouldn't be asked why, if he wanted to attack a hill fort, he avoided the real prize.'

'Numantia.' The youngsters nodded. Titus declined to say that he had first recommended an attack on Numantia as a young tribune, when he was not much older than these young men, but he still posed the question, just to see if the answer differed from the conclusions he had reached all those years ago. 'Why?'

Marcellus shot him a swift glance. He knew full well that Titus had been harping on about this for years.

'Because the biggest, the hardest to attack, with the toughest, most numerous tribe of them all, is the Duncani. Their leader has been at odds with the Republic for thirty years, yet he won't come out to fight. Our information is that he hopes we will attack, so that he can inflict a resounding defeat that will spell the end of Roman rule in Hispania. It's a good job he wasn't at Pallentia. He would have put every one of our men to the sword.'

'Could we isolate Numantia?' asked Marcellus. 'If we took all the other forts?'

'We lack the means,' said Gnaeus. 'There are dozens of them now, but there is nothing as formidable as Numantia. Destroy it, raze it to the ground, and the rest will know that they have no chance against Rome. Leave it standing and the war will last another thirty years.'

'Is this the advice of your centurion?' asked Titus.

'No. His advice is to isolate it by making peace with every tribe between Brennos and us, fighting and subduing those we have to, and being lenient with the rest. Once we have made our peace, it must be rigidly maintained, with no back-sliding by avaricious consuls.'

'So, he too is afraid of Numantia?'

'No, Titus, he is not,' insisted Publius. 'He knows as well as anyone it is the key, but he also knows he is under the command of a body of men who will never give anyone the means and the time to take it.'

* * *

'Well, Brother?' said Titus, in a non-committal way, as Quintus put aside what Marcellus's scribe had recorded.

They were usually guarded in each other's presence, and were so now, though the elder brother had kept his promise to Claudia by helping Titus to the consulship. Quintus had provided his support with little grace, yet now he was grateful for that pressure, in a way he had not anticipated. Mancinus had been appointed to Spain by him as reward for his senatorial support; now, because of the actions of the fool, the whole careful structure of personal power he had built up since the death of Lucius Falerius threatened to come down about his ears.

In the same period, Titus had risen to become Rome's most successful soldier, having fought all around the Middle Sea wherever trouble threatened: endless campaigning that had never risen, anywhere, to the heights of an all-out war. Because of this he had one precious asset, a record of unbroken success: Quintus had kept him away from Spain, that bottomless pit of wealth being reserved for his uncritical supporters. Now that things had gone so badly wrong, he needed his brother to pull his chestnuts out of the fire. It was to Titus's credit that he took no advantage of this.

'Impeachment is too good for him,' said Quintus. 'The cretin should be thrown from the Tarpeian Rock.'

Titus could not resist a little jibe. 'Agreed, but Mancinus has powerful friends in the Senate.'

'Who will cover their heads with shame when they read this.'

He waved the scroll that Titus had brought from Marcellus's house, more damning than the official report, while entirely ignoring the fact that, as a 'friend' of Mancinus, he was talking about himself – so much so that Titus was moved to wonder at the kind of man his brother had become. He seemed to be able to shift his ground without effort, while all the time prattling on about his principles. Quintus had not always been like that: indeed there had been a time when Titus looked up to him as a worthy elder brother. Yet that had changed and it could be dated from the time, immediately after the death of Aulus at Thralaxas, when Lucius Falerius had drawn Quintus into his orbit. The prospect of power had seduced Quintus to the point where he had actually embraced Vegetius Flaminus, the man responsible for the death of his own father.

'So we move to impeach him?' he asked, well aware that Quintus would guess he was pursuing his own agenda. If Mancinus could be brought before a court, so too could Vegetius Flaminus, even after all these years. 'And this time you can leave him to his fate. That will appease the knights.'

Quintus frowned, evidence that he was aware of the trap. He had still not forgiven Titus for the statute on *Equites* participating in juries, so the danger was neatly side-stepped.

'It's worse than that, Brother. This is not a matter for a court, senatorial or otherwise. The *Comitia Centuriata* is clamouring for the right to try him in open session. Egged on by the knights, of course. They don't trust us to do the proper thing.'

Titus pulled a wry face. 'I wonder why?'

'Once let them convict a senator, and we'll all be at risk!'

It was not the time for Titus to say that, unlike Quintus, he was prepared to take his chances, yet he was curious about his brother's attitude, for he seemed unconcerned about the threat from the knights, or the representatives of the tribes that made up the Comitia. He was clearly more worried about the views of his fellow senators.

'Do you have a plan to head them off?'

'Oh, yes,' Quintus replied, smiling for the first time since his brother had arrived. 'All we have to do is threaten to try the tribunes who served with

Mancinus as well. Quite a few of them are the sons of knights.'

'So what you're saying is this; for the first time in living memory, the Senate is so angry it's prepared to condemn one of its own?' Quintus nodded slowly. 'Do you want me to move the motion for impeachment?'

'Not for impeachment, Brother. I think the loss of a whole Roman army calls for something a little more – how shall I say? – permanent.'

'What if I were to say to you, Brother, that I'm not prepared to go to Spain unless you agree to do something about Vegetius Flaminus?'

'I would say you are mad. I've arranged proconsular powers that have nothing to do with being a serving consul. You have as long as you like and can ask for what troops you want.'

'With those powers, why don't you go yourself?'

'You know the answer to that as well as I do. I dare not leave Rome after what Mancinus has done.'

He had to press; Titus had him in a position that would be unlikely to recur at some future date, either because his brother was too feeble, or too secure. Quintus was weakened by what had happened at Pallentia, so being absent represented too much of a risk, even if a final victory in Spain was the best way to restore his power. Time was the problem, and the risk of his enemies making mischief while he was out of Rome, was, for him, too great. The only other people he could send might garner enough credit to prove a threat on their return, but, if another Cornelii pulled off the ultimate success, he could claim most of the benefits.

'I'm sorry, Quintus.'

'Doesn't family honour mean anything to you?'

Titus started to explode, but his brother saw it coming and, consummate as ever, spoke quickly to head it off. 'I've always intended to bring down Vegetius Flaminus, but I need the power to do so. If you can win in Spain, I'll be unassailable.'

'I want your sworn word, Brother.'

'By any god you wish,' replied Quintus, reaching over to grasp his brother's forearm.

Titus dined with the family that night, witnessing an exchange between Claudia and her husband that left him wondering what she was up to, for his stepmother had changed. Physically, of course, since even her great beauty was showing signs of her age, but it was more in her attitude. Gone was the cynical smile, and the slightly barbed comments that were so effective in puncturing pomposity. This had been replaced by a stern quality, almost entirely lacking in humour, so that even her eyes, which Titus recalled as dancing, had a more determined look. Certainly that was the case now, when she was trying to persuade her dolt of a husband to do something that clearly did not appeal to him.

'Sicily is a province,' she insisted.

'I know that,' replied Sextius, who was not really trying to dissuade her. Part of him was wondering why she had chosen to bring up the subject with Titus present, but mostly he was wondering how he could contrive to stay on the Italian mainland and send Claudia over to the island.

'I think the comparison would add weight to the survey, the difference between Rome and a province. Are more children exposed? Do they behave in the same way, taking them and rearing them? After all, the island is very different. It's almost entirely Greek.'

'Of course it is,' said Sextius, for the first time showing real interest.

'Are you still engaged in that same survey, Claudia?' asked Titus. She swung round to look at him, giving him such a glare that he changed the subject. 'Did I tell you, by the way, I've asked Marcellus Falerius to join me in Spain?'

* * *

'Let us just say that it would please me more if you leave that young man, and his future, to me.'

Titus emitted a short laugh. 'You've taken care of his future to date. He's been sent to every dead-end posting in the empire.'

'I don't want to risk him.'

Titus knew that was probably a lie. 'It's a long-standing promise.'

Quintus's face took on that sly look. 'But did Marcellus remind you of it, Titus?'

'No, he did not.'

Titus was not honouring a promise to Marcellus, but one made to his father. Lucius had been cunning; having done Titus a service, forcing Quintus to aid him in gaining the required junior magistries needed for a successful career, he had asked for nothing specific in return. He knew that the younger Cornelii would decline to do anything he might consider questionable, but he had trusted him to do what was right when the time came, and now old Lucius's words made sense. Titus could see him in his mind's eye now; as thin as a rake, with a high domed forehead to attest to his intelligence, and that slight smile with which he had delivered what he sought in return for his assistance.

'You will do me a service, but it won't feel that you're doing anything for me at all.'

How could the old man have seen so far ahead? How could he have known the way his brother would behave? Getting Marcellus out from under the yoke which Quintus was using to keep him down was the repayment of that obligation, and, as Lucius had also known, one he was happy to make.

'If Marcellus did not remind you of it, then surely you could let it lapse.'

Titus fought to control his anger. At another time he would have let fly, but right now he was constrained by the need to avoid giving Quintus an excuse. Given a sliver of an escape route, Quintus would renege on the vow he had made him take at the Temple of Jupiter Maximus, a vow that would finally provide vengeance for his father and the legionaries who had perished with him at Thralaxas.

But he had to say something to make his displeasure obvious. 'Sometimes I wonder if we are bred from the same father.'

'I am sure you will be brave, Husband,' said Claudanilla, rubbing her distended belly with one hand. 'Though I would rather you were here when your child is born.'

'He will be as sturdy as his brothers, Claudanilla. You have no fear in that respect.'

Here, in his own house, Marcellus recalled his wedding night and the taking of the virginity of the then slight creature. That was gone, first through age and secondly through the bearing of children. He rarely did his duty by his wife, but she had a natural fecundity that had initially shocked him. Having had three children, two boys and a girl, four miscarriages and one still-born infant, his wife was round and maternal. Her breasts were no longer underdeveloped, quite the reverse, they matched the wide hips and spreading waist that Claudanilla kept hidden under her voluminous garments. Marcellus, for once, made no allusion to that, for he was in a state of near-elation, finally going somewhere to fight a war. Yet, happy as he was, he could not leave Claudanilla without a warning.

'I have said this before, but I'll say it again, since I know you take some advantage of my absences. You are not to interfere in the boys' schooling, do you understand?'

Claudanilla's plump face took on a look of pure misery. 'It is hard for a mother to stand by and watch her children so cruelly used.'

'If their teacher sees fit to punish them, then that is his duty. How are they to become soldiers if they're not allowed the odd wound? If you are tempted to interfere, then think of me. I had the same kind of education, and it has not done me any harm.'

Claudanilla dropped her eyes, lest Marcellus see that she disagreed; to her he was anything but normal. Immediately on his return to Rome, he visited the ranch where he had installed the Greek girl, just before he made several visits to the Vispanii house – visits that always took place when Gallus was absent. Clearly, he derived little pleasure from these; they always left him bad-tempered and hurtful, as though whatever happened made him want to take his revenge out on her. In many respects, she was glad he was going away.

CHAPTER FIFTEEN

———◆———

Mancinus was determined to brazen it out, though he must have known that being superseded by the brother of Quintus Cornelius boded ill for his future. Titus listened, without comment, to the litany of excuses. Everyone else was to blame but him. Titus could ask the priests, who had cast the corn before the sacred chickens and pronounced, confidently, that the omens were propitious for the venture.

'Did you take the priests and their chickens with you?'

Mancinus gave Titus a black look, as though offended that he could make jokes at a time like this. 'Of course I didn't.'

'Pity, Senator, because if you had, they might have foreseen that, like your legions, their bellies would be empty.' Titus stood up, towering over the other man. 'It might have also been more help if you'd taken some responsibility upon yourself, but no, you blame the state of the army, the poor quality of the information you were given...'

The superseded senator cut in, his expression one of innocent protest. 'The man I sent to reconnoitre the place said it would fall easily.'

'Fool,' replied Titus, shaking his head. 'Too many people survived, Mancinus. They made you eat the grass on the battlefield, then let you go. What did you promise them in return?'

'What else could I say? I promised Rome would pay an indemnity for the lives of our soldiers.'

'Without knowing that it's true?'

'What if it's a lie? Who cares about these Iberian scum?'

Titus walked to the entrance to the tent. Marcellus and the Calvinus twins stood outside, beside the lictors that accompanied the consul everywhere. Slightly behind them, purposefully standing apart, stood a tall centurion, his uniform covered in decorations. From his height and the colour of his hair, Titus assumed that he was the man he had heard so much about. Publius caught his eye, and gave him a quick nod to indicate that the praetorian guards had been changed; Mancinus's men had gone, to be replaced by those chosen by Aquila Terentius.

Titus indicated to the centurion that he should

enter and Aquila did so, halting at attention in the middle of the tent. The salute was sharp and loud, but plainly directed away from his titular commander and it was obvious by the glare on Mancinus's face that he had noticed the deliberate insult. Titus then called in the lictors who held his symbols of office and represented his consular power. Satisfied with the arrangements, he put his hand into the folds of his toga and produced a tightly wound scroll, which he opened slowly.

'In my capacity as consul and by order of the Senate of the Roman Republic, I hereby relieve you of all responsibility for the operations in this province.'

Mancinus had been sitting bolt upright; he now let his shoulders sag, as though finally relieved to hear the words. 'I shall be glad to be back in Rome.'

'I don't think so,' said Titus evenly.

The seated man's face took on a foxy look. 'They won't impeach me, Titus Cornelius. There are too many skeletons in the cupboard for that. If I go down, you can be sure that your brother will come with me.'

'You're right, Mancinus, no one is going to impeach you.' He turned to Aquila. 'Centurion, take this man into custody. He is to speak with no one.'

The man was halfway out of his chair. 'You can't imprison me, I'm a senator.'

'No one is going to imprison you, Mancinus.' The look of confusion did not last long, being swiftly replaced by a look of absolute terror as Titus finished giving Aquila his orders. 'Take this scum to Pallentia under a sign of truce. Tell the inhabitants that he lied to them. Rome will not pay them an indemnity, but if they swear a treaty of peace we will leave them be.'

'And then, General?' asked Aquila, clearly intrigued.

'Then hand him over as a gift from the Senate in Rome. They can do with him what they wish.'

'It's not envy,' Marcellus insisted. 'In fact, I'm full of admiration for your centurion.'

'He's a tribune now, remember,' Gnaeus replied.

'All right,' sighed Marcellus. 'Your tribune.'

'You sound as though you don't think he deserves it?'

'Perhaps he does, then again perhaps not.' Marcellus heard the exasperated intake of breath and spoke quickly. 'He's brave, yes. A good soldier...'

'Brilliant.'

Marcellus merely nodded. 'But it's the manner

of his speech that rankles. He showed Titus Cornelius scant respect.'

Gnaeus shrugged. 'He has little time for senators. He's seen too many who would steal the eyes out of your head.'

'Are those his words?'

'They are. He added that, having stolen the eyes, they'd likely come back for the holes.'

Marcellus had been quietly fuming since the conference, and he knew precisely why. Despite his anger at the way it was delivered, the advice that Aquila had given Titus was exceedingly sound. He knew the terrain, the language, and had a comprehensive knowledge of the Celt-Iberian tribes and knew how to fight them, as well.

'They've learnt these last years. You'll be offered no pitched battles in open country. Neither will you be allowed to march anywhere without being ambushed. Even the whole army's not safe. They know they can't defeat Rome in strength, but they can discourage us by drawing the legions into difficult and dangerous country.'

Marcellus cut in. 'Perhaps with a little cunning we could trap them.'

His initial anger stemmed from the way the newly elevated tribune peremptorily dismissed his suggestion. Aquila made no attempt to hide the contempt in his eyes, remembering the elevated Marcellus Falerius better than the other man knew.

'A waste of time! As soon as they feel threatened they retire to their forts, which we lack the ability to take, and if we do decide to invest them, then all the tribes gather to oppose us. If we are in one place, they will be there too. We'll find ourselves up against the Lusitani, the Bregones, the Leonini and a dozen other tribes, all combined under the leadership of Brennos. You may come here from Rome thinking that the solution is easy, Marcellus Falerius, but you'll discover that you're just as fallible as the rest!'

'We've taken fortresses in the past,' said Titus, cutting across Marcellus, whose noble blood was plainly up. He looked set to try to put Aquila Terentius in his place.

'Not with what you've got to hand. You lack siege equipment and the army is in a mess, General, more concerned with creature comforts than fighting.'

Titus dismissed that with a wave of the hand. 'Most soldiers are.'

'That's rubbish, General, and you should know it. Mind, the shit starts at the top, then filters down. Properly led, these men are as good as any in the Republic.'

Titus took that statement better than
Marcellus. He flushed angrily to see a Roman
consul talked down to in such a disdainful
manner; on top of the way Aquila had treated
him, it was intolerable. Titus was far from
pleased himself, but he did keep any hint of that
out of his next question.

'Do you often address your superiors like this?'

Aquila looked Titus right in the eye,
unblinking. 'I do.'

Titus looked grim. 'Then it's a wonder you're
still alive, Aquila Terentius.'

'Not really, General, the wonder is that all
those turds they sent us from Rome got back in
one piece. I've been sorely tempted to intervene
and lop off their heads. Rome would be better
served by the public piss-gatherers than senators
with ox-dung where they should have a brain.'

Those around the table gasped. The coarseness
of his speech was understandable, after all the
man was an illiterate peasant, but the bearing,
and the way he spoke, was downright mutinous.
Titus and Aquila were staring at each other,
neither blinking.

'I shall make you apologise for speaking to me
like that,' said Titus coldly.

Aquila's voice was as unperturbed as his look.
'I don't know how, General.'

'I was sent here, by the Senate, to finally put an end to the fighting in Hispania and that I intend to do. I'll take your rabble and remould them into fighters. Then you can forget the other hill forts; we will attack and subdue Numantia.'

'In a year?'

'No, Soldier. I will be here for as long as it takes, and before you tell me that I don't know what I'm talking about, I was here in this province for quite a few years myself. I have fought the tribes and competed with several of their leaders in peaceful games, and at one time I could have truthfully said some of them were my friends. You are not the only one who knows a thing or two about this frontier. I wrote a report for the Senate on Brennos, and in it I said that he was a menace whom we would one day have to remove, because we would never have peace as long as he lived. And my father, who fought him and beat him, said exactly the same thing before me. So don't presume to offer me advice in that tone of voice again, because even if it causes a mutiny, I'll break you at the wheel, then decimate the 18th Legion to show them who is really in command.'

Aquila smiled for the first time since the conference had started, and it made an enormous difference to his battle-hardened face. The blue eyes ceased to appear icy, instead becoming warm, the creases on the tanned face looked welcoming instead of threatening.

'Maybe I will apologise, at that, General,' he said. 'Who knows, if I get to see Italy again, I may even say thank you.'

Gnaeus was still talking about his 'tribune', annoying Marcellus by the way he passed on the fellow's radical notions verbatim. 'You can't blame him, Marcellus. He's been here for nearly twelve years, and all he's seen is dead bodies and a succession of men, already wealthy, trying to enrich themselves even more.'

'So he would happily see the whole system, which made Rome great, cast aside for the bad behaviour of a few rotten apples.'

'Don't underestimate Aquila, Marcellus,' said Gnaeus. 'You said he was an illiterate peasant—'

'He is,' snapped Marcellus, interrupting. 'And I might add his manners are a disgrace. I remember him being just as rude to Quintus Cornelius years ago.'

Gnaeus knew that story – after all it was part of the Terentius legend. He rarely subscribed to the generally held view that Marcellus was a stuck-up prig, but he did now and his voice, when he spoke, was unusually sharp. 'Believe me,

Marcellus, if Aquila is proud of anything, it is his Roman citizenship.'

'Then he should learn to respect it properly, and avoid insulting men who are consuls. If he were still on his farm, any noble landowner he addressed like that would flog him through the district for insolence.'

'I rather like the fact that he's not very refined,' said Gnaeus.

'I think I already referred to his illiteracy. It's a disgrace that someone who can't read and write properly is a tribune.'

'But he can speak Greek.'

'The accent is appalling.'

Gnaeus was now genuinely shocked; such condescension was most unlike his oldest friend and he just had to put him in his place. 'That was unworthy of a Roman, Marcellus.'

He could not know that his companion, as he spoke, could have bitten his tongue and was prepared to curse himself for such a remark. Had Gnaeus known how much this Aquila had got under Marcellus's skin then perhaps he would have been more forgiving. What was most galling was the way the centurion, now tribune by order of Titus Cornelius, had, in the time they had spent with him, suborned his friends.

'I withdraw the remark and apologise,' he said, stiffly.

They walked on in silence, Gnaeus wishing that Marcellus would just spend some time with Aquila, as he had before, during and after the siege of Pallentia. Perhaps then he could be brought to see how rotten the system had become, where poor people lost their land to men already too wealthy to know what to do with their money, where the rich hogged all the power to themselves and, when they were forced to hand some on, only let it slip so far. Not all senators were filthy rich, of course, but these men, in their purple-bordered togas, raised armies and led them either to disaster, or used them as a private band of robbers. They called on the whole of Italy, who had little to gain from the power of Rome, and forced them, as subject peoples, to provide the Republic with yet more blood to spill, denying those same people the rights of Roman citizenship. After two months with Aquila, Gnaeus had ended up ashamed to be rich or associated with the senatorial class.

'You must understand, my friend,' Marcellus insisted, 'what Rome needs is a stronger ruling class, not a weaker one. If we once allow decisions to be made by a mob, then Rome will fall apart.'

'That's only part of Aquila's argument. I think he's more in favour of one man having the power to sort out the mess first.'

Marcellus's voice was like a whip. 'A dictator, is that what he wants? No prizes for guessing who he sees in the role. Well, thank the gods that he's only a military tribune, so none of these wild notions are likely to get very far.'

'I cannot come with you, Lady,' said Cholon. 'I am already committed to join Titus in Spain.'

'Then I shall just have to redouble my efforts with Sextius, though I fear some of his friends have quite undermined my attempt to paint a rosy picture of Sicily.'

'You have yet to tell me why you are so keen to go there?'

Valuing Cholon's friendship, Claudia hesitated, but set against her desire to find her son that was as nothing. The question, once posed, would open a breach between them, one that could perhaps never be closed. She had undertaken, many years ago, not to ask where he and Aulus had exposed her son, yet she had no choice but to probe and the answer was vital. If it was affirmative, she would go to Sicily on her own and if Sextius baulked at this, he would have outlived his usefulness, so since they were not married in the strict form, she would offer him a divorce.

'As you know, I travel everywhere with my husband.'

'It has always amazed me that you do,' replied Cholon smoothly.

He failed to add that, to him, the act of journeying was less mysterious than the person she chose to journey with. The Greek had suffered many an evening in Sextius's company, purely for Claudia's sake. The man was a bore, forever preening his perfect Roman countenance and his attempts to hide his true inclinations behind a façade of Roman virility were risible. Sextius was locked into the past, unaware that times had changed, that with the increasing influx of Greek ideas into the Republic, no one in Rome gave a damn these days about a man's sexual orientation. Claudia stood up and went to a chest set against the wall, opened it and took out a number of lined scrolls, before turning round to face her guest.

'What have we here?' he asked.

'You must have wondered, once or twice, why I chose to marry Sextius?'

Good manners fought with veracity in Cholon's breast and throat. The result was a sound that was neither affirmative nor negative, but it would have been recognisable in a man with a heavy cold trying to clear his windpipe.

Claudia smiled. 'I've always admired your eloquence, Cholon.' He just pointed to the scrolls in her hand, not trusting himself to speak. 'Sextius owns land all around Rome. It is an added advantage that he is friendly with all the other landowners.' Cholon bowed his head, acknowledging the truth of what she said. 'That is why I married him.'

The Greek was as devious as he was clever, so she waited to see if he would make the connection. He shook his head slowly, like a man who has hold of only part of an idea. 'I asked you a question once, which you declined to answer.' Claudia let fall one of the linen scrolls. 'I have here a survey I have undertaken, which Sextius will present to the Senate in his name, detailing the incidence of infant exposures in Rome and the immediate surrounding areas of Latinum.'

The Greek's eyebrows were up now, and he shifted his position, adopting a more guarded pose as she continued. 'It's incomplete of course. I've naturally been constrained in what I can ask. Only a properly empowered praetor could demand answers, but, as you will see, my survey is quite comprehensive.'

'I thought you had put that matter out of your mind,' he said.

She ignored that and pointed to the scroll, but her eyes never left the Greek's face. 'There's a place near Aprilium, right by the River Liris. A child was exposed there, on the night of the Feast of Lupercalia, which, as you know, is the exact time my son was born.'

Cholon kept his face as stiff as a thespian's mask, but he could not stop the flicker in his eyes, which was enough to satisfy Claudia.

'I must go,' he said standing up.

'Yes,' his hostess replied. 'You'd better, before I'm tempted to break a promise.'

Cholon was afraid that his resolve would weaken, so the farewell was as hurried as it was unpleasant. Her words had taken him back to that night, so many years before, when he and his master, Aulus, had ridden many leagues from the empty villa where Claudia had just given birth to a bastard son. The child had lain in the saddlebag beneath him as he rode, and still he could recall the eyes that had stared at him in the reflected moonlight, bright blue as he had seen by the candles which illuminated the actual birth.

They had placed the child where he could not be found; Aulus wanted no disgrace of his name, but, noble as always, he was not prepared to bring opprobrium on the head of the woman he loved. Many times he had wondered what became of that little body in the swaddling cloth; many times he had prayed to his gods to forgive him for what had to be a sin. And, loyal to his late master, when pressed, not that he knew precisely, he had declined to tell Claudia the area in which the child had been exposed.

There had been a river gurgling in the woods where they had lain him down, that he recalled, and a mountain-top silhouetted in the moonlight, it being a cold, clear night, with a strange cap shaped like a votive cup. He had asked a surgeon about death by cold, and had been assured that, as the body cooled, the person dropped into a slumber from which they did not wake, so the child would have felt no pain.

It was only when he was in the street outside Claudia's house that he realised that he had forgotten to ask her why, when she had mentioned the River Liris and Aprilium, in his mind likely locations, she was so intent on going to Sicily.

Titus knew that he had to split them up. They were not working together – just the opposite – and if he left Aquila and Marcellus together too long, one of them would kill the other. It seemed as if the differences in birth and background somehow served to compound the mutual antipathy. Marcellus could not accept the new tribune as his equal. Aquila, aware that Marcellus Falerius had little battle experience, took every chance he could to remind him of the fact. It was as hard to know who to blame as it would be to find the seat of their quarrel, but Titus knew that a decision had to be made. Yet the most simple one, of sending Marcellus back to Rome, was debarred to him and not only because it would break a commitment; it would be a dishonourable thing to do.

He needed Aquila Terentius to help him retrain the legions, as well as the Iberian levies he had raised from the coastal plains. Not only that, the whole army, except those men he had brought to Spain himself, knew him. Titus was the kind of general who talked to his troops, so he heard repeatedly how much both Aquila and that charm he wore round his neck were seen as lucky symbols. There was an element of legend about the tales they told; even the men who had passed under the yoke before Pallentia credited his new tribune with saving their lives. And his elevation to what was a rich man's rank made every man in the army proud, leaving him in no doubt that they would feel more comfortable attacking

Numantia with this man by his side.

Yet he was bound to Marcellus by a tie of loyalty that went back a long way, to a time before the young Falerii had donned his manly gown. Quintus always claimed he was doing something, but he seemed to want Marcellus to take on his first magistracy without ever having spilt blood, something that would hamper the young man's future career. The solution came to him through Aquila, who, at a conference, asked the general what steps he was going to take to ensure that the Lusitani, more numerous than any of the other tribes excepting the Duncani, could not interfere with his operations around Numantia.

'I'm sure you have some suggestions to make, Aquila Terentius,' said Marcellus, sarcastically, ignoring the sour look Titus gave him for his interjection.

'Perhaps we should send you to confront them, Marcellus Falerius. After all, a soldier with your reputation will scare them shitless.'

'Enough!' snapped Titus, glaring at Aquila. 'Please be so good as to leave your rankers' language outside my tent.'

'I do have a suggestion, General, but it's not one you're likely to welcome.'

'Which is?'

'Postpone the campaign for this year. Raise ten more legions, get some good officers, and attack both the Lusitani and the Duncani at the same time.'

'Why would I be so against such a suggestion, always assuming it made military sense?'

'Your year as a consul will be up, Titus Cornelius. There will be some other bugger champing at the bit soon, especially if they think you're doing nothing. You might be blessed with an open-ended proconsulship now, but I'll bet a sestertius to a bent ass that you're recalled. I'll say it now, and stand by it. You're a proper soldier, but I don't think even you'll want to go home and leave somebody else to grab all the glory.'

Titus frowned at that, then he looked around the assembled officers, all junior, since he had sent all the senior men, those who had served with Mancinus, back to Rome.

'Listen well. I am here as proconsul of both provinces of Spain. I am here to fight a war, not just a campaign. When I leave this land, it will be at peace and my soldiers will be able to go home with me. There will be no more commanding generals coming out from Rome. Do I make myself clear?'

Marcellus was pleased to see Titus finally put

the upstart in his place. The general's brother had promised him the words he had just said were true, but Titus knew he would be a fool to place unlimited trust in Quintus. Just as telling was that Aquila had spoken the truth: something had to be done to contain the Lusitani, to at least keep them occupied till he had reached and invested Numantia. They, in the field and allied to the Duncani, might prove too much for the forces he could dispose. Many times in his life, a thought on some related subject had crystallised in his mind while he was talking, and that had happened now.

'As it happens, gentlemen, I have a plan to keep the Lusitani occupied. I leave for the province of Outer Spain in the morning. Aquila Terentius, you will assume command in my absence.' Marcellus opened his mouth to protest, so upset that he, even with his upbringing, was prepared to openly question his commander's orders. Titus's next words cut him off.

'And you, Marcellus Falerius, will accompany me!'

CHAPTER SIXTEEN

To anyone who knew him, the face of Sextius Paullus, as he was helped down the ramp at Messana, would have reduced them to helpless mirth. He looked like a man being lowered into a legionary latrine, just at the point where the contents had reached his lower lip. To say that the senator was not a happy man was a definite understatement. He could not comprehend what had come over Claudia; from being the perfect wife, kind, attentive and fully aware of his innate superiority, she had turned into a screeching shrew. The word 'divorce' horrified him, and at least she had undertaken never to mention that again. So here he was in Sicily, having been positively bundled out of Neapolis before he had had a chance to look up old acquaintances, only to be stuck, because of bad weather, in Rhegnum, a beastly port full of ruffians. Claudia had behaved as though that were his fault too. The crossing had been undertaken before the storm had properly moderated, which had made him sick, then the master of the vessel, well within sight of the harbour mouth, had demanded an increased fee to land them, saying that the swell made such a prospect dangerous.

His steward had at least secured the services of a gig and they set off for the governor's palace in silence. Claudia, beside him, craned out of the window in a most unseemly fashion, as though she were a fishwife calling out to passing friends. But he forbore to tell her to desist, aware that nothing he said, these days, produced anything other than abuse.

Titus Cornelius, having been given proconsular powers over the whole of the Iberian Peninsula, also displaced the governor of the southern province, Hispania Ulterior. That fellow, no less venal than Mancinus, took being superseded with more grace, but then he was going back to Rome, not being delivered into the hands of his enemies, with the prospect of suffering torture and abuse, before finally being burnt alive in a wicker cage. The troops in this province, although a lot less numerous, were in the same condition as those who had served under Mancinus, and the enemy, to the north and west, was even stronger, less exposed to Rome and its civilising influence.

Marcellus, given the rank of *legatus* by Titus, set to work straight away, instituting a tough new regime in the legion, with dire, sometimes fatal results for transgressors, and he questioned the available officers, trying to get a proper appraisal of the current situation. Here the problem was different, since they were exposed to the activities of seaborne raiders as well as the incursions of the Lusitani from the north. Lacking real experience to handle the solution himself, luck intervened, for in Regimus, an old and experienced sailor, he found just the man he was looking for.

They spent a long time together, both in the headquarters and on the seashore until finally Marcellus hired a ship, disappearing with his new-found companion for a week. That suited Titus; away from his main camp in the north and the day-to-day problems of training an army, he could give some thought to how he was going to beat Brennos. He knew that if he failed to find the right method, his army would suffer a worse fate than had been afforded them when they surrendered before Pallentia: Brennos would seek no truce, only the total destruction of his enemies. Of all people, Titus Cornelius knew that the defeat of his legions was, for Brennos, but one step in a greater and more dangerous plan.

Slowly, as he examined the problem, the germ of a solution presented itself, but it only had validity if he could control, in the initial attacks, the numbers he faced. Try as he might, he could think of no way to stop the Lusitani from reinforcing his main enemy.

It was plain, as soon as he returned, that whatever plan Marcellus had hatched to deal with this had got him excited. Calling for a series of maps, he rushed through the basic details without pausing for breath, failing to notice his general did not wholly share his enthusiasm.

'It depends on how quickly they hear that we are besieging Numantia,' Titus said.

'Are you going to besiege it?'

'If I can, I have to get to the place first.'

'Communications are good and they share a tribal border. There is nothing to stop the Lusitani coming to the aid of Numantia before you've had a chance to launch your first attack. That is, unless someone distracts their attention.'

Titus looked at the map of the western seaboard that Marcellus then placed in front of him, smiling slightly. 'Perhaps you are going to tell me Marcellus Falerius can do this?'

The younger man ran his finger along the

indentations on the coastline, trying to contain his delight. He had never supposed that Titus, land-minded like most Roman generals, would see the logic of his ideas, but at least he was open-minded enough to listen.

'We can't besiege Numantia and fight the Lusitani in a land campaign, so we must find a way to occupy them with the forces we already have. One thing that will keep them busy is concern for their own possessions. These are the main river outlets to the sea, and if we can establish a presence on any one of them, we can raid into the interior. They'll be so busy trying to dislodge us they won't have time to support Brennos.'

'What about their ship-borne raiders?'

'We will attack them first, if they show themselves. Their craft are small and unarmed, no match for a quinquereme.'

'Which we don't have,' said Titus, 'and I'm not sure that the Senate will agree to send any, quite apart from the time it would take.'

'Then we'll build them. We have the wood in abundance, and I undertake to train the rowers. I even have an old decurion who was at sea for years, a fellow called Regimus. He says we can make up the ships' crews.'

'From the legions?'

Marcellus nodded. Titus however, shook his head. 'It's no good, you'll need proper sailors. Remember that fight we had with the Sicilian slaves off Agrigentum? We could cast our spears all right, but it took proper seafarers to get us to a point where we could fight.'

'One sailor per oar, perhaps, that and a crew to steer and set the sails.'

'That's still a lot of men we do not have.'

'The harbour of Portus Albus is full of trading ships, we'll take what we need.'

Titus favoured the younger man with a wry smile. 'I can almost hear the words of my indictment. Who do you think owns those trading ships? A good number, if not most of them, are the property of my fellow senators.'

'Write to Quintus. He'll keep them off your back.'

The smile remained. 'You have lofty ideas of my brother's power, let alone his willingness to sacrifice himself for me. Terentius had a point about my being recalled, even though I glossed it over. Understand, Marcellus, Quintus will only continue to support this operation and me as long as it suits his purpose. If he once feels his position to be threatened he will drop me like a new moulded brick, and you with me.'

Marcellus, if asked, would have denied he was

desperate, but that was the naked truth; all these years of being sent to safe places had made him so. They were just enough to justify his candidacy for the *cursus honorum* and Quintus never tired of telling him, before despatching him to some backwater, that he would inherit his father's power, but he never quite said how long the son would have to wait. Marcellus suspected that he would have trouble extracting anything from Quintus on his deathbed and, for that reason alone, he had kept his father's private papers secret, waiting until the time when they could be used for his political benefit, the moment when he first challenged Quintus to block his path to the leadership of the *optimates*.

'If I were to guarantee that Quintus would not only back you, but have the power to do so, would you accept my word?'

Titus hid his surprise well, just as he masked his curiosity. He looked long and hard at the young man before him; the boy he had first come across boxing in the Campus Martius, the young man he had taught to drive a chariot was now gone for good. Tall, dark, with that direct gaze, which, allied to his innate honesty, most men found disconcerting. Quintus certainly did, but only because his brother was unprincipled and shifty. Marcellus was anything but – indeed Titus could recall no occasion where he even suspected this young man of lying to him. On the journey from New Carthage he had asked him to put personalities aside and tell him what he thought of Aquila Terentius. Marcellus was well aware that his general esteemed the man, having handed over control of the northern legions to his care and giving him the temporary rank of quaestor. Most men would have praised Aquila's soldierly qualities to his face and, because they disliked or envied him, damned him behind Titus's back.

Not Marcellus Falerius. 'I don't doubt his competence, Titus Cornelius, nor his bravery, but he is an uncouth ruffian raised on a farm. He has no education and no knowledge of anything higher than a horse's groin. He talks about reform as though it was his business, instead of realising that, with his birth, he must do what he is told by better men. You will damn me for this, but I wonder whether it is desirable to elevate such a man above his natural station.'

Titus made no effort to hide the fact that he was less than pleased. 'Are you saying I should get rid of him?'

'No, but you command the legions and you do so by right, as well as ability. I would not want this Aquila to rise any further than he has already, otherwise he may try to usurp your prerogative. Then he may seek to take your birthright as well.'

'That's nonsense, Marcellus, and is it not your birthright you are really talking about. You make it sound as though he wants to take over the Republic. Can't you just admit the man is a soldier, and a damn good one?'

'Rome has no shortage of soldiers, Titus. You are proof of that.'

He could have looked for flattery in that remark, but it would be a waste of time, it being another one of Marcellus's habits, his disinclination to praise people unless they deserved it, and rarely then. Many a senator, having dealt with him, had been heard to remark that it was worse than doing business with the boy's father. But ruminating on that would get them nowhere; Titus was being asked to put his entire career, his hard-won reputation, perhaps even his life, in this young man's hands, and it was plain he would have to take the whole risk on trust.

'You doubt my word?' asked Marcellus.

'Never,' said Titus truthfully. 'But you ask a great deal.'

'What if I were to tell you that what I'll give your brother, if we do not succeed, will make him as powerful as my father—'

Titus interrupted. 'If that's the case, it seems a lot to pay.'

'Do I have to explain to you?'

'No, Marcellus, you don't, but ask yourself this. Is what you have, that will so enhance my brother's prestige and power, worth throwing away on a small independent command?'

Marcellus, usually so grave, smiled suddenly. 'I'm quite shocked that you ask.'

Titus remained silent for a full minute, and all the time Marcellus's eyes never left his face. Finally he nodded. 'Then so be it. Take what you need.'

'Thank you, Titus.'

There was no smile of agreement on the older man's face, no gentleness in the voice. Both were as hard as they had been when he arrested Mancinus. 'You'd better succeed, Marcellus. I don't care what you give to Quintus, fail and we'll lose at Numantia. Then, even assuming we survive to face their retribution, they'll combine to tear us both apart. Now I must go and see how the other arm of my command is faring.'

'I want the shops shut, and the brothels. All the women out of the camp as well, including soldiers' wives.'

The looks of protest were universal. Even

Fabius, newly appointed as his 'uncle's' orderly, was palpably shocked, nearly spilling the cup of wine he was pouring for himself, just out of sight of the assembled officers. Getting rid of the merchants, the wine shops and the brothels was one thing, but the camp wives?

'There will be a mutiny,' said Gaius Trebonius, one of the few tribunes who had served under Mancinus that, out of a favour to Marcellus, the new proconsul had allowed to remain.

'He's right, Aquila,' said Publius Calvinus.

The blue eyes blazed with anger. 'If the general were here, would you question him?' Everyone shook their heads. 'Then don't presume to question the man he left in command. Some of these men have been here for fourteen years. They have wives and families at home. Tell them that's where they will be going soon. Home.'

'I doubt they'll believe it.'

'Then I'll tell them myself!' snapped Aquila.

He ordered the horns to be sounded, calling men to the oration platform on the *Via Principalis* and stood, impatiently, waiting for them to arrive, pacing up and down the elevated rostrum. If anything demonstrated to Aquila how lax the legions had become, it was the time they took to form up.

'What a bunch of old women you lot are,' he

said, when they had finally quietened down. He turned right round, looking at the platform, with a meaningful stare. 'I've often wondered what it's like to be up here. Somehow I thought the air would smell different, more refined and pleasant, but it doesn't. It still smells of you and horses' piss, in that order.'

They laughed as he held his nose. 'Mind, we've heard some ripe old lies told from up here, lads, haven't we?' Some of the other tribunes looked at each other with alarm as the men cheered loudly in agreement. 'We've been promised everything under the sun from the bastards that have used this spot.'

Now even some of the men looked uneasy. Aquila was pushing it; calling senators of good family bastards, however far away they were, was dangerous stuff. None of them realised how nervous he was, nerves not being something they associated with their temporary commander.

'Well let me tell you, that you're now looking at the biggest bastard ever to tread these boards.'

'I second the motion,' said Fabius from behind him.

That was all right, because only those on the platform could hear him. Aquila walked to the very edge and took his gold eagle in his hand. Not a single eye missed that movement and those who had served alongside him knew that when he did that, he was about to make a vow. Odd, when his fingers closed round the charm, the fear that he had that he would make a fool of himself immediately evaporated.

'Why am I a bigger bastard, indeed a bigger shit, than the others? It's not 'cause I'm rich, is it? It's not because I'm greedy, since I wouldn't see any of you dead to earn myself a triumph, or even a silver denarius. No, lads, I'm a bastard and a shit because, for the first time in years, you see standing up here someone who's going to tell you the truth.'

He had their complete attention now. 'Now what happens normally? The general gets on his hind legs and tells you you're all wonderful soldiers and brave fellows. I can't do that, since I've promised to tell you the truth.'

The voice dropped slightly, so that they had to strain to hear.

'You're not wonderful, lads. Barring a few men from the 18th, you're soft, full of wine, meat and the comfort of women. What general will tell you this, even if it's what he thinks? No, having praised you to the skies, he now tells you that he's planned a small campaign, nothing dangerous, just a little skirmish against a few ill-prepared barbarians, that's necessary for the safety of the

Republic. He promises you plenty of food, comfortable camps, an ill-prepared enemy and few casualties.'

He paused again, lifting the charm higher so it stood out from his neck. The sun caught it, causing it to flash like a message from the gods. 'But I won't lie to you. We're going to war, boys, *real* war this time. We're going to take on the largest and most dangerous bunch of local tribesmen I can find. These sods are holed up in a near-impregnable fortress, so there won't be one battle. In fact, I'll be surprised if we don't see a round dozen before we even get near the place. As for casualties, if we get it right, at least one man in five of you won't be coming back. If we get it wrong, none of us will.'

'Then why the fuck are we goin'?' said a voice from the ranks.

'I said I won't lie to you. It's not for glory and it's certainly not an excuse to line some consul's pockets, but going we are. It's the battle we should have fought years ago, and when we leave this camp we're going to be the best men that Rome can put in the field. You're all about to lose some weight, just as you're all about to lose those comforts that have become part of your lives.'

There was a loud murmur, like a wave going through the massed ranks of legionaries.

'This camp goes on a war footing as from today. Only soldiers, grooms and armourers will be allowed in the camp.' Aquila paused, letting the import of his words sink in, then took a spear from one of the praetorian guards. 'Anybody who doesn't like it, can come and see me.'

'It's robbery,' said the fat captain, chins wobbling as he protested.

'Very likely,' replied Marcellus. 'But at least you'll have the satisfaction of knowing you helped to save the Republic.'

'Bugger the Republic,' he replied, though he recoiled quickly enough when he felt Marcellus's sword at his throat.

'Never say that again! And just so you'll remember where you loyalties should lie, I'll take twice the number of your men than I'm taking from the other ships.'

'I won't be able to move from Portus Albus. The owner will flay me alive.'

If he had hoped to dent Marcellus's determination he was sadly disappointed. His rowers were marched ashore and, once assembled, led along the beach to the platforms that the young tribune had erected. These were surrounded by piles of newly cut sweeps, as well as legionaries, who looked as unsure of their reasons for being there as the newly pressed sailors. Marcellus jumped up onto the first step and addressed them.

'Right now, every shipwright in the whole of the province is busy building a fleet of quinqueremes, the most powerful weapon afloat. Once they're built, I'm going to sail north and attack the Lusitani.' He looked around slowly to gauge the effect of his words. 'We could wait for the ships to be ready and then spend months learning to row them, but there's no time for that. Instead we will use these platforms to practise on, one sailor to four soldiers. You seafarers will teach them to row on dry land. By the time the ships are built, I intend to put straight to sea. If you're any good, we'll win. If not, we'll probably all drown.'

The local people came to stare, the children to jeer, as they watched grown men sitting on dry land, rowing furiously and unevenly. It started out as chaos, with oars going in all directions as the soldiers tried to get used to them, but order came eventually and it was possible to see that a few of the oars were keeping time with the beat of the drum. Marcellus made sure that they had plenty of food and water available, knowing it was exhausting work on the sun-drenched beach. He also had a strict guard mounted, to make sure that none of his precious sailors escaped.

* * *

'We do not allow civilians in the camp,' said Aquila again, 'and I am not much given to repeating myself.'

Cholon gave him the full shocked treatment, the 'how dare you speak to me like that?' look. It had no effect whatever.

'I would remind you that I'm here at the personal invitation of Titus Cornelius.'

'How can you remind me of something I don't know?'

'That's sophistry, young man.'

'What the hell is sophistry?' Aquila saw that Cholon was about to explain and held up his hand. 'Don't bother to explain. I've got through this far in life without knowing, so it's obviously something I can do without.'

Cholon bridled. 'Has anyone ever told you that you're an insolent swine?'

'From the day I was born and every waking moment since, but I'm also in charge here. Now do me a favour and piss off out of the camp.'

'Titus Cornelius will hear of this.'

The shout nearly knocked Cholon over. 'Guards, get this man out of here and remind the sentries on the gate: no civilians allowed, regardless of what fairy story they come up with!'

The young tribune escorting him tried to ease

the pain caused by Aquila's words. 'The general will be back soon, sir. I'm sure that everything will work out all right in the end.'

The tribune, who was more afraid of Aquila than the comfort of this Greek civilian, was hurrying Cholon along at a terrific pace, which made his response sound like that of a man just arrested protesting his innocence.

'Not with people like that in positions of power. The man is a positive oaf. I don't know what the legions are coming to, letting men like that become officers. What did you say the fellow's name was?'

'Aquila Terentius, sir,' said the tribune.

'Well, he's a barbarian,' replied Cholon, but he was also wondering, vaguely, where he'd heard the name before.

Titus Cornelius returned to a different camp. Now it resounded to the clashing of swords, instead of the calls of the traders and any pained shouts came from soldiers, not abused and fractious camp wives. The ragged children who had run half-naked through the streets were gone too, leaving the horses free from torment. Aquila had built another camp five miles away to house them, which he kept supplied by a levy on his soldiers, as well as the Iberian auxiliaries.

And they were soldiers again; that was obvious by the efficient way they moved into position around the oration platform. But Titus had known before that, from the guard at the main gate, smart and alert; indeed the horns had sounded when he was half a league away. By the time he had reached the camp, the proconsul found a hot bath waiting, as well as all his officers eager to discuss forthcoming operations. Before he changed, they held a conference and Aquila was not the only one surprised by his stated intention to set off for the interior straightaway.

'Don't be fooled by a bit of spit and polish, General,' he said. 'If you tell these men that they're goin' to march into the middle of Iberia, they won't go.'

'Not even if you tell them?'

'I can't lie to them!'

'I don't want you to. Why can't we attack now?'

Aquila sighed, and he could not hide his disappointment at having to explain to one of the first consuls he had ever admired why it couldn't be done. 'All the conditions that applied to Pallentia apply here, tenfold. We've got further to go. Instead of building a few bridges, we'll have to construct a dozen. Every inch of the road we build will have to be guarded if supplies are to get through. If we do that, we won't have the troops to attack.'

'I don't intend to attack, at least not right away.'

'Then forgive me, General, but how in the name of Hades Hall do you expect to win?'

Titus indicated the map on the table and gestured for those present to come closer. 'We march straight to our goal. We will bridge only those rivers we can't ford and we'll destroy them behind us. Once we get to Numantia we'll need to live off the land for perhaps a month, then I can release two legions to build a road back to the coast so that we can be supplied.'

'And Brennos, what will he be doing? Not to mention the Lusitani.'

Titus interrupted Aquila, speaking with a confidence that he certainly did not completely feel. 'Marcellus Falerius will take care of the latter, and before you ask how, I'm not going to say anything other than this; that he has my full confidence.'

'That still leaves Brennos.'

'Don't worry about him, Aquila Terentius. I have a plan that will take care of him and his hill fort.'

* * *

Freshly washed and in his purple-bordered toga, Titus walked onto the oration platform. He looked around the massed rank of legionaries, all at attention, staring straight ahead. He quite deliberately saluted them, something no senator had ever done, unbidden, to a soldier. A loud and spontaneous cheer followed a moment's silence as Titus turned and indicated that Aquila should join him on the platform.

'Soldiers. I hate making speeches as much as you hate listening to them. My father used to tell my mother, when I wouldn't sleep at night, that he'd repeat to me some of the things he'd heard said from up here. He claimed even the noisiest baby would be out cold within minutes.'

Titus paused then linked his arm with Aquila, who had come to stand beside him. 'My father, Aulus Cornelius Macedonicus, was a great soldier, one of the best Rome ever had. I'm not a patch on him, so I intend to take out a bit of insurance.' He walked forward to the edge of the platform, dragging Aquila with him. 'As you know, when I came here, I sent packing the quaestor and the legates that Mancinus had brought out from Rome. I was tempted to send them in the same direction as Mancinus, but I didn't.'

An angry growl came from twenty thousand throats.

'I also sent for new senior officers and they have yet to arrive. I didn't think I'd need them for a few months yet, but I can tell you're ready for battle. That anyone could turn you from what you were – a rabble – back into soldiers, in such a short time, is amazing. So, I'm not going to wait for my legates, who're on the way from Rome, nor the quaestor I asked for. In fact, when it comes to a second-in-command, I cannot think of anyone more suited to the post than Aquila Terentius.'

They must have guessed what was coming. Titus could feel the tension becoming unbearable as he spoke. He took Aquila by the shoulders and embraced him. The men let forth the greatest cheer he had ever heard in all his years as a soldier.

It was with some difficulty that Aquila made himself heard. 'We're ready to march at forty-eight hours' notice, General.'

'Good.'

Then Aquila smiled, and as the noise died down he spoke again. 'I think I owe you an apology.'

'Do I still have to wait for the "thank you"?' asked Titus, with a smile.

'After Numantia,' replied the new quaestor, who then lifted his gold eagle and publicly kissed it.

CHAPTER SEVENTEEN

———•———

Marcellus got his first ship to sea in record time, thanks to the engineering skills of Regimus and the work-rate of the local shipwrights. The old sailor, now once more a decurion, was a real find. 'Can't be done' was not an expression he understood. From bare ribs, the ships started to take rapid shape, and the old man was proud, in more ways than one, of what the shipwrights had achieved.

'They build better than anyone else I've seen, which is just as well. The conditions here, beyond the Pillars of Hercules, are nothing like the Middle Sea.'

Marcellus had been interested in all things nautical since his first trip aboard a trireme, and sailors loved to talk, though some caution had to be exercised to avoid falling for their endemic exaggerations. He had heard about the tidal rise and fall from those he had questioned, but the stories about the outer sea could be hair-raising. Some of the trading captains had sailed so far north that ice islands, floating on the surface, had turned them back. These men traded in amber and other precious objects, like tin and silver. Wonderful woollen cloaks came from the Pretanic Islands, easy to reach since they were a mere twenty-five leagues from the shore of northern Gaul. They were hard to believe, these tales he had been told, of storms where the waves had risen above the height of the masts, of whales ten times the size of the ship who sang to each other, yet swam alongside and never harmed men; and he had disbelieved more than he should.

Now, at sea, he would readily admit to being wrong. Nothing had quite prepared him for the sheer volume of water and the way it behaved, once you got out beyond the narrow entrance to the Middle Sea, and that alone took some doing due to the current, a boat being forced to hug the northern shore, and that only possible with a good following wind. The waves could indeed be huge! White-capped, whipped onwards by a screaming wind, curling over themselves to form dark cavities, rushing at phenomenal speed, then crashing onto rocks that had been worn down over time into fantastic shapes. Other days would see the same water a huge and gentle swell with troughs deep enough to hide you from land. And the smell was different, with air that had travelled over an ocean that seemed to have no end, all the way from the very rim of the world, carrying with it magical elements that could make you dizzy.

'It's not magic, Marcellus. You'll get used to it,' said Regimus as he staggered out of the steady wind, and the old seafarer was right; he had.

Marcellus was amidships, one hand holding on to the mast, his hair whipping about in the breeze, nose up and his eyes gleaming with pleasure, while beneath his feet the oars dipped evenly into the water, carrying the first of his ships forward at a steady pace. He turned to shout to Regimus, who stood with his arms around the great sweep.

'Used to it, man? I love it! I think *Neptune* must be somewhere in my bloodline. Standing here, I feel at one with the gods.'

They had sacrificed a bull before sailing, as well as listening carefully to the augurs, but the gods were fickle, inclined to smite foolish mortals. The augurs and their corn-fed chickens guaranteed nothing; it was a reading of the sky, the shape and direction of the clouds, the state of the sea, a careful watch on the behaviour of the seabirds, the smell of the spume by those who had sailed these waters before, that provided some feeling of security.

'Put her before the wind, Regimus. Let's get that sail up and see how she handles.'

The old man called the orders and most of the oars were lifted and shipped, only those needed to steady the ship and hold her head true remaining in the water. He leant on the heavy sweep bringing the quinquereme round so that the wind was dead astern. They rose on the swell and the coast lay clear ahead: rocky, with narrow sandy bays and the mountains rising into a blue haze behind. Men hauled on ropes and the boom holding the huge square sail rose up the mast, then they lashed it taut and it took the wind, bowing out as though it would tear. Water started to run white along the ship's side and Marcellus ran forward, dodging round the *corvus*, to observe the sea cream under the bows.

He moved back to the stern, took the sweep from Regimus, edging it this way and that, trying to find out how far he could steer off true before the sail flapped uselessly and the ship lost speed. Finally satisfied, he took in the sail, ordered the men back to their oars and sent the head oarsman to beat his tattoo on the great block of wood that stood just before the well of the ship. It was nothing like a trireme, built to ram the enemy; the heavy quinquereme was built to carry soldiers into battle, but speed could still be a prerequisite of a successful manoeuvre, placing the Roman ship in an advantageous position when faced with the much lighter ships Marcellus would need to engage.

They raced through the water as the drumbeat increased. The land, so recently a strip on the horizon, was now close enough for each feature to be clear to the naked eye. The rowers bent and strained, bent and strained, the sweat running freely from their bodies. Marcellus could not see their faces, but he knew, from his own experience, that they would be screwed up in pain, fighting to fill their lungs with air. Mentally he willed them to greater efforts, watching carefully for the first sign of collapse. One oar, wrongly handled, could throw out the whole rhythm of a galley. The heaving noise of snatched breath was clear above the sound of wind and sea, so the legate gave the order and the oars were shipped again, this time with exhausted rowers collapsing over them, as if suddenly dead.

'Excellent,' said Marcellus. 'Back to Portus Albus, Regimus, let us see how our other ships and crews are doing.'

* * *

Brennos knew they were coming long before the first legionary put a boot outside the camp gate. He felt it in his bones as he awoke from his dream; not pain, for it was like an ache lifted. He looked at Galina, asleep by his side, the one person who had kept faith with him out of love rather than fear, never doubting that his prediction would come true. Not that anyone had dared to say anything to his face, but Brennos could see into men's minds, so he knew they thought him mad, obsessed with the defeat of Rome. He never tried to explain, since that first battle against Aulus Cornelius, that it was the triumph of the Celts he sought; that he would have fought Carthage, Rome's predecessors in Iberia, with equal venom. His hand ran softly over Galina's thigh and she murmured in her sleep, while his other hand took the gold eagle that he always wore round his neck, the personal talisman that he believed would decide his fate.

Gifted to him by his uncle, a senior Druid who had helped him to escape from the hole in the ground in which he had been placed, as well as death at the hands of those who hated and feared him in the Druid community, it had been with him ever since that day, only ever removed when washing. Taken by his namesake, Brennos, from the Temple of Delphi, hundreds of years before he had been told it had magical powers, though it had as yet failed to fulfil the prophesy which went with it; that one day he who wore it would stand triumphant in the Temple of Jupiter Maximus high on the Capitoline Hill in Rome, a man who had conquered the legions and the city.

Finally, after all these years of trying to tempt them, his enemies were coming to meet their nemesis. In his mind's eye, he could see the fields around Numantia filled with the bleached bones of the Romans. Once they had been defeated here, once he had proved that he was the true heir to the first Brennos, the Celts, the most numerous of peoples fractured by tribal rivalries, would come together under his rule. He would create and lead the greatest army the Celts had ever put in the field, then do what his predecessor had not done. First, Brennos would take enough gold to retire from Rome; they would not bribe him, he would raze their city state to the ground, destroy its temples and enslave its people.

Yet there were doubts; not everything was certain, and not just because the gods were fickle; he should have achieved this already. He had fought Aulus Cornelius, he had even captured the man's wife and become her lover, more at her bidding than his own. Celibacy was his duty, the Lady Claudia Cornelia had taken that from him.

He recalled the day he had to tell her to leave, though he did not tell her it was because his revolt had failed, that her husband was winning his war of attrition. The tribes had been deserting him, making peace, and he could no longer protect her and the child she carried. Why had he not succeeded in fulfilling the prophecy? Would he do so now?

He leant over the girl, his movement waking her, and held the charm up to her half-open eyes. 'I'm old, Galina, yet I believed once that I would conquer Rome. The man who wears this has that as his destiny. I cannot believe absolutely now that it will be me, so I must have a son. This will pass to him and even if he has to breed sons and pass it on, one day my bloodline will conquer.'

Brennos pushed Galina gently on to her back and the action of his hands brought a smile to her lips. He kept the gold charm in his hand, and he felt the power course through his loins, certain that for the first time in thirty years he could really feel the force in the charm, the same kind of power he had felt that dark night when it had been placed in his hand. Despite being a passionate creature, Galina had never conceived, perhaps because she feared he would do as he had to his other offspring and kill the child. But he knew, with absolute certainty, that she would now give him the son he needed, one he would cherish and raise to fulfil his destiny.

Brennos was in the central arena long before the sun came up, reciting, from memory, the sagas that he had learnt so many years before. He could feel the years slip away, making him strong again, as if his life had gone into reverse, and as the sun came up he watched for the moment at which it first touched the altar in the middle of the square. The gold light crept slowly down the walls of the surrounding buildings, and all the time he talked. People had gathered to listen, never having seen their chieftain like this. He seemed taller than ever, more imposing, and just before the sunlight touched the altar, it lit his silver hair, making it shine. It was as though the Great Earth God had blessed him and a huge shout sprang from his lips at the sacred moment, when the sunlight lit the altar, startling those watching. Then he spun round, looking at them with a fearsome gaze, and started to issue the commands that would make Numantia ready for the invaders.

They had expected the march to Numantia to be hard, but not even Aquila, with his dire warnings and elaborate precautions, was prepared for the tenacity with which the tribes tried to block their passage. Brennos wanted them weakened before they arrived and had bent all his persuasive power to the task of ensuring a rough passage for the Romans. Every hill had to be taken by assault, each narrow valley outflanked and every river bridged under a rain of spears and arrows. They cut a makeshift road through the huge forests – a straight Roman road, ignoring the terrain. If they succeeded, it would become permanent, opening up the interior of the land to Roman civilisation; if they failed, it would disappear, an overgrown testament to the demise of a whole army.

The new quaestor had known for years that the formation of the army, with its complicated baggage train, had previously militated against success, for, when fighting such an enemy, in such country, speed and mobility were paramount and he had been worried at the outset when Titus pushed his army hard, letting the tribes occupy the route to their rear. These legionaries had grown up with a method of fighting and it was common sense to Aquila that a sudden change of basic tactics, in a situation where battle is imminent, could lead to total disaster.

One asset was Titus himself. The men had, for once, a general who led from the front; in fact, he could not be kept away from a fight, despite continual pleading that the loss of his life could be fatal to the enterprise. Titus trusted the gods with his person and the men beneath him with his legions. Aquila noticed right away, that, given the responsibility to make their own decisions, few officers let their general down, since the only requirement the consul had of them was that they avoid being foolish. So the individual tribunes were encouraged to innovate.

Aquila himself had instituted a way of pushing the entire force of *velites*, as well as the Iberian auxiliaries, forward at a rapid pace. These skirmishers, gathered from all the legions, added to the fighters from the coastal plain, being numerous, forced the tribesmen to spring their ambushes too early, and, facing lightly armed Romans, they were drawn into pressing home their attacks, from which they found it difficult to swiftly disengage. The bulk of the army, without the usual baggage train and camp followers, was moving at a hitherto unprecedented pace, so, in the first few weeks of the march they caught their enemies engaged time and time again. But Brennos, if indeed it was he who was directing the tribal effort, soon learnt the lesson and, with a firm grasp of the properties afforded him by the rugged landscape, he eschewed ambush, instead setting up defensive positions that had to be taken by assault.

'These are mere pinpricks, Fabius,' said Aquila, as they formed up yet again to attack a steep ridge. 'The real fighting is still to come.'

'That's one of the things that's wrong about you. You can't tell a pin from a knitting needle, and as for a prick...'

Aquila yelled out his commands and the skirmishers started forward, darting about before the enemy to draw their fire and reduce their stock of spears. Success would mean they would have less to cast at the following heavy infantry. Titus for once stayed back, as a general should, standing on a rock to observe the action, all his army spread out around him in battle array. Cholon sat beside him, a papyrus roll on his lap, his eyes darting from the battle taking place ahead, then down to the paper for a quick notation. The commotion from the rear took them both by surprise. A huge mass of mounted tribesmen had appeared across the road back to the coast, formed up and ready to attack. Too small a force to defeat the Romans, their presence was, nevertheless, demoralising. They were living proof to all the legionaries that they were cut off in enemy territory and any attack they delivered, even partially successful, would lead to casualties that Titus could ill afford.

The general was off his perch in a flash,

mounting his horse to ride to the scene of the trouble. Publius and Gnaeus Calvinus, in command of the lightly armed rearguard, had calmly wheeled their men round, forming two lines, as the mounted tribesmen came rushing forward. They kept their voices steady, raising them only as much as was needed for their orders to be understood. Their first line knelt at the command, their shields angled over their heads and their spears dug into the ground, forming a frieze before them that would impale any mounted attacker. The second line immediately formed into threes, one behind the other. Titus hauled on his reins, watching the next line of legionaries, heavy infantry to the rear of the Calvinus twins, as they swung expertly into place, forming up into four lines, with the proper gap between each group. That would allow the Calvinus cohorts to withdraw in safety. It was a set-piece manoeuvre, carried out as if being executed on the Campus Martius.

For all the pride in Roman arms that Titus Cornelius had experienced as a soldier, nothing equalled this, because it was being carried out, not on a practice field, but in broken country. That iron discipline, the ability to manoeuvre under attack, plus sheer raw courage by officers and men alike, when properly employed, made

Roman legions invincible. Cholon had joined him, abandoning his chair and his note-taking. Titus looked over his shoulder to check that Aquila's attack was proceeding successfully, noting that the *velites* and auxiliaries had scaled the escarpment and were now engaged in hand-to-hand combat with the defenders.

'Write this up, Cholon. This is the very best you'll ever see. A Roman army attacking in two directions at once.'

'But they're not attacking,' said Cholon, pointing to the men withdrawing under the orders of their officers. 'They're retreating.'

'Watch!'

Publius and Gnaeus led their men safely back, one defensive line slipping through another, with the three men coming abreast immediately the last man escaped, never leaving the attacker anything but certain impalement to face. Finally, when they were close enough to the heavier infantry, they broke and ran to safety. The gaps closed immediately and the rear cohorts filled in. The orders were given, and the Celt-Iberian tribesmen found themselves facing an unbroken line of advancing troops. Having milled around uselessly, their horses were winded, so they broke at the first cast of the spears, leaving dead men and screaming animals pinned to the ground by Roman javelins.

A great shout rent the air and both Cholon and Titus turned in their saddles, just in time to see Aquila, at the head of the *princeps* of the 18th Legion, take the crest of the ridge, his enemies in full flight before him.

Their next battle was at a heavily contested river-crossing, the main problem being that there was no room on the opposite bank to deploy, since, apart from a narrow strip of land, the rock rose sheer for a hundred feet. Titus had searched the river up and down its length for an easier passage, but in his bones he knew there was nothing. The mere presence of his enemies, in such force, on the opposite hills was proof of that. But the one asset that the Roman legion had in this situation was that they could all swim; the other advantage lay in their discipline. A well-trained army could attack at night – something denied to wild hordes of barbarians. Titus rested his men throughout the day, with only the rearguard engaged in any meaningful way, and stood down his auxiliaries; this was no task for local troops.

Then, using the cover of cloud, interspersed with fitful moonlight, he threw a line of cavalry across the river, well downstream, each soldier and horse roped to the other. These men and their horses would stay there all night, set to catch anyone swept away by the force of the water. Then, in almost pitch darkness, the most experienced heavy infantrymen, with ropes tied round their middle and stakes lashed to their backs, followed the *velites* into the water, holding clear their great metal-topped hammers. Aquila was at their head, his red-gold hair with the white band lashed round it picking up what little light existed. He swam swiftly to the other bank, forming the skirmishers into a defensive screen that would allow their comrades to work. The first the defenders knew of the coming assault was the sound of those stakes being driven into the damp riverside earth. The ropes were lashed to the stakes and at a steady pace Titus pushed his infantry across.

Aquila had already led his skirmishers up the steep slope, so that the tribesmen found themselves engaged in battle before they were properly awake. Fighting in the dark is terrifying, never knowing where the enemy is; or if the ghostly shape in front of you is friend or foe. Such hand-to-hand combat required a steely determination that the defenders lacked. Titus had the horns sounded continuously, and out of tune, from the moment the first stake was driven into the earth. This cacophony bounced off the rocks, multiplying and, added to the screams of the attackers, making the defenders feel that they were under attack from some horrifying monster. Each of Aquila's men had, like him, a white cloth tied round his head. The Romans, even in the dim light, could identify their enemies, and they extracted a heavy toll long before the heavier troops arrived to take over the assault.

Yet someone gathered them into a cohesive line, shouting commands that Aquila heard clearly. He sent a messenger back to warn Titus, well aware that the effect, initially, would be minimal. The Celts started to throw their javelins over the heads of the Romans on the cliff, aiming them in the general direction of the river. With such a mass of men in the water, struggling across the foaming torrent on dozens of ropes, many found a target. The screams of the wounded added to all the other noises of battle that echoed off the rock face, and, downstream, the line of cavalry found that they were indeed required, if only to stop the bodies of drowned men flowing all the way to the sea.

When they ran out of spears, a distinct horn sounded, and the defence evaporated, leaving the Romans no one to fight.

CHAPTER EIGHTEEN

The fog swirled around them, making their long, curled brass horns sound like something from the underworld. Few would have sailed into this, but Marcellus blessed the mist, for it could mean he would get his men ashore unopposed. They had spotted the first of the Lusitani the day before on the eastern shore, following them on land as the fleet made its way north. As darkness fell, beacons were lit on the hilltops so that the message would proceed ahead of those on foot, who could not be expected, in the dark, to match the pace of well-rowed galleys. To the west lay an endless expanse of sea and beyond that the edge of the world, peopled by demons and sea-nymphs who fed on human flesh and turned the wits of those they did not eat.

Nothing could be seen of east or west in this mist. In the bows, the slow chant of the leadsman, calling out the depth of water beneath the keel, added a nerve-jangling litany to the ethereal call of the horns. Marcellus was with the fellow doing the casting, listening carefully to the depths, for they were in shoal water, perhaps surrounded by jagged rocks, with his ship in the very lead, each galley in the fleet taking station right behind the one ahead. If he could get through whatever they faced, so could they.

'Sand on the line,' called the leadsman, before casting it ahead again.

The quinquereme rowed on slowly, its forward movement carrying it to a point where the line was vertical. The leadsman hauled quickly, pulling it out of the water, examining the tallow at the end to see what lay on the bottom, then, swinging it in an ever-widening circle, cast it forward again.

'Give the order for silence,' said Marcellus to a sailor standing behind him. 'No more horns. And you, leadsman, whisper to me.'

The sailor rushed to obey and his young commander strained forward. They were close inshore now, and the sound of the waves would tell him if he had guessed right. If they crashed unevenly and noisily, he would be on a rocky shore, in grave danger of holing his ship and sinking, but if he heard the hiss of water running evenly up a beach, then he would be safe. Marcellus could put men ashore and start to build the first Roman stockade in Lusitani territory.

The fog lifted like a curtain suddenly whisked aside. Marcellus did not look back to see if the other galleys were still hidden, being too taken by the sight that greeted him on the sandy shore: rows and rows of Lusitani tribesmen, their spear tips glinting in the watery sun, lined the golden beach. A great roar welcomed him, with the spears jabbing impatiently, and threateningly, in the air. In the middle of the throng stood a magnificently clad chieftain, who opened his arms, shield in one hand, sword in the other, in a gesture intended to invite them to do battle.

'Steer parallel to the shore,' he called and the galley swung round, each ship emerging from the fog doing likewise, eventually anchoring in a line that matched the serried ranks of warriors waiting for them to try and wade ashore.

'Well, Regimus, what do you think?'

The older man rubbed his short, iron-grey hair. 'Not a single ship. We've haven't seen one the whole way here.'

'No,' replied Marcellus. 'Yet these Lusitani are here. It's as though they knew in advance that this were where we intended to land.'

'Oh, they knew all right. All that beacon-burning was just to make sure we came as far as this bay. I daresay everyone in Portus Albus knew where we were headed by the time we sailed.'

Marcellus stood still, his eyes fixed on the edge of the shore. He could see the line of weed by the feet of the front rank of warriors; between that and the sea, the sand was wet, which told him they had been there since high tide. If the warriors had waited that long on land, then it was a fair bet that the ships would be at sea, full of men, ready to fall on their rear.

'Well, *Legatus*?' asked Regimus, neatly underlining, by the unusual use of Marcellus's rank, that the sole responsibility lay with him.

Marcellus smiled. 'I've no intention of retreating, Regimus, though I'm not averse to letting them think I am.'

He turned and looked at the bank of offshore fog. The indentation on the shore was like a capsule, with the mountains at the back, the arms of the bay on each side running into the fog, forming an impenetrable wall to the rear.

'I think they're hoping we'll attack.'

Marcellus interrupted, still smiling. 'At which point their ships will come in and try to catch us in the water as we wade ashore.'

'That thought might cheer you up, Marcellus

Falerius, but it makes my blood go cold.'

The young legate laughed. 'Don't be silly, Regimus. Can't you see we've got them in a trap?'

The rings of earthworks, in the morning light, seemed to rise one upon the other like some gigantic temple. Below Numantia, in front of their position, two rivers cut a wide swathe through the countryside. The only route of attack lay between those rivers; the other sides of the hill fort had approaches that were too steep for a proper assault.

'As you said, Aquila, if this place falls, it will break the spirit of Iberian resistance.' Aquila smiled, knowing that his general, who was not one for hyperbole, had not finished. 'The question is, will our spirit survive to see it destroyed?'

Aquila felt that he was seeing something familiar that he recognised from a dream, but it was hard to tell if that was true or just wild imagination. He had heard so many tales about the place, he felt he knew every stone and earthwork by heart. All around them the legionaries were hard at work constructing a camp, which seemed the wrong course of action. As always, when faced with a problem, he took his eagle in his hand, something Titus observed.

'Does that bird have the power to divine the future?'

The quaestor smiled at him. 'Many people have thought so.'

'Like every man in the legions,' he continued, answering the look on Aquila's face. 'I've had no end of hints, friend, that I should consult your charm, so that we can all get out of this alive. The men have great faith in it and no faith at all in the priests and their chickens.'

Titus looked again at the fortress of Numantia, a place so much stronger than he had ever imagined, a site that truly lived up to its reputation. For the first time since they had set out, he considered that he might have to order a retreat, wondering if even the novel tactic he had decided to employ would work on such a formidable obstacle. His mind went back to the conference he held on his return from the south, to the looks on the faces of his officers as he outlined his plan to turn Brennos's great defensive bastion into a trap.

'Our weapon, gentleman, is a combination of action and inaction. We will make breaches in the wall of the fort, and men will die doing so, but we will have plenty of time to rest between assaults.'

The eyes that had fixed on him then, in a look

brazenly enquiring, had been those of his quaestor and they had quite plainly posed the question: what are we going to do about all the tribesmen not in the hill fort? Titus knew he had truly gained Aquila Terentius's trust at that point, for as he spoke, the look in the eyes changed from challenge to wonder. He told them that he intended to build a wall all the way round Numantia, interspersed with forts that Brennos's allies would have to attack. He would besiege the enemy within, while those without would be forced to attack him in a situation heavily to their disadvantage. Such a situation would discourage them, and once that happened, he would detach enough men to fight their way back to the coast, opening up a supply route which meant he could stay in front of Numantia forever.

Like all plans, it looked good on paper; now, with the task visible before him, it was less so. But Aquila's next words, delivered with such heart-warming conviction, chased any thoughts of failure away. 'If we can eat, General, and they can't, then they must eventually surrender.'

Titus looked at the terrain. Apart from the fertile strip by the river it was rocky and inhospitable, no place to camp an army unless regular supplies could be guaranteed. He would have to forage for several weeks, living off the land, but it was also no place for the people inside the fortress to grow food other than that one plateau, which could not sustain them forever. Their hillsides were more barren than the plain.

'A tough nut, Aquila, but seemingly not impossible. I suggest we ride round the place and see where we should site our forts before it gets dark.'

They all knew Marcellus's orders, nor had he missed the looks – part uncertainty, part mistrust. The galleys weighed anchor and, to loud cheers from the massed ranks of the Lusitani, they swung their bows to head out of the bay. The warrior chieftains might have wondered why they formed up and rowed out to sea abreast of each other – a manoeuvre Marcellus had been forced to employ, and there was no way of knowing if that would allow those on the beach to guess the truth. The fog was thinning as the morning sun burnt it off, but it was still enough to swallow them up, while all the time his single drum beat the pace for the whole fleet.

'I see no other way to split them up,' he said to Regimus. 'If we decline to go ashore and wait until the fog lifts, then their ships will simply run away. They know they can't stand against quinqueremes.'

'Would that not count as a victory?' asked Regimus.

'No!' snapped Marcellus. 'We have to land sometime and beat them in battle, and that applies to their ships as well. We're here to stay.'

'I still think you're taking a terrible risk, *Legatus*,' said Regimus, who had remained formal ever since he had issued his commands.

Marcellus ignored him, calling softly to the oar master to keep his time steady. Another man stood beside him counting off the number of strokes and, as he reached a thousand, the oar master gave a quick drum roll. Regimus pushed the sweep and the rowers on one side lifted their oars so that the galley swung round in its own length. Timing at this point was crucial and Marcellus left the decision as to when they were fully round to Regimus. The older man called to the oar master, who gave another quick roll on the drum, before reinstating his steady beat, which increased slowly as the oars bit into the water. By the time the line of galleys emerged once more from the fog, they were going at battle speed, racing towards the shore in line abreast, Marcellus, in the bows, relieved to see that his enemies had done that which he expected; he had no need to abort his progress. Instead he called for more effort.

The Lusitani, thinking the Romans had departed, had broken ranks and they were milling about like a mob, half still on shore, the rest anything from ankle- to knee-deep in the shallows. The horns sounded in panic as their chieftains tried to reform them, which only added to the confusion. The gorgeously clad warrior who had challenged them to battle was in the water, in front of his men, using the boss of his shield to try to get them back into line. Marcellus watched the shore eagerly as it came near, and also the two galleys on either side as they edged slightly closer to his vessel. The men in the bows were standing by to release the *corvus*, the bridge that dropped from the front of the ship, which would provide a dry and defensible route for his soldiers to get ashore.

The Lusitani, still disordered, swept forward to form a ragged line in the shallows, just behind their leader, their indiscipline playing further into their enemies' hands. They expected the Romans to heave to, anchor, then wade ashore. It was impossible to count how many, hemmed in by those behind them, died in the shallow water, crushed by the quinqueremes' bows as Marcellus drove all his ships at ramming speed into the soft sand of the beach. Their leader was one of them, his gold-embossed metal breastplate cracking like a nutshell as the prow drove over him, sending his blood flowing outwards to stain the clear blue water. The wooden bridges, with their evil spikes, dropped onto the heads of the tribesmen, disabling even more and, as Marcellus's troops careered across them, the Lusitani found the Romans in their midst. The sailors, obeying their orders, rushed like Egyptian acrobats along the oars, which were raised out of the water, with each galley now so close that they interlocked. Quickly they lashed them together so that the entire fleet presented a solid line that could not be penetrated, either by the warriors on the shore, or the ships that would come in to aid them, should the fog disperse.

To begin with, it was a series of individual combats, not a battle, but the Romans had the advantage. They could, if driven back, retire to a safe and unassailable base: their galleys. Once they gained a foothold on the beach, they could be reinforced, fanning out to form a proper line. The battle raged back and forth, but every movement, in either direction, cost the lives of more Lusitani warriors than Romans. Marcellus, once he was sure his fleet was secure, personally led the main assault from his galley, for the first time in his life truly at liberty to use those skills he had learnt as a boy and a man on the Campus Martius.

He was the first to get a sizeable body of legionaries ashore. The men at the oars, now armed and numerous, poured onto the beach behind him, his advance party forming a line that the tribesmen could neither breach nor destroy. The men from the next galley to the right, after a hard fight, linked up; and, in time, the same thing happened on the left, until the entire foreshore was in Roman hands. The legionaries, at the command, advanced steadily, pushing back the tribesmen until the majority of them were penned against the rocks that surrounded two sides of the bay. Some escaped up the gentle incline in the centre, driven hard by the pursuit, but most died where they stood, their blood turning the golden sand to deep red.

Marcellus had floated his ships off on the rising tide before the fog lifted. The small Lusitani ships, numerous and loaded with men, looked upon a scene they had never thought to see. Floating before them lay an impenetrable line of battle-ready quinqueremes, while just inland the Romans were occupied building a stockade.

Their horses' heads drooped wearily by the time Titus and Aquila returned; the sun was well down in the sky and would be gone within the hour. Their tents were up, with hot water waiting and the air full of the smell of food. Fabius, with his usual scrounger's ability, had found the ingredients for a sumptuous meal, including several large fish from the nearby river.

'What's the point of me doing all this if you're not going to use it?' said Fabius, pointing angrily at the steaming bath in the middle of the tent.

Ever since Aquila's elevation, Fabius had been trying to pamper him. His 'nephew's' efforts had fallen on stony ground. 'If I need a wash, there's a perfectly good river nearby.'

'Which comes straight out of the mountain snows. Dive in that and your nuts will drop off. I can just hear you on the oration platform. You'll open your mouth to speak and find out that you've turned into a eunuch.'

Aquila smiled, the last part of this stricture being delivered in a high-pitched voice. He began to strip off his armour and decorations. 'You're so feeble, you city folk. No wonder Rome's in so much trouble.'

'Are we in trouble?' Fabius asked the question eagerly, for he made a tidy sum, these days, out of letting slip information to the troops.

'Ask me tomorrow.'

Aquila took the large robe that Fabius had laid out for him and went out of the tent. He was not alone in his desire to bathe in the river and the gates of the camp were guarded but open, while the men on duty lined the route to protect the swimmers. Fabius was right about the water, it was icy, but after such a hot, tiring day, it was a blessed relief. He emerged onto the bank to find Cholon standing by his clothes. They had hardly exchanged a word since the day Aquila had thrown him out of the camp, and every time the Greek had thrown a glance at the new quaestor, it had immediately turned to a sour frown. Yet now the man was smiling, and he even picked up and offered Aquila his robe, at the same time indicating the men splashing about.

'I've often wondered at your Roman love of water, Aquila Terentius.'

The younger man was not one to bear a grudge against someone like Cholon, who had, after all, been invited to come to the base camp, and he knew that Titus, who had issued that invitation, held the man in high regard, so he smiled back at him, making the peace.

'A distinct advantage, having soldiers who can swim. I hope you have noted in your history how it won us that battle at the river.'

Cholon's eyes were fixed on Aquila's neck, with the gold eagle swinging back and forth as he roughly towelled his naked body.

'Will it win you this one?' asked the Greek, pointing to the water from which he had just emerged. Clearly it was a way in and out of the defender's perimeter.

'It might,' replied Aquila thoughtfully, nodding towards the fort, huge and menacing on the hill above them. 'It depends on whether they can swim too.'

Having surveyed the terrain, Titus called a conference of all the officers in his army, down to the rank of centurion. Only the most senior knew what was coming, but before them all lay a map of the fort and the surrounding countryside, with a great ring running like a line of blood at the extremity.

'We will build forts of our own at these seven points. I want them joined by a palisade, permanently guarded, with a mobile reserve standing by in each fort to sally out and hold the line if it's attacked.' Titus stabbed his finger at various points. 'I want all these trees cleared and one or two of the hills close by flattened. No one is to get in, or out, unless we wish it.'

'The rivers will still be open, sir,' said Publius Calvinus.

Titus looked up from the table, his face hard.

'That will be the last thing we will seal. I want

a pontoon of bridges over them, backed by booms and chains. We will cut Numantia off from the outside world, and if we have to stay here forever, we will starve them out.'

'You speak the language,' said Titus. 'And anyway, it's a bad idea for a commander to negotiate personally.'

'Why?' asked Aquila, puzzled. He put down his knife, stopped chewing and looked hard at his general.

'Because his word would be final,' added Cholon.

Aquila half-suspected this whole scheme was his idea. They might be at peace with each other now, but he suspected that Cholon was a slippery customer.

'Is that a bad thing?'

Cholon smiled, increasing Aquila's discomfort. 'An envoy makes proposals but he can always pretend that there is a point beyond which he cannot proceed and, should he go too far, his commander can always reprimand him and revoke the agreement.'

Cholon was basing his attitude on what he had achieved as an envoy in Sicily all those years ago, acting on behalf of Lucius Falerius Nerva. The old senator might have set them, but it was he who had negotiated the terms that saw the slave leaders desert their followers, though one, a Celt, had proved intransigent and died for his stubbornness. For a moment, he contemplated giving Aquila an explanation of those events so he would comprehend what Cholon was driving at – for he had always had the ability to deny things on the grounds that his superior would not agree – or go back to the table and say some previously agreed point was not acceptable, but he decided against it as being too distracting.

Aquila, who was looking at him very directly, took another mouthful of food, chewing slowly while he ruminated. 'So what you're saying is this: that I should go into the hills, talk to a tribal chief called Masugori, an ex-client of Rome, who would like to do nothing more than stick a spear so far up my arse that it comes out of my mouth, and make promises that you might decide not to keep?'

Cholon winced at the way that Aquila had reached his conclusions, though he replied calmly enough. 'That, as an interpretation, is somewhat crude.'

'Get stuffed!'

Titus burst out laughing, while Cholon's face took on a hurt expression.

'If I make an agreement,' said Aquila, his blue

eyes now boring into those of the Greek, 'Rome keeps it, never mind Titus Cornelius.'

'So?'

'You've met this Masugori, you said, so you should know.'

'It was a long time ago, before I even put on my manly gown.'

'But you trusted him?'

'I think it's worth a try.'

Again Aquila thought long and hard before replying. The attacks on the legions had ceased as soon as they reached Numantia, and both he and Titus knew what that meant; the enemy was chary about facing the whole of Titus Cornelius's force in full battle, but they wanted them to stay, and they were giving them a breathing space to get well dug in. The attacks would be resumed just as soon as they commenced the assault and the tribesmen thought the Romans, being both occupied and taking casualties, and running short on supplies, would be so weakened that they could be defeated.

Masugori held the key. His tribe was the closest, and barring the Lusitani, the most numerous. They had once signed a peace with the general's father that had held until later commanders had so abused their office. If the chief of the Bregones could be brought back to neutrality, it would ease Titus's task immensely, since supplying the army would become relatively straightforward. It was the life of one man put at risk to save the lives of many. He looked at the two other men, who were watching him closely to see what he would decide, so he just nodded and went back to his food.

CHAPTER NINETEEN

———•———

'Why me?' asked Fabius for the twentieth time, with that truly agonised expression he could produce on demand.

It was a litany that Aquila had become used to, but he knew that his 'nephew' would have killed anyone who sought to accompany the quaestor in his place. It was part of Fabius's way to play the endemic coward, just as he reserved the right to steal the officers' food and wine; and if he had stopped moaning, Aquila would have been seriously worried.

'What am I doing out here, in the company of a madman in his underwear, with not even a pin to protect myself? No sword, no spear, nothing! Well, I tell you, "Uncle", if those tribesmen come anywhere near me, before they stick a weapon in me, I'm going to hoist up my kilt and give them a good look at my bare arse.'

'That might make them keep you alive?'

Fabius pulled a face. 'I wonder if it's truly a fate worse than death?'

Aquila raised his hand slowly. 'Now's your chance to find out.'

Fabius followed the finger to observe that the ridge in front of them was full of horsemen, who had appeared as if by magic. 'What are the chances?' he asked. There was no fear in his voice, but he was not joking either.

'If they charge, none. If they stay still, evens.'

Aquila raised his hands, holding his horse by the knees. Fabius followed suit, praying silently that these Celt-Iberians would recognise that Aquila wanted to talk peace. The only sound was that of their hooves as they rode slowly uphill. The chieftain of those before them was an easy man to spot; everything he wore, from the gold-decorated helmet, to the silver and gold on his shield and breastplate and the richly carved metal greaves, spoke of his elevated station. But even at this distance they could see he was quite elderly.

The quaestor of the Roman army looked like nothing by comparison, wearing a simple purple-edged smock, with no decoration except the gold eagle around his neck; no weapons and no helmet. The distance was closing and the chieftain, surrounded by his tribesmen, knew he was at no risk, knew he could kill these messengers before or after he spoke with them, aware that prudence demanded he listen to what they had to say. The wrinkled face was set stiff, as if he had no intention of conceding anything, but as Aquila came closer, that changed, and it was not just the chieftain's face that altered. Other men murmured and pointed, setting up a babble of noise.

'That bloody hair of yours is going to get us killed,' said Fabius out of the corner of his mouth.

'Maybe you're right,' his uncle replied.

The chieftain raised his garlanded spear, the sun catching the torques of gold on his arm and his guttural cry stifled the noise, which ceased abruptly and he spoke again, quietly this time. Then he rode forward, with just one warrior on either side of him. Aquila halted and waited for him to approach.

'Ye gods, he's an ugly bastard,' said Fabius softly. 'Whatever you do, don't ask him if he's got a sister.'

He had dark skin and black marks on his face to match his eyes. They stopped a few feet away, staring at each other for what seemed an age. Then Aquila spoke, with the chieftain's face registering deep shock at being addressed in his own tongue by someone he thought was a

Roman, a race that if they condescended to talk to you at all, spoke Latin and used interpreters.

'I am Aquila Terentius, quaestor to Titus Cornelius, commander of the Roman army besieging Numantia.'

No one said anything for a while, except of course Fabius, to whom a long silence was anathema. 'Chatty bunch!'

Aquila ignored him and began speaking in the Celtic tongue again, outlining what they were here to do and how the Romans intended to do it. 'We are strong and we will build forts that you cannot safely attack. Numantia will be cut off, then we will bring in food on a proper Roman road, if necessary with an escort too strong to attack.'

'No escort is that strong,' said the chieftain, speaking for the first time.

Aquila's blue eyes never blinked, nor did his voice alter. 'If you attack us, we won't need supply columns, we'll just come and take the food out of your mouths.'

The chieftain dropped his spear, pushing it forward. It was hard for Aquila to hold still with the spear coming at him, but he did. The tip stopped just below his neck, then it was jerked so that it just caught the golden charm, causing the eagle to swing back and forth across the chest of his smock.

'Have you taken Numantia already?'

The question surprised Aquila, and for the first time he blinked. 'No. But we will. If you attack us, we will let them be and turn on your tribe and destroy you.'

'So we should just let you kill our cousins in Numantia?'

'Why not? Are you really friends with them? You've spent years watching them grow, stealing a bit of land here, more there, until you must bow the knee to them. Are you to be made beggars while they increase their riches?' The face opposite still showed no expression, nor did the eyes lift from his breast to his face, so Aquila ploughed on. 'Ask yourself this. If you are prepared to come to the aid of the Duncani, what will they do if we attack you? Will you suffer the same fate as the Averici, who looked in vain to the west? Brennos left them to die, and he would see your bones bleached before he would venture out of his fortress. He speaks of an alliance, when what he means is this: you die for the greater glory of me.'

The spear tip flicked again, moving the charm once more. 'Truly, you would know this.'

'Who am I addressing?' asked Aquila.

'Masugori.'

'Chief of the Bregones?'

The man nodded and the spear tip flicked the eagle again. 'This thing, how did you come by it?'

He had been asked that question many times, and usually refused to answer; in fact he had even concocted the odd lie to deflect curiosity, or at least allowed others to draw conclusions he declined to refute. But something told him that the truth, on this occasion, would serve him better.

'It was put round my foot when I was born. Where it comes from originally, I do not know.'

Masugori pushed his horse forward slightly and touched the eagle, then he looked at Aquila, with his height and his red-gold hair. Finally, he tugged at his reins, turning his horse.

'Follow me!'

The Bregones were one of the few tribes who had never built a fort. Partly this stemmed from the peace they had once enjoyed with Rome, but it also had something to do with a numerical strength that made them less fearful than their neighbours. The huge encampment – more of a city – named Lutia, lay in a fertile plain, with huts stretching as far as the eye could see. Aquila tried to count them so as to guess at the number of warriors, but he gave up after a while, aware that it ran into thousands. Masugori handed Fabius over to someone else to be entertained, took Aquila into his own hut, and then sent for his priests.

They came and pored over Aquila, touching his body and hair. He refused to remove the charm, afraid that it might not be returned, but he lifted it so that the priests could finger that too. The entire party was then moved outside, so that the priests could perform their magic, casting bones very much as old Drisia the sorceress had done all those years before outside Fulmina's hut. Then there was a long moaning incantation while their leading shaman held his charm again, all this taking place at the same time as some mystical ceremony involving earth, fire and water. When they had finished, the priests went into a whispered conclave with Masugori, who emerged from the throng and invited Aquila and Fabius back into his tent.

'You were not born in these lands?'

Aquila shook his head. 'Italy, just south of Rome.'

'Your father is—'

'Is unknown to me,' Aquila interrupted, sharply. It had always been a subject on which he was touchy, and one his fellows knew not to ask. The last thing he intended to do was discuss it with a barbarian chief, diplomacy be damned, yet the way he spoke had not, it seemed, offended his host, who extended one gnarled finger towards his neck.

'Take that eagle in your hand.' Aquila did so. 'Will you win, Roman?'

He nodded. 'Without doubt!'

The Bregones chieftain sat, head bowed for a while, obviously thinking. Then he raised his eyes, surrounded by crow's feet, and looked at his strange visitor.

'My priests said that was so. They have seen the hill of Numantia bare of earthworks. They have also looked into the past.' Masugori paused, as though he was unsure of what to say. When he did continue, Aquila had the distinct impression that he was leaving something out. 'Then there is you, coming to me with nothing but your eagle to protect you. It is very strange that the gods should bring you here, of all places. They must have a purpose and I am advised not to anger them. We will not interfere in your siege, nor with your supplies.'

'The price?' demanded Aquila.

'There is no price for you.'

'The land around Numantia. True peace with Rome after that,' said Aquila.

'We ask for nothing. If you win, perhaps you will give us these things. If you lose, because of

folly or fickle predictions, you will leave the
bleached bones of your legions in the hills as a
testimony to your failure. Now we will eat and
talk, and you will swear by your gods that you
are who you are, and that the words you speak
are the truth.'

*The Roman ability to build never ceased to
amaze those they fought and conquered, but then
they could not comprehend the stock from which
Roman military ideas had sprung. It was the
solid, hard-working farmer who had made the
legions feared, not gaudily dressed warriors who
saw husbandry and farming as effete.*

Cholon put aside his stylus and looked around
him, as the very evidence for that sentence lay
before him. It was typical of the people he lived
amongst to go about a siege this way: no
imaginative attacks, nor a search for a refreshing
form of tactics. Just plain hard work and time,
which produced a slow but certain result. Every
one of the seven forts was a complete Roman
camp, able to house the entire army in an
emergency. The palisade, fifteen feet high, with
projecting towers at regular intervals, ran in a
straight line, regardless of the state of the ground,
from one fort to the next, stopping only at the
banks of the river.

Across that stream they had laid a boom of thick logs, chained together to prevent boats coming or going, with razor-sharp blades hanging deep in the water. At night, the wall was manned at regular intervals, with flaring torches between the guards to throw some light onto the deep ditch that ran along the outer edge. Special squads, made up of the best swimmers, stood sentinel at the riverbank, ready to plunge into the icy stream and fight those trying either to escape from Numantia, or bring in news and supplies.

Thinking about guards reminded Cholon of a note he must make regarding the Roman system, and he picked up his stylus again.

Each guard is issued with a wooden token before taking up his post. This token must be handed to an officer at an unspecified time during the night. These rounds are distributed after the guards have taken up their posts, and who visits whom is entirely at the discretion of the duty tribune. Thus it is easy to discover who has fallen asleep at his post, thereby endangering the entire legion, since that man will still have his token in the morning. The penalty for such an offence is a horrible death, delivered by the other soldiers, whose life this man put at risk.

He looked up to see Titus standing over him,

politely waiting so as not to interrupt. 'I hope you're doing as you said, Cholon, and sticking to a general military history.'

'You do not wish to be recorded for distant posterity?' asked the Greek.

Titus smiled. 'Not without reading what is said about me.'

'You have nothing to fear, Titus, nothing at all, but I daresay some of your predecessors, and some senators at Rome, might cringe at what is implied.'

'I've come to ask a favour.'

Cholon put aside his stylus and scroll. 'Ask away!'

'As you know, I've elevated Aquila Terentius to a position he could never have dreamt of. If he thought of the future at all, he would have seen himself as a retired *primus pilus*, who with luck would, on leaving service, have enough money to join the class of knights.'

'He may have dreamt of something better than that,' said Cholon, ever literal in his interpretation of words.

'Since he has never been taught, he cannot read. That should be remedied.'

Cholon frowned. 'He also speaks Greek like a Piraeus dock worker. Mind, since he says he's never been out of Italy, it's a wonder he speaks

Greek at all. It would be interesting to know where he learnt it.'

'His past is a mystery. I have spent some time with him these last months and he will talk of little but his service in the legions. I know he was raised on a farm near Aprilium.'

There was a nagging sensation in the Greek's mind that somehow what Titus was saying should mean something, but he couldn't fix it. 'What about that relative of his?'

'Fabius Terentius? He's from the back streets of Rome. It would be like trying to get blood out of a stone for someone like me to ask him anything.'

'Is this merely curiosity, Titus?'

The senator shook his head slowly. 'I've raised him above his natural station. Once this campaign is over, and assuming we succeed, where does he go? His appointment as quaestor is my personal gift, yet I cannot see him going back to his previous rank; besides which, he will be a very wealthy man if we take Numantia. After me, he will have the pick of anything that can be made out of this godforsaken land and that will most certainly give him the means to become a senator.'

'Goodness, Titus. Imagine Aquila Terentius in the Senate, with his language!'

'It would be fun to watch, that's for certain.'

'I should let the gods decide his future. It's not for men to interfere.'

Titus smiled. 'Would a little teaching be interference? And who knows, in the process you might unravel the mystery of his birth.'

It was a slave who recognised the drawing: a plump, homely girl of Greek extraction, who worked for the overseer of Cassius Barbinus's warehouse. That they were staying in the man's house at all was a constant source of complaint from the fastidious Sextius, who moaned about the size of the accommodation, the conversation of their host, the heat, the flies, the tedious landscape full of wheat, the rumbling of that damned volcano and the smell of the natives. He frowned mightily when Claudia told him to shut up, and if his personality had been as strong as his countenance, more people than his wife would have trembled at the looks he could produce.

Sextius was one of those people who managed to look better the older he became, his profile seeming ever more Roman, the stuff of which sculptors dreamt, and it was that which produced the idea of the drawing. In a rare effort to mollify her carping spouse, Claudia suggested he have a bust done in the fine marble that was locally quarried in this part of the island. Almost by habit, she asked the sculptor – without success – if he had ever heard of a man called Aquila Terentius, so she went on to describe the charm she had so lovingly put round the infant's foot. All the while, Sextius sat mopping his sweating brow and complaining that this was going to take long enough without Claudia disturbing the 'poor man' at his work.

'Would it help if I drew it for you, Lady?'

'Drew it?'

'Yes. This charm. If you describe it to me, I will do the best I can, to give you something you can show to others.'

'Claudia,' snapped Sextius, his lips pursed in frustration.

'Please do so.'

'I distinctly remember you calling him a "poor man",' said Claudia. She was sitting at a table while the Greek maid dressed her hair for dinner with the Barbinus overseer.

'Well, he's not poor now,' replied Sextius, sourly. 'I've never been charged so much for a bust in my life.'

'It must be the cost of the stone.'

Her husband just grunted; really he was wondering if he could get the Greek girl to dress his hair as well. Claudia slipped the drawing out to sneak another look and the girl's sharp intake of breath merged with Claudia's yell of pain, as her hair was tugged violently by the heavy tongs.

'What happened?' asked Sextius. 'Did she burn you?'

'An accident, Master,' said the girl, still looking at the piece of linen in Claudia's hand. The hair trapped between the hot tongs started to smoulder and the girl pulled it abruptly away. Sextius stood up, towering over her. 'If you pull my wife's hair, or burn her again, I'll see you whipped.'

'Why don't you go and have some wine, Sextius,' said Claudia, with a tremor in her voice.

She had noticed that, denied any outlet for his main pleasure in life, he had taken to drinking a great deal. Sextius looked at the back of Claudia's head, then at the girl who had tugged her locks so painfully. The smell of burnt hair lingered in the atmosphere and he ran his hand over his smooth silver thatch, thinking perhaps it would be a bad idea for him to put himself at similar risk. He fixed the girl again with his sternest Roman frown and left the room.

'You recognise this?' Claudia demanded, her heart beating wildly as she held up the linen.

The girl shook her head violently. No slave

volunteered information to anyone; it usually got them, or someone they cared for, into trouble. Claudia fought to stop herself shouting at the girl, knowing instinctively that to do so would be fatal; instead she reached out and lifted the tongs out of the girl's hands.

'Your name, child?' she asked, though the girl was far too old for the title.

'Phoebe,' she responded, so quietly that it was hard to hear.

'You're frightened, aren't you?'

Claudia was cursing Sextius as a bully; clearly part of the girl's fear would be a hangover from his strictures. Phoebe nodded, forcing her eyes away from the drawing, lest by looking at it she betray herself. Claudia felt an ache in her belly, being so close to the truth, yet so far away. If she pressured this girl, she would shut up completely, and Claudia was in no position to call the master of the house and threaten to have the information beaten out of her.

'Do you have any children, Phoebe?' she asked, her voice as soft as she could make it. The girl nodded slowly, as Claudia continued. 'Can you imagine how you would feel, if your child had been taken from you at birth, and you'd never seen him since that day?'

She looked Phoebe in the eye as she said that,

encouraging the younger woman to respond to her next question. 'Does the name Aquila Terentius mean anything to you?'

Sextius came back in to find the slave girl in floods of tears, and Claudia sat frozen in her chair, her face a mask. She's beaten the wretch, he thought. Serve her right. A bit of pain will do her good. He was wrong of course; all the pain was in the heart of the stony-faced woman who was not crying.

'I cannot fathom women at all, Barbinus. Perhaps you can tell me what makes them the way they are?'

Sextius took another large gulp of wine. He was very pleased to be back in what he considered to be near civilisation. He would be home tomorrow, for this, near Aprilium, was the last stop before Rome, brought about by Claudia's insistence that she be allowed to buy the Greek girl Phoebe and her daughter.

'It's not sex, is it?' asked Barbinus, who owned Phoebe, as well as her child, and was afire to know why they had brought her all the way back here to secure his agreement.

Sextius fixed him with a jaundiced eye. Barbinus was flabby now, with all the texture gone from his skin. He still tried to be the man he was as a youth, though the years were against him. Not only that, the potions and love philtres he was constantly swallowing in the hope of reviving his flagging libido had taken their toll on his complexion as well.

'For if it is,' he continued, 'you can have her for free if I'm allowed to watch Claudia with her.'

Sextius gave him what he considered was his manliest look. 'The gods will have fun with you, Barbinus. I've never met such a rogue.'

'You haven't answered my question.'

'It most certainly is not, and if you see them together you'd wonder at why Claudia wants the girl. All they seem to do in each other's company is cry. It's a mystery to me.'

'Well, if Claudia insists on having her, take her as a gift.'

'No, no, friend. She will insist on paying.'

'Do you think she might pay in kind? She's still a handsome woman.'

Sextius snorted. 'I have a terrible fear, Barbinus. There is an eastern cult that believes that when we die, we return to the earth as animals.'

'So what's your fear?'

'I'd hate to return as one of yours, say a pig or a sheep.'

Barbinus grinned, his lopsided lips thick, wet and red. 'Nice idea. I could roger you, then have you for dinner.'

The shared memory was important to Claudia, even the knowledge her son had grown up, only to become a rebel against Rome – perhaps because it was in his blood – but not before he had enjoyed a relationship with Phoebe and left her pregnant.

'He went with the overseer, Didius Flaccus, to Messana,' said Phoebe, 'and that was the last time I saw him. All I know is that Flaccus came back in a towering rage and, after accusing me of being to blame, he sent me away. I heard later that Aquila had joined the slave army to fight Rome, but after their defeat I heard no more.'

Then he had disappeared, a victim, no doubt, of Rome's revenge in the clampdown that had followed the collapse of the revolt. Sometimes she harboured a feeling that he might have survived, but Phoebe insisted that, if he had, he would have come back to her. That produced a slight twitch of jealousy, since this girl had experienced a love that she had been denied. They walked by the riverbank, trailed by the girl that Phoebe had borne after being sent packing by Flaccus.

She was tall for her age, with long raven hair

that, when it caught the sun, had a tinge of fire to it; and she was beautiful, with pale skin like alabaster. Looking up from the gurgling waters of the Liris to the mountains in the distance, they could see the extinct volcano with that strange-shaped top that looked like a votive cup. Where had they put him? Claudia wanted to know, wanted to ask Cholon, who would surely tell her now that the boy was certainly dead. She would erect a small shrine on the spot, as a memory to him.

The young man tickling fish in the river was so intent on what he was doing that he failed to hear them approach. This was Barbinus's land, not that she cared, except perhaps that she should buy the whole place from him, then she would know that the land on which her little boy had been laid was definitely hers. The poacher stood up abruptly, water dripping from his arm and he turned to face them with a nervous smile. Something about his looks tugged at Claudia's memory, so she walked closer and addressed him directly.

'Do I know you?'

Rufurius Dabo could see that she was rich. She wore enough to buy ten farms on her neck alone and he dreamt of owning a farm, but Annius, his elder brother, had got everything when their father died. The younger Dabo had just built a hut on a vacant spot, which someone informed him was the place where old Clodius Terentius and his wife Fulmina had lived. Given the stories he had heard about that peasant, Rufurius often wondered if that was why he stayed poor.

He replied to Claudia's question with due deference. 'No, Lady.'

'Odd, I thought I did.' Claudia smiled, and indicated his dripping arm. 'I shouldn't let Cassius Barbinus find you doing that. He'll feed you to his dogs.'

CHAPTER TWENTY

'I think Fabius enjoyed it more than me,' said Aquila. 'They thought he was a general too, and entertained him accordingly.'

Talking about Fabius was a blind; he was determined to stay off the subject of what had happened to him at the Bregones encampment, given that he had much to ponder, and none of it was any business of his general or Cholon the Greek. His situation, as an envoy of Titus, had precluded questions, and to show curiosity about what was happening might have jeopardised the whole prospect of a truce. Aquila's height and colour had attracted attention all his life, as had the charm he wore round his neck, but both had deeply affected Masugori and his priests, and had in some way contributed to, if not brought about, the final decision to leave Numantia and Brennos to their fate.

He took the charm in his hand; perhaps, as

Fulmina had insisted, it had some magic potency. Though he saw it as his lucky talisman, the prospect had always alarmed him and he had no desire that it should be more than that, especially if he was unable to understand its meaning. Suddenly he realised that both the other men were waiting for him to elaborate and he dragged his thoughts back to Fabius.

'Don't be surprised if be behaves like a patrician from now on.'

'Did he learn anything of use?' asked Titus, slightly terse at what he saw as levity in a situation that demanded that his envoy be serious.

'He informs me that, though the Bregones women are ugly by thirty, they are fine at around fifteen, though the drink they brew, a coarse grain spirit, seriously interferes with a man's ability to test out the notion.'

'I suppose we should be grateful he came back.' Titus liked Fabius, because the ranker insisted that no Roman citizen need be overly polite to another, a right he exercised whether he was talking to a consul or a quaestor. Cholon frowned darkly, since another Fabian maxim was that Romans should always be rude to Greeks. 'But I am less interested in what he was up to, Aquila, than what you did.'

'I have told you, you have your truce.'

'Well, all I do is repeat our congratulations. You've succeeded beyond my wildest hopes, but I still don't quite understand how you managed it?'

He lied smoothly. 'It was so easy, General. I can only think I was telling them what they wanted to hear.' Then he waited, hoping the look on his face would deter further enquiry.

'Will they keep their word?' asked Cholon,

'I'd say yes,' Aquila replied. 'But I am, by nature, a man disinclined to trust anyone too much.'

'You're right, you can never totally trust the Celt-Iberians,' said Cholon, emphatically.

'I wasn't just talking about them,' replied Aquila coldly, still convinced that notion of sending him off alone had emanated from the Greek's mind. 'I mean everybody.'

'Cholon is writing a section of his history on the Duncani chieftain.' said Titus, as the Greek flushed with embarrassment. 'As you know, I've had a lifelong interest in the man.'

'Brennos?' asked Cholon, looking at Aquila. 'You say that it's not a common Celt-Iberian name?'

Aquila's eyes flashed angrily; Masugori had told him that he looked very like Brennos, just as he had also told him where Brennos came from. 'Did I?'

Titus put his hands up, slightly alarmed, to stop the Greek. 'No, Cholon, it was I who told you that. Tell me what you found out about him that we don't already know.'

Cholon reached over to pick up his wax tablet. 'It would be helpful to me, as well. The more complete my history, the more it will serve as a guide to others. The Romans must learn to make peace as well as war.'

'Your legate, Marcellus Falerius, seems to be doing well,' said Aquila, desperate to change the subject. 'We haven't even had a sniff of the Lusitani.'

The *legatus* in question was often prey to doubts, for, mostly alone, thinking about the numerous nature of his enemies, as well as the limited force he had at his disposal, he could easily imagine them being pushed back into the sea. When they had first landed he had had no idea of the magnitude of the task facing him. As the largest single tribal grouping in the Iberian Peninsula, with an identity quite distinct from most of their Celt-Iberian neighbours, the Lusitani boasted a more unified command, one that could put warriors into the field in quantities that he could never defeat. That he held on at all was a testimony to both his determination and his inventiveness.

Normally it was the tribes that avoided pitched battles with Roman forces; here in the west it was Marcellus Falerius, with the small comfort that, by his presence, he was keeping them from interfering in Titus's operations around Numantia. These were the spectres of the dark hours of the night; in the morning, his diligent nature would force him to a more positive approach and he would put aside the thoughts that he considered unworthy of a man of his breeding. Never mind if others won triumphs, received the thanks of the Senate, and rode garlanded down the Sacred Way. He was doing his duty and that was enough.

Marcellus had constructed his stockade further up the coast, where his ships could anchor in some safety in a horn-shaped bay, protected by two long spits of sand visible at low tide, the open shore being deadly when the weather turned foul. This was his base camp from which he emerged to engage in a war of skirmish and raid, using the marching ability of his men, in combination with the power and mobility of his ships, to outwit the Lusitani, his aim to use their country against them instead of the other way round. Two things were paramount: he must never allow them to assemble against him in any strength, and he could never risk a defeat at sea. Fortunately, the Lusitani ships seemed disinclined to test out the heavier quinqueremes, especially in deep water.

The place he was now using as a base presented a strong fortified position: his stockade built with great ingenuity, the natural defensive nature of the shoreline being enhanced by two small strongholds at the head of the bay. With steep cliffs on both sides, he was safe from any outflanking manoeuvre, while the great bight of water narrowed to an entrance where the two sandbars kept out both the weather and anyone inclined to attack him from the sea. On the landward side, the shape of the steep-sided ravine, enhanced by earthworks, channelled the attackers into a narrow approach that nullified their numerical superiority; but that same defensive network hemmed him in too, forcing him to undertake a voyage every time he wanted to mount an attack.

It was the ships that allowed him to keep his enemies guessing. Regimus had charted the coast, sailed it with him, and now knew every bay and landing place for a hundred leagues, as well as every hazard they could possibly face, so the

Lusitani, never knowing where he might strike next, were forced to extend themselves to contain him. If Marcellus had a true worry, one that survived into the hours of daylight, it was that war was a matter of luck and one day his luck, which had held till now, could run out.

'If the Roman soldier dreams of anything, it is this,' said Marcellus. The flickering torch, catching the surfaces of gold and silver, and winking off the precious stones, seemed to increase the size of the hoard. Regimus, his nose tickled by the dust that had risen off the wrappings, sneezed loudly.

'No wonder they stood and fought,' he said, wiping his nose.

'Guard it, Regimus!'

Marcellus turned and walked out of the hut to see that the bodies of the Lusitani warriors had been cleared away and that his men were now standing around, whispering excitedly, because they all knew that this camp that they had just taken was different.

'Any sign of women and children?' asked Marcellus.

All the replies were negative, which only confirmed his original suspicion that this was some kind of sacred place. It had a circle of large upright stones, which stood like sentinels in the moonlight, surrounding a flat, raised rock, seven sided, that could only be an altar. Added to that, the huts were of a more solid construction than those normally found in Lusitani settlements, but that was as nothing to the hoard of gold and silver objects he had just been shown. Those on long wooden shafts were, no doubt, designed to stand upright in the holes which had been made in each corner of the altar, but there were many more objects, all with that intricate craftsmanship in precious metals for which the Celtic nations were famous. These stones formed some kind of temple and the treasure was for use in whatever rituals took place at this spot.

Was it his imagination, or did the night air seem colder here than elsewhere, as though the spirits of the dead were in residence? He was a Roman, and traditionally he respected the gods of others as much as his own, so the feel of the place affected him deeply. In peace, it would not be beyond his imagination to see himself worshipping here, sacrificing some animal as an offering to an alien deity, who, in truth, would be the same as a Roman god, only with a different name.

All his instincts told him to leave everything as it was and get back to his ships with all haste, for he could not be certain that his men had killed all the guards, so some might have got away. The trouble with that idea was that his men knew about the find, since one of their number had been the first to discover it. He would have a revolt if he suggested they leave such a treasure behind, and what would they say in Rome when they heard that he had had a fortune at his fingertips, the possessions of an enemy of the Republic, and had just left them to be repossessed?

He would try in vain to find a satisfactory explanation, yet standing here it was obvious. He had fought his campaign in a deliberately low-key way, doing just enough to harass his enemy and keep him occupied without ever troubling the Lusitani enough to make his removal a matter of paramount tribal survival. That this strategy had been forced on him by his limited resources in no way altered anything, but if he despoiled this sacred site, that could all change. Nothing would enrage them more than that their sacred objects should fall into the hands of an enemy and they would muster all their forces to attack him, with the sole aim of getting them back. Yet to leave it be would send an even less palatable signal; it would imply that Rome was afraid of the power of the Lusitani gods; so afraid, that, having killed the warriors left to guard it, the legions had been forced to flee without touching anything.

'Ropes and shovels,' he shouted. 'At the double!'

The tall circle of stones was held in place by its own weight, which over the years had allowed them to sink into the ground, so he set half his men to digging at one side of the base, while the others formed a human pyramid, so that one of their number could get high enough to lash a rope around the very top. Regimus was given the task of laying out the treasure; the route back to the beach was too rough for carts so each man would be given so much to carry, though Marcellus suspected that he would never get back with the entire hoard. Some would be filched, but that was the price he would have to pay.

The diggers had finished their task, hacking away at the earth until they reached the base of the stones lying on the bedrock. One of them went over on its own, without warning, nearly crushing the diggers, and as the work continued many a prayer was offered, silently, to Roman gods, for this was seen as a manifestation of the wrath of Celtic ones. The rest were pulled over, until every stone lay untidily on the thick grass.

Then they lined up and filled their pouches

with booty. Some had knotted their cloaks and slung them over their shoulders. Marcellus watched, noticing, in the torchlight, the fine craftsmanship that had gone into the making of these objects. He also saw the naked greed in the eyes of his men and the thought occurred that, with such valuable objects about their person, some of them might try to desert.

'Back to the beach and we stop for nothing. Anyone wounded is to be left.'

'What about the stuff he's carrying?' asked a voice in the dark.

'That will just have to be left with him. You might just have time to put him out of his misery and say a prayer for him. After what we've done tonight, I wouldn't want anyone to fall into the hands of the men who know we despoiled their sacred temple. Whoever does will end up on that altar, wide awake, while they slowly cut out his heart.'

The sky was tinged with grey and the sun was about to rise, so they had stayed there far too long already, and it was long past the time to go, so they set off at a steady trot, the laden legionaries following in single file. Marcellus had stood to count his men, tallying them off as they ran past him, when he first saw the pursuit. The glint of the rising sun, flashing off metal spear tips caught his eye, making him stare harder at the ridges on either side of the long broad valley. The movement of the tiny figures became apparent, riding at a steady pace on small ponies, easily overhauling his foot-slogging legionaries. He tried to calculate how far they had come, what the chances were of reaching the beach before these horsemen caught up with them; indeed, whether it would be better to stand and fight.

His mind was made up by what he saw next: Lusitani on foot, so numerous he could not count them, pouring over one of the ridges and running to catch them. They were a long way away, but those horsemen had been sent to cut them off from their escape route, so that together they could overwhelm his small force. Marcellus threw off most of the things he was carrying, keeping only his weapons and those precious objects that they hacked off their wooden poles. He ran up the line, ordering his men to do the same, to drink their water and cast aside what they could not consume, to throw away their sacks of polenta, salt and bread and to run, each man at his own pace. He kept looking back, sure that the tribesmen on foot were not gaining, but the horsemen were already abreast while they were still a long way from the beach and the safety of their ship.

Running alongside Regimus, he saw that the older man was puffing hard, his legs being more accustomed to the deck of a ship than this exertion on dry land, while in his mind he ran through various options. The horsemen would get ahead of him, he had no doubt of that, and they would have to break through or face a horrible death, quite possibly, as he had already said, strapped to that sacrificial altar. They could break into smaller groups and try to escape over the more broken ground of the rock-strewn hillsides, but then the other warriors behind them would have the advantage of level ground, which would bring them on much faster.

By the time these thoughts had crystallised, the horsemen were past them and he saw the lead riders on each side turn their ponies' heads and descend from the ridges, followed in single file by the rest. From that vantage point they would have picked their spot to halt the Romans and they would assume, from their own experience, that the legionaries would form up in a defensive line to face cavalry, just as he knew that ultimately that would suit their purpose.

'Phalanx!' he shouted to Regimus.

The older man looked at him wild-eyed, as though he had no notion of what his leader was saying, till Marcellus grabbed his arm and slowed him, holding up his other hand to halt the rest. It was quite possibly a mad idea, since Roman javelins were nothing like the fearsome spears of Alexander's Macedonian infantry, but it had the single virtue as a tactic that the Lusitani would not expect it, and quite possibly confused, they would yield before a determined charge by a solid triangle of spears.

There was no time for neatness, no time even to attempt perfection, and he did his best to impart the theory of this strange manoeuvre to his men as he pushed them into place, telling them to cover their heads with their shields and point the spears out at the same angle to the man in front. Then, raising his voice to the loudest tone of command, he ordered them to move, taking the point of the triangle himself so as to regulate the pace. The horsemen were strung across the broad valley floor, more numerous in the middle than they were on the flanks. Marcellus, spear pointed straight forward, turned slightly to the right as they came within casting distance, away from the heaviest concentration of his foes.

Sweat was running in his eyes, making it hard to see properly, but he felt that his tactic had them confused. The men in the centre, seeing him turn a flank to them, did not wait to find out what would happen next but charged at the array of spears. Marcellus turned again to face them, aiming for the dog-leg gap that had opened up between those who had charged and the others, on his right flank, who had held their ground. As the galloping horsemen swerved to engage, it was like the meeting of two irresistible forces, the Romans, to a man, knowing that they would all die if they even paused. The Lusitani horsemen at the front of the charge were pushed onto the Roman spears by those behind and there was a moment, brief but frightening, when Marcellus thought that their forward movement had been arrested.

But the legionaries, with the single order to close up to the soldier in front and to keep going at all costs, managed to maintain some momentum. In this they were aided by the Lusitani horses, which tended to shy away from the unbroken line of spears. Those on the flanks were now charging to close the gap, but before him he could just see the silver glint of the sea at the point where the valley met the beach. His ships, he hoped, were out of sight below the rise. If they had their *corvii* out and they could keep moving, his troops had a chance; if they had decided to stand off for safety's sake, then he and his men were doomed.

The improvised phalanx was no triangle now, it was a knot of men jabbing and running at the same time, each one trying to fend off an attacking horseman. The Lusitani swung their great swords, lopping off arms with spears still in the hands, getting under the raised shields to decapitate those who had dropped their guard. Men stumbled and fell, bringing down the unwary to their rear, the heaps of bodies quickly surrounded, to be remorselessly speared by screaming tribesmen, but at the head of that mass they were through, though the earth beneath their feet worked against them as it turned to soft sand.

Marcellus, head down, sweat dripping from his forehead, watched as the mixture changed, losing the colour of burnt earth, until his feet, seemingly weighed down by heavy stones, rose and fell on the clinging fine sand of the golden beach. Lifting his eyes he saw his ships, bridges down, with the men who manned the oars rushing to their stations. Those marines left to guard the ships were armed and they rushed down the *corvus* and formed up in a defensive 'V' to receive their fleeing companions.

Marcellus, aware of his duty as much as he was of the knot of terror in his stomach, dashed to one side, hoarsely urging his men up the ramp.

He could scarcely breathe from the heat and the weight of his helmet, so he tore it off his head and threw it into the ship, immediately feeling the welcome wind on his sweaty face. His sword was out, whipping the back of his men if they showed the slightest intention of delaying.

The Lusitani horsemen, several with Roman heads impaled on their spears, had formed up to charge the puny line of marines. Marcellus yelled an order, fearing that his voice would not work and the instructions would not carry, but a marine beside him, wiser than his fellows, bellowed out the instructions in a fresh, full voice as the Lusitani charged. From the line on the beach to every man on the ships who could find the space, a wall of javelins hit the charging horsemen. Animals went over, riders thrown forward into the sand. Those behind fared little better, their forelegs taken by the horses in front, struggling to rise in the sucking, awkward ground.

Marcellus ordered his men up the ramps at the double, waiting till all were aboard before himself walking slowly up. He gave the orders for the *corvus* to be raised, for the pole-men to fend off, and felt relieved as the oars bit and the ships began to move till they pulled away from the beach. A vast array of Lusitani infantry, all screaming at the departing Romans, mounted the ridge that formed the barrier between the valley and the beach.

'Bring those poles,' Marcellus called to the men who had pushed them off the beach. He called for ropes and ordered the sacred objects they had taken from the grove to be tied to the poles, and at his command they were all raised at once, these sacred symbols. A huge cry, more like a collective moan, filled the air as the Lusitani saw the ancient totems of their faith glinting and flashing in the hands of their enemies.

CHAPTER TWENTY-ONE

Marcellus was tired, with every bone aching from battle and lack of sleep. The Lusitani had overrun everything but the final wooden palisade that marked the boundary of his stockade. Most of his stores had been loaded overnight, between assaults, and after the last attack so had the majority of his surviving men, so it was only the rearguard who needed to get aboard before he fired the huts and barracks. Grimly he watched as the sun rose, knowing his enemies would attack again with that behind them, as they always did, but this time they only had one wall to scale in order to get to and massacre the garrison. They would kill them all, and painfully, for the tribesmen were fired by an almost desperate determination, seemingly oblivious to any fear of death. He had held them for three weeks, which, given the odds, was a remarkable achievement, yet he was being driven out of his base, so he could not dispel the gloom that filled his heart. If he established another, they would boot him out of that too, and all because he had removed the tribal symbols of their religion, something their chiefs and shamans seemed to be prepared to pay any price to recover.

Should he wait, blunt the first attack, and then retire to his ships? Or was he just sustaining casualties for the sake of his honour? Enough of his men had died to keep this fort in existence, so really it was time to go, before the sun rose just high enough to make the attackers nearly invisible against the glare. Marcellus issued the orders and the last of his men filed off the walls and streamed towards the boats. He waited till the last designated man was aboard, waited till he heard the first of the war cries that signalled a new attack, then indicated to those with the torches to set everything alight.

It burnt merrily, their stockade, sending a cloud of smoke into the still morning air, swirling round the few warriors who now stood silently on the beach, watching as the Roman galleys drifted out of the bay. No shout, no imprecations came from their throats; they merely stared long and hard, before the horns blew and they turned and left the beach.

'We could land somewhere else,' said Regimus,

in a vain attempt to cheer him up.

'Not without more men,' replied Marcellus.

His losses amounted to half of the force with which he had set out from Portus Albus, and there was no point in attempting what might be an opposed landing with what he had left. Nor did he really have enough soldiers, or the time, to build the kind of defences he had erected on this shore even if he could land unopposed, and the idea that he could return south and get reinforcements was not possible, for the province of Outer Hispania could not provide them without being denuded of any prospect of defence. He would have to go south, but only to warn them to man their outposts, before heading round to New Carthage. If Titus was still besieging Numantia, he would have trouble raising more soldiers there, though that would point to the consul's success, but even that thought brought more grief. He had failed, for while he was gone, the Lusitani were free to go east and fall on the rear of the besieging force.

The cry from the lookout made him spin round and run from the stern to the bows. Every free eye was straining forward, towards the line of ships that blocked the exit to the bay. The foreshore, the twin sandbars that narrowed the entrance on either side were thick with men, silently waiting for their quarry, for the tide was out and much of the sandbar lay exposed. Marcellus cursed under his breath, then ordered the oars to be shipped so he could examine the situation. They had known he had chosen this day to leave; indeed, if he had waited for that assault, instead of taking to the ships at sunrise, he would have realised how few men were left before him.

'And I thought they'd given up on the idea of fighting with ships,' said Regimus, who was standing by his shoulder.

'No, friend. They have waited for this. In these confined waters, with the tide low, we'll lose a great deal of our advantage.'

'Do we fight?' asked the older man.

'We certainly won't surrender!' snapped Marcellus. 'Feed the men, Regimus, and call the masters aboard. I think we're in for a long day.'

'They will seek to drive us into shallow water,' said Marcellus, as all the other masters fingered the copies of their charts, knowing what that meant. Once beached, they would be at the mercy of the Lusitani on the shore. 'We must seek to avoid that, to spin out the battle. Time is on our side if we can just hold them off. Remember the tide. It is making now, and once it is full the entrance will be that much wider and they will not have enough ships to block our escape.'

'Do we run all the way to Portus Albus?' asked one of the men.

'No. Once we are out of the bay, and if they follow us, we will sink every one of the Lusitani ships that have survived, something that will be a lot easier once we have plenty of sea room. They can't stand against a quinquereme at ramming speed and they know that as well as we do.'

It was plain that they did not believe him; they suspected that they were going to die in this bay.

'We have three hours before the tide is full,' said Regimus, in a voice that left it open as to whether he thought that was too much time or too little.

Marcellus spoke again, repeating the orders he had already given. 'Once we've undertaken the original manoeuvre and inflicted some damage, back off. Keep moving, ram them if you have to, but just hard enough to make them sheer off. Don't get stuck in their planking, and protect your oars. If they snap those, you're dead. Use your charts. Let them chase us all round the bay if they wish, but survive to get to open water.'

The masters went back to their own ships, each deck emitting smoke from the cauldrons of charcoal, while leather buckets were over the side, ready to be used for fire fighting, for the Romans intended to shoot flaming arrows at their enemies and without doubt the Lusitani would do the same in reply. The quinqueremes got under way as soon as their opponents weighed, their oars striking the water in a steady tattoo. Marcellus knew the odds were against them in such confined waters, for the enemy would seek to pit several of their ships against each one of his.

They would make no attempt, initially, to board or ram, being too light, individually, in both construction and manpower, but if they could disable one of his quinqueremes enough so that several could attack at once, they would have a chance of taking a Roman ship and there was always the prospect of driving them aground on those warrior-filled sandbars. Their smaller galleys were just coming on, with no seeming plan, but everyone suspected that they had already decided on their targets, and once they were closer they would split into groups. They would expect the Roman ships to stick together, just as they were now, relying on mutual support to nullify their numerical advantage. Marcellus intended to surprise them.

The horn sounded and each ship adopted a different course. Some went left, others right.

Some increased their rowing, the rest shipped their oars, then spun to head back the way they had come. Those who kept on fanned out towards the shore on either side, forcing the enemy to split up, creating the impression that if they had a plan, it was one they abandoned by going for the nearest ships. Once they were committed, Marcellus showed them why they had made a mistake, for the horns blew again and the ships that had been heading back for the ruined stockade spun in their own length, their oars biting into the water at an increasing rate, propelling them forward. The other quinqueremes did likewise, their pace taking them past the outside of the attackers. They now spun on the oars and the Lusitani ships, for all their numerical superiority, found themselves assailed on all sides.

'It's a matter of discipline,' Marcellus had said to the masters, time and again. 'We know we can evolve a plan and stick to it, and if our enemy can't, then we will win our way out of this trap.'

Nothing should have been proved to be more correct. Once they had abandoned their original intention, the Lusitani lacked the kind of central direction or an overall tactic that would allow those manning the ships to combine. All were individuals and they reacted as such, and having selected their targets they went after them, but Marcellus had split his fleet so that the ships were in totally different positions, causing their opponents to ram each other and sheer friendly oars in an attempt to go after their personal quarry – all this while the enemy was bearing down on them in heavy quinqueremes that could smash through these lightly built vessels two at a time.

Panic added to the confusion as some of the Lusitani masters tried to get away, but the Roman attack was a bluff. They had no intention of becoming embroiled in a mêlée; Marcellus wanted sea room to fight and the furthest he was prepared to go was a swift descent, a quick hail of flaming shafts, then it was back to working the oars to get out of danger. The Romans fired their arrows together, sending hundreds of burning pinpoints into the Lusitani fleet to keep them busy, then they were round, heading away quickly so that their enemy could not return the compliment.

'Now, Regimus, we'll see how good your charts are,' said Marcellus, turning to his ship's master.

The arrow took him high on the right shoulder, the wad of flame extinguished with a horrible hiss as it entered the soft flesh. Regimus let go of the sweep and leapt forward as Marcellus fell and in one swift movement he hauled the arrow out of his commander's back, ignoring the pain it must have caused. He called for a bucket of seawater and threw the entire contents over the legate's back.

'Get me up,' said Marcellus struggling to his knees.

'Lie still, Marcellus Falerius.'

'Damn you man, help me! Do you want everyone to think I'm dead?'

Regimus obeyed as others came forward to help, only to be pushed away. Even Regimus, once he was on his feet, was told to desist. Their leader's face was grey, but only those close to him could see that, just as only they could see the way he swayed back and forth, fighting to keep his balance on the swaying deck. Regimus stepped forward again, to ensure he did not fall.

'Leave me be,' hissed Marcellus, slightly hunched, his fists clenched in determination.

He pulled himself upright, the pain of that simple action searing across his face, then, slowly, with deliberate steps, he walked all the way to the mast, and leant on that to recover some strength before making his way to the bows. On every ship they had seen him fall, and most had shipped their oars. If their leader was dead, the heart would go out of them.

Marcellus had brought them here, when most would have said it was impossible, made a land base against all the odds and raided the interior with seeming impunity, and that was before he found the Lusitani temple and brought out enough booty to make them all comfortable for the rest of their lives. He would have been angry if he had known how much they admired him, would have coldly reminded them that he was but a servant of the Republic, and that anyone of his class, given loyal troops and hard-rowing sailors, could have achieved precisely the same.

They cheered, on his ship as well as all the others, as he staggered along the deck. The oars bit the water again as he raised his arm in a triumphal salute, marching back down the ship to take station by the sweep. Only those close to him saw the agony, because that raised arm was from the shoulder that had taken the arrow.

In the open sea they could have out-rowed and out-manoeuvred their enemy, but in these confined waters numbers told. Only one galley ran aground, a tribute to the charts that Regimus had made, yet he would have happily burned them all to avoid seeing the slaughter that followed. The land-based Lusitani waded out by the hundreds to surround the ship. No amount of heroism could save the crew, and any galley going to its rescue would only suffer the same fate. Two of Marcellus's quinqueremes had rammed Lusitani ships, and become locked to them in an embrace that could only end in death, while others were alight from end to end, with men jumping into the water to avoid the flames. Another pair, in desperation, had rowed straight at the ships still guarding the entrance to the bay. They were now surrounded by smaller galleys, like wasps around an empty wine goblet, selling their lives for as high a price as they could extract, since to surrender meant a worse death than a spear or a sword in the guts.

Marcellus's ship, with the six remaining members of his fleet, used every trick they knew to avoid close entanglements, managing to ground some of their enemies, who did not know this bay, though not for long, given the numbers available to re-float them. What fires were started aboard the remaining quinqueremes by flaming arrows they put out before they became serious, this while they rowed in circles so tight that their attackers collided, all the time fighting off boarding parties without once allowing an oar to be snapped. The tide steadily rose, opening up the bottleneck at the end of the bay, until the remaining Roman vessels could attack it as one.

Those still in the line who had stuck to their orders and not engaged were too few and the quinqueremes sliced through them like a house slave cutting cheese with a wire. Marcellus, standing with his eyes tight shut, lashed by a rope to the side of the ship to keep him upright, felt the bows of his quinquereme lift and drop as they reached deep blue water and he managed a smile before he passed out. Regimus cut him down and had him carried below, then, turning his bow to the south, he gave the signal for what was left of the fleet to make all speed for home.

The wound, once the surgeon had said it was on the mend, ceased to exist as far as the legate was concerned. No amount of pleading would persuade Marcellus that anyone else could carry the message to Titus; it was his responsibility alone. At least he travelled by sea to New Carthage, in good weather, which was a lot less tiring than a land journey, and that in itself went some way to restoring his health. He suffered a slight relapse once he transferred to a chariot, and had to endure the indignity of making a large part of his journey by litter, but Marcellus had made sure he had a horse along, determined he was not going to arrive in Titus's encampment, before Numantia, like an invalid.

He made his report to his mentor alone, crisply and comprehensively, detailing his losses in men and ships, ending, his face sad, with an apology for having failed.

'But you have not failed, Marcellus,' said Titus.

'If the Lusitani come...'

His general interrupted him. 'They will be too late. We have so weakened the defence of Numantia that we can easily put an army in the field against them.'

Titus looked at his young protégé, the lines of exhaustion clearly visible in his face. He needed rest, but he was young and would recover. 'Despite what you say, Marcellus, you have succeeded beyond my wildest dreams. The truly wonderful thing is that you will be here to see Numantia fall.'

Aquila had left Titus with Marcellus Falerius, having listened as a far happier man had reprised his report for the assembled officers and, though he was reluctant to admit it, what he had heard of the legate's exploits had impressed him – and not just because the idea of fighting on a ship was anathema to someone who loathed the motions of the sea. He smiled, suddenly conscious of the fact that he was guarding a fast-flowing river, standing in the pitch dark, listening to the sound of the water as it hurried by.

There was no moon and heavy cloud cover, so if any of the besieged tribesmen in Numantia were going to get away, then these were perfect conditions. If they had not seen his boats, they were in for a horrible surprise; if they had, they would decline to come, so nothing would be lost. He knew they were starving in the hill fort, since no food had got through to them for almost a year, so most of the populace would be too weak to move. Only the best, the warriors, would have the stamina to try and escape, perhaps leaving the rest to surrender.

The boats had been built upriver, out of sight; flat-bottomed and broad, they were of little use on fast water, but lashed together they formed a proper bridge. Planks had been laid from one boat to the next, and stationed on this platform a line of soldiers stood, weapons in hand, ready to spear the tribesmen like fish. Torches were at hand, ready to be lit, so that the soldiers could see the victims of this proposed execution, while behind them was a boom of thick logs chained together, acting as a second line of defence.

The clouds broke suddenly, turning the Stygian blackness pale blue and the river, picking up the light, became a silver ribbon. The huge log, sharpened at the end, dark and menacing, was going very fast, propelled by the boats lashed to either side. It hit Aquila's bridge with an almighty crunch and the sound of smashing wood filled the air, topped with the cries of men as they toppled into the river. The log sliced through his line of boats, which were then flung to the river-banks by the force of the current, before nearly coming to a halt in the middle of the stream, with half the oarsmen on the boats at its side trying to get it going again, while the rest jabbed ferociously at Aquila's men, struggling in the water.

His voice rose above the screams and cries of battle, and he plunged into the river without waiting to find out if his men would obey. The spear he had been holding was abandoned as he waded out into the middle of the stream, grappling to remove his armour, for this was no place for a heavily laden man to fight; it needed a sharp sword, a knife and the freedom to swim.

Aquila struck out for one of the boats, swimming awkwardly to keep his sword above water. The spearman saw him coming and he jabbed with as much force as he could muster. No need to kill; one decent wound would be enough and, after that, the river would do the rest. Aquila took a great gulp of air as he went under, trying to go deep enough to avoid the tips of the spears. His hand touched the keel of the boat and he used that to drag himself beneath it until his fingers felt the bottom of the rough log.

In the pitch darkness it was all touch. His lungs were bursting and he moved hand over hand, trying to find the end. It was luck and the stump of a sawn-off branch that made him grab it as it went slowly by. He hung on, dragging himself up, and the buoyancy of the water helped him lift his body as he heaved, landing belly down on the top of the log. The men in the boats were too intent on their other tasks, rowing or killing Romans, to notice him behind them.

Aquila lifted his sword in the air, but not to strike at the boatmen, for there was no need. The blade swept down in a flashing arc, slicing through the ropes that held the boats to the log, and, as soon as it was free, it spun, throwing him back into the river. Under the water again, swimming downstream, his fingers reached out once more, to feel for one of the boats. What he felt was a leg, which kicked furiously as he used it to claw his way to the surface, where he found himself staring into a pair of wild and frightened eyes. The fellow seem to be tied to some kind of float, which hampered his movement as he swung a weapon at him, more to fend his attacker off than to wound. The blow that Aquila tried to strike at his chest, in reply, was feeble, hampered by being underwater, but it hit something and his adversary seemed to ignore him in his panic, his arms and legs flailing wildly as he slowly sank beneath the surface.

Others surrounded Aquila, bobbing along with their arms grasping the sheep's-belly floats in front of them. His sword jabbed remorselessly and he heard the cries of the men in the boats as they were capsized, easy now that they were free of their lashing. The water around him was full of guttural Celtic cries, not of men fighting, but of men dying by drowning. It was only when he got back on shore, soaked to the skin and freezing, that he heard another party of Celts had assaulted the perimeter wall, got over in numbers, stolen Roman horses, and made their getaway. The news, after what he and his men had suffered in the water, sent him into a towering rage.

Marcellus awoke refreshed, unaware that he had slept through the alarms and incursions of the night before. His dread of the day, of the accusation of failure, evaporated as he remembered Titus's warm words. The Calvinus twins were early visitors, as was Gaius Trebonius, but nothing reassured him more than the visit from Titus Cornelius himself. The general's solicitations, his reiteration of his satisfaction, warmed Marcellus in a way he scarcely thought possible. That was, of course, before he heard of Aquila Terentius's rank.

'Quaestor!' he shouted.

'Calm yourself, Marcellus,' said Gnaeus. 'The appointment has been a great success.'

'Titus, the fool, has allowed himself to be blinded by that peasant.'

'I would have a care how loudly you say that, Marcellus Falerius.' Aquila was standing in the doorway, framed against the bright morning sun. 'You may say what you like about me, though if you go too far we may find ourselves with swords in our hands, but I will not stand by and allow you to casually insult our commanding officer.'

Marcellus allowed his anger to run away with his tongue. He also ignored Gnaeus's hand on his good arm. 'You dare to preach proper behaviour to me?'

Being in silhouette, Marcellus could not see if he was smiling, but the words certainly sounded like sarcasm to a man, slightly feverish, who was still suffering the effects of a wound. 'I have no choice, Marcellus Falerius. It is my duty as your senior officer.'

Then he was gone and Marcellus, who had been too taken with the title to realise the full import of what he had been told, was obliged to sit down suddenly when he realised that this man he thought an upstart could actually order him about.

'I must see Titus. He has to do something about this. Rome is full of men, good soldiers from good families, who would give their eye-teeth for such an appointment. How can he allow himself to give it to a man so coarse? Swabbing the seats in the officer's latrine is about as close as he should come to nobility.'

'That is unworthy,' said Publius, coldly.

'Perhaps it would be better if you went back to sea,' added Gnaeus, sadly.

It was not jealousy, though he had no end of trouble trying to convince his friends that this was so. They failed utterly to see what he could see, it being the same problem as that identified by Titus, who confirmed it to Marcellus during a private interview. That had been hard, with the young man forced to chide a general and a consul he admired, only to find himself rebuked for his temerity. Marcellus walked the entire perimeter of Titus's walls, turning over the problem in his mind, and what he concluded made him even more uncomfortable. A man who had been a quaestor during a triumphant campaign, a man who could claim some credit for that success, and who was about to come into a great deal of wealth, was not about to just disappear off the face of the earth. In fact, if he was ambitious, he would go to Rome, to be greeted with a degree of honour only marginally less than that granted to Titus. Such acclaim was not for a man like Aquila Terentius.

Yes, men rose from obscurity to become senators, new men, but they could speak Greek and write Latin. Educated, they had studied rhetoric and knew how to plead in the courts, had been born to parents who owned a decent house, had slaves and had accrued wealth. They did not come from farms in the deepest countryside and they certainly did not come armed with radical ideas that questioned the foundations of the state. Even his friends from good patrician families seemed to have fallen under his spell, taking on board any rubbish he chose to spout. All they saw was a brilliant soldier; Marcellus could see that too, but he also observed the way that the men in the legions felt about Aquila Terentius. They thought him immortal and no one deserved that, going, as it did, way beyond admiration to something that, he felt instinctively, was dangerous.

He questioned his friends carefully, to ensure that what he had heard about this man's beliefs were not mere whims, expressed to shock. They seemed proud to tell him that their paragon believed in all the things his father had fought against for years. True, they were rough in outline, but it was easy to see Aquila Terentius, with his peasant background, supporting land reform, just as there was no doubt at all that he held Rome's allies to be badly treated, thought all senators crooks and stated, quite openly, that those who starved in the streets of Rome should take what they wanted from their greedy betters by force.

At the conclusion of his enquiries he was even more disturbed than he been at the outset. His father had left him a legacy and a vow: Rome first and always, and never to allow the mob to rule or let fools elevate a man above the Senate. He must make sure that the kind of adulation with which Aquila was treated in Spain did not transfer itself to the streets of Rome, where the rabble, granted a hero from their own ranks, could be an unstable instrument. Admittedly, it was unlikely that a city state like Rome would be troubled and the fellow would probably, after the first flush of fame, disappear into obscurity. The

Republic could put his soldierly qualities to good use provided he knew, and observed, his place; just as long as he stayed out of politics. Not that Marcellus rated him very highly in that area; Aquila was not equipped for the life, even if Cholon Pyliades had begun to instruct him in reading and numeracy.

The Greek he spoke was as risible as ever, and the Latin not much better, so the first time he stood to address anything other than a bunch of roughnecked soldiers, he would be laughed off the rostrum. All that was required to keep him in check was a careful eye. His friends may laugh at the need, but caution was something he had learnt from the best brain he had ever encountered, that of his own father, Lucius Falerius Nerva. That, and the need to take a very long view of public affairs.

CHAPTER TWENTY-TWO

Masugori watched as the horsemen rode into his camp at Lutia. Brennos was at the head of the column, he alone looking as though he had the energy to continue, still managing to look like a chieftain, with his silver hair showing that hint of gold at the very tips that denoted its earlier colouring. His dress was, as always, plain, the single gold eagle at his neck was all he wore; that and a braided band to keep his long hair in check. Brennos slipped off the Roman horse with the ease of long practice and walked through the silent line of Bregones warriors to confront their chieftain, who had so signally failed to come to his aid.

'Why, Masugori?'

No preamble; no polite expressions of esteem. Brennos behaved as he always had, with an arrogance that bordered on contempt for his fellow man.

'Are the Romans worse than you, Brennos?'

The tall man's blue eyes flashed and his voice grew loud as he sought to include everyone present. 'You ask me that? I have spent my life trying to tell you all, and here you are, sitting by, watching the Romans subdue the best hope of Celtic independence.'

'The best hope of Brennos,' relied Masugori.

'Someone must take the lead,' said the Duncani chieftain.

Masugori had never been able to talk to Brennos like this; in common with most of the Celt-Iberian chiefs, he had been obliged to sit and listen to endless lectures from this man about what he should do, how he should fight, when and whom. And why? Because this interloper had climbed over a mountain of bodies to take the leadership of a tribe, turning it into something so strong that he dominated them all. Yet there was no pleasure in seeing him like this, reduced to begging for help.

'You are not of this land, Brennos, yet you came here years ago to fight Rome. Why? To help us or to help yourself? The tribes refused to unite under you, so you went away. We paid the price for that, then you came back again, angry and full of hate, instead of the love of freedom you had expressed before. You have blooded us to the point where Rome, the enemy, now looks like a friend.'

The warriors had gathered to listen to this exchange, and some were murmuring unhappily. Masugori had not convinced them all that his course of action was the right one. Many wanted to fight, not necessarily for any cause but for the sheer love of battle, but he had forbidden them to go. Brennos's presence here had awakened their interest and he knew he would have more trouble now, and perhaps, at his age, more than he could cope with.

'I am begging you, which is what in your mind I see you want.' Masugori went white. This ability Brennos had to see into a man's thoughts had always frightened him. 'If you will attack the Romans, then we can get supplies into Numantia. The Lusitani will come to our aid.'

'Will they, Brennos?'

'Yes, they will. They have defeated the Romans that troubled them. I can count on their support, but only if you give us the time to fight.'

'I made a peace, Brennos, with a man who was so like you he could have been your son.'

Masugori was looking at the charm, so familiar, shaped like an eagle in flight, that hung around the other man's neck. Brennos knew the direction of his gaze and, as if afraid, put his hand up to touch it. 'The man who came, the Roman, he had the eagle.'

'The eagle?'

'Around your neck. It's the only thing you wear. I know you feel it gives you power. He had one just like it. His name is Aquila Terentius and he is quaestor to the man who opposes you. At first we thought this Aquila had taken the charm off you, but then we found he had had it since birth. I consulted the priests and they felt its strength, called it a gift from the gods. They saw you, Brennos, with the aid of that eagle, a disgraced Druid forced to flee from his northern home, a man who broke his vows again and planted his seed in the heart of his own enemy. Then they counselled a truce, telling me that we cannot fight such a man, a man who will, one day, subdue Rome.'

Something went out of Brennos at that point, as though he was sustained by an injection of air that had been removed. He held the eagle charm in his hand, as if, once more, trying to draw strength from it. 'And that is why you failed me?'

Masugori nodded. 'Once we could not fight you, and that was when you had nothing with which to stop us. I wondered if it was our own stupidity that allowed you to establish yourself with the Duncani. Now perhaps I think it was magic, a magic you no longer possess.'

Brennos turned and went back to his horse. He mounted it and left the camp without a word.

They were out of sight of the Bregones camp when Brennos stopped and those with him did likewise. He turned suddenly, his blue eyes ablaze with anger and his finger shot out and pointed to one of his men.

'There are warriors in Lutia willing to fight. Go amongst them and help them defy their traitor chief.'

The finger spun round to a second companion. 'You. Go to the Romans. Surrender, and they will let you live. Tell them that the Bregones are intending to attack them at the next night of new moon. Go!'

The young man rode away and Brennos turned to the others. 'We must ride to the Lusitani.'

'It's too far, Brennos,' replied one of the men. A murmur of discontent swept the small troop, and Brennos sensed their thoughts about Masugori, his prediction, and the omens that had been provided by their Celtic gods. When he spoke, it was in a quiet voice.

'Don't fear the gods. I've defied them. I won't stop now.'

*   *   *

'Marcellus Falerius was my legate in Outer Hispania, Aquila.'

'Very good, General,' replied Aquila stiffly.

He was not going to tell Titus that he had only gone to the Falerii tent to enquire after the man's wound, just as he would never say what words he had overheard. Titus frowned at the stiff military response, for he had become close to Aquila Terentius during this siege, close enough to consider him more than just a subordinate, and he had gone to some lengths to defend him when Marcellus complained of his elevation.

'Nothing would please me more than that you two should be friends.'

'Unfortunately, Titus Cornelius, that is something not even you can command.'

The tribune burst in, which cut off the rebuke that Titus was about to deliver. 'A prisoner, General. He's given himself up. He says he has information about a possible attack.'

Titus was on his feet and out of the tent in a flash. Surrounded by every officer in the camp, he listened carefully as the man outlined the Bregones' plans.

'I don't believe it,' said Aquila. 'Why wait this long?'

'I don't disagree with you,' said Titus, 'but it does require some reaction. We can't just sit here hoping that the man is a liar.'

'I am happy to go alone...'

'No!' the General snapped, so harshly that Aquila was shocked, for Titus had not spoken to him in such a tone for months. 'Marcellus Falerius. Take two legions and surround Lutia. I want to be absolutely sure that nothing against us is planned.'

'And if it is?' asked Marcellus.

Titus was looking at Aquila when he replied. 'You are my legate. Act as you see fit.'

Aquila waited until they were alone. 'What was that, Titus, loyalty to your class?'

Brennos knew that all was lost before he even spoke to the Lusitani envoys. If his shoulders had been slumped before, they were hunched now. They had lost their tribal ornaments, either to the Romans or the sea, and the Lusitani priests, convinced that their gods had deserted them, counselled against going to the aid of Numantia. He turned his horse round and, despite the pleading of his escort that he head north, set its head back to the hill fort which he had created over so many years.

This Roman was not like the other one. The height, yes, and the build, but black hair and dark skin. The arm in a white sling meant nothing, just a wound, but the compassion was absent. This was Rome as Masugori remembered it, the stern conqueror on whose doorstep he had lived all his life.

'It is a tradition in the legions,' said Marcellus, 'to stifle revolt.'

What could he say? A great many of his warriors, disgusted at his rejection of Brennos, had indeed set out for Numantia, putting their blood loyalty to their fellow Celts above that of their obligations to the tribe. Four thousand men, and they had run right into two whole Roman legions. Now his city was surrounded and at the slightest sign of disagreement the whole place would be put to the torch.

'Please understand that I accept your explanation, but you must realise that this cannot be allowed to go unpunished.'

It really was, as this legate claimed, quite a merciful solution. Most Romans would have killed the lot out of hand, then sacked Lutia, carrying off all precious objects and the inhabitants as slaves. Masugori nodded his agreement and Marcellus turned to his senior centurion and issued his orders.

'One in ten.'

'Decimate them, sir?' asked the centurion.

'No, these people are really our allies. One in ten of the warriors we captured on the way here. Cut off their right hands.'

*   *   *

'The same rule applies here,' said Cholon, archly. 'I will not become involved, just as I refuse to have anything to do with your quarrel with Marcellus, nor can I interfere when Titus makes a decision.'

'It was your idea, Cholon. I made promises to the Bregones, yet at the first sign of trouble, Titus sends someone else to investigate.'

Cholon held up his hand as Titus entered the tent. His face, normally so relaxed, was screwed up with tension. The Bregones were forgotten when he informed them that the people of Numantia had sent envoys asking for terms of surrender.

'I should go to treat with them myself,' he said.

Both Aquila and Cholon said 'No' together. Cholon did so because he believed it to be right; Aquila said no because, for the first time, he had seen in his commander's face the strain the man had been under all these months. The final indication that what he sought to achieve was possible seemed to drain him. Of the two, Aquila's observations made the most sense; all he did was advance ideas that he and Titus had discussed many times.

'What do you need to treat with them for? If they've sent envoys it's because they've no chance of holding out. We require unconditional surrender and a handing-over of Roman deserters. The hill fort is to be cleared of all inhabitants so that it can be razed to the ground. Anyone can do that.'

Titus turned his tired eyes towards his second-in-command and nodded, then he sat in a chair, slumped down and wept. Cholon started to move towards him, but Aquila stopped him. The Greek probably would not comprehend that, at a time like this, any good general would be thinking of the men he had lost and the mistakes he had made, not of the victory gained.

Numantia smelt of death; it was in his nostrils from half a league away. The gates were open, with a small party of the leading men there to treat with him. He assumed they were slack-jawed through hunger and fatigue, presumed they accepted his terms in silence because they had no choice, yet when he turned his back they started to talk, with great animation, accompanied with much wailing and crying to their gods. He knew the language and wondered why, after all these months of siege, they could even contemplate the use of the word betrayal.

Brennos slipped through the Roman lines with ease. He put this down to skill, not aware that all the legions knew the fight was over, so they were lax to a degree not seen before. He had more trouble getting into Numantia, and when they did finally open the gates he found himself walking between two lines of silent scarecrows. There was a crowd in the central space, the large area that stood in front of the temple, and as they parted, Brennos closed his eyes. The shattered body of Galina lay on the altar, the embryo that had been his second child torn from her womb. One voice spoke, the words like a knell of doom.

'He came, Brennos, like your double. The same height, your colour when you were young, he even had about his neck the golden eagle that you wear.'

Brennos turned to explain, just as the first stone hit him. Everyone had a rock to throw at the man they now saw as a traitor, and even in their feeble state it was not long before their chieftain was dead.

The inhabitants came out at dawn, thin, wasted creatures barely able to walk through the lines of Roman soldiers. Titus Cornelius stood, Aquila and Marcellus at his side, as they stumbled past, to be corralled by their captors, their plight recorded by the ever-present Cholon. The Romans were in Numantia before the last defender had departed, already beginning the destruction of the town and fort that would erase it from the landscape. The body of Brennos was on a handcart, barely recognisable, and the men pushing it did not, as they should, approach Titus. Instead they came to stand in front of Aquila, their heads bowed.

'This is the body of Brennos. It was our right to kill him, but it falls to you to bury him.'

With that, the oldest scarecrow pressed a charm into Aquila's hand. It was gold, finely wrought, and it looked very like an eagle in flight. With one set of fingers on that, he touched the eagle round his neck, knowing they were the same, then he turned and looked at the smashed body being trundled towards the Roman camp.

Their bodies were foul, their hair and nails long, and they were smeared with dirt. In their eyes, a fearful expression; an expression of anger, pain, weariness and bewilderment. They had, in their extremity, eaten human flesh and this seemed to show deep in their eyes.

'Careful, Cholon,' he said to himself, putting aside his wax tablet. 'You're getting carried away here.'

'Select fifty of the leading warriors,' said Titus, his voice now full of strength. 'And set aside the finest armour for them to wear. Tell the men of the other tribes round Numantia that I want riders sent in every direction. Those thinking of resistance to Rome should come here first, look upon this place, and decide whether what they plan is worth the pain.'

'And us?' asked Aquila, who held the charm in his hand, without knowing why he had it, or what to do with it.

'We march back to New Carthage. I leave it to you to choose the legion we will take back to Italy.'

'And me?'

Titus smiled at Aquila the quaestor, now wondering if he would revert to his previous rank of centurion.

'You will lead the legion home, Aquila Terentius. I want you and Marcellus Falerius there, in Rome, behind me, as I make my way down the Via Sacra. The Senate will honour me, but a great deal of this, at least, truly belongs to you both.'

Aquila was made welcome by Masugori, Fabius by some of those young women he had met on their previous visit. Aquila and Masugori talked for a long time, and the younger man learnt all that the Bregones chieftain knew about Brennos. What he heard in Lutia made him sombre, and when he returned to the camp outside Numantia, his first act was to go and see Titus and ask if they could talk alone.

'I require your permission to execute a personal obligation.'

'Which is?'

'Sorry, General, I haven't finished. I also want you to take the most solemn oath that I never asked for this; that what I'm about to propose was your idea, and that you will never tell a living person, nor commit to any written record what I'm about to say.'

'That's a lot to require from a favour you've yet to propose.'

'In return, I will release you from any obligation you feel you have to me.'

Titus tried to be flippant, answering with a wry smile. 'You're sure I have one?'

'Yes!' replied Aquila without even a trace of humour.

'I dislike open-ended commitments.'

His quaestor took his eagle charm in his hand, like a man looking for support. 'Have you never, ever given one?'

The image of old Lucius Falerius sprung immediately to his mind, that day in his house when Titus had accepted his help without any clue as to how to repay the man. Lucius had been wise enough to see that Titus would do for

Marcellus what he had done for the younger Cornelii, so he found himself nodding before he had really thought that through.

'If what you ask does not damage me, or Rome, I will grant your request.'

'I want to take the body of Brennos back to Rome. You may display him in your triumph if you wish. After that, he is mine.'

'He'll be a rank thing by then.'

'I have had his carcass placed in a vat of that Iberian spirit that Fabius is so fond of. I need to know, do you accede to my request?'

'Granted,' said Titus, curious about the stiff quality of a man normally very relaxed, but also too polite to enquire. 'Now, let's see to the destruction of Numantia. I want a plateau at the top of that hill, one where nothing will grow.'

Since Titus could not enter the city until the day he celebrated his triumph, Claudia came out to welcome him home. Cholon had less reason to stay with him and she half-suspected it was to avoid an invitation to dine with Sextius. The greetings were warm, as they always are when old friends reunite. Another man came into the room just as they finished their embrace, a soldier by his bearing, tall with red-gold hair, and the sight of him made her draw her breath sharply.

Titus stood up, a wide grin on his face.

'Stepmother, allow me to introduce the man who did more than any man alive to subdue Numantia. My quaestor, Aquila Terentius.'

Marcellus copied everything, then took the Cornelii family papers, and those relating to Vegetius Flaminus, out of the chest. As he gave half the contents to Quintus, you could see the greed in the man's eyes, mixed with disquiet, as he looked through them, and the conversation that followed was a lesson in double dissimulation. Quintus wanted to know if he had everything; Marcellus wanted something for the remainder without asking. It was not long before the older man caught his drift.

'By the way,' Quintus said, 'you must announce your candidacy for the aedileship.'

The senator smiled at Marcellus, in a way he had not done since Lucius was alive. 'A mere formality, of course. You have my full support, as always.'

When Quintus was gone, Marcellus placed the scroll he had brought from Numantia in the chest. He too had talked to Masugori, and had learnt a great deal about Brennos, though he could not put aside the feeling that the Bregones chieftain was holding something back, not telling him everything he knew about the ex-Druid. He had also assiduously questioned the skeletons who had survived the siege and noted that when he mentioned Aquila Terentius, they became less willing to speak, as though the name terrified them.

There was a mystery about the man he knew he would have to discover, because now that he had been brought back to Rome, elevated by Titus, and given his radical ideas, there was no doubt he could pose a threat to the Republic.

Cholon was patting her hand. 'You fainted, Claudia. It must have been the journey from Rome. It can be very fatiguing on a hot day. Titus has gone to fetch a physician.'

Behind Cholon's shoulder she could see the tall young man and she could also see, flashing on his chest, the charm in the shape of an eagle, the mark that, even more than the name and the appearance, identified him as her son.

'Could you fetch me something to drink, Cholon?'

'Of course, Lady,' said the Greek.

He stood up and scurried out of the room. Claudia signalled to Aquila to come close and as he leant over her she reached up and took the charm in her hand. 'Would you do one thing for me, Aquila Terentius?'

'Most certainly, Lady.'

The deep voice thrilled her as much as the looks.

'I would like you to call on me, alone.'

He raised an eyebrow slowly, and smiled faintly as a prelude to a refusal, but Claudia tugged on the chain. 'You were found by the River Liris, near Aprilium, with this round your foot. I would want to tell you how and when you acquired it.'

His face went as hard as stone, though Claudia never did find out what he would have said, because Cholon came rushing back into the room.

CHAPTER TWENTY-THREE

They were all awake well before dawn, to ensure that all the arrangements for the day were in place; gleaming chariots ready with well-greased wheels; the horses fed and watered, hooves blacked, accoutrements polished, then groomed until their hides shone. The whole courtyard of the *Villa Publica* outside the *Porta Triumphalis* was a hive of activity, while two leagues away the tribunes that Titus had commanded in Spain had risen even earlier, marshalling the 18th Legion, home after a decade in Hispania. The general had chosen them as the troops who would march behind him to receive the well-deserved cheers of the Roman crowd, and to these Titus had added the sailors who had served under Marcellus.

Once assembled and inspected, they were marched to the Campus Martius, arranged in order, to await their commander. The carts containing the spoils of this latest war were already there, some piled high with armour, spears and swords, others containing the gold and silver as well as the precious stones the Romans had looted from Numantia's temple. The objects from the Lusitani temple, once more mounted on poles, stood up like a frisson of temptation from the long four-wheeled wagon on which they had been mounted, the conveyance now panelled to look like a quinquereme.

The body of Brennos lay on a special handcart, set to be pulled by two of his own yoked warriors – this a combined symbol of servitude to Roman power and death at the Republic's hands. Aquila and Marcellus, each in his own chariot, took station at the front of the parade. The former was as tall and imposing as ever with his red-gold hair hidden under a plumed helmet and wearing all his decorations: the civic crown of oak leaves, of no intrinsic value yet so highly prized that men died in droves trying to gain one; four torques adorned his arms, while his breastplate bore the rest of his many decorations. Beside him stood Fabius, the silver-tipped spear held upright, happy to be seen this day at his 'uncle's' right hand.

Marcellus wore the naval crown, the gold of decoration, the motif of a ship's forepeak catching the morning sun, sending flashing rays of light in all directions. They held their animals steady, with minor tugs of the traces, and both men exchanged not a single word while studiously avoiding any form of eye contact. A hush fell over the whole proceedings as the lictors rushed around making sure that all was well, jabbing their rods of office at anything which they considered less than perfect. Finally Titus appeared, his face and upper body painted red. He wore a purple cloak, shot through with gold designs. On his brow rested the laurel crown of the victor. As soon as he stepped into his chariot, a slave got up behind him, ready to whisper the words of caution that were delivered to all *triumphatores*, that all glory was fleeting and that they should remember that they were merely men.

The lictors took station behind the leaders, and Titus raised an arm. In his hand he had the rods surrounding the small axe, the symbol of his consular *imperium*. As soon as he signalled, the great gates in the Servian walls opened to admit him, the cheers of the multitude rushing through the gap in an overwhelming burst of adulation. At that point, Aquila pulled on the chain that held his charm, pulling it out from under his tunic to lay, for all to see, in the middle of his polished leather breastplate.

The streets of Rome had been crowded for hours, since long before cock-crow, as the population jostled for the best places. Calpurnia was there, in a special place in the central isle of the *Circus Maximus*, secured for her by her brother Fabius, one that would allow her to see the whole parade. The noise rose to a crescendo as Titus came through the gate, his fiery black horses pawing the ground, half-alarmed by the noise, half-filled with the desire to race through the gap in the crowds.

The city cohorts lined the route, each soldier's arm raised in salute. Those behind them threw flowers and blossoms that paved the cobbled roadway, turning it from a mere street into what looked like a pathway to the heavens. Having traversed the *Velabrum*, the *Forum Boracum*, the parade entered the crowded, oval-shaped circus. Here assembled were some of the elite of Rome, those who did not qualify to attend the actual ceremonies, and who had bought places that afforded them the best view. Men, women and children cheered themselves hoarse, jabbing the air with laurel branches as a salute to Titus Cornelius, but cheers went to his subordinates too, and both Aquila and Marcellus were at liberty to acknowledge the accolades of the crowd, while behind them officers like the

Calvinus twins and Gaius Trebonius had to keep their heads rigidly to the front, ignoring the cries of admiration.

Exiting from the *Circus Maximus,* they made their way down the roadway named for the purpose, the *Via Triumphalis,* then turned into the *Via Sacra.* This ran in a wide arc, ending alongside the open debating space of the *Forum Romanum,* with the Senate meeting place, the *Curia Hostilia,* standing in paramount splendour. The road rose steeply up the side of the Capitoline Hill, till it terminated in the great open space before the temple of *Jupiter Optimus Maximus.* Here stood the men who ruled Rome, the patrician and plebeian senators, all in specially whitened togas, those who had served as consuls marked out by the thick purple stripe that bordered the garment.

Claudia had secured a place from which to observe her son, her breast swelling with pride as he entered the plaza behind Titus. Even in the uniform of a high-ranking Roman officer, he looked like his father. Then she turned her gaze towards Titus, for here was a truly noble man, who had sought nothing but victory in arms. Now he would have a wealth to rival that of his father and a reputation that would place his family mask high in the decorated cupboards of the Cornelii chapel after he was gone.

She caught her breath as the cart containing the body of Brennos came into the square. She could not know what he looked like before this, since Aquila had ordered the undertakers to restore his features. Gone was the battered and bloody face that had taken so many stones; now he lay there, in seeming repose, hands across the silk tunic he wore, his silver hair well dressed and held back by a braided band. The two warriors pulling the cart, prodded by their jailers, swung it round towards the temple and the sun caught the single object that lay on the cadaver's breast. Claudia knew, even from the great distance at which she stood, that it was that same gold charm she had seen so many times, that same eagle she had clutched in her hand the day that Aquila was conceived.

Titus swung his chariot round until his horses faced the temple steps. Men rushed forward to hold the bridles as he dismounted, and he walked over to Brennos's cart and looked at the body of his enemy. There was no hint of triumphalism in this, even though those present raised an extra cheer. If anything, he looked sad, as though he regretted that his actions had ended in this death. Then he looked at Aquila, still mounted, and nodded. Titus turned, and, followed by his lictors, he entered the temple of the premier Roman deity to dedicate his laurel wreath, and his victory in battle, to the gods.

Aquila spoke to Fabius, who dismounted and took charge of the cart containing Brennos's body, and men of the 18th Legion, who unyoked the two warriors and personally dragged the vehicle away, suddenly replaced the guards who had escorted it. Fabius signalled to more of his men, who formed an escort for the two Celt-Iberian warriors. They were obviously not going to be killed, as was the custom, and they would need those escorts to protect them from some of the more over-enthusiastic members of the Roman mob.

As Titus entered the temple, the assembled senators pushed forward, cutting Claudia off from any further view of the proceedings. She was gone by the time Titus exited from the temple, did not see Quintus embrace his brother, nor observe the question and the response, but others did, and it was the talk of Rome for days.

'Is this the right time to remind you of your vow, Quintus?' said Titus, half-turning to indicate the temple where it had been sworn.

Quintus raised his arms, his face concerned, trying to convey both exasperation and pity simultaneously. 'Look around you, Brother, at all these august senators. You will look in vain for the face of Vegetius Flaminus.'

'What's happened to him?' Titus hissed.

'I blame myself, Brother,' Quintus replied. 'Since I intended to bring a case before him in the house, I felt it only fair to show Vegetius the detail of the charges.'

'He knew those very well!'

'Not all of them. Nor could he know that father wrote to Lucius Falerius listing them in detail. I'm afraid that when he saw what I had he was very downcast. Poor man went home and opened his veins. I'm afraid that Vegetius is dead.'

The sound that Titus emitted, halfway between a growl and a roar, affected his brother not at all. Quintus continued as calmly as if he had not heard Titus's displeasure.

'Never fear, Brother, our father is avenged, even if it's not as tidy as it should be.'

Aquila called on Claudia while the triumphal feast was still in progress, having changed out of his uniform and now wearing a plain white toga. The streets outside were crowded with the same multitude who had watched the parade, but now they were carousing, drunk and noisy, still celebrating. The first greeting was stiff and formal, made more so by the presence of

Claudia's curious maid, Callista. But once she had dismissed her, she walked over and took his hands in hers. They stared at each other for a long time before she spoke.

'I have dreamt of this so often, and shed so many tears.'

Her son, so much taller than she, leant forward and kissed her on the forehead. The crying, which she had fought so hard to contain, began immediately.

They sat by the window, looking at the stars up above. Claudia had sent Phoebe and her daughter to the country because she did not want her son to feel he had an obligation to either of them after all these years, and, in truth, she wanted him to herself. But it was difficult; both were nervous and strangers to each other. Slowly, with many a pause and a lot of sighs, Aquila persuaded his mother to tell him everything, especially of her capture and subsequent treatment.

'Out in the streets they are singing songs that say Brennos was a beast and a murderer. Perhaps he was, Aquila, though it ill becomes Romans to throw out such an accusation. All I can say with certainty was that he was never like that with me. Oh, I daresay I felt the same as that mob when I was captured. In truth, at that time I despised him and showed it. Yet, he stood between me and death. The other chieftain wanted to send my head back to Aulus. It was only the force of his personality that kept me alive. Then, for safety, he accommodated me in his own tent.

'We spent nearly two years together. I was shown all respect; in fact, I was pampered. Over time I learnt to trust him, and then, when I allowed my Roman pride to subside, I actually listened to what he had to say. We are born and educated to see the Roman way as perfect, so it comes as something of a shock to find out otherwise, but in time, I came to esteem him. He was clever, wise and dedicated to his goal of subduing Rome. I fought him on that, of course, but my will to defend my homeland wore thin. Months spent close to someone of his power wove a spell I couldn't resist. And finally, one night...'

Claudia dropped her head at that point. 'When Quintus found me, he sent for my husband, his father, to come to that covered wagon. I suggested to Aulus that he put me aside, but he assumed that I was with child because I'd been abused. Yet it was not like that, it was something that I sought myself. When Brennos looked into my eyes, I found I couldn't resist him. Perhaps he cast a spell over me, who's to tell, but I wanted his child. You! I was going to the north, to safety, when the wagon was intercepted. If that hadn't happened, I would never have seen Rome again, never have wounded Aulus, who was such an honourable man, and you would never have ended up on that riverbank.'

He touched the chain on his neck. 'And this?'

'I loved that charm. If anything, that shows he wasn't an ogre. Brennos had a copy made for me. That one you're wearing is Brennos's own. I so wanted something of his to take with me when I left his encampment, so I exchanged them while he slept. The one round his neck today was the copy he made for me.'

Aquila held out his hand as he stood up. 'Come.'

'Where to?'

He put his finger to his lips, and as she gazed into his compelling blue eyes she saw there that same power that Brennos had exercised. She stood and he led her across the atrium to the gate. It opened to reveal his legionary escort. The leader was grinning from ear to ear, no doubt taking hold of entirely the wrong impression when he saw his 'uncle' holding the hand of an older, but still handsome, Roman noblewoman. A glare from Aquila had him eyes front and they marched off, making their way through the celebrating throng towards the Esquiline Hill.

As they walked out onto the open space at the crest, Claudia recognised the cart that had carried Brennos's body. It was sitting there, still guarded, now empty, but a high pile of wood stood a few yards away, with his body just visible on the top. Both stood for a moment in silent prayer, before one of the soldiers brought Aquila a torch. He tried to pass it to Claudia, but she refused.

'It falls to a son to carry out the funeral rites of his father, in the Celtic religion as well as the Roman one.'

He stepped forward and jabbed the flaming torch into the dry kindling. It took immediately and the flames shot up to engulf the body. Soaked as it was in that potent grain spirit which had preserved it all the way back from Spain, the corpse flared in a great whoosh of flame that made Aquila's men jump backwards.

'He even weaves spells in death,' said Claudia, with wonder.

Aquila turned to his mother. In his hand he held the gold eagle that had been given to him by those scarecrows outside the walls of Numantia.

'It's time you had your own property back.'

With that, he tried to put the gold charm, with the wings that made it look so like an eagle in flight, over his mother's head. Claudia put a hand up to stop him, then took it herself, holding it out so that the precious metal picked up the flickering light from the billowing flames.

'No. Let Brennos take it with him. He always believed that he would conquer Rome. Now, his ashes will. He cannot be allowed to go to his resting place without some symbol of his dream.'

Claudia kissed the eagle, then threw it into the flames.